The Secret Pilgrim

'He will be remembered as perhaps the most significant novelist of the second half of the twentieth century in Britain. He will have charted our decline and recorded the nature of our bureaucracies like no one else has. But that's just been his route into some profound anxiety in the national narrative. Most writers I know think le Carré is no longer a spy writer. He should have won the Booker Prize a long time ago. It's time he won it and it's time he accepted it. He's in the first rank' Ian McEwan, *Daily Telegraph*

'No other writer has charted – pitilessly for politicians but thrillingly for readers – the public and secret histories of his times, from the Second World War to the "War on Terror"' *Guardian*

'John le Carré is as recognisable a writer as Dickens or Austen' *Financial Times*

'A writer of towering gifts . . . le Carré is one of the great analysts of the contemporary scene, who has a talent to provoke as well as unsettle' *Independent*

'The premier spy novelist of his time. Perhaps of all time' *Time*

'One of those writers who will be read a century from now' Robert Harris

'The great master of the spy story . . . the constant flow of emotion lif   nse novelists, but ab   *ial Times*

'The mast

D1350098

LM 1391998 9

'Our greatest living master of espionage fiction . . . Le Carré is one of our great writers of moral ambiguity, a tireless explorer of that darkly contradictory no-man's land' Tim Rutten, *Los Angeles Times*

'Le Carré is not just today's gold standard, but the best there ever was' *The Huffington Post*

'No other contemporary novelist has more durably enjoyed the twin badges of being both well-read and well-regarded' Scott Turow

'Le Carré is one of the best novelists – of any kind – we have' *Vanity Fair*

'He can communicate emotion, from sweating fear to despairing love, with terse and compassionate conviction. Above all, he can tell a tale' Susan Hill, *Sunday Times*

'A masterly understanding of moral complexity . . . the signature clarity of his prose is matched only by the distinctive murkiness of what it describes' *Guardian*

'Brilliant, morally outraged works that mine rich veins of post-Cold War venality' *Seattle Times*

'The world's greatest fictional spymaster' *Newsweek*

ABOUT THE AUTHOR

John le Carré was born in 1931 and attended the universities of Bern and Oxford. He taught at Eton and served briefly in British Intelligence during the Cold War. For the last fifty years he has lived by his pen. He divides his time between London and Cornwall.

JOHN LE CARRÉ

The Secret Pilgrim

with an Afterword by the author

PENGUIN BOOKS

PENGUIN CLASSICS

Published by the Penguin Group
Penguin Books Ltd, 80 Strand, London WC2R ORL, England
Penguin Group (USA) Inc., 375 Hudson Street, New York, New York 10014, USA
Penguin Group (Canada), 90 Eglinton Avenue East, Suite 700, Toronto, Ontario,
Canada M4P 2Y3 (a division of Pearson Penguin Canada Inc.)
Penguin Ireland, 25 St Stephen's Green, Dublin 2, Ireland (a division of Penguin Books Ltd)
Penguin Group (Australia), 707 Collins Street, Melbourne, Victoria 3008, Australia
(a division of Pearson Australia Group Pty Ltd)
Penguin Books India Pvt Ltd, 11 Community Centre, Panchsheel Park,
New Delhi – 110 017, India
Penguin Group (NZ), 67 Apollo Drive, Rosedale, Auckland 0632, New Zealand
(a division of Pearson New Zealand Ltd)
Penguin Books (South Africa) (Pty) Ltd, Block D, Rosebank Office Park,
181 Jan Smuts Avenue, Parktown North, Gauteng 2193, South Africa

Penguin Books Ltd, Registered Offices: 80 Strand, London WC2R ORL, England

www.penguin.com

First published in Great Britain by Hodder & Stoughton 1991
Published in Penguin Classics 2011
004

Set in 11.25/14 pt Dante MT Std
Typeset by Jouve (UK), Milton Keynes
Printed in England by Clays Ltd, St Ives plc

ISBN: 978-0-141-19636-7

www.greenpenguin.co.uk

MIX
Paper from
responsible sources
FSC
www.fsc.org   FSC™ C018179

Penguin Books is committed to a sustainable
future for our business, our readers and our planet.
This book is made from Forest Stewardship
Council™ certified paper.

For Alec Guinness
with affection and thanks

I

Let me confess to you at once that if I had not, on the spur of the moment, picked up my pen and scribbled a note to George Smiley inviting him to address my passing-out class on the closing evening of their entry course – and had Smiley not, against all my expectations, consented – I would not be making so free to you with my heart.

At the most, I would be offering you the sort of laundered reminiscence with which, if I am honest, I was a bit too inclined to regale my students: feats of secret chivalry, of the dramatic, the resourceful and the brave. And always, of course, the useful. I would be enthralling you with memories of night drops into the Caucasus, hazardous crossings by fast boat, beach landings, winking shore lights, clandestine radio messages that ceased in mid-transmission. Of silent heroes of the Cold War who, having made their contribution, modestly went to earth in the society they had protected. Of defectors-in-place snatched in the nick of time from the jaws of the opposition.

And to a point, yes, that is the life we lived. In our day we did those things, and some even ended well. We had good men in bad countries who risked their lives for us. And usually they were believed, and sometimes their intelligence was wisely used. I hope so, for the greatest spy on earth is worth nothing when it isn't.

And for the lighter note, over a second whisky in the Probationers' Mess, I would have picked out for them the occasion when a three-man reception team from the Circus, operating inside East Germany, and gallantly led by myself, lay freezing on a ridge in the Harz Mountains, praying for the flutter of an unmarked plane with its engines cut, and the blessed black parachute floating in its wake. And what did we find when our prayer was answered and we had slithered down an icefield to claim our treasure? Stones, I would tell my wide-eyed students. Chunks of honest Argyll granite. The despatchers at our Scottish airbase had sent us the training canister by mistake.

That tale, at least, found a certain echo, even if some of my other offerings tended to lose their audience halfway through.

I suspect that my impulse to write to Smiley had been brewing in me longer than I realised. The idea was conceived during one of my regular visits to Personnel to discuss the progress of my students. Dropping in on the Senior Officers' Bar for a sandwich and a beer, I had bumped into Peter Guillam. Peter had played Watson to George's Sherlock Holmes in the long search for the Circus traitor, who turned out to be our Head of Operations, Bill Haydon. Peter had not heard from George for – oh, a year now, more. George had bought this cottage in North Cornwall somewhere, he said, and was indulging his dislike of the telephone. He had some kind of sinecure at Exeter University, and was allowed to use their library. Sadly I pictured the rest: George the lonely hermit on an empty landscape, taking his solitary walks and thinking his thoughts. George slipping up to Exeter for a little human warmth in his old age while he waited to take his place in the spies' Valhalla.

And Ann, his wife? I asked Peter, lowering my voice as one

does when Ann's name comes up – for it was an open secret, and a painful one, that Bill Haydon had counted among Ann's many lovers.

Ann was Ann, said Peter, with a Gallic shrug. She had bits of family with grand houses on the Helford Estuary. Sometimes she stayed with them, sometimes she stayed with George.

I asked for Smiley's address. 'Don't tell him I gave it you,' said Peter as I wrote it down. With George, there had always been that certain kind of guilt about passing on his whereabouts – I still don't quite know why.

Three weeks later Toby Esterhase came down to Sarratt to give us his celebrated talk on the arts of clandestine surveillance on unfriendly soil. And of course he stayed for lunch, which was greatly enhanced for him by the presence of our first three girls. After a battle lasting as long as I had been at Sarratt, Personnel had finally decided that girls were all right after all.

And I heard myself trailing Smiley's name.

There have been times when I would not have entertained Toby in the woodshed, and others when I thanked my Maker I had him on my side. But with the years, I am pleased to notice, one settles to people.

'Oh look here, my God, Ned!' Toby cried in his incurably Hungarian English, smoothing back his carefully pomaded mane of silver hair. 'You mean you haven't heard?'

'Heard what?' I asked patiently.

'My dear fellow, George is chairing the Fishing Rights Committee. Don't they tell you anything down here in the sticks? I think I better take this up with the Chief actually, one to one. A word in his ear at the Club.'

'Perhaps you'd tell me first what the Fishing Rights Committee is,' I suggested.

'Ned, you know what? I think I get nervous. Maybe they took you off the list.'

'Maybe they did at that,' I said.

He told me anyway, as I knew he would, and I duly acted astonished, which gave him an even greater sense of his importance. And there is a part of me that remains astonished to this day. The Fishing Rights Committee, Toby explained for the benefit of the unblessed, was an informal working party made up of officers from Moscow Centre and the Circus. Its job, said Toby – who I really believe had lost any capacity to be surprised – was to identify intelligence targets of interest to both services and thrash out a system of sharing. 'The idea actually, Ned, was to target the world's trouble spots,' he said with an air of maddening superiority – 'I think they fix first the Middle East. Don't quote me, Ned, okay?'

'And you're telling me Smiley *chairs* this committee?' I asked incredulously when I had attempted to digest this.

'Well, maybe not much longer, Ned – Anno Domini and so forth. But the Russians were so frightfully keen to meet him, we brought him in to snip the tape. Give the old fellow a treat, I say. Stroke him a bit. Bunch of fivers in an envelope.'

I didn't know which to marvel at the more: the notion of Toby Esterhase tripping to the altar with Moscow Centre, or of George Smiley presiding over the marriage. A few days later, with Personnel's permission, I wrote to the Cornish address Guillam had given me, adding diffidently that if George loathed public speaking half as much as I did, he should on no account accept. I had been a bit in the dumps till then, but when his prim little card arrived by return declaring him delighted, I felt a probationer myself, and just as nervous.

Two weeks after that, wearing a brand-new country suit

for the occasion, I was standing at the barrier at Paddington Station, watching the elderly trains disgorge their middle-aged commuters. I don't think I had ever been quite so aware of Smiley's anonymity. Wherever I looked, I seemed to see versions of him: tubby, bespectacled gentlemen of a certain seniority, and every one of them with George's air of being slightly late for something he would rather not be doing. Then suddenly we had shaken hands and he was sitting beside me in the back of a Head Office Rover, stockier than I remembered him, and white-haired, it was true, but of a vigour and good humour I had not seen in him since his wife had her fatal fling with Haydon.

'Well, well, Ned. How do you like being a schoolmaster?'

'How do you like retirement?' I countered, with a laugh. 'I'll be joining you soon!'

Oh, he loved retirement, he assured me. Couldn't get enough of it, he said wryly; I should have no fears of it at all. A little tutoring here, Ned, the odd paper to deliver there; walks, he'd even acquired a dog.

'I hear they hauled you back to sit on some extraordinary committee,' I said. 'Conspiring with the Bear, they say, against the Thief of Baghdad.'

George does not gossip, but I saw his smile broaden. 'Do they now? And your source would be Toby, no doubt,' he said, and beamed contentedly upon the dismal subtopian landscape while he launched into a diversionary story about two old ladies in his village who hated each other. One owned an antique shop, the other was very rich. But as the Rover continued its progress through once-rural Hertfordshire, I found myself thinking less about the ladies of George's village than about George himself. I was thinking that this was a Smiley reborn, who told stories about old ladies, sat on committees with Russian spies and gazed on the overt world with the relish of someone who has just come out of hospital.

That evening, squeezed into an elderly dinner jacket, the same man sat at my side at Sarratt high table, peering benignly round him at the polished plate candlesticks and old group photographs going back to God knows when. And at the fit, expectant faces of his young audience as they waited on the master's word.

'Ladies and gentlemen, Mr George Smiley,' I announced severely as I rose to introduce him. 'A legend of the Service. Thank you.'

'Oh, I don't think I'm a legend at all,' Smiley protested as he clambered to his feet. 'I think I'm just a rather fat old man wedged between the pudding and the port.'

Then the legend began talking, and I realised that I had never heard Smiley address a social gathering before. I had assumed it was a thing he would be congenitally bad at, like forcing his opinions on people, or referring to a joe by his real name. So the sovereign way in which he addressed us surprised me before I had begun to fathom the content. I heard his first few sentences and I watched my students' faces – not always so obliging – lift and relax and light to him as they gave him first their attention, then their trust and finally their support. And I thought, with an inner smile of belated recognition: yes, yes, of course, this was George's other nature. This was the actor who had always lain hidden in him, the secret Pied Piper. This was the man Ann Smiley had loved and Bill Haydon had deceived and the rest of us had loyally followed, to the mystification of outsiders.

There is a wise tradition at Sarratt that our dinner speeches are not recorded and no notes are taken, and that no official reference may afterwards be made to what was said. The guest of honour enjoyed what Smiley in his Germanic way called 'the fool's freedom', though I can think of few people less qualified for the privilege. But I am nothing if not a professional, trained to listen and remember, and you must understand also that Smiley had not spoken many words before I realised – as my students were not slow to notice – that he was speaking straight into my heretical heart. I refer to that other, less obedient person who is also inside me and whom, if I am honest, I had refused to acknowledge since I had embarked on this final lap of my career – to the secret questioner who had been my uncomfortable companion even before a reluctant joe of mine called Barley Blair had stepped across the crumbling Iron Curtain and, for reasons of love, and some sort of honour, had calmly kept on walking, to the incredulity of the Fifth Floor.

The better the restaurant, we say of Personnel, the worse the news. 'It's time you handed on your wisdom to the new boys, Ned,' he had told me over a suspiciously good lunch at the Connaught. '*And* to the new *girls*,' he added, with a loathsome smirk. 'They'll be letting them into the Church next, I suppose.' He returned to happier ground. 'You know the tricks. You've kicked around. You've had an impressive last lap running Secretariat. Time to put it all to advantage. We think you should take over the Nursery and pass the torch to tomorrow's spies.'

He had used a rather similar set of sporting metaphors, if I remembered rightly, when in the wake of Barley Blair's defection he had removed me from my post as Head of the Russia House and consigned me to that knacker's yard, the Interrogators' Pool.

He ordered up two more glasses of Armagnac. 'How's your Mabel, by the way?' he continued, as if he had just remembered her. 'Somebody told me she'd got her handicap down to twelve – ten, by God! Well. I trust you'll keep her away from me! So what do you say? Sarratt in the week, home to Tunbridge Wells at weekends, sounds to me like the triumphant crowning of a career. What do you say?'

So what *do* you say? You say what others have said before you. Those who can, do. Those who can't, teach. And what they teach is what they can't do any more, because either the body or the spirit or both have lost their singleness of purpose; because they have seen too much and suppressed too much and compromised too much, and in the end tasted too little. So they take to rekindling their old dreams in new minds, and warming themselves against the fires of the young.

And that brings me back to the opening bars of Smiley's speech that night, for suddenly his words were reaching out and grasping me. I had invited him because he was a legend of the past. Yet to the delight of all of us, he was turning out to be the iconoclastic prophet of the future.

I'll not bother you with the finer points of Smiley's introductory tour of the globe. He gave them the Middle East, which was obviously on his mind, and he explored the limits of colonial power in supposedly post-colonialist times. He gave them the Third World and the Fourth World and posited a Fifth World, and pondered aloud whether human despair and poverty were the serious concern of any wealthy nation. He seemed pretty confident they weren't. He scoffed at the idea that spying was a dying profession now that the Cold War had ended: with each new nation that came out of the ice, he said, with each new alignment, each rediscovery of old identities and passions, with each erosion of the old sta-tus quo, the spies would be working round the clock. He spoke, I discovered afterwards, for twice the customary length, but I didn't hear a chair creak or a glass clink – not even when they dragged him to the library and sat him in the throne of honour before the fire for more of the same, more heresy, more subversion. My children, hardened cases all of them, in love with George! I didn't hear a sound beyond the confident flow of Smiley's voice and the eager burst of laughter at some unexpected self-irony or confession of failure. You're only old once, I thought, as I listened with them, sharing their excitement.

He gave them case histories I had never heard, and which I was certain nobody in Head Office had cleared in advance – certainly not our Legal Adviser Palfrey, who in response to the openness of our former enemies had been battening down and double-locking every useless secret he could lay his obedient hands on.

He dwelt on their future role as agent-runners and, apply-ing it to the altered world, vested in it the traditional Service image of mentor, shepherd, parent and befriender, as prop and marriage counsellor, as pardoner, entertainer and pro-tector; as the man or woman who has the gift of treating the outrageous premise as an everyday affair, and so becomes his agent's partner in illusion. None of that had changed, he said. None of it ever would. He paraphrased Burns: 'A spy's a spy for all that.'

But no sooner had he lulled them with this sweet notion than he warned them of the death of their own natures that could result from the manipulation of their fellow men, and the truncation of their natural feeling.

'By being all things to all spies, one does rather run the

risk of becoming nothing to oneself,' he confessed sadly. 'Please don't ever imagine you'll be unscathed by the methods you use. The end may justify the means – if it wasn't supposed to, I dare say you wouldn't be here. But there's a price to pay, and the price does tend to be oneself. Easy to sell one's soul at your age. Harder later.'

He mixed the deadly serious with the deadly frivolous and made the difference small. Between whiles he seemed to be asking the questions I had been asking of myself for most of my working life, but had never managed to express, such as: 'Did it do any good?' And 'What did it do to me?' And 'What will become of us now?' Sometimes his questions were answers: George, we used to say, never asked unless he knew.

He made us laugh, he made us feel and, by means of his inordinate deference, he shocked us with his contrasts. Better still, he put our prejudices at risk. He got rid of the acceptance in me and revived the slumbering rebel that my exile to Sarratt had silenced. George Smiley, out of a clear sky, had renewed my search and confused me wonderfully.

Frightened people never learn, I have read. If that is so, they certainly have no right to teach. I'm not a frightened man – or no more frightened than any other man who has looked at death and knows it is for him. All the same, experience and a little pain had made me a mite too wary of the truth, even towards myself. George Smiley put that right. George was more than a mentor to me, more than a friend. Though not always present, he presided over my life. There were times when I thought of him as some kind of father to replace the one I never knew. George's visit to Sarratt gave back the dangerous edge to my memory. And now that I have the leisure to remember, that's what I mean to do for you, so that you can share my voyage and ask yourself the same questions.

2

'There are some people,' Smiley declared comfortably, favouring with his merry smile the pretty girl from Trinity Oxford whom I had thoughtfully placed across the table from him, 'who, when their past is threatened, get frightened of losing everything they thought they had, and perhaps everything they thought they were as well. Now I don't feel that one bit. The purpose of *my* life was to end the time I lived in. So if my past were still around today, you could say I'd failed. But it's not around. We won. Not that the victory matters a damn. And perhaps we didn't win anyway. Perhaps they just lost. Or perhaps, without the bonds of ideological conflict to restrain us any more, our troubles are just beginning. Never mind. What matters is that a long war is over. What matters is the hope.'

Removing his spectacles from his ears, he fumbled distractedly with his shirt front, looking for I could not imagine what, until I realised that it was the fat end of the necktie on which he was accustomed to polish his lenses. But an awkwardly assembled black bow tie provides no such conveniences, so he used the silk handkerchief from his pocket instead.

'If I regret anything at all, it's the way we wasted our time and skills. All the false alleys, and bogus friends, the misapplication of our energies. All the delusions we had about who we were.' He replaced his spectacles and, as I fancied, turned his smile upon myself. And suddenly I felt like one of my own students. It was the sixties again. I was a fledgling spy, and George Smiley – tolerant, patient, clever George – was observing my first attempts at flight.

We were fine fellows in those days, and the days seemed longer. Probably no finer than my students today, but our patriotic vision was less clouded. By the end of my new-entry course I was ready to save the world if I had to spy on it from end to end. We were ten in my intake and after a couple of years of training – at the Sarratt Nursery, in the glens of Argyll and battle camps of Wiltshire – we waited for our first operational postings like thoroughbreds pining for the chase.

We too in our way had come to maturity at a great moment in history, even if it was the reverse of this one. Stagnation and hostility stared at us from every corner of the globe. The Red Peril was everywhere, not least on our own sacred hearth. The Berlin Wall had been up two years and by the looks of it would stay up for another two hundred. The Middle East was a volcano, just as it is now, except that in those days Nasser was our chosen British hate object, not least because he was giving Arabs back their dignity and playing hookey with the Russians into the bargain. In Cyprus, Africa and South-East Asia the lesser breeds without the law were rising against their old colonial masters. And if we few brave British occasionally felt our power diminished by this – well, there was always Cousin America to cut us back into the world's game.

As secret heroes in the making, therefore, we had everything we needed: a righteous cause, an evil enemy, an indulgent ally, a seething world, women to cheer us, but only from the touchline, and best of all the Great Tradition to inherit, for the Circus in those days was still basking in its wartime glory.

Almost all our leading men had earned their spurs by spying on the Germans. All of them, when questioned at our earnest, off-the-record seminars, agreed that when it came to protecting mankind against its own excesses, World Communism was an even darker menace than the Hun.

'You gentlemen have inherited a dangerous planet,' Jack Arthur Lumley, our fabled Head of Training, liked to tell us. 'And if you want my personal opinion, you're bloody lucky.'

Oh, we wanted his opinion all right! Jack Arthur was a derring-do man. He had spent three years dropping in and out of Nazi-occupied Europe as if he were a regular house-guest. He had blown up bridges single-handed. He had been caught and escaped and caught again, no one knew how many times. He had killed men with his bare fingers, losing a couple in the fray, and when the Cold War came along to replace the hot one, Jack hardly noticed the difference. At the age of fifty-five he could still shoot you a grin on a man-sized target with a 9-millimetre Browning at twenty paces, pick your door lock with a paper clip, booby-trap a lavatory chain in thirty seconds or pin you helpless to the gym-mat in one throw. Jack Arthur had despatched us by parachute from Stirling bombers and landed us in rubber boats on Cornish beaches and drunk us under the table on mess nights. If Jack Arthur said it was a dangerous planet, we believed him to the hilt!

But it made the waiting all the harder. If I hadn't had Ben Arno Cavendish to share it with, it would have been harder still. There are only so many attachments you can serve around Head Office before your enthusiasm turns to gall.

Ben and I had been born under the same star. We were the same age, the same schooling, the same build, and within an inch of the same height. Trust the Circus to throw us together – we told each other excitedly; they probably knew it all along!

We both had foreign mothers, though his was dead – the Arno came from his German side – and were both, perhaps by way of compensation, determinedly of the English extrovert classes – athletic, hedonistic, public-school, male, born to administer if not to rule. Though, as I look at the group photographs of our year, I see that Ben made a rather better job of the part than I did, for he possessed an air of maturity that in those days eluded me – he had the widow's peak and the confirmed jaw, a man superior to his youthfulness.

Which, for all I knew, was why Ben got the coveted Berlin job instead of me, running flesh-and-blood agents inside East Germany, while I was once more put on standby.

'We're lending you to the watchers for a couple of weeks, young Ned,' said Personnel, with an avuncular complacency I was beginning to resent. 'Be good experience for you, and they can do with a spare pair of hands. Plenty of cloak-and-dagger stuff. You like that.'

Anything for a change, I thought, putting a brave face on it. For the past month I had bent my ingenuity to sabotaging the World Peace Conference in – let's say – Belgrade, from a dark desk on the Third Floor. Under the instruction of a slow-spoken superior who lunched for hours on end in the Senior Officers' Bar, I had enthusiastically re-routed delegates' trains, blocked their hotel plumbing and made anonymous bomb threats to their conference hall. For the month before that, I had crouched bravely in a stinking cellar next to the Egyptian Embassy at six every morning, waiting for a venal charlady to bring me, in exchange for a five-pound note, the contents of the Ambassadorial waste paper basket from the previous day. By such modest standards, a couple of weeks riding around with the world's best watchers sounded like a free holiday.

'They're assigning you to Operation Fat Boy,' Personnel

said, and gave me the address of a safe house off Green Street in the West End. I heard the sound of ping-pong as I walked in, and a cracked gramophone record playing Gracie Fields. My heart sank, and once again I sent a prayer of envy to Ben Cavendish and his heroic agents in Berlin, the spy's eternal city. Monty Arbuck, our section leader, briefed us the same evening.

Let me apologise for myself in advance. I knew very little of other ranks in those days. I was of the officer caste – literally, for I had served with the Royal Navy – and found it perfectly natural that I had been born into the upper end of the social system. The Circus is nothing if not a little mirror of the England it protects, so it seemed equally right to me that our watchers and allied trades, such as burglars and eavesdroppers, should be drawn from the artisan community. You cannot follow a man for long in a bowler hat. A honed BBC voice is no passport to unobtrusiveness once you are outside London's golden mile, least of all if you are posing as a street hawker or a window cleaner or a post-office engineer. So you should see me, at best, as a callow young midshipman seated among his more experienced and less privileged shipmates. And you should see Monty not as he was, but as I saw him that evening, as a taut-minded gamekeeper with a chip on his shoulder. We were ten, including Monty: three teams of three, therefore, with a woman to each so that we could cover ladies' lavatories. That was the principle. And Monty our controller.

'Good evening, College,' he said, placing himself before a blackboard and talking straight to me. 'Always nice to have a touch of quality to raise the tone, I say.'

Laughter all round, loudest from myself, a good sport to his men.

'Target for tomorrow, College, is His Right Royal Sovereign Highness Fat Boy, otherwise known as—'

Turning to the blackboard, Monty helped himself to a piece of chalk and laboriously scratched up a long Arab name.

'And the nature of our mission, College, is PR,' he resumed. 'I trust you know what PR is, do you? I have no doubt they teach you that at the spies' Eton?'

'Public Relations,' I said, surprised to occasion so much merriment. For alas it turned out that in the watchers' vernacular the initials stood for Protect and Report, and that our task for tomorrow, and for as long as our royal visitor chose to remain our charge, was to ensure that no harm came to him, and to report to Head Office on his activities, whether social or commercial.

'College, you're with Paul and Nancy,' Monty told me, when he had provided us with the rest of our operational intelligence. 'You'll be number three in the section, College, and you'll kindly do *exactly* as you are told, irregardless.'

But here I prefer to give you the background to Fat Boy's case not in Monty's words but in my own, and with the benefit of twenty-five years of hindsight. Even today, I can blush to think who I thought I was, and how I must have appeared to the likes of Monty, Paul and Nancy.

Understand first that licensed arms dealers in Britain regard themselves as some kind of rough-edged élite – did then, do now – and that they enjoy quite disproportionate privileges at the hands of the police, the bureaucracy and the intelligence services. For reasons I have never understood, their grisly trade puts them in a relationship of confidence with these bodies. Perhaps it's the illusion of reality they impart, of guns as the earthy truth of life and death. Perhaps, in the tethered minds of our officials, their wares suggest the same authority that is exerted by those who use them. I don't know. But I've seen enough of the street side of life in the years between to know that more men are in love with war than ever get a chance to fight one, and that more guns are bought to satisfy this love than for a pardonable purpose.

Understand also that Fat Boy was a most valued customer of this industry. And that our task of Protecting and Reporting was only one small part of a far larger undertaking; namely, the care and cultivation of a so-called friendly Arab state. By which was meant, and is meant to this day, currying favour, suborning and flattering its princelings with our English ways, wheedling favourable concessions in order to satisfy our oil addiction – and, along the way, selling enough British weaponry to keep the Satanic mills of Birmingham turning day and night. Which may have accounted for Monty's rooted distaste for our task. I like to think so anyway. Old watchers are famous for their moralising – and with reason. First they watch, later they think. Monty had reached the thinking stage.

As to Fat Boy, his credentials for this treatment were impeccable. He was the wastrel brother of the ruler of an oil-rich sheikdom. He was capricious, and prone to forget what he had bought before. And he arrived as billed, in the ruler's Boeing jet, at a military airport near London specially cleared for him, to have himself a little fun and do a little shopping – which we understood would include such fripperies as a couple of armoured Rolls-Royces for himself, half the trinkets at Cartier's for his women friends around the globe, a hundred or so of our not quite latest ground-to-air missile launchers, and a squadron or two of our not quite latest combat fighters for his royal brother. Not forgetting a succulent British government contract for spares, services and training which would keep the Royal Air Force and the arms manufacturers in clover for years to come. – Oh, and oil. We would have oil to burn. Naturally.

His retinue, apart from private secretaries, astrologers, flatterers, nannies, children and two tutors, comprised a personal doctor and three bodyguards.

Lastly there was Fat Boy's wife, and her codename is irrelevant because from Day One Monty's watchers dubbed her 'the Panda' on account of the dark circles round her eyes when she was unveiled, and her wistful and solitary deportment, which gave the air of an endangered species. Fat Boy had a string of wives, but the Panda, though the oldest, was the most favoured, and perhaps the most tolerant of her husband's pleasures around town, for he liked nightclubs and he liked to gamble – tastes for which my fellow watchers cordially loathed him before he arrived, since it was known of him that he seldom went to bed before six in the morning, and never without losing about twenty times their combined annual salaries.

The party had rooms at a grand West End hotel, on two floors linked by a specially installed lift. Fat Boy, like many forty-year-old voluptuaries, was worried about his heart. He was also worried about microphones, and liked to use the lift as his safe room. So the Circus listeners had thoughtfully provided a microphone in the lift for him as well, which was where they reckoned to pick up their tidbits about the latest palace intrigues, or any unforeseen threat to Fat Boy's military shopping list.

And everything was running smoothly until Day Three, when one small unknown Arab man in a black overcoat with velvet collars appeared silently on our horizon. Or more accurately, in the ladies' lingerie department of a great Knightsbridge department store, where the Panda and her attendants were picking their way through a stack of frilly white undergarments spread over the glass counter. For the Panda also had her spies. And word had reached her that, on the day before, the Fat Boy himself had brooded fondly over the same articles, and even ordered a few dozen to be sent to an address in Paris where a favoured lady friend constantly awaited him in subsidised luxury.

Day Three, I repeat, and the morale of our three-strong unit under strain. Paul was Paul Skordeno, an inward man with a pocked complexion and a talent for ferocious invective. Nancy told me he was under a cloud, but wouldn't say what for.

'He *hit* a girl, Ned,' she said, but I think now that she meant more than merely hit.

Nancy herself was all of five feet tall and in appearance a kind of licensed bag-lady. For her standard, as she called it, she wore lisle stockings and sensible rubber-soled walking shoes, which she seldom changed. What more she needed – scarves, raincoats, woollen hats of different colours – she took in a plastic carrier.

On surveillance duty our section worked eight-hour shifts always in the same formation, Nancy and Paul playing forward, young Ned trailing along behind as sweep. When I asked Skordeno whether we could vary the formation, he told me to get used to what I'd got. On our first day we had followed Fat Boy to Sandhurst, where a lunch had been organised in his honour. The three of us ate egg-and-chips in a café close to the main gates while Skordeno railed first against the Arabs, then against the Western exploitation of them, then to my distress against the Fifth Floor, whom he described as Fascist golfers.

'You a Freemason, College?'

I assured him I was not.

'Well, you'd best hurry up and join then, hadn't you? Haven't you noticed the saucy way Personnel shakes your hand? You'll never get to Berlin if you're not a Mason, College.'

Day Two had been spent hanging around Mount Street while Fat Boy had himself measured for a pair of Purdy shotguns, first precariously brandishing a try-gun round the premises, then throwing a tantrum when he discovered he would have to wait two years before they were ready. Paul ordered me twice into the shop while this scene was unfolding, and seemed pleased when I told him the staff were becoming suspicious of my frivolous enquiries.

'I'd have thought it was your kind of place,' he said, with his skull-like grin. 'Huntin', shootin' and fishin' – they like that on the Fifth Floor, College.'

The same night had found us sitting three up in a van outside a shuttered whorehouse in South Audley Street, and Head Office in a state of near panic. Fat Boy had only been holed up there two hours when he had telephoned the hotel and ordered his personal doctor to attend immediately. His heart! we thought in alarm. Should we go in? While Head Office dithered, we entertained visions of our quarry dead of a heart attack in the arms of some over-conscientious whore before he had signed the cheque for his obsolete fighter planes. It was not till four o'clock that the listeners laid our fears to rest. Fat Boy had been afflicted by a spell of impotence, they explained, and his doctor had been summoned to inject an aphrodisiac into the royal rump. We returned home at five, Skordeno drunk with anger, but all of us consoled by the knowledge that Fat Boy was due in Luton at midday to attend a grand demonstration of the nearly latest British tank, and we could count on a day's rest. But our relief was premature.

'The Panda wants to buy herself some pretties,' Monty announced to us benignly on our arrival in Green Street. 'Your lot's on. Sorry about that, College.'

Which brings us to the lingerie department of the great Knightsbridge store, and to my moment of glory. Ben, I was thinking; Ben, I would trade one day of yours for five of mine. Then suddenly I wasn't thinking of Ben any more and I had ceased to envy him. I had drawn back into the privacy of a doorway and was speaking into the mouthpiece of the cumbersome radio set, which in those days was the best there was. I had selected the channel which gave me a direct line to base. It was the one Skordeno had told me not to use.

'The Panda's got a monkey on her back,' I informed Monty in my calmest voice, using the approved watchers' jargon to describe a mysterious follower. 'Five five, black curly hair, heavy moustache, aged forty, black overcoat, rubber-soled black shoes, Arab appearance. He was at the airport when Fat Boy's plane came in. I remember him. It's the same man.'

'Stay on him,' came Monty's laconic reply. 'Paul and Nancy stick with the Panda, you stick with the monkey. Which floor?'

'One.'

'Stay on him wherever he goes, keep talking to me.'

'He could be carrying,' I said as my eyes again fixed surreptitiously on the subject of my call.

'You mean he's pregnant?'

I didn't think that very funny.

Let me see the scene precisely, for it was more complicated than you may suppose. Our trio was not alone in following the Panda's retinue on its snail-paced shopping expedition. Wealthy Arab princesses do not arrive unannounced at great Knightsbridge stores. In addition to a pair of floorwalkers in black jackets and striped trousers, two very obvious house detectives had placed themselves at either archway with their feet apart and their hands curled at their sides, ready at any moment to grapple with whirling dervishes. As if that were not enough, Scotland Yard had that morning taken upon itself to provide its own brand of protection in the form of an iron-faced man in a belted raincoat who insisted on placing himself beside the Panda and glowering at anyone who came near. And finally, you must see Paul and Nancy in their Sunday best, their backs turned to everyone while they affected to study trays of négligés, and watched our quarry in the mirrors.

And all of this again, you understand, set in the hushed and scented privacy of the harem; in a world of flimsy undergarments, deep-pile carpets and languorous half-naked dummies – not to mention those kindly grey-haired lady attendants in black crêpe who, at a certain age, are deemed to have achieved a sufficiently unthreatening demeanour to preside over shrines of female intimacy.

Other men, I noticed, preferred not to enter the lingerie department at all, or hurried through it with averted gaze. My instinct would have been the same, had it not been for my recognition of this melancholy little man with his black moustache and passionate brown eyes, who unswervingly trailed the Panda's retinue at fifteen paces. If Monty had not appointed me sweep, I might not have seen him at all – or not then. But it was quickly clear that both he and I, by virtue of our different trades, were obliged to keep the same distance from our target – I with nonchalance, he with a kind of intense and mystical dependence. For his gaze never wavered from her. Even when he was unsighted by a pillar or a customer, he still contrived to crane his dark head this way or that until he had locked her once more in his zealous and – I was now convinced – fanatical gaze.

I had first sensed this fervour in him when I had spotted him in the arrivals hall at the airport, pressing himself on tiptoe against the long window as he wriggled to get a better view of the royal couple's approach. I had made nothing so special of him then. I was subjecting everyone to the same critical examination. He had seemed to be just another of the gaggle of diplomats, retainers and hangers-on who formed the royal welcome party. Nevertheless his intensity had struck a chord in me: So this is the Middle East, I had mused as I watched him squeeze his hollowed face against the glass. These are the heathen passions my Service must contain if we are to drive our cars and heat our houses and sell our weaponry in peace.

The monkey had taken a couple of steps forward and was peering at a cabinet of ribbons. His gait – exactly like that of his namesake – was wide but stealthy; he seemed to move entirely from the knees, in conspiratorial strides. I selected a display of garters next to him and peered into it while I again furtively examined him for tell-tale bulges round the waist and armpits. His black overcoat was of the classic gunman's shape: voluminous and without a belt, the kind of coat that covers effortlessly a long-barrelled pistol fitted with a suppressor, or a semi-automatic slung beneath the arm.

I studied his hands, my own nervously prickling. His left hung loosely at his side, but his right, which looked the stronger, kept travelling towards his chest and withholding, as if he were preparing himself to pluck up courage for the final act.

A right-handed cross-draw, I thought; most likely to the armpit. Our weapons trainers had taught us all the combinations.

And his eyes – those dark, slow-burning, soulful zealot's eyes – even in profile they seemed fixed upon the afterlife. Had he sworn vengeance on her? On her household? Had fanatical mullahs promised him a place in heaven if he did the deed? My knowledge of Islam was scant, and what there was of it was drawn from a couple of background lectures and the novels of P. C. Wren. Yet it was enough to warn me that I was in the presence of a desperate fanatic who counted his own life cheap.

As to myself, alas, I was unarmed. It was a sore point with me. Watchers would never dream of carrying weapons on normal duty, but covert protection work is a different type of watching, and Paul Skordeno had been allocated a sidearm from Monty's safe.

'One's enough, College,' Monty had told me, with his old man's smile. 'We don't want you starting World War Three, now do we?'

All that was left to me, therefore, as I rose and softly followed him again, was to select in advance one of the blows we had been taught to master in our silent-killing classes. Should I count on attacking him from behind – with a rabbit punch? – with a double simultaneous blow over the ears? Either method could kill him instantly, whereas a live man can still be questioned. Then would I do better breaking his right arm first, hoping to take him with his own weapon? Yet if I let him draw, might I myself not go down in a hail of bullets from the several bodyguards around the room?

She had seen him!

The Panda had looked straight into the eyes of the monkey, and the monkey had returned her stare!

Had she recognised him? I was certain she had. But had she recognised his purpose? And was she, perhaps, in some strange turn of Oriental fatalism, preparing herself for death? The lurid possibilities went racing through my mind as I continued to observe their mysterious exchange. Their eyes met, the Panda froze in mid-gesture. Her jewelled, crabby little hands, plundering the clothing on the counter, kept still – and then, as if to his command, slipped passively to her sides. After which she stood motionless, without will, without even the strength to detach herself from his penetrating stare.

At last, with a forlorn and strangely humble air, she turned away from him, murmured something to her lady companions and, holding out her hand to the counter, released whatever frilly thing she was still clutching in it. She was wearing brown that day – if she had been a man, I would be tempted to say a Franciscan habit – with wide sleeves longer than her arms, and a brown headband bound tightly across her brow.

I saw her sigh, then slowly and, I was sure, resignedly, she led her entourage towards the archway. After her went her personal bodyguard; after him the Scotland Yard policeman. Then came the ladies of her train, followed by the floorwalkers. And finally came Paul and Nancy, who, with a show of indecision, had torn themselves away from their study of the négligés and were sauntering like any shoppers in the party's wake. Paul, who had surely overheard my conversations with Monty, vouchsafed me not the smallest glance. Nancy, who prided herself on her amateur dramatics, was pretending to pick a marital dispute with him. I tried to see whether Paul had unbuttoned his jacket, for he too favoured the cross-draw. But his broad back was turned away from me.

'All right, College, show me,' said Monty brightly into my left ear, appearing beside me as if by magic. How long had he been there? I had no idea. It was past midday and our time for standing down, but this was no moment to change the guard. The monkey was not five yards from us, stepping lightly but determinedly after the Panda.

'We can take him at the stairs,' I murmured.

'Speak louder,' Monty advised me, in the same unabashed voice. 'Speak normally, no one listens to you. Mutter, mutter out of the corner of your mouth, they think you've come to rob the till.'

Since we were on the first floor, the Panda's party was sure to take the lift, whether they went up or down. Beside the lift stood a pair of swing doors opening on to what in those days was a stone emergency staircase, rather dank and insanitary, with linoleum treads. My plan, which I outlined to Monty in staccato sentences as we followed the monkey towards the archway, was simplicity itself. As the party approached the lift, Monty and I would close on him from either side, grab an arm each and sweep him into the staircase. We would subdue him with a blow to the groin, remove his weapon, then spirit him to Green Street where we would invite him to make a voluntary statement. In training exercises we had done such things a dozen times – once, to our embarrassment, to an innocent bank clerk who was hurrying home to his wife and family, and whom we had mistaken for a member of the training staff.

But if Monty heard me, to my frustration he gave no sign of having done so. He was watching the floorwalkers clear a path through the crowd to the lift so that the Panda's party could ride in privacy. And he was smiling like any casual commoner who stumbles on a glimpse of royalty.

'She's going down,' he declared with satisfaction. 'Pound to a penny it's the costume jewellery she's after. You'd think the Gulfies wouldn't bother with the artificial stuff, but they can't get enough of it; they think it's got to be a bargain. Come on, son. This is fun. Let's go and take a look.'

I like to think that even in my perplexity I recognised the excellence of Monty's tradecraft. The Panda's exotic entourage, mostly in Arab dress, was arousing lively curiosity among the shoppers. Monty was just another punter, enjoying the spectacle. And yes, he was right again, their destination was the costume jewellery department, as the monkey also had divined, for as we emerged from our lift the monkey scampered ahead of the party to take up a favoured place alongside the glittering displays, his left shoulder nearest to the wall, exactly as required of a right-handed gunman who draws across his chest.

Yet, far from choosing a strategic position from which to return fire, Monty merely wandered after him, and, having placed himself next to him, beckoned me to join them, and in such a way that I had no alternative but to leave Monty, not the monkey, at the centre of our trio.

'This is why I always come to Knightsbridge, son,' Monty was explaining, loudly enough for half the floor to hear. 'You never know who you're going to meet. I brought your mother last time – *you* remember – we'd gone to the Harrods Food Hall. I thought: "*Hullo*, I know you, you're Rex Harrison." I could have held out my hand and touched him but I didn't. It's the crossroads of the world, Knightsbridge is, don't you agree, sir?' – lifting his hat to the monkey, who smiled wanly in return. 'Now I wonder where this lot would be from. Arabs, by the look of them, with the wealth of Solomon at their fingertips. And they don't even pay taxes, I dare say. Not royalty, well, they wouldn't have to. There isn't a royal household in the world pays taxes to itself, it wouldn't be logical. See the big policeman there, son? He'll be Special Branch, you can tell by his stupid scowl.'

The Panda's party meanwhile was distributing itself among the illuminated glass counters while the Panda, in barely concealed agitation, was requiring that the trays be taken out for her inspection. And soon, as in the lingerie department, she was picking out one object after another, turning it critically under the inspection light, then setting it down and taking up another. And yet again, as she continued to appraise and relinquish each piece in turn, I saw her worried gaze slip towards us, first to the monkey, then to myself, as if she had seen in me her one hope of protection.

Yet Monty, when I glanced at him for confirmation, was still smiling.

'That's exactly what happened in the lingerie department,' I whispered, forgetting his instruction to speak normally.

But Monty continued his noisy monologue. 'But underneath, son – I always say this – underneath, royals or not, they're the same as what we are, through and through. We're all born naked, we're all on our way to the grave. Your wealth is your health, better to be rich in friends than money, I say. We've all got the same appetites, the same little weaknesses and naughty ways.' And on he ran, as if in deliberate contrast to my extreme alertness.

She had ordered up more trays. The counter was covered with sumptuous paste tiaras, bracelets and rings. Selecting a three-string necklace of imitation rubies, she held it to her throat, then took up a hand mirror to admire herself.

And was it my imagination? It was not! She was using the mirror to observe the monkey and ourselves! First one dark eye, then the other fixed upon us; then the two of them together, warning us, imploring us, before she set the mirror down again and turned her back to us, and swept as if in anger along the edge of the glass counter, where a fresh display awaited her.

At the same moment, the monkey took a step forward and I saw his hand rise to the opening of his overcoat. Throwing caution aside, I too stepped forward, my right arm drawn back, the fingers of my right hand flexed, palm parallel to the ground in the approved Sarratt manner. I had decided on an elbow to the heart, followed by a side-of-hand to the upper lip, to the point where the nose cartilage joins the top half of the jaw. A complicated network of nerves has its meeting point here, and a well-aimed blow can immobilise the victim for some while. The monkey was opening his mouth and breathing in. I anticipated a cry to Allah, or perhaps the screamed slogan of some fundamentalist sect – though I am no longer sure how much we knew or cared in those days about fundamentalist Arabs. I at once determined to scream myself, not only in order to confuse him, but because a deep breath would put more oxygen into my bloodstream and so increase my striking power. I was actually drawing this breath when I felt Monty's hand lock like an iron ring round my wrist and, with unpredicted power, immobilise me as he drew me back to him.

'Now don't do that, son, this gentleman was before you,' he said in a matter-of-fact voice. 'He's got a little confidential business to transact, haven't you, sir?'

He had indeed. And Monty's grasp did not release me until I had observed the nature of it. The monkey was speaking. Not to the Panda, not to her retinue, but to the two floor-walkers in striped trousers who were inclining their heads to listen to him, at first condescendingly, then with startled interest as their gaze switched to the Panda.

'Alas, gentlemen, Her Royal Highness prefers to make her purchases informally, you see,' he was saying. 'Without the inconvenience of a wrapping or an invoice, let us put it that way. It is her time of life. Three and four years ago, she was a most expert bargainer, you know. Oh yes. She would negotiate a most competitive discount for everything she wished to buy. But today, at her time of life, she is taking matters most literally into her own hands, you see. Or should I say into her sleeve, oh dear? I am therefore charged by His Royal Highness to make a most bountiful settlement for all such informal purchases, on the very clear understanding that no breath of publicity reaches the public ear, gentlemen, whether in the written or the spoken word, if you understand me.'

Then from his pocket he drew not, alas, a deadly Walther automatic, not a Heckler & Koch sub-machine gun, not even one of our beloved standard Browning 9-millimetres, but a tooled Moroccan leather wallet stuffed with his master's banknotes in a variety of denominations.

'I counted, I believe, three fine rings, sir, one in artificial emerald, two in paste diamond, also a fine artificial ruby necklace, gentlemen, three strings. It is the wish of His Royal Highness that our settlement should take generous account of any inconvenience suffered by your most excellent staff, you see. Also commission to your good selves, on the understanding already stated regarding publicity.'

Monty's grip on me had at last relaxed, and as we walked

towards the hall I dared to glance at him, and saw to my relief that his expression, though thoughtful, was surprisingly gentle.

'That's the trouble in our job, Ned,' he explained content-edly, using my Christian name for the first time. 'Life's looking one way, we're looking the other. I like an honest-to-God enemy myself sometimes, I don't mind admitting. Take a lot of finding, though, don't they? Too many nice blokes about.'

3

'Now do please remember,' Smiley piously exhorted his young audience, in much the tone he might have selected if he had been asking them to put their offerings in the collection box as they were leaving, 'that the privately educated Englishman – and Englishwoman, if you will allow me – is the greatest dissembler on earth.' He waited for the laughter to subside. 'Was, is now and ever shall be for as long as our disgraceful school system remains intact. Nobody will charm you so glibly, disguise his feelings from you better, cover his tracks more skilfully or find it harder to confess to you that he's been a damned fool. Nobody acts braver when he's frightened stiff, or happier when he's miserable; nobody can flatter you better when he hates you than your extrovert Englishman or woman of the supposedly privileged classes. He can have a Force Twelve nervous breakdown while he stands next to you in the bus queue, and you may be his best friend, but you'll never be the wiser. Which is why some of our best officers turn out to be our worst. And our worst, our best. And why the most difficult agent you will ever have to run is yourself.'

In his own mind, I had no doubt, Smiley was talking about the greatest deceiver of us all, Bill Haydon. But for me, he was talking about Ben – and yes, though it's harder to admit, about the young Ned, and perhaps the old one too.

It was the afternoon of the day I had failed to immolate the Panda's bodyguard. Tired and dispirited, I arrived at my flat in Battersea to find the door on the latch and two men in grey suits sifting through the papers in my desk.

They barely looked at me as I burst in. The nearer of them was Personnel and the second an owlish, ageless, tubby man in circular spectacles who eyed me with a sort of baleful commiseration.

'When did you last hear from your friend Cavendish?' said Personnel, scarcely glancing at me before returning to my papers.

'He *is* your friend, isn't he?' said the owlish man unhappily while I struggled to collect myself. 'Ben? Arno? Which do you call him?'

'Yes. He is. Ben is. What is this?'

'So when did you last hear from him?' Personnel repeated, shoving aside a pile of letters from my girlfriend of the time. 'Does he ring you? How do you keep in touch?'

'I had a postcard from him a week ago. Why?'

'Where is it?'

'I don't know. I destroyed it. If it isn't in the desk. Will you kindly tell me what's going on?'

'Destroyed it?'

'Threw it away.'

'*Destroy* sounds deliberate, doesn't it? What did it look like?' Personnel said, pulling out another drawer. 'Stay where you are.'

'It had a picture of a girl on one side and a couple of lines from Ben on the other. What does it matter what it had on it? Please get out of here.'

'Saying?'

'Nothing. It said, this is my latest acquisition. "Dear Ned, this is my new catch, so glad you're not here. Love, Ben." Now get out!'

'What did he mean by that?' – pulling out another drawer.

'Glad I wouldn't cut him out with the girl, I suppose. It was a joke.'

'Do you usually cut him out with his women?'

'We've no women in common. We never have had.'

'What *do* you have in common?'

'Friendship,' I said angrily. 'What the hell are you looking for actually? I think you'd better leave at once. Both of you.'

'I can't find it,' Personnel complained to his fat companion as he tossed aside another wad of my private letters. 'No post-card of any kind. You're not lying, are you, Ned?'

The owlish man had not taken his eyes off me. He continued to regard me with a wretched empathy, as if to say it comes to all of us and there's nothing we can do. 'How was the postcard *delivered*, Ned?' he asked. His voice, like his demeanour, was tentative and regretful.

'By post, how else?' I replied rudely.

'The open mail, you mean?' the owlish man suggested sadly. 'Not by Service bag, for instance?'

'By Forces mail,' I replied. 'Field Post Office. Posted Berlin with a British stamp on it. Delivered by the local postman.'

'Do you remember the Field Post Office *number*, by any chance, Ned?' the owlish man enquired with enormous diffidence. 'On the postmark, I mean?'

'It was the ordinary Berlin number, I imagine,' I retorted, struggling to keep up my indignation in the face of someone so exquisitely deferential. 'Forty, I think. Why's it so important? I've had enough of this.'

'But you'd say it was definitely posted in Berlin anyway? I mean, that was your impression at the time? So far as you recall it now? The Berlin number – you're sure?'

'It looked exactly like the others he'd sent me. I didn't submit it to a minute examination,' I said, my anger rising again as I saw Personnel yank yet another drawer from my desk and tip out its contents.

'A *pin-up* sort of girl, Ned?' the owlish man enquired, with a hangdog smile, which was evidently intended to apologise for Personnel as well as for himself.

'A nude, yes. A tart, I assume, looking over her bare backside. That's why I threw it away. Because of my cleaning lady.'

'Oh, so you remember now!' Personnel cried, swinging round to face me. ' "I threw it away." Pity you didn't bloody say so at once!'

'Oh, I don't know, Rex,' said the owlish man placatingly. 'Ned was very confused when he came in. Who wouldn't be?' His worried gaze settled once more upon myself. 'You're doing a stint with the watchers, isn't that right? Monty says you're rather good. Was she in colour, by the way? Your nude?'

'Yes.'

'Did he always send postcards, or sometimes letters?'

'Only postcards.'

'How many?'

'Three or four since he's been there.'

'Always in colour?'

'I don't remember. Probably. Yes.'

'And always of girls?'

'I think so.'

'Oh, but you remember, really. Of course you do. And always naked too, I expect?'

'Yes.'

'Where are the others?'

'I must have thrown them away too.'

'Because of your cleaning lady?'

'Yes.'

'To protect her sensitivities?'

'Yes!'

The owlish man took his time to consider this. 'So the dirty postcards – forgive me, I don't mean that offensively, really not – they were a sort of running joke between you?'

'On his side, yes.'

'But you didn't send him any in return? Please say if you did. Don't be embarrassed. There isn't time.'

'I'm not embarrassed! I didn't send him any. Yes, they were a running joke. And they were getting increasingly *risqué*. If you want to know, I was becoming slightly bored with seeing them laid out on the hall table for my collection. So was Mr Simpson. He's the landlord. He suggested I write to Ben and tell him to stop sending them. He said it was getting the house a bad name. Now will you please, one of you, tell me what the hell's going on?'

This time Personnel replied. 'Well, that's what we thought you might be able to tell *us*,' he said in a mournful voice. 'Ben Cavendish has disappeared. So have his agents, in a manner of speaking. A couple of them are featured in this morning's *Neues Deutschland*. British spy ring caught red-handed. The London evening papers are running the story in their late editions. He hasn't been seen for three days. This is Mr Smiley. He wants to talk to you. You're to tell him whatever you know. And that means anything. I'll see you later.'

I must have lost my bearings for a moment, because when I saw Smiley again he was standing at the centre of my carpet, gloomily peering round him at the havoc he and Personnel had wreaked.

'I've a house across the river in Bywater Street,' he confessed, as if it were a great burden to him. 'Perhaps we ought to pop round there, if it's all the same to you. It's not *terribly* tidy, but it is better than this.'

We drove there in Smiley's humble little Austin, so slowly you would have supposed he was conveying an invalid, which was perhaps how he regarded me. It was dusk. The white lanterns of Albert Bridge floated at us like waterborne coach-lights. Ben, I thought desperately, what have we done? Ben, what have they done to you?

Bywater Street was jammed, so we parked in a mews. Parking for Smiley was as complicated as docking a liner, but he managed it and we walked back. I remember how impossible it was to keep alongside him, how his thrusting roundarm waddle somehow ignored my existence. I remember how he steeled himself to turn the key of his own front door, and his alertness as he stepped into the hall. As if home were a danger-ous place for him, as I know now that it was. There was a couple of days' milk in the hall and a half-eaten plate of chop and peas in the drawing room. The turntable of a gramophone was silently revolving. It didn't take a genius to surmise that he had been called out in a hurry – presumably by Personnel yes-terday evening – while he was tucking into his chop and listening to a spot of music.

He wandered off to the kitchen in search of soda for our whiskies. I followed him. There was something about Smiley that made you responsible for his solitude. Open tins of food lay about and the sink was crammed with dirty plates. While he mixed our whiskies, I started clearing up, so he fished a teacloth from the back of the door and set to work drying and putting away.

'You and Ben were considerable partners, weren't you?' he asked.

'We shared a cabin at Sarratt, yes.'

'So that's what – kitchen, couple of bedrooms, bathroom?'

'No kitchen.'

'But you were twinned for your training course as well?'

'For the last year of it. You choose an oppo and learn to work to each other.'

'Choose? Or have chosen for you?'

'Choose first, then they approve or break you up.'

'And after that, you're landed with each other for better for worse?'

'Pretty much, yes.'

'For the whole of the last year? For half the course, in fact? Day and night, as it were? A total marriage?'

I could not understand why he was pressing me about things he must have known.

'And you do everything together?' he continued. 'Forgive me but it's some time since I was trained. Written, practical, physical, you mess together, share a cabin – a whole life, in fact.'

'We do the syndicate work together, and the strongarm stuff. That's automatic. It begins with being roughly the same weight and physical aptitude.' Despite the disturbing tendency of his questions, I was beginning to feel a great need to talk to him. 'Then the rest sort of follows naturally.'

'Ah.'

'Sometimes they split us up – say, for a special exercise or if they think one person is relying too much on his oppo. But as long as it's fifty-fifty they're happy for you to keep together.'

'And you won everything,' Smiley suggested approvingly, helping himself to another wet plate. 'You were the best pair. You and Ben.'

'It was just that Ben was the best student,' I said. 'Whoever had him would have won.'

'Yes, of course. Well, we all know people like that. Did you know each other before you joined the Service?'

'No. But we'd run parallel. We were at the same school, different houses. We were at Oxford, different colleges. We both read languages but we still never met. He did a short service commission in the army, I did the same in the navy. It took the Circus to bring us together.'

Taking up a delicate bone-china cup, he peered doubtfully into it, as if searching for something I had missed. 'Would *you* have sent Ben to Berlin?'

'Yes, of course I would. Why not?'

'Well, why?'

'He's got perfect German from his mother. He's bright. Resourceful. People do what he wants them to do. His father had this terrific war.'

'So did your mother, as I remember.' He was referring to my mother's work with the Dutch Resistance. 'What did *he* do – Ben's father, I mean?' he continued, as if he really didn't know.

'He broke codes,' I said, with Ben's pride. 'He was a wrangler. A mathematician. A genius, apparently. He helped organise the double-cross system against the Germans – recruit their agents and play them back. My mother was very small beer by comparison.'

'And Ben was impressed by that?'

'Who wouldn't be?'

'He talked of it, I mean,' Smiley insisted. 'Often? It was a big matter for him. You had that impression?'

'He just said it was something he had to live up to. He said it was the up-side of having a German mother.'

'Oh dear,' said Smiley unhappily. 'Poor man. And those were his words? You're not embellishing?'

'Of course I'm not! He said that with a background like his, in England you had to run twice as fast as everyone else, just to keep up.'

Smiley seemed genuinely upset. 'Oh dear,' he said again. 'How unkind. And do you think he has the stamina, would you say?'

He had once more stopped me short. At our age, we really didn't think of stamina as being limited.

'What for?' I asked.

'Oh, I don't know. What kind of stamina would one need for running twice as fast as everyone else in Berlin? A double ration of nerves, I suppose – always a strain. A doubly good head for alcohol – *and* where women are concerned – never easy.'

'I'm sure he's got whatever it takes,' I said loyally.

Smiley hung his teacloth on a bent nail which looked like his own addition to the kitchen. 'Did you ever talk politics, the two of you?' he asked as we took our whiskies to the drawing room.

'Never.'

'Then I'm sure he's sound,' he said, with a sad little laugh, and I laughed too.

Houses always seem to me, at first acquaintance, to be either masculine or feminine, and Smiley's was undoubtedly feminine, with pretty curtains and carved mirrors and clever woman's touches. I wondered who he was living with, or wasn't. We sat down.

'And is there any reason why you *mightn't* have sent Ben to Berlin?' he resumed, smiling kindly over the top of his glass.

'Well, only that I wanted to go myself. Everybody wants a Berlin break. It's the front line.'

'He simply disappeared,' Smiley explained, settling back and appearing to close his eyes. 'We're not keeping anything from you. I'll tell you what we know. Last Thursday he crossed into East Berlin to meet his head agent, a gentleman named Hans Seidl – you can see his photograph in *Neues Deutschland*. It was Ben's first solo meeting with him. A big event. Ben's superior in the Berlin Station is Haggarty. Do you know Haggarty?'

'No.'

'Have you heard of him?'

'No.'

'Ben never mentioned him to you?'

'No. I told you. I've never heard his name.'

'Forgive me. Sometimes an answer can vary with a context, if you follow me.'

I didn't.

'Haggarty is second man in the Station under the Station Commander. Did you not know that either?'

'No.'

'Has Ben a regular girlfriend?'

'Not that I know of.'

'Irregular?'

'You only had to go to a dance with him, they were all over him.'

'And after the dance?'

'He didn't brag. He doesn't. If he slept with them, he wouldn't say. He's not that kind of man.'

'They tell me you and Ben took your bits of leave together. Where did you go?'

'Twickenham. Lord's. Bit of fishing. Mainly we stayed with one another's people.'

'Ah.'

I couldn't understand why Smiley's words were scaring me. Perhaps I was so scared for Ben that I was scared by everything. Increasingly I had the feeling Smiley assumed I was guilty of something, even if we had still to find out what. His recitation of events was like a summary of the evidence.

'First comes *Willis*,' he said, as if we were following a difficult trail. 'Willis is the Berlin Head of Station, Willis has overall command. Then comes *Haggarty*, and Haggarty is the senior field officer under Willis and Ben's direct boss. Haggarty is responsible for the day-to-day servicing of the Seidl network. The network is twelve agents strong, or was – that is to say, nine men and three women, now all under arrest. An illegal network of that size, communicating partly by radio and partly by secret writing, requires a base team of at least the same number to maintain it, and I'm not talking about evaluating or distributing the product.'

'I know.'

'I'm sure you do, but let me tell you all the same,' he continued at the same ponderous pace. 'Then you can help me fill in the gaps. Haggarty is a powerful personality. An Ulsterman. Off duty, he drinks, he's noisy and unpleasant. But when he's working he's none of those things. He's a conscientious officer with a prodigious memory. You're sure Ben never mentioned him to you?'

'I told you. No.'

I had not intended this to sound so adamant. There's always a mystery about how often you can deny a thing without beginning to sound like a liar, even to yourself; and of course this was the very mystery Smiley was playing upon in order to bring hidden things to the surface in me.

'Yes, well, you *did* tell me no,' he agreed with his habitual courtesy. 'And I did *hear* you say no. I merely wondered whether I had jogged your memory.'

'No.'

'Haggarty and Seidl were *friends*,' he continued, speaking, if it were possible, even more slowly. 'So far as their business allowed, they were *close* friends. Seidl had been a prisoner of war in England, Haggarty in Germany. While Seidl was working as a farm labourer near Cirencester in 1944, under the relaxed conditions for German prisoners of war that prevailed by then, he succeeded in courting an English landgirl. His guards at the camp took to leaving a bicycle for him outside the main gates with an army greatcoat tossed over the handlebar to cover Seidl's prisoner-of-war tunic. As long as he was back in his own bed by reveille, the guards turned a blind eye. Seidl never forgot his gratitude to the English. When the baby came along, Seidl's guards and fellow prisoners came to the christening. Charming, isn't it? The English at their best. But the story doesn't ring a bell?'

'How could it? You're talking about a joe!'

'A blown joe. One of Ben's. Haggarty's experiences of German prison camp were not so uplifting. Never mind. In 1948, while Haggarty was nominally working with the Control Commission, he picked up Seidl in a bar in Hanover, recruited him and ran him back into East Germany, to his home town of Leipzig. He has been running him ever since. The Haggarty–Seidl friendship has been the linchpin of the

Berlin Station for the last fifteen years. At the time of his arrest last week, Seidl was fourth man in the East German Foreign Ministry. He had served as their Ambassador in Havana. But you've never heard of him. Nobody ever mentioned him to you. Not Ben. Not anyone.'

'No,' I said, as wearily as I could manage.

'Once a month Haggarty was accustomed to going into East Berlin and debriefing Seidl – in a car, in a safe flat, on a park bench, wherever – the usual thing. After the Wall there was a suspension of service for a while, before the meetings were cautiously resumed. The game was to cross in a Four Power vehicle – say, an army jeep – introduce a substitute, hop out at the right moment and rejoin the vehicle at an agreed point. It sounds perilous and it was, but with practice it worked. If Haggarty was on leave or sick, there was no meeting. A couple of months ago Head Office ruled that Haggarty should introduce Seidl to a successor. Haggarty is past retiring age, Willis has had Berlin so long he's blown sky high, and besides he knows far too many secrets to go wandering round behind the Curtain. Hence Ben's posting to Berlin. Ben was untarnished. Clean. Haggarty in person briefed him – I gather exhaustively. I'm sure he was not merciful. Haggarty is not a merciful man, and a twelve-strong network can be a complicated matter: who works to whom and why; who knows whose identity; the cut-outs, codes, couriers, covernames, symbols, radios, dead-letter boxes, inks, cars, salaries, children, birthdays, wives, mistresses. A lot to get into one's head all at once.'

'I know.'

'Ben told you, did he?'

I did not rise to him this time. I was determined not to. 'We learned it on the course. *Ad infinitum*,' I said.

'Yes. Well, I suppose you did. The trouble is, the theory's never quite the same as the real thing, is it? Who's his best friend, apart from you?'

'I don't know.' I was startled by his sudden change of tack. 'Jeremy, I suppose.'

'Jeremy who?'

'Galt. He was on the course.'

'And women?'

'I told you. No one special.'

'Haggarty wanted to take Ben into East Berlin with him, make the introduction himself,' Smiley resumed. 'The Fifth Floor wouldn't wear that. They were trying to wean Haggarty away from his agent, and they don't hold with sending two men into badland where one will do. So Haggarty took Ben through the rendezvous procedures on a street map, and Ben went into East Berlin alone. On the Wednesday, he did a dry run and reconnoitred the location. On the Thursday he went in again, this time for real. He went in legally, driven in a Control Commission Humber car. He crossed at Checkpoint Charlie at three in the afternoon and slipped out of the car at the agreed spot. His substitute rode in it for three hours, all as planned. Ben rejoined the car successfully at six-ten, and recrossed into West Berlin at six-fifty in the evening. His return was logged by the checkpoint. He had himself dropped at his flat. A faultless run. Willis and Haggarty were waiting for him at Station Headquarters, but he telephoned from his flat instead. He said the rendezvous had gone to plan, but he'd brought nothing back except a high temperature and a ferocious stomach bug. Could they postpone their debriefing till morning? Lamentably they could. They haven't seen him or heard from him since. He sounded cheerful despite his ailment, which they put down to nerves. Has Ben ever been ill on you?'

'No.'

'He said their mutual friend had been in great form, a real character and so forth. Obviously he could say no more on the open telephone. His bed wasn't slept in, he took no extra clothes with him. There's no proof that he was in his flat when he rang, there's no proof he's been kidnapped, there's no proof he hasn't been. If he was going to defect, why didn't he stay in East Berlin? They can't have turned him round and played him back at us or they wouldn't have arrested his network. And if they wanted to kidnap him, why not do it while he was their side of the Wall? There's no hard evidence that he left West Berlin by any of the approved corridors – train, autobahn, air. The controls are not efficient, and as you say, he was trained. For all we know, he hasn't left Berlin at all. On the other hand, we thought he might have come to you. Don't look so appalled. You're his friend, aren't you? His best friend? Closer to him than anyone? Young Galt doesn't compare. He told us so himself. "Ben's great buddy was Ned," he said. "If Ben was going to turn to any of us, it would have to be Ned." The evidence rather bears that out, I'm afraid.'

'What evidence?'

No pregnant pause, no dramatic change of tone, no warning of any kind: just dear old George Smiley being his apologetic self. 'There's a letter in his flat, addressed to you,' he said. 'It's not dated, just thrown in a drawer. A scrawl rather than a letter. He was probably drunk. It's a love letter, I'm afraid.' And, having handed me a photocopy to read, he fetched us both another whisky.

Perhaps I do it to help me look away from the discomfort of the moment. But always when I set that scene in my memory

I find myself switching to Smiley's point of view. I imagine how it must have felt to be in his position.

What he had before him is easy enough to picture. See a striving trainee trying to look older than his years, a pipe-smoker, a sailor, a wise nodder, a boy who could not wait for middle age, and you have the young Ned of the early sixties.

But what he had behind him was not half so easy, and it was capable of altering his reading of me drastically. The Circus, though I couldn't know it at the time, was in low water, dogged by unaccountable failure. The arrest of Ben's agents, tragic in itself, was only the latest in a chain of catastrophes reaching across the globe. In northern Japan, an entire Circus listening station and its three-man staff had vanished into thin air. In the Caucasus, our escape lines had been rolled up overnight. We had lost networks in Hungary, Czechoslovakia and Bulgaria, all in a space of months. And in Washington our American Cousins were voicing ever-louder dissatisfaction with our reliability, and threatening to cut the special cord for good.

In such a climate, monstrous theories became daily fare. A bunker mentality develops. Nothing is allowed to be accident, nothing random. If the Circus triumphed, it was because we were allowed to do so by our opponents. Guilt by association was rife. In the American perception, the Circus was nurturing not one mole but burrows of them, each cunningly advancing the career of every other. And what joined them was not so much their pernicious faith in Marx – though that was bad enough – it was their dreadful English homosexuality.

I read Ben's letter. Twenty lines long, unsigned, on white unwatermarked Service stationery, one side. Ben's handwriting but awry, no crossings out. So yes, probably he was drunk.

It called me 'Ned my darling.' It laid Ben's hands along my face and drew my lips to his. It kissed my eyelids and my neck and, thank God, on the physical front it stopped there.

It was without adjectives, without art, and the more appalling for its lack of them. It was not a period piece, it was not affected. It was not arch, Greek or nineteen-twenties. It was an unobstructed cry of homosexual longing from a man I had known only as my good companion.

But when I read it, I knew it was the real Ben who had written it. Ben in torment confessing feelings I had never been aware of, but which when I read them I accepted as true. Perhaps that already made me guilty – I mean, to be the object of his desire, even if I had never consciously attracted it, and did not desire him in return. His letter said sorry, then it ended. I didn't think it was unfinished. He had nothing more to say.

'I didn't know,' I said.

I handed Smiley back the letter. He returned it to his pocket. His eyes didn't leave my face.

'Or you didn't know you knew,' he suggested.

'I didn't know,' I repeated hotly. 'What are you trying to make me say?'

You must try to understand Smiley's eminence, the respect his name awoke in someone of my generation. He waited for me. I shall remember all my life the compelling power of his patience. A sudden shower of rain fell, with the handclap that London rain showers make in narrow streets. If Smiley had told me he commanded the elements, I would not have been surprised.

'In England you can't tell anyway,' I said sulkily, trying to collect myself. God alone knows what point I was trying to make. 'Jack Arthur's not married, is he? Nowhere to go in the evenings. Drinks with the lads till the bar closes. Then drinks a bit more. No one says Jack Arthur's queer. But if they arrested him tomorrow in bed with two of the cooks, we'd say we'd known it all along. Or I would. It's imponderable.' I stumbled on, all wrong, groping for a path and finding none. I knew that to protest at all was to protest too much, but I went on protesting all the same.

'Anyway, where was the letter found?' I demanded, trying to recover the initiative.

'In a drawer of his desk. I thought I told you.'

'An empty drawer?'

'Does it matter?'

'Yes, it does! If it was jammed in among old papers, that's one thing. If it was put there to be found by you people, that's another. Maybe he was forced to write it.'

'Oh, I'm sure he was forced,' said Smiley. 'It's just a question of what by. Did you know he was so lonely? If there was no one in his life but you, I'd have thought it would have been rather obvious.'

'Then why wasn't it obvious to Personnel?' I said, bridling again. 'My God, they grilled us for long enough before they appointed us. Sniffed round our friends and relations and teachers and dons. They know far more about Ben than I do.'

'Why don't we just assume that Personnel fell down on the job? He's human, this is England, we're the clan. Let's begin again with the Ben who's disappeared. The Ben who wrote to you. There was no one close to him but you. Not anyone that you knew of, anyway. There could have been lots of people you *didn't* know of, but that's not your fault. As far as you knew, there was no one. We have that settled. Don't we?'

'Yes!'

'Very well then, let's talk about what you *did* know. How's that?'

Somehow he brought me down to earth and we talked into the small grey hours. Long after the rain had stopped and the starlings had begun, we were talking. Or I was – and Smiley was listening as only Smiley can, eyes half closed, chins sunk into his neck. I thought I was telling him everything I knew. Perhaps he thought I was too, though I doubt it, for he understood far better than I the levels of self-deception that are the means of our survival. The phone rang. He listened, muttered 'Thank you' and rang off. 'Ben's still missing and there are no new pointers,' he said. 'You're still the only clue.' He took no notes that I remember and I don't know to this day whether he had a recorder running. I doubt it. He hated machines, and besides, his memory was more reliable than theirs.

I talked about Ben but I talked as much about myself, which was what Smiley wanted me to do: myself as the explanation for Ben's actions. I described again the parallel nature of our lives. How I had envied him his heroic father – I, who had no father to remember. I made no secret of our shared excitement, Ben's and mine, when we began to discover how much we had in common. No, no, I said again, I knew of no one woman – except his mother, who was dead. And I believed myself, I am sure I did.

In childhood, I told Smiley, I used to wonder whether somewhere in the world there was not another version of myself, some secret twin who had the same toys and clothes and thoughts that I did, even the same parents. Perhaps I'd read a book based on this story. I was an only child. So was Ben. I told Smiley all this because I was determined to talk directly to him from my thoughts and memories as they came to me, even if they incriminated me in his eyes. I only know that, consciously, I held nothing back from him, even if I reckoned it potentially ruinous to myself. Somehow Smiley had convinced me that was the least I owed to Ben. Unconsciously – well, that's another matter altogether. Who knows what a man hides, even from himself, when he is telling the truth for his survival?

I told him of our first meeting – mine and Ben's – in the Circus training house in Lambeth where the newly selected entrants were convened. Until then, none of us had met any of his fellow novices. We had hardly met the Circus either, for that matter, beyond the recruiting officer, the selectors and the vetting team. Some of us had only the haziest notion of what we'd joined. Finally we were to be enlightened – about each other, and about our calling – and we gathered in the waiting room like so many characters in a Foreign Legion novel, each with his secret expectations and his secret reasons for being there, each with his overnight bag containing the same quantity of shirts and underpants, marked in Indian ink with his personal number, in obedience to the printed instructions on the unheaded notepaper. My number was nine and Ben's was ten. There were two people ahead of me when I walked into the waiting room, Ben and a stocky little Scot called Jimmy. I nodded at Jimmy, but Ben and I recognised each other at once – I don't mean from school or university but as people who bear a physical and temperamental similarity to one another.

'Enter the third murderer,' he said, shaking my hand. It seemed a wonderfully inappropriate moment to be quoting Shakespeare. 'I'm Ben, this is Jimmy. Apparently we've got no surnames any more. Jimmy left his in Aberdeen.'

So I shook Jimmy's hand as well, and waited on the bench beside Ben to see who came through the door next.

'Five to one he's got a moustache, ten to one a beard, thirty to one green socks,' said Ben.

'And evens on a cloak,' I said.

I told Smiley about the training exercises in unfamiliar towns when we had to invent a cover story, meet a contact and withstand arrest and interrogation. I let him sense how such exploits deepened our companionship, just as sharing our first parachute jumps deepened it, or compass-trekking at night across the Scottish Highlands, or looking out dead-letter boxes in godforsaken inner cities, or making a beach landing by submarine.

I described to him how the directing staff would sometimes drop a veiled reference to Ben's father, just to emphasise their pride in having the son to teach. I told him about our leave weekends, how we would go once to my mother's house in Gloucestershire and once to his father's in Shropshire. And how, each parent being widowed, we had amused ourselves with the notion that we might broker a marriage between them. But the chances in reality were small, for my mother was stubbornly Anglo-Dutch, with jolly sisters and nephews and nieces who all looked like Brueghel models, whereas Ben's father had become a scholarly recluse whose only known surviving passion was for Bach.

'And Ben reveres him,' said Smiley, prodding again at the same spot.

'Yes. He adored his mother but she's dead. His father has become some sort of icon for him.'

And I remember noticing to my shame that I had deliberately avoided using the word 'love', because Ben had used it to describe his feelings for me.

I told him about Ben's drinking, though again I think he knew. How Ben normally drank little and often nothing at all, until an evening would come along – say, a Thursday and the weekend already looming – when he would drink insatiably, Scotch, vodka, anything, a shot for Ben, a shot for Arno. Then reel off to bed, speechless but inoffensive. And how on the morning after, he looked as if he had undergone a fortnight's cure at a health farm.

'And there was really nobody but you?' Smiley mused. 'Poor you, what a burden, coping with all that charm alone.'

I reminisced, I wandered, I told him everything as it came to me, but I knew he was still waiting for me to tell him something I was keeping back, if we could find out what it was. Was I conscious of withholding? I can only reply to you as I afterwards replied to myself: I did not know I knew. It took me a full twenty-four hours more of self-interrogation to winkle my secret out of its dark corner. At four a.m., he told me to go home and get some sleep. I was not to stray from my telephone without telling Personnel what I was up to.

'They'll be watching your flat, naturally,' he warned me as we waited for my cab. 'You won't take it personally, will you? If you imagine being on the loose yourself, there are really very few ports you'd feel safe to head for in a storm. Your flat could rank high on Ben's list. Assuming there isn't anybody else except his father. But he wouldn't go to him, would he? He'd be ashamed. He'd want you. So they watch your flat. It's natural.'

'I understand,' I said as a fresh wave of disgust swept over me.

'After all, there's no one of his age whom he seems to like better than you.'

'It's all right. I understand,' I repeated.

'On the other hand of course, he's not a fool, so he'll know how we're reasoning. And he could hardly imagine you would hide him in your priest-hole without telling us. Well, you wouldn't, would you?'

'No. I couldn't.'

'Which if he's halfway rational he would also know, and that would rule you out for him. Still, he might drop by for advice or assistance, I suppose. Or a drink. It's unlikely, but it's not an assumption we can ignore. You must be far, far and away his best friend. Nobody to compare with you. Is there?'

I was wishing very much he would stop talking like this. Until now, he had shown the greatest delicacy in avoiding the topic of Ben's declared love for me. Suddenly he seemed determined to reopen the wound.

'Of course he *may* have written to other people apart from you,' he remarked speculatively. 'Men or women, both. It's not so unlikely. There are times when one's so desperate that one declares one's love to all sorts of people. If one knows one's dying or contemplating some desperate act. The difference in their case would be, he posted the letters. Still, we can't go round Ben's chums asking them whether he's written them a steamy letter recently – it wouldn't be secure. Besides, where would one start? That's the question. You have to put yourself in Ben's position.'

Did he deliberately plant the germ of self-knowledge in me? Later, I was certain he did. I remember his troubled, perspicacious gaze upon me as he saw me to the cab. I remember looking back as we turned the corner, and seeing his stocky figure standing in the centre of the street as he peered after me, ramming his last words into my departing head. 'You have to put yourself in Ben's position.'

I was in vortex. My day had begun in the small hours in South Audley Street and continued with barely pause for sleep through the Panda's monkey and Ben's letter until now. Smiley's coffee and my sense of being the prisoner of outrageous circumstance had done the rest. But the name of Stefanie, I swear it, was still nowhere in my head – not at the front, not at the back. Stefanie still did not exist. I have never, I am sure, forgotten anyone so thoroughly.

Back in my flat, my periodical spurts of revulsion at Ben's passion gave way to concern for his safety. In the living room I stared theatrically at the sofa where he had so often stretched out after a long day's street training in Lambeth: 'Think I'll bunk down here if you don't mind, old boy. Jollier than home tonight. Arno can sleep at home. Ben sleeps here.' In the kitchen I laid the palm of my hand on the old iron oven where I had fried him his midnight eggs: 'Christ Almighty, Ned, is that a stove? Looks more like what we lost the Crimean War with!'

I remembered his voice, long after I had switched out my bedside light, rattling one crazy idea after another at me through the thin partition – the shared words we had, our insider language.

'You know what we ought to do with Brother Nasser?'

'No, Ben.'

'Give him Israel. Know what we ought to do with the Jews?'

'No, Ben.'

'Give them Egypt.'

'Why, Ben?'

'People are only satisfied with what doesn't belong to them. Know the story of the scorpion and the frog crossing the Nile?'

'Yes, I do. Now shut up and go to sleep.'

Then he'd tell me the story, nevertheless, as a Sarratt case history. The scorpion as penetration agent, needing to contact his stay-behind team on the opposite bank. The frog as double agent, pretending to buy the scorpion's cover story, then blowing it to his paymasters.

And in the morning he was gone, leaving behind him a one-line note saying, 'See you at Borstal,' which was his name for Sarratt. 'Love, Ben.'

Had we talked about Stefanie on those occasions? We hadn't. Stefanie was someone we discussed in motion, glancingly, not side by side through a stationary wall. Stefanie was a phantom shared on the run, an enigma too delightful to dissect. So perhaps that's why I didn't think of her. Or not yet. Not knowingly. There was no dramatic moment when a great light went up and I sprang from my bath shouting, '*Stefanie!*' It simply didn't happen that way, for the reason I am trying to explain to you; somewhere in the no-man's-land between confession and self-preservation, Stefanie floated like a mythic creature who only existed when she was owned up to. As best I remember, the notion of her first came back to me as I was tidying up the mess left by Personnel. Stumbling on my last year's diary, I began flipping through it, thinking how much more of life we live than we remember. And in the month of June, I came on a line drawn diagonally through the two middle weeks, and the numeral '8' written neatly beside it – meaning Camp 8, North Argyll, where we did our paramilitary training. And I began to think – or perhaps merely to sense – yes, of course, Stefanie.

And from there, still without any sudden Archimedean revelation, I found myself reliving our night drive over the moonlit Highlands: Ben at the wheel of the open Triumph roadster, and myself beside him making chatty conversation in order to keep him awake, because we were both happily exhausted after a week of pretending we were in the Albanian mountains raising a guerrilla army. And the June air rushing over our faces.

The rest of the intake were travelling back to London on the Sarratt bus. But Ben and I had Stefanie's Triumph roadster because Steff was a sport, Steff was selfless, Steff had driven it all the way from Oban to Glasgow just so that Ben could borrow it for the week and bring it back to her when the course restarted. And that was how Stefanie came back to me – exactly as she had come to me in the car – amorphously, a titillating concept, a shared woman – Ben's.

'So who or what *is* Stefanie, or do I get the usual loud silence?' I asked him as I pulled open the glove compartment and looked in vain for traces of her.

For a while I got the loud silence.

'Stefanie is a light to the ungodly and a paragon to the virtuous,' he replied gravely. And then, more deprecatingly: 'Steff's from the Hun side of the family.' He was from it himself, he liked to say in his more acerbic moods. Steff was from the Arno side, he was saying.

'Is she pretty?' I asked.

'Don't be vulgar.'

'Beautiful?'

'Less vulgar, but still not there.'

'What is she, then?'

'She is perfection. She is luminous. She is peerless.'

'So beautiful, then?'

'No, you lout. Exquisite. *Sans pareil*. Intelligent beyond the dreams of Personnel.'

'And otherwise – to you – what is she? Apart from being a Hun and the owner of this car?'

'She is my mother's eighteenth cousin dozens of times removed. After the war she came and lived with us in Shropshire and we grew up together.'

'So she's your age, then?'

'If the eternal is to be measured, yes.'

'Your proxy sister, as it were?'

'She was. For a few years. We ran wild together, picked mushrooms in the dawn, touched wee-wees. Then I went off to boarding school and she returned to Munich to resume being a Hun. End of childhood idyll and back to Daddy and England.'

I had never known him so forthcoming about any woman, nor about himself.

'And now?'

I feared he had switched off again, but finally he answered me. 'Now is less funny. She went to art school, took up with a mad painter and settled in a dower house in the Western Isles of Scotland.'

'Why's it less funny? Doesn't her painter like you?'

'He doesn't like anyone. He shot himself. Reasons unknown. Left a note to the local council apologising for the mess. No note to Steff. They weren't married, which made it more of a muddle.'

'And now?' I asked him again.

'She still lives there.'

'On the island?'

'Yes.'

'In the dower house?'

'Yes.'

'Alone?'

'Most of the time.'

'You mean you go and see her?'

'I *see* her, yes. So I suppose I *go* too. Yes. I go and see her.'

'Is it serious?'

'Everything to do with Steff is massively serious.'

'What does she do when you're not there?'

'Same as she does when I'm there, I should think. Paints. Talks to the dickie birds. Reads. Plays music. Reads. Plays music. Paints. Thinks. Reads. Lends me her car. Do you want to know any more of my business?'

For a while we remained strangers, until Ben once more relented. 'Tell you what, Ned. Marry her.'

'Stefanie?'

'Who else, you idiot? That's a bloody good idea, come to think of it. I propose to bring the two of you together to discuss it. You shall marry Steff, Steff shall marry you, and I shall come and live with you both, and fish the loch.'

My question sprang from a monstrous, culpable innocence: 'Why don't you marry her yourself?' I asked.

Was it only now, standing in my flat and watching the slow dawn print itself on the walls, that I had the answer? Staring at the ruled-out pages of last June and remembering with a jolt his dreadful letter?

Or was it given to me already in the car, by Ben's silence as we sped through the Scottish night? Did I know even then that Ben was telling me he would never marry any woman?

And was this the reason why I had banished Stefanie from my conscious memory, planting her so deep that not

even Smiley, for all his clever delving, had been able to ex-
hume her?

Had I looked at Ben as I asked him my fatal question? Had
I looked at him as he refused, and went on refusing, to reply?
Had I deliberately *not* looked at him at all? I was used to his
silences by then, so perhaps, having waited in vain, I pun-
ished him by entering my own thoughts.

All I knew for certain was that Ben never answered my
question, and that neither of us ever mentioned Stefanie
again.

Stefanie his dream woman, I thought as I continued to examine the diary. On her island. Who loved him. But should
marry me.

Who had the taint of death about her that Ben's heroes
always seemed to need.

Eternal Stefanie, a light to the ungodly, luminous, peerless, German Stefanie, his paragon and proxy sister – mother
too, perhaps – waving to him from her tower, offering him
sanctuary from his father.

You have to put yourself in Ben's position, Smiley had said.

Yet even now, the open diary in my hands, I did not allow
myself the elusive moment of revelation. An idea was forming in me. Gradually it became a possibility. And only gradually
again, as my state of physical and mental siege bore in on me,
did it harden into conviction, and finally purpose.

It was morning at last. I hoovered the flat. I dusted and
polished. I considered my anger. Dispassionately, you understand. I reopened the desk, pulled out my desecrated private
papers and burned in the grate whatever I felt had been irrev-
ocably sullied by the intrusion of Smiley and Personnel: the
letters from Mabel, the exhortations from my former tutor

to 'do something a bit more fun' than mere research work at the War Office.

I did these things with the outside of myself while the rest of me grappled with the correct, the moral, the decent course of action.

Ben, my friend.

Ben, with the dogs after him.

Ben in anguish, and God knew what more besides.

Stefanie.

I took a long bath, then lay on my bed watching the mirror on the chest of drawers because the mirror gave me a view of the street. I could see a couple of men whom I took to be Monty's, dressed in overalls and doing something long-winded with a junction box. Smiley had said I shouldn't take them personally. After all, they only wanted to put Ben in irons.

It is ten o'clock of the same long morning as I stand purposefully to one side of my rear window, peering down into the squalid courtyard, with its creosoted shed that used to be the old privy, and its clapboard gate that opens on the dingy street. The street is empty. Monty is not so perfect after all.

The Western Isles, Ben had said. A dower house on the Western Isles.

But which isle? And Stefanie who? The only safe guess was that if she came from the German side of Ben's family and lived in Munich, and that since Ben's German relatives were grand, she was likely to be titled.

I rang Personnel. I might have rung Smiley but I felt safer lying to Personnel. He recognised my voice before I had a chance to state my business.

'Have you heard anything?' he demanded.

'Afraid not. I want to go out for an hour. Can I do that?'

'Where to?'

'I need a few things. Provisions. Something to read. Thought I'd just pop round to the library.'

Personnel was famous for his disapproving silences.

'Be back by eleven. Ring me as soon as you get in.'

Pleased by my cool performance, I went out by the front door, bought a newspaper and bread. Using shop windows, I checked my back. Nobody was following me, I was sure. I went to the public library and from the reference section drew an old copy of *Who's Who* and a tattered *Almanach de Gotha*. I did not pause to ask myself who on earth, in Battersea of all places, could have worn out the *Almanach de Gotha*. I consulted the *Who's Who* first and turned up Ben's father, who had a knighthood and a battery of decorations: '*1936, married the Gräfin Ilse Arno zu Lothringen, one son Benjamin Arno.*' I switched to the *Almanach* and turned up the Arno Lothringens. They rated three pages, but it took me no time to identify the distant cousin whose first name was Stefanie. I boldly asked the librarian for a telephone directory for the Western Isles of Scotland. She hadn't one, but allowed me to call enquiries on her telephone, which was fortunate for I had no doubt my own was being tapped. By ten-forty-five I was back at the telephone in my flat talking to Personnel in the same relaxed tone as before.

'Where did you go?' he asked.

'To the newsagent. And the baker's.'

'Didn't you do the library?'

'Library? Oh yes. Yes, I did.'

'And what, pray, did you take out?'

'Nothing, actually. For some reason I find it hard to settle to anything at the moment. What do I do next?'

Waiting for him to reply, I wondered whether I had given too many answers but decided I had not.

'You wait. The same as the rest of us.'

'Can I come in to Head Office?'

'Since you're waiting, you might as well wait there as here.'

'I could go back to Monty, if you like.'

It was probably my over-acute imagination at work, but I had a mental image of Smiley standing at his elbow, telling him how to answer me.

'Just wait where you are,' he said curtly.

I waited, Lord knows how. I pretended to read. I dramatised myself and wrote a pompous letter of resignation to Personnel. I tore up the letter and burned the pieces. I watched television, and in the evening I lay on the bed observing the changing of Monty's guard in the mirror and thinking of Stefanie, then Ben, then Stefanie again, who was now firmly lodged in my imagination, always outside my reach, dressed in white, Stefanie the immaculate, Ben's protector. I was young, let me remind you, and in matters of women less experienced than you would have suspected if you had heard me speak of them. The Adam in me was still pretty much a child, not to be confused with the warrior.

I waited till ten, then slipped downstairs with a bottle of wine for Mr Simpson and his wife, and sat with them while we drank it, watching more television. Then I took Mr Simpson aside.

'Chris,' I said. 'I know it's daft but there's a jealous lady stalking me and I'd like to leave by the back way. Would you mind letting me out through your kitchen?'

An hour later, I was on the night sleeper to Glasgow. I had obeyed my counter-surveillance procedures to the letter and

I was certain I was not being followed. At Glasgow Central Station, all the same, I took the precaution of dawdling over a pot of tea in the buffet while I cocked an eye for potential watchers. As a further precaution, I hired a cab to Helensburgh on the other side of the Clyde, before joining the Campbeltown bus to West Loch Tarbert. The ferry to the Western Isles sailed three days a week in those days, except for the short summer season. But my luck held: a boat was waiting, and she sailed as soon as I had boarded her, so that by early afternoon we had passed Jura, docked at Port Askaig and were heading out to the open sea again under a darkening northern sky. We were down to three passengers by then, an old couple and myself, and when I went up on deck to fend off their questions, the first mate cheerfully asked me more of his own: Was I on holiday now? Was I a doctor then? Was I married at all? Nevertheless, I was in my element. From the moment I take to the sea, everyone is clear to me, everything possible. Yes, I thought excitedly, surveying the great crags as they approached, and smiling at the shrieking of the gulls, yes, this is where Ben would hide! This is where his Wagnerian demons would find their ease!

You must understand and try to pardon my callow susceptibility in those days to all forms of Nordic abstraction. What Ben was driven by, I pursued. The mythic island – it should have been Ossian's! – the swirling clouds and tossing sea, the priestess in her solitary castle – I could not get enough of them. I was in the middle of my Romantic period, and my soul was lost to Stefanie before I met her.

The dower house was on the other side of the island, they told me at the shop, better ask young Fergus to take you in his jeep. Young Fergus turned out to be seventy, if a day. We passed between a pair of crumbling iron gates. I paid off young Fergus and rang the bell. The door opened; a fair woman stared at me.

She was tall and slim. If it was really true that she was my own age – and it was – she had an authority it would take me another lifetime to acquire. She wore, instead of white, a paint-smeared smock of dark blue. She held a palette knife in one hand, and as I spoke she raised it to her forehead and pushed away a stray bit of hair with the back of her wrist. Then lowered it again to her side, and stood listening to me long after I had finished speaking, while she pondered the resonance of my words inside her head and compared them with the man or boy who stood before her. But the strangest part of this moment is also the hardest for me to relate. It is that Stefanie came closer to the figure of my imagination than made sense. Her pallor, her air of uncorrupted truthfulness, of inner strength, coupled with an almost pitiable fragility, corresponded so exactly with my expectation that, had I bumped into her in another place, I would have known that she was Stefanie.

'My name's Ned,' I said, speaking to her eyes. 'I'm a friend of Ben's. Also a colleague. I'm alone. No one knows I'm here.'

I had meant to go on. I had a pompous speech in my head that said something like, 'Please tell him that whatever he's done, it makes no difference to me.' But the steadiness of her gaze prevented me.

'Why should it matter who knows that you are here and who does not?' she asked. She spoke without accent, but with a German cadence, making tiny hesitations before the open vowels. 'He is not hiding. Who is looking for him except you? Why should he hide?'

'I understood he might be in some kind of trouble,' I said, following her into the house.

The hall was half studio, half makeshift living room. Dust-sheets covered much of the furniture. The remains of a meal lay on the table: two mugs, two plates, both used.

'What kind of trouble?' she demanded.

'It's to do with his work in Berlin. I thought perhaps he would have told you about it.'

'He has told me nothing. He has never talked to me about his work. Perhaps he knows I am not interested.'

'May I ask what he does talk about?'

She considered this. 'No.' And then, as if relenting, 'At present he does not talk to me at all. He seems to have become a Trappist. Why not? Sometimes he watches me paint, some-times he fishes, sometimes we eat something or drink a little wine. Quite often he sleeps.'

'How long's he been here?'

She shrugged. 'Three days?'

'Did he come straight from Berlin?'

'He came on the boat. Since he does not speak, that's all I know.'

'He disappeared,' I said. 'There's a hue and cry for him. They thought he might come to me. I don't think they know about you.'

She was listening to me again, listening first to my words and then my silence. She seemed to be without embarrass-ment, like a listening animal. It's the authority of suffering, I thought, remembering her lover's suicide; she cannot be reached by small worries.

'*They*,' she repeated with puzzlement. 'Who are *they*? What is there to *know* about me that is so particular?'

'Ben was doing secret work,' I said.

'*Ben?*'

'Like his father,' I said. 'He was tremendously proud of following in his father's steps.'

She was shocked and agitated. 'Why? Who for? *Secret* work? What a fool!'

'For British Intelligence. He was in Berlin, attached to the Military Adviser's office, but his real work was intelligence.'

'*Ben?*' she said as the disgust and disbelief gathered in her face. 'All those *lies* he must tell? Ben?'

'Yes, I'm afraid so. But it was duty.'

'How *terrible*.'

Her easel stood with its back to me. Placing herself the other side of it, she began mixing her paints.

'If I could just talk to him,' I said, but she pretended to be too much lost to her painting to hear me.

The back of the house gave on to parkland, then a line of pines hunchbacked by the wind. Beyond the pines lay a loch surrounded by small mauve hills. On its far bank I made out a fisherman standing on a collapsed jetty. He was fishing but not casting. I don't know how long I watched him, but long enough to know that it was Ben, and that he had no interest in catching fish. I pushed open the French windows and stepped into the garden. A cold wind was ruffling the surface of the loch as I tiptoed along the jetty. He was wearing a tweed jacket that was too full for him. I guessed it had belonged to her dead lover. And a hat, a green felt hat that, like all hats with Ben, looked as though it had been made for him. He didn't turn, though he must have felt my footsteps. I placed myself beside him.

'The only thing you'll catch like that is pneumonia, you German ass,' I said.

His face was turned against me, so I remained standing

beside him, watching the water with him and sensing the nudge of his shoulder as the rocking jetty threw us carelessly together. I watched the water thicken and the sky turn grey behind the mountains. A few times I watched the red float of his line vanish below the oily surface. But if a fish had struck, Ben made no effort to play it or reel it in. I saw the lights go on in the house, and the figure of Stefanie standing at her easel, adding a brush stroke, then backing her wrist against her brow. The air turned cold and the night gathered, but Ben didn't move. We were in competition with each other, as we had been during our strongarm training. I was demanding, Ben was refusing. Only one of us could have his way. If it took me all night and all tomorrow, and if I starved in the process, I wasn't going to yield till he'd acknowledged me.

A half moon came up, and stars. The wind dropped and a silver ground mist formed across the blackened heather. And still we stood there, waiting for one of us to surrender. I was nearly sleeping on my feet when I heard the rattle of his reel and saw the float lift from the water and the bare line after it, flashing in the moonlight. I didn't move and didn't speak. I let him reel in and make his hook fast. I let him turn to me, because he had to if he wanted to walk past me down the jetty.

We stood face to face in the moonlight. Ben looked downwards, apparently studying my feet to see how he could step round them. His gaze travelled up to my face, but nothing changed in his expression. His locked features stayed locked. If they betrayed anything, it was anger.

'Well,' he said. 'Enter the third murderer.'

This time neither of us laughed.

*

She must have sensed our approach and removed herself. I heard music playing in another part of the house. When we reached the hall, Ben headed for the stairs but I grabbed his arm.

'You've got to tell me,' I said. 'There's never going to be anyone better to tell. I broke ranks to come here. You've got to tell me what happened to the network.'

There was a long drawing room beyond the hall, with shuttered windows and more dustsheets over the sofas. It was cold, but Ben still had his jacket on and I my greatcoat. I opened the shutters and let the moonlight in. I had an instinct that anything brighter would disturb him. The music was not far away from us. I thought it was Grieg. I wasn't sure. Ben spoke without remorse and without catharsis. He had confessed enough to himself, all day and night, I knew. He talked in the dead tone of somebody describing a disaster he knows that nobody can understand who was not part of it, and the music kept playing below his voice. He had no use for himself. The glamorous hero had given up as one of life's contenders. Perhaps he was a little tired of his guilt. He spoke tersely. I think he wanted me to go.

'Haggarty's a shit,' he said. 'World class. He's a thief, he drinks, he rapes a bit. His one justification was the Seidl network. Head Office were trying to wheedle him away from it and give Seidl to new people. I was the first new person. Haggarty decided to punish me for taking away his network.'

He described the studied insults, the successive night duties and weekends, the hostile reports passed back to Haggarty's supporters' club in Head Office.

'At first he wouldn't tell me anything about the network. Then Head Office bawled him out, so he told me everything. Fifteen years of it. Every tiny detail of their lives, even the joes who'd died on the job. He'd send files to me in pyramids, all flagged and cross-referred. Read this, remember that. Who's she? Who's he? Note this address, the name, these covernames, those symbols. Escape procedures. Fallbacks. The recognition codes and safety procedures for the radio. Then he'd test me. Take me to the safe room, sit me across the table, grill me. "You're not up to it. We can't send you in till you know your stuff. You'd better stay in over the weekend and mug it up. I'll test you again on Monday." The network was his life. He wanted me to feel inadequate. I did and I was.'

But Head Office did not give in to Haggarty's bullying, neither did Ben. 'I put myself on an exam footing,' he said.

As the day of his first meeting with Seidl approached, Ben assembled for himself a system of mnemonics and acronyms that would enable him to encompass the network's fifteen years of history. Seated night and day in his office at Station Headquarters, he drew up consciousness charts and communications charts and devised systems for memorising the aliases, covernames, home addresses and places of employment of its agents, sub-agents, couriers and collaborators. Then he transferred his data to plain postcards, writing on one side only. On the other, in one line, he wrote the subject: 'dead-letter boxes', 'salaries', 'safe houses'. Each night, before going back to his flat or stretching out in the Station sick-room, he would play a game of memory with himself, first putting the cards face downward on his desk, then comparing what he had remembered with the data on the reverse side.

'I didn't sleep a lot but that's not unusual,' he said. 'As the day came up, I didn't sleep at all. I spent the whole night mugging up my stuff, then I lay on the couch staring at the ceiling.

When I got up I couldn't remember any of it. Sort of paralysis. I went to my room, sat down at the desk, put my head in my hands and started to ask myself questions. "If covername Margaret-stroke-two thinks he's under surveillance, whom does he contact how, and what does the contact then do?" The answer was a total blank.

'Haggarty wandered in and asked how I was feeling and I said "fine". To do him justice, he wished me luck and I think he meant it. I thought he'd shoot some trick question at me and I was going to tell him to go to hell. But he just said, "*Komm gut heim*," and patted my shoulder. I put the cards in my pocket. Don't ask me why. I was scared of failure. That's why we do everything, isn't it? I was scared of failure and I hated Haggarty and Haggarty had put me to the torture. I've got about two hundred other reasons why I took the cards, but none of them help a great deal. Perhaps it was my way of committing suicide. I quite like that idea. I took them and I went across. We used a limousine, specially converted. I sat in the back with my double hidden under the seat. The Vopos weren't allowed to search us, of course. All the same, switching with a double as you turn a sharp corner is a bloody hairy game. You've got to sort of roll out of the car. Seidl had provided a bike for me. He believes in bicycles. His guards used to lend him one when he was a prisoner of war in England.'

Smiley had told me the story already, but I let Ben tell it to me again.

'I had the cards in my jacket pocket,' he went on. 'My inside jacket pocket. It was one of those blazing-hot Berlin days. I think I unbuttoned my jacket while I bicycled. I don't know. When I try to remember, I sometimes unbuttoned it and I sometimes didn't. That's what happens to your memory when you work it to death. It does all the versions for you. I got to the rendezvous early, checked the cars, the usual bullshit, went in. It had all come back to me by then. Taking the cards with me had done the trick. I didn't need them. Seidl was fine. I was fine. We did our business, I briefed him, gave him some money – all just like Sarratt. I rode back to the pick-up point, ditched the bike, dived into the car and as we crossed into West Berlin I realised I hadn't got the cards. I was missing the weight of them, or the pressure or something. I was in a panic but I always am. Deep down, I'm in a panic all the time. That's who I am. This was just a bigger panic. I made them drop me at my flat, rang Seidl's emergency number. No one answered. I tried the fallback. No answer. I tried his stand-in, a woman called Lotte. No answer. I took a cab to Tempelhof, made a discreet exit, came here.'

Suddenly there was only Stefanie's music to listen to. Ben had finished his story. I didn't realise at first that this was all there was. I waited, staring at him, expecting him to go on. I had been wanting a kidnapping at least – savage East German secret police rising from the back of his car, sandbagging him, forcing a chloroformed mask on him while they rifled his pockets. It was only gradually that the appalling banality of what he had told me got through to me: that you could lose a network as easily as you could lose a bunch of keys or a cheque book or a pocket handkerchief. I was craving for a greater dignity, but he had none to offer me.

'So where did you last have them?' I said stupidly. I could have been talking to a child about his lost schoolbooks, but he didn't mind, he had no pride any more.

'The cards?' he said. 'Maybe on the bicycle. Maybe rolling out of the car. Maybe getting back into it. The bike has a security chain to lock round the wheel. I had to stoop down to put it on and take it off. Maybe then. It's like losing anything. Till you find it, you never know. Afterwards, it's obvious. But there hasn't been an afterwards.'

'Do you think you were followed?'

'I don't know. I just don't know.'

I wanted to ask him when he had written his love letter to me, but I couldn't bring myself to. Besides, I thought I knew. It was in one of his drinking sessions when Haggarty was riding him hardest and he was in despair. What I really wanted him to tell me was that he had never written it. I wanted to put the clock back and make things the way they had been until a week ago. But the simple questions had died with the simple answers. Our childhoods were over for good.

They must have surrounded the house, and certainly they never rang the bell. Monty was probably standing outside the window when I opened the shutters to let the moonlight in, because when he needed to, he just stepped into the room, looking embarrassed but resolute.

'You did ever so nicely, Ned,' he said consolingly. 'It was the public library gave you away. Your nice librarian lady took a real shine to you. I think she'd have come with us if we'd let her.'

Skordeno followed him, and then Smiley appeared in the other doorway, wearing the apologetic air that frequently accompanied his most ruthless acts. And I recognised with no particular surprise that I had done everything he had wanted me to do. I had put myself in Ben's position and led them to my friend. Ben didn't seem particularly surprised either. Perhaps he was relieved. Monty and Skordeno moved into place either side of him, but Ben remained sitting among the dustsheets, his tweed jacket pulled around him like a rug. Skordeno tapped him on the shoulder; then Monty and Skordeno stooped and, like a pair of furniture removers used to one another's timing, lifted him gently to his feet. When I protested to Ben that I had not knowingly betrayed him, he shook his head to say it didn't matter. Smiley stepped aside to let them by. His myopic gaze was fixed on me enquiringly.

'We've arranged a special sailing,' he said.

'I'm not coming,' I replied.

I looked away from him and when I looked again he was gone. I heard the jeep disappearing down the track. I followed the music across the empty hall into a study crammed with books and magazines and what appeared to be the manuscript of a novel spread over the floor. She was sitting sideways in a deep chair. She had changed into a housecoat and her pale golden hair hung loose over her shoulders. She was barefoot, and did not lift her head as I entered. She spoke to me as if she had known me all her life, and I suppose in a way she had, in the sense that I was Ben's familiar. She switched off the music.

'Were you his lover?' she asked.

'No. He wanted me to be. I realise that now.'

She smiled. 'And I wanted him to be my lover, but that wasn't possible either, was it?' she said.

'It seems not.'

'Have you had women, Ned?'

'No.'

'Had Ben?'

'I don't know. I think he tried. I suppose it didn't work.'

She was breathing deeply and tears were trickling down her cheeks and neck. She climbed to her feet, eyes pressed shut, and, like a blind woman, stretched out her arms for me to embrace her. Her body squeezed against me as she buried her head in my shoulder and shook and wept. I put my arms round her but she pushed me away and led me to the sofa.

'Who made him become one of you?' she said.

'No one. It was his own choice. He wanted to imitate his father.'

'Is that a choice?'

'Of a sort.'

'And you too, you are a volunteer?'

'Yes.'

'Whom are *you* imitating?'

'No one.'

'Ben had no capacity for such a life. They had no business to be charmed by him. He was too persuasive.'

'I know.'

'And you? Do you need them to make a man of you?'

'It's something that has to be done.'

'To make a man of you?'

'The work. It's like emptying the dustbins or cleaning up in hospitals. Somebody has to do it. We can't pretend it isn't there.'

'Oh, I think we can.' She took my hand and wound her fingers stiffly into mine. 'We pretend a lot of things aren't there. Or we pretend that other things are more important. That's how we survive. We shall not defeat liars by lying to them. Will you stay here tonight?'

'I have to go back. I'm not Ben. I'm me. I'm his friend.'

'Let me tell you something. May I? It is very dangerous to play with reality. Will you remember that?'

I have no picture of our leave taking, so I expect it was too painful and my memory has rejected it. All I know now is, I had to catch the ferry. There was no jeep waiting so I walked. I remember the salt of her tears and the smell of her hair as I hurried through the night wind, and the black clouds writhing round the moon and the thump of the sea as I skirted the rocky bay. I remember the headland and the stubby little lighted steamer starting to cast off. And I know that for the entire journey I stood on the foredeck and that for the last part of it Smiley stood beside me. He must have heard Ben's story by then, and come up on deck to offer me his silent consolation.

I never saw Ben again – they kept me from him as we disembarked – but when I heard he had been discharged from the Service I wrote to Stefanie and asked her to tell me where he was. My letter was returned marked 'Gone Away.'

I would like to be able to tell you that Ben did not cause the destruction of the network, because Bill Haydon had betrayed it long before. Or better, that the network had been set up for us by the East Germans or the Russians in the first place, as a means of keeping us occupied and feeding us disinformation. But I am afraid the truth is otherwise, for in those days Haydon's access was limited by compartmentation, and his work did not take him to Berlin. Smiley even asked Bill, after his capture, whether he had had a hand in it, and Bill had laughed.

'I'd been wanting to get my hooks on that network for years,' he'd replied. 'When I heard what had happened, I'd a bloody good mind to send young Cavendish a bunch of flowers, but I suppose it wouldn't have been secure.'

The best I could tell Ben, if I saw him today, is that if he hadn't blown the network when he did, Haydon would have blown it for him a couple of years later. The best I could tell

Stefanie is that she was right in her way, but then so was I, and that her words never left my memory, even after I had ceased to regard her as the fountain of all wisdom. If I never understood who she was – if she belonged, as it were, more to Ben's mystery than my own – she was nevertheless the first of the siren voices that sounded in my ear, warning me that my mission was an ambiguous one. Sometimes I wonder what I was for her, but I'm afraid I know only too well: a callow boy, another Ben, unversed in life, banishing weakness with a show of strength, and taking refuge in a cloistered world.

I went back to Berlin not long ago. It was a few weeks after the Wall had been declared obsolete. An old bit of business took me, and Personnel was pleased to pay my fare. I never was formally stationed there, as it worked out, but I had been a frequent visitor, and for us old cold warriors a visit to Berlin is like returning to the source. And on a damp afternoon I found myself standing at the grimy little bit of fencing known grandly as the Wall of the Unknown Ones, which was the memorial to those killed while trying to escape during the sixties, some of whom did not have the foresight to give their names in advance. I stood among a humble group of East Germans, mostly women, and I noticed that they were examining the inscriptions on the crosses: unknown man, shot on such-and-such a date, in 1965. They were looking for clues, fitting the dates to the little that they knew.

And the sickening notion struck me that they could even have been looking for one of Ben's agents who had made a dash for freedom at the eleventh hour and failed. And the notion was all the more bewildering when I reflected that it was no longer we Western Allies, but East Germany itself, which was struggling to snuff out its existence.

The memorial is gone now. Perhaps it will find a corner in a museum somewhere, but I doubt it. When the Wall came down – hacked to pieces, sold – the memorial came down with it, which strikes me as an appropriate comment on the fickleness of human constancy.

4

Somebody asked Smiley about interrogation, yet again. It was a question that cropped up often as the night progressed – mainly because his audience wanted to squeeze more case histories out of him. Children are merciless.

'Oh, there's *some* art to faulting the liar, of course there is,' Smiley conceded doubtfully, and took a sip from his glass. 'But the real art lies in recognising the truth, which is a great deal harder. Under interrogation, nobody behaves normally. People who are stupid act intelligent. Intelligent people act stupid. The guilty look innocent as the day, and the innocent look dreadfully guilty. And just occasionally people act as they are and tell the truth as they know it, and of course they're the poor souls who get caught out every time. There's nobody less convincing to our wretched trade than the blameless man with nothing to hide.'

'Except possibly the blameless woman,' I suggested under my breath.

George had reminded me of Bella and the ambiguous Sea Captain Brandt.

He was a big, rough flaxen fellow, at first guess Slav or Scandinavian, with the roll of a landed seaman and the far eyes of an adventurer. I first met him in Zurich where he was in hot water with the police. The city superintendent called me in the middle of the night and said, 'Herr Konsul, we have somebody who says he has information for the British. We have orders to put him over the border in the morning.'

I didn't ask which border. The Swiss have four, but when they are throwing somebody out they're not particular. I drove to the district prison and met him in a barred interviewing room: a caged giant in a roll-neck pullover who called himself Sea Captain Brandt, which seemed to be his personal version of *Kapitän zur See*.

'You're a long way from the sea,' I said as I shook his great, padded hand.

As far as the Swiss were concerned, he had everything wrong with him. He had swindled a hotel, which in Switzerland is such a heinous crime it gets its own paragraph in the criminal code. He had caused a disturbance, he was penniless and his West German passport did not bear examination – though the Swiss refused to say this out loud, since a fake passport could prejudice their chances of getting rid of him to another country. He had been picked up drunk and vagrant and he blamed it on a girl. He had broken someone's jaw. He insisted on speaking to me alone.

'You British?' he asked in English, presumably in order to disguise our conversation from the Swiss, though they spoke better English than he did.

'Yes.'

'Prove, please.'

I showed him my official identity card, describing me as Vice-Consul for Economic Affairs.

'You work for British Intelligence?' he asked.

'I work for the British government.'

'Okay, okay,' he said, and in sudden weariness sank his

head into his hand so that his long blond hair flopped forward, and he had to toss it back again with a sweep of his arm. His face was chipped and pitted like a boxer's.

'You ever been in prison?' he asked, staring at the scrubbed white table.

'No, thank God.'

'Jesus,' he said, and in bad English told me his story.

He was a Latvian, born in Riga of Latvian and Polish parents. He spoke Latvian, Russian, Polish and German. He was born to the sea, which I sensed immediately, for I was born to it myself. His father and grandfather had been sailors, he had served six years in the Soviet navy, sailing the Arctic out of Archangel, and the Sea of Japan out of Vladivostok. A year back he had returned to Riga, bought a small boat and taken up smuggling along the Baltic coast, running cheap Russian vodka into Finland with the help of Scandinavian fishermen. He was caught and put in prison near Leningrad, escaped and stowed away to Poland, where he lived illegally with a Polish girl student in Cracow. I tell you this exactly as he told it to me, as if stowing away to Poland from Russia were as self-evident as catching a number 11 bus or popping down the road for a drink. Yet even with my limited familiarity with the obstacles he had overcome, I knew it was an extraordinary feat – and no less so when he performed it a second time. For when the girl left him to marry a Swiss salesman, he headed back to the coast and got himself a ride to Malmö, then down to Hamburg where he had a distant cousin, but the cousin was distant indeed, and told him to go to hell. So he stole the cousin's passport and headed south to Switzerland, determined to get back his Polish girl. When her new husband wouldn't let her go, Brandt broke the poor man's jaw for him, so here he was, a prisoner of the Swiss police.

All this still in English, so I asked him where he'd learned it. From the BBC, when he was out smuggling, he said. From his Polish girl – she was a language student. I had given him a packet of cigarettes and he was devouring them one after another, making a gas chamber of our little room.

'So what's this information you've got for us?' I asked him.

As a Latvian, he said in preamble, he felt no allegiance to Moscow. He had grown up under the lousy Russian tyranny in Latvia, he had served under lousy Russian officers in the navy, he had been sent to prison by lousy Russians and hounded by lousy Russians, and he had no compunction about betraying them. He hated Russians. I asked him the names of the ships he had served on and he told me. I asked him what armament they carried and he described some of the most sophisticated stuff they possessed at that time. I gave him a pencil and paper and he made surprisingly impressive drawings. I asked him what he knew about signals. He knew a lot. He was a qualified signalman and had used their latest toys, even if his memory was a year old. I asked him, 'Why the British?' and he replied that he had known 'a couple of you guys in Leningrad' – British sailors on a goodwill visit. I wrote down their names and the name of their ship, returned to my office and sent a flash telegram to London because we only had a few hours' grace before they put him over the border. Next evening Sea Captain Brandt was undergoing rigorous questioning at a safe house in Surrey. He was on the brink of a dangerous career. He knew every nook and bay along the south Baltic coast; he had good friends who were honest Latvian fishermen, others who were black marketeers, thieves and disaffected drop-outs. He was offering exactly what London was looking for after our recent losses – the chance to build a new supply line in and out of northern Russia, across Poland into Germany.

I have to set the recent history for you here – of the Circus, and of my own efforts to succeed in it.

After Ben, it had been touch and go for me whether they promoted me or threw me out. I think today that I owed more to Smiley's backstairs intervention than I gave him credit for at the time. Left to himself, I don't think Personnel would have kept me five minutes. I had broken bounds while under house arrest, I had withheld my knowledge of Ben's attachment to Stefanie, and if I was not a willing recipient of Ben's amorous declarations, I was guilty by association, so to hell with me.

'We rather thought you might like to consider the British Council,' Personnel had suggested nastily, at a meeting adorned not even by a cup of tea.

But Smiley interceded for me. Smiley, it appeared, had seen beyond my youthful impulsiveness, and Smiley commanded what amounted to his own modest private army of secret sources scattered around Europe. A further reason for my reprieve was provided – though not even Smiley could have known it at the time – by the traitor Bill Haydon, whose London Station was rapidly acquiring a monopoly of Circus operations worldwide. And if Smiley's questing eye had not yet focused on Bill, he was already convinced that the Fifth Floor was nursing a Moscow Centre mole to its bosom, and determined to assemble a team of officers whose age and access placed them beyond suspicion. By a mercy, I was one.

For a few months I was kept in limbo, devilling in large back rooms, evaluating and distributing low-grade reports to Whitehall clients. Friendless and bored, I was seriously beginning to wonder whether Personnel had decided to post me to death, when to my joy I was summoned to his office and in Smiley's presence offered the post of second man in Zurich, under a capable old trooper named Eddows, whose stated principle was to leave me to sink or swim.

Within a month I was installed in a small flat in the Altstadt, working round the clock eight days a week. I had a Soviet naval attaché in Geneva who loved Lenin but loved a French air hostess more, and a Czech arms dealer in Lausanne who was having a crisis of conscience about supplying the world's terrorists with weapons and explosives. I had a millionaire Albanian with a chalet in St Moritz who was risking his neck by returning to his homeland and recruiting members of his former household, and a nervous East German physicist on attachment to the Max Planck Institute in Essen who had secretly converted to Rome. I had a beautiful little microphone operation running against the Polish Embassy in Bern and a telephone tap on a pair of Hungarian spies in Basel. And I was by now beginning to fancy myself seriously in love with Mabel, who had recently been transferred to Vetting Section, and was the toast of the Junior Officers' Bar.

And Smiley's faith in me was not misplaced, for by my own exertions in the field, and his insistence upon rigid need-to-know at home, we succeeded in netting valuable intelligence and even getting it into the right hands – and you would be surprised how rarely that combination is achieved.

So that when after two years of this the Hamburg slot came up – a one-man post, and working directly to London Station, now willy-nilly the operational hub of the Service – I had Smiley's generous blessing to apply for it, whatever his private reservations about Haydon's widening embrace. I angled, I was not brash, I reminded Personnel of my naval background. I let him infer, if I did not say it in as many words, that I was straining at the bonds of Smiley's old-world caution. And it worked. He gave me Hamburg Station on the Haydon ticket, and the same night, after a romantic dinner at Bianchi's, Mabel and I slept together, the first time for each of us.

My sense of the rightness of things was further increased when, on looking over my new stocklist, I saw to my amusement that one Wolf Dittrich, alias Sea Captain Brandt, was a leading player in my new cast of characters. We are talking of the late sixties now. Bill Haydon had three more years to run.

Hamburg had always been a good place to be English, now it was an even better place to spy. After the lakeside gentility of Zurich, Hamburg crackled with energy and sparkled with sea air. The old Hanseatic ties to Poland, northern Russia and the Baltic states were still very much alive. We had commerce, we had banking – well, so had Zurich. But we had shipping too, and immigrants and adventurers. We had brashness and vulgarity galore. We were the German capital of whoredom and the press. And on our doorstep we had the secretive lowlands of Schleswig-Holstein, with their horizontal rainstorms, red farms, green fields and cloud-stacked skies. Every man has his price. To this day, my soul can be bought for a jar of Lübeck beer, a pickled herring and a glass of schnapps after a trudge along the dykes.

Everything else about the job was equally pleasing. I was Ned the Assistant Shipping Consul; my humble office was a pretty brick cottage with a brass plate, handy enough for the Consulate General, yet prudently apart from it. Two clerks on secondment from the Admiralty performed my cover work for me, and kept their mouths shut. I had a radio and a Circus cypher clerk. And if Mabel and I were not yet engaged to be married, our relationship had reached a stage when she was ready to clear her decks for me wherever I popped back to London for a consultation with Bill or one of his lieutenants.

To meet my joes, I had a safe flat in Wellingsbüttel overlooking the cemetery, on the upper floor of a flower shop managed by a retired German couple who had belonged to us in the war. Their busiest days were Sundays, and on Monday mornings a queue of kids from the housing estate sold them back the flowers they had sold the day before. I never saw a safer spot. Hearses, covered vans and funeral cortèges rolled past us all day long. But at night the place was literally as quiet as the grave. Even the exotic figure of my sea captain became unremarkable when he donned his black hat and dark suit and swung into the brick archway of our shop and, with his commercial traveller's briefcase bouncing at his side, stomped up the stairs to our innocent front door marked 'Büro'.

I shall go on calling him Brandt. Some people, however much they change their names, have only one.

But the jewel in my crown was the *Margerite* – or, as we called her in English, the *Daisy*. She was a fifty-foot clinker-built, double-ended fishing boat converted to a cabin cruiser, with a wheelhouse, a main saloon and four berths in the foc'sle. She had a mizzen mast and sail to steady her from rolling. She had a dark-green hull with light-green gunnels and a white cabin roof. She was built for stealth, not speed. In poor light and choppy water, she was invisible to the naked eye. She had sparse top-hamper, and lay close to the water, which gave her a harmless image on the radar screens, particularly in heavy weather. The Baltic is a vengeful sea, shallow and tideless. Even in a mild wind, the waves come steep and nasty. At ten knots and full throttle, the *Daisy* pitched and rolled like a pig. The only speedy thing about her was the fourteen-foot Zodiac dinghy hoisted as the ship's lifeboat and lashed to the cabin roof, with a Johnson 50-horsepower to whisk our agents in and out.

For her berth she had the old fishing village of Blankenese on the river Elbe, just a few short miles out of Hamburg. And there she lay contentedly among her equals, as humble an example of her kind as you could wish. From Blankenese, when she was needed, she could slip upriver to the Kiel Canal, and crawl its sixty miles at five knots before hitting open sea.

She had a Decca navigator that took readings from slave stations on the shore, but so did everyone. She had nothing inside or out that was not consistent with her modesty. Each of her three-man crew could turn his hand to everything. There were no specialists, though each had his particular love. When we needed expert despatchers or fitters, the Royal Navy was on hand to help us.

So you can see that, what with a new dynamic team to back me up at London Station, and a full hand of sources to test my versatility, and the *Daisy* and her crew to manage, I had everything that a Head of Station with salt water in his blood could decently inherit.

And of course I had Brandt.

Brandt's two years before the Circus mast had altered him in ways I at first found hard to define. It was not so much an aging or a hardening I observed in him, as that wearying alertness, that overwakefulness, which the secret world with time imprints upon even the most relaxed of its inhabitants. We met at the safe flat. He entered. He stopped dead and stared at me. His jaw fell open and he let out a great shout of recognition. He seized my arms in a sultan's greeting and nearly broke them. He laughed till the tears came, he held me away to look at, then hauled me back to hug against his black overcoat. But his spontaneity was strained by watchfulness. I knew the signs. I had seen them in other joes.

'God damn, why they don't tell me nothing, Herr Konsul?' he cried as he embraced me yet again. 'What damn game they playing? Listen, we do some good things over there, hear me? We got good people, we beat those damn Russians to death, okay?'

'I know,' I said, laughing back at him. 'I heard.'

And when night fell he insisted on seating me among the coils of rope in the back of his van and driving me at breakneck speed to the remote farmhouse that London had acquired for him. He was determined to introduce me to his crew and I looked forward to it. And I looked forward even more to getting a sight of his girlfriend Bella, because London Station was feeling a little queasy about her recent arrival in his life. She was twenty-two years old and had been with him three months. Brandt was looking hard at fifty. It was midsummer, I remember, and the inside of the van smelt of freesias, for he had bought her a bunch at the market.

'She's a number one girl,' he told me proudly as we entered the house. 'Cooks good, makes good love, learns English, everything. Hey, Bella, I brought you new boyfriend!'

Painters and sailors make the same kind of houses, and Brandt's was no exception. It was scant but homely, with brick floors and low, white-raftered ceilings. Even in the darkness it seemed to usher in the outside light. From the front door we stepped straight down into the drawing room. A wood fire smouldered in the hearth and a ship's lamp shone on the naked flank of a girl as she lay reading on a heap of cushions. Hearing us enter, she sprang excitedly to her feet. Twenty-two and going on eighteen, I thought as she grabbed my hand and gaily pumped it up and down. She was wearing a man's shirt and very short shorts. A gold amulet glinted at her throat, declaring Brandt's possession of her: this is my woman, wearing my badge of ownership. Her face was peasant and Slav and naturally happy, with clear, wide eyes, high cheeks and a tipped-up smile even when her lips were in repose. Her bare legs were long and tanned to the same gold colour as her hair. She had a small waist, high breasts and full hips. It was a very beautiful, very young body, and whatever Brandt was thinking, it belonged to no one of his age, or even mine.

She set his freesias in a vase and fetched black bread and pickles and a bottle of schnapps. She was carelessly provocative in her movements. Either she knew exactly, or not at all, the power of each slight gesture she made. She sat beside him at the table, smiled at me and threw her arm around him, letting her shirt gape. She took possession of his hand and showed me by comparison the slenderness of her own, while Brandt talked recklessly about the network, mentioning joes and places by name, and Bella measured me with her frank eyes.

'Listen,' Brandt said, 'we got to get Aleks another radio, hear me, Ned? They take it apart, they put new spares, batteries, that radio's lousy. That's a bad-luck radio.'

When the phone rang, he answered it imperiously: 'Listen, I'm busy, okay? . . . Leave the package with Stefan, I said. Listen, have you heard from Leonids?'

The room gradually filled up. First to enter was a darting, bandy-legged man with a drooping moustache. He kissed Bella rapturously but chastely on the lips, punched Brandt's forearm and helped himself to a plateful of food.

'That's Kazimirs,' Brandt explained, with a jab of his thumb. 'He's a bastard and I love him. Okay?'

'Very okay,' I said heartily.

Kazimirs had escaped three years ago across the Finnish border, I remembered. He had killed two Soviet frontier guards along his way, and he was crazy about engines – never happier than when he was up to his elbows in oil. He was also the respected ship's cook.

After Kazimirs came the Durba brothers, Antons and Alfreds, stocky and pert like Welshmen, and blue-eyed like Brandt. The Durbas had sworn to their mother that they would never go to sea together, so they took it in turns, for the *Daisy* handled best with three, and we liked to leave space for cargo and unexpected passengers. Soon everyone was talking at once, shooting questions at me, not waiting for the answers, laughing, proposing toasts, smoking, reminiscing, conspiring. Their last run had been bad, really bad, said Kazimirs. That was three weeks ago. *Daisy* had hit a freak storm off the Gulf of Danzig and lost her mizzen. At Ujava on the Latvian coast, they had missed the light signal in the fog, said Antons Durba. They had fired a rocket and God help them, there was this whole damned reception party of crazy Latvians standing on the beach like a delegation of city fathers! Wild laughter, toasts, then a deep Nordic silence while everyone but myself was struck by the same solemn memory.

'To Valdemars,' said Kazimirs, and we drank a toast to Valdemars, a member of their group who had died five years ago. Then Bella took Brandt's glass and drank too, a separate ceremony while she watched me over the brim. 'Valdemars,' she repeated softly, and her solemnity was as beguiling as her smile. Had she known Valdemars? Had he been one of her lovers? Or was she simply drinking to a brave fellow country-man who had died for the Cause?

But I have to tell you a little more about Valdemars – not whether he had slept with Bella or even how he had died, for no one knew for sure. All that was known was that he had been put ashore and never heard of again. One story said he had managed to swallow his pill, another that he had given orders to his bodyguard to shoot him if he walked into a trap. But the bodyguard had disappeared too. And Valdemars was not the only one who had disappeared during what was now remembered by the group as 'the autumn of betrayal'. In the next few months, as the anniversaries of their deaths came round, we drank to four other Latvian heroes who had per-ished unaccountably in the same ill-starred period – delivered, it was now believed, not to partisans in the forest, nor loyal reception parties on the beach, but straight into the hands of Moscow Centre's chief of Latvian operations. And if new networks had been cautiously rebuilt meanwhile, five years later the stigma of these betrayals still clung to the survivors, as Haydon had been at pains to warn me.

'They're a careless bunch of sods,' he had said with his usual irreverence, 'and when they're not being careless, they're duplicitous. Don't be fooled by all that Nordic phlegm and backslapping.'

I was remembering his words as I continued my mental reconnaissance of Bella. Sometimes she listened resting her head on her clenched fist, sometimes she laid her head on Brandt's forearm, dreaming his thoughts for him while he plotted and drank. But her big, light eyes never ceased visiting me, working me out, this Englishman sent to rule our lives. And occasionally, like a warm cat, she shook herself free of Brandt and took time to groom herself, recrossing her legs and primly correcting the fit of her shorts, or twisting a hank of hair into a plait, or drawing her gold amulet from between her breasts and examining it front and back. I waited for a spark of complicity between herself and other members of the crew, but it was clear to me that Brandt's girl was holy ground. Even the ebullient Kazimirs deadened his face to talk to her. She fetched another bottle, and when she returned she sat down beside me and took hold of my hand and opened my palm on the table, examining it while she spoke in Latvian to Brandt, who broke into a gust of laughter which the rest of them took up.

'You know what she say?'

'I'm afraid I don't.'

'She says English make damn good husband. If I die, she going to have you instead!'

She clambered back to him and, laughing, wriggled into his embrace. She didn't look at me after that. It was as if she didn't need to. So I avoided her eyes in return, and thought dutifully about her history as told to London Station by Sea Captain Brandt.

She was the daughter of a farmer from a village near Jelgava, who had been shot dead when security police raided a secret meeting of Latvian patriots, Brandt had said. The farmer was a founder member of the group. The police wanted to shoot the girl as well, but she escaped into the forest and joined up with a band of partisans and outlaws who passed her round among them for a summer, which did not seem to have upset her. By stages she had made her way to the coast and, by a route that was still mysterious to us, got word to Brandt, who, without troubling to mention her to London in advance, picked her off a beach while he was landing a new radio operator to replace another who had had a nervous breakdown. Radio operators are the opera stars of every network. If they don't have breakdowns, they have shingles.

'Great guys,' said Brandt enthusiastically as he drove me back to town. 'You like them?'

'They're terrific,' I said, and meant it, for there is no better company anywhere than men who love the sea.

'Bella want to work with us. She want to kill the guys who shoot her father. I say no. She's too young. I love her.'

A fierce white moon shone on the flat meadows, and by its light I saw his craggy face in profile, as if set against the storm to come.

'And you knew him,' I suggested, affecting to recapitulate something I vaguely remembered. 'Her father. Feliks. He was a friend of yours.'

'Sure I knew Feliks! I love him! He was a great guy! The bastards shot him dead.'

'Did he die immediately?'

'They shoot him to pieces. Kalashnikovs. They shoot everybody. Seven guys. All shot.'

'Did anyone see it happen?'

'One guy. He see it, run away.'

'What became of the bodies?'

'Secret police take them. They're scared, those police guys. Don't want no trouble from the people. Shoot the partisans, throw them in a truck, drive away to hell.'

'How well did you know him – her father?'

Brandt made his sweeping gesture with his forearm. 'Feliks? He was my friend. Fought at Leningrad. Prisoner of war in Germany. Stalin didn't like those guys. When they came home from Germany, he sent them to Siberia, shot them, gave them a bad time. What the hell?'

But London Station had picked up a different story, even if at this stage it was only a whisper. The father had been the informant, said the whisper. Recruited in Siberian captivity and sent back to Latvia to penetrate the groups. He had called the meeting, tipped off his masters, then climbed out of the back window while the partisans were being slaughtered. As a reward, he was now managing a collective farm near Kiev, living under a different name. Somebody had recognised him and told somebody else who had told somebody else. The source was delicate, checking would be a lengthy process.

So I was warned. Watch out for Bella.

I was more than warned. I was disturbed. In the next weeks I saw Bella several times, and each time I was obliged to record my impressions on the encounter sheet which London Station now insisted must be completed each time she was sighted. I made a rendezvous with Brandt at the safe flat, and to my alarm he brought her with him. She had spent the day in town, he said. They were on their way back to the farmhouse, why not?

'Relax. She don't speak no English,' he reminded me with a laugh, noticing my discomfort.

So I kept our business short, while she lounged on the sofa and smiled and listened to us with her eyes, but mostly she listened to me.

'My girl's studying,' Brandt told me proudly, patting her on the backside as we prepared to separate. 'One day she be a big professor. *Nicht wahr, Bella? Du wirst ein ganz grosser Professor, du!'*

A week later, when I took a discreet look at the *Daisy* at her berth in Blankenese, Bella was there again, wearing her shorts and scampering over the deck in her bare feet as if we were planning a Mediterranean cruise.

'For heaven's sake. We can't have girls aboard. London will go mad,' I told Brandt that night. 'So will the crew. You know how superstitious they are about having women on the ship. You're the same yourself.'

He brushed me aside. My predecessor had raised no objection, he said. Why should I?

'Bella makes the boys happy,' he insisted. 'She's from home, Ned, she's a kid. She's a family for them, come on!'

When I checked the file, I discovered he was half right. My predecessor, a seconded naval officer, had reported that Bella was 'conscious to' the *Daisy*, even adding that she seemed to 'exert a benign influence as ship's mascot'. And when I read between the lines of his report of the *Daisy*'s most recent operational mission, I realised that Bella had been there on the dockside to wave them off – and no doubt to wave them safely back as well.

Now of course operational security is always relative. I had never imagined that everything in the Brandt organisation was going to be played by Sarratt rules. I was aware that in the cloistered atmosphere of Head Office it was too easy to mistake our tortuous structures of codenames, symbols and cut-outs for life on the ground. Cambridge Circus was one thing. A bunch of volatile Baltic patriots risking their necks was another.

Nevertheless the presence of an uncleared, unrecruited

camp-follower at the heart of our operation, privy to our plans, and conversations, went beyond anything I had imagined – and all this in the wake of the betrayals five years earlier. And the more I worried over it, the more proprietorial, it seemed to me, did Brandt's devotion to the girl become. His endearments grew increasingly lavish in my presence, his caresses more demonstrative. 'A typical older man's infatuation for a young girl,' I told London, as if I had seen dozens of such cases.

Meanwhile a new mission was being planned for the *Daisy*, the purpose to be revealed to us later. Twice, three times a week, I found myself of necessity driving out to the farmhouse, arriving after dark, then sitting for hours at the table while we studied charts and weather maps and the latest shore observation bulletins. Sometimes the full crew came, sometimes it was just the three of us. To Brandt it made no difference. He clasped Bella to him as if the two of them were in the throes of constant ecstasy, fondling her hair and neck, and once forgetting himself so far as to slip his hand inside her shirt and cup her naked breast while he gave her a prolonged kiss. Yet as I discreetly looked away from these disturbing scenes, what remained longest in my sight was Bella's gaze on me, as if she were telling me she wished that it was I, not Brandt, who was caressing her.

'Explicit embraces appear to be the norm,' I wrote drily on the encounter sheet, Hamburg to London Station, late that night in my office. And in my nightly log: 'Route, weather and sea conditions acceptable. We await firm orders from Head Office. Morale of crew high.'

But my own morale was fighting for survival as one calamity followed upon another.

There was first the unfortunate business of my predecessor,

full name Lieutenant Commander Perry de Mornay Lipton, DSO, RN, retd., sometime hero of Jack Arthur Lumley's wartime irregulars. For ten years until my arrival, Lipton had cultivated the role of Hamburg character, by day acting the English bloody fool, sporting a monocle and hanging around the expatriate clubs ostensibly to pick up free advice on his investments. But come nightfall, he put on his secret hat and went to work briefing and debriefing his formidable army of secret agents. Or so the legend, as I had heard it from Head Office.

The only thing that had puzzled me was that there had been no formal handover between us, but Personnel had told me tersely Lipton was on a mission elsewhere. I was now admitted to the truth. Lipton had departed, not on some life-and-death adventure in darkest Russia, but to southern Spain, where he had set up house with a former Corporal of Horse named Kenneth, and two hundred thousand pounds of Circus funds, mainly in gold bars and Swiss francs, which he had paid out over several years to brave agents who did not exist.

The mistrust shed by this sad discovery now spilled into every operation Lipton had touched, including inevitably Brandt's. Was Brandt too a Lipton fiction, living high on our secret funds in exchange for ingeniously fabricated intelligence? Were his networks, were his vaunted collaborators and friends, many of whom were drawing liberal salaries?

And Bella – was Bella part of the deception? Had Bella softened his head and weakened his will? Was Brandt too feathering his nest before retiring with his loved one to the south of Spain?

A procession of Circus experts passed through the doors of my little shipping office. First came an improbable man called Captain Plum. Crouched in the privacy of my safe room, Plum and I pored over the *Daisy*'s old fuel dockets and mileage records and compared them with the perilous routes that Brandt and the crew claimed to have steered on their missions along the Baltic coast. The ship's logs were sketchy at best, as most logs are, but we read them all, alongside Plum's records of signals intercepts, radar stations, navigational buoys and sightings of Soviet patrol boats.

A week later Plum was back, this time accompanied by a foul-mouthed Mancunian called Rose, a former Malayan policeman who had made himself a name as a Circus sniffer dog. Rose questioned me as roughly as if I were myself a part of the deception. But when I was about to lose my temper he disarmed me by declaring that, on the evidence available, the Brandt organisation was innocent of misdoing.

Yet in the minds of such people as this, suspicions of one kind only fired suspicions of another, and the question mark hanging over Bella's father, Feliks, had not gone away. If the father was bad, then the daughter must know it, went the reasoning. And if she knew and had not said it, then she was bad as well. Moscow Centre, like the Circus, was well known for recruiting entire families. A father-and-daughter team was eminently plausible. Soon, without any solid evidence I was aware of, London Station began to peddle the notion that Feliks had been responsible for the betrayals five years ago.

Inevitably, this placed Bella in an even more sinister light. There was talk of ordering her to London and grilling her, but here my authority as Brandt's case officer held sway. Impossible, I advised London Station. Brandt would never stand for it. Very well, came the answer – typical of Haydon's cavalier approach – bring them both over and Brandt can sit in while we interrogate the girl. This time I was sufficiently moved to fly back to London myself, where I insisted on stating my case personally to Bill. I entered his room to find him stretched out on a chaise longue, for he affected the eccentricity of never sitting at his desk. A joss stick was burning from an old ginger jar.

'Maybe Brother Brandt isn't as prickly as you think, Master Ned,' he said accusingly, peering at me over his half-framed spectacles. 'Maybe *you're* the prickly one?'

'He's besotted with her,' I said.

'Are you?'

'If we start accusing his girl in front of him, he'll go crazy. He lives for her. He'd tell us to go to hell and dismantle the network, and I doubt whether anyone else could run it.'

Haydon pondered this: 'The Garibaldi of the Baltic. Well, well. Still, Garibaldi wasn't much bloody good, was he?' He waited for me to answer but I preferred to take his question as rhetorical. 'Those jokers she shacked up in the forest with,' he drawled finally. 'Does she talk about them?'

'She doesn't talk about any of it. Brandt does, she doesn't.'

'So what does she talk about?'

'Nothing much. If she says anything of significance, it's usually in Latvian and Brandt translates or not as he thinks fit. Otherwise she just smiles and looks.'

'At you?'

'At him.'

'And she's quite a looker, I gather.'

'She's attractive, I suppose. Yes.'

Once more he took his time to consider this. 'Sounds to me like the ideal woman,' he pronounced. 'Smiles and looks, keeps quiet, fucks – what more can you ask?' He again examined me quizzically over his spectacles. 'Do you mean she doesn't even speak *German*? She must do, coming from up there. Don't be daft.'

'She speaks German reluctantly when she's got no choice. Speaking Latvian's a patriotic act. German isn't.'

'Good tits?'

'Not bad.'

'Couldn't you get alongside her a bit more? Without rocking the lovers' boat, obviously. Just the answers to a few basic questions would be a help. Nothing dramatic. Just whether she's the real thing, or whether Brother Brandt smuggled her into the nest in a warming pan – or whether Moscow Centre did, of course. See what you can get out of her. He's not her natural father, you realise that, I suppose. He can't be.'

'Who isn't?' For a confused moment I had thought he was still talking about Brandt.

'Her daddy. Feliks. The one who got shot or didn't. The farmer. According to the record, she was born January '45, wasn't she?'

'Yes.'

'Ergo, conceived around April '44. At which time – if Brother Brandt's to be believed – her supposed daddy was languishing in a prisoner-of-war camp in Germany. Mind you, we shouldn't be too straitlaced about it. No great feat of skill, I suppose, to get yourself knocked up while your old man's in the pen. Still every little helps when we're trying to decide whether to abort a network which may have run its course.'

I was grateful for Mabel's company that night, even if we had not yet found our form as the great lovers we were so anxious to become. But of course I didn't tell her anything of my business, least of all about Bella. As a Vetting girl, Mabel was on the routine side of the Circus. It would have been quite improper for me to share my problems with her. If we had already been married – well, that might have been a different thing. Meanwhile, Bella must remain my secret.

And she did. Back in my solitary bed in Hamburg I thought of Bella and little else. The double mystery of her – as a woman and as a potential traitor – elevated her to an object of almost unlimited danger to me. I saw her no longer as a fringe figure of our organisation but its destiny. Her virtue was ours. If Bella was pure, so was the network. But if she was the plaything of another service – a deceiver planted on us to tempt and weaken and ultimately betray us – then the integrity of those round her was soiled with her own, and the network would indeed, as Haydon put it, have run its course.

I closed my eyes and saw her gaze upon me, sunny and beckoning. I felt again the softness of her kisses each time we greeted one another – always, as it seemed to me, held for a fraction longer than formality required. I pictured her liquid body in its different poses, and turned it over and over in my imagination in the same way that I contemplated the possibilities of her treason. I remembered Haydon's suggestion that I should try to 'get alongside her', and discovered I was incapable of separating my sense of duty from my desires.

I retold myself the story of her escape, questioning it at every stage. Had she got away before the shooting or during it? And how? Had some lover among the security troops tipped her off? Had there been a shooting at all? And why did she not grieve more for her dead father, instead of making love to Brandt? Even her happiness seemed to speak against her. I imagined her in the forest, with the cut-throats and outlaws. Did each man take her at his will, or did she live now with this one, now with that? I dreamed of her, naked in the forest, and myself naked with her. I awoke ashamed of myself and put through an early-morning call to Mabel.

Did I understand myself? I doubt it. I knew little about women, beautiful women least of all. I am sure it never occurred to me that finding fault with Bella might be my way of weakening her sexual hold on me. Determined on the straight path, I wrote to Mabel daily. Meanwhile I fixed on the *Daisy*'s forthcoming mission as the perfect opportunity to undertake a hostile questioning of Bella. The weather was turning foul, which was what suited the *Daisy* best. It was autumn and the nights were lengthening. The *Daisy* liked the dark too.

'Crew stand by to sail Monday,' said London Station's first signal. The second, which did not arrive till Friday evening, gave their destination as the Narva Bay in northern Estonia, not a hundred miles west of Leningrad. Never before had the *Daisy* ventured so far along the Russian seaboard; only rarely had she been used in support of non-Latvian patriots.

'I would give my eyes,' I told Brandt.

'You're too damn dangerous, Ned,' he replied, clapping me on the shoulder. 'Be seasick four days, lie in your bunk, get in the way, what the hell?'

We both knew it was impossible. The most Head Office had ever granted me was a night spin round the island of Bornholm, and even that had been like drawing teeth.

On the Saturday night we gathered in the farmhouse. Kazimirs and Antons Durba arrived together in the van. It was Antons's turn to go to sea. With such a small operational crew, everyone had to know everything, everyone had to be interchangeable. There was no more drink. From now on, they were a dry ship. Kazimirs had brought lobsters. He cooked them elaborately, with a sauce that he was famous for, while Bella played cabin girl to him, fetching and carrying and being decorative. When we had eaten, Bella cleared the table and I spread the charts under the hanging overhead lamp.

Brandt had said six days. It was an optimistic guess. From the Kieler Förde the *Daisy* would make for open sea, passing Bornholm on the Swedish side. On reaching the Swedish island of Gotland she would put in at Sundre on the southern tip, refuel and top up her provisions. While refuelling, she would be approached by two men, one of whom would ask if they had any herring. They were to reply: 'Only in tins. There have been no herring in these waters for years.' All such exchanges sound fatuous in cold blood, and this one reduced Antons and Kazimirs to fits of nervous laughter. Returning from the kitchen, Bella joined in.

One of the men would then ask to come aboard, I continued. He was an expert – I did not say in sabotage, because the crew had mixed feelings on the matter. His name for the trip would be Volodia. He would be carrying a leather suitcase and, in his coat pocket, a brown button and a white button as proof of his good faith. If he did not know his name, or carried no suitcase, or did not produce the buttons, they were to put him back on shore alive, but return to Kiel at once. There was an agreed radio signal for this eventuality. Otherwise they should make no signals whatever. A moment's silence gripped us, and I heard the sound of Bella's bare feet on the brick floor as she fetched more firewood.

From Gotland they should head north-east through international waters, I said, and steer a central course up the Gulf of Finland, until they were lying off the island of Gogland, where they should idle till dusk, then head due south for Narva Bay, reckoning to make landfall by midnight.

I had brought large-scale charts of the Bay and photographs of the sandy coastline. I spread them on the table and the men gathered to my side to look at them. As they did so, something made me glance up and I caught sight of Bella, curled up in her own corner of the room, her excited eyes full upon me in the firelight.

I showed them the point on the beach that the Zodiac should make for, and the point on the headland where they should watch for signals. The landing party would be wearing ultra-violet glasses, I said; the Estonian reception party would be using an ultra-violet lamp. Nothing would be visible to the naked eye. After the passenger and his suitcase had been landed, the dinghy should wait no more than two minutes for any possible replacement before heading back for the *Daisy* at full speed. The dinghy should be crewed by one man only, so that if necessary he could take a second passenger on the return run. I recited the recognition signals to be exchanged with the reception party, and this time nobody laughed. I gave the shelving and gradients of the landing beach. There would be no moon. Bad weather was expected, and surely hoped for. Bella brought us tea, brushing carelessly against us as she set out the mugs. It was as if she were harnessing her sexuality to our cause. Reaching Brandt, who was still stooped over the beach chart, she gravely caressed his broad back with both her hands as if filling him with her youthful strength.

I returned to my flat at five in the morning with no thought of sleep. In the afternoon I rode with Brandt and Bella to Blankenese in the van. Antons and Kazimirs had been with the boat all day. They were dressed for the voyage, in bobble hats and oilskin trousers. Orange life jackets were airing on the deck. Shaking hands with each man in turn, I passed round the seaproofed capsules that contained their lethal pills of pure cyanide. A grey drizzle was falling; the little quay was deserted. Brandt walked to the gangway, but when Bella made to follow him, he stopped her.

'No more,' he told her. 'You stay with Ned.'

She was wearing his old duffle coat, and a woollen hat with earflaps, which I suspected she had been wearing when he rescued her. He kissed her and she hugged him till he pushed her off and went aboard, leaving her at my side. Antons stepped into the engine house and we heard the engine cough and come to life. Brandt and Kazimirs cast off. Nobody looked at us any more. The *Daisy* cleared the quay and headed sedately for the centre of the river. The three men's backs remained turned against us. We heard the hoot of her ship's horn, and watched her until she had slipped behind the curtain of grey mist.

Like abandoned children, Bella and I walked hand in hand up the ramp to Brandt's parked van. Neither of us spoke. Neither of us had anything to say. I glanced back for a last sight of the *Daisy*, but the mist had swallowed her. I looked at Bella and saw that her eyes were unusually bright, and that she was breathing fast.

'He'll be all right,' I assured her, releasing her hand while I unlocked the door. 'They're very experienced. He's a great man.' Even in German, it sounded rather silly.

She got into the van beside me and took back my hand. Her fingers were like separate lives inside my palm. Get alongside her, Haydon had kept insisting. In my most recent signal, I had assured him I would try.

★

At first we drove in companionable silence, joined and separated by our shared experience. I was driving cautiously because I was taut, but my hand still held hers to give her comfort, and when I was obliged to take a firmer grasp of the steering wheel, I saw that her hand stayed beside me, fingers upward, waiting for me to come back. Suddenly I was terribly concerned about where to take her. Absurdly so. I thought of an elegant basement restaurant with tiled alcoves where I took my banking joes. The elderly waiters would provide her with the kind of reassurance she needed. Then I remembered she was wearing Brandt's duffle coat, jeans and rubber boots. I was no better dressed myself. So where? I wondered anxiously. It was getting late. Through the mist, lights were coming on in the cottages.

'Are you hungry?' I asked.

She put her hand back on her lap.

'Should I find us somewhere to eat?' I asked.

She shrugged.

'Shall I take you to the farmhouse?' I suggested.

'What for?'

'Well, I mean, how are you going to spend the next few days? What did you do the last time he was away?'

'I rested from him,' she said, with a laugh I had not expected.

'Then tell me how you would like to wait for him,' I suggested magnanimously, with a hint of rank. 'Do you prefer to be alone? Meet up with other exiles and have gossips? What's best?'

'It's not important,' she said, and moved away from me.

'Tell me all the same. Help me.'

'I shall go to cinemas. Look at shops. Read magazines. I shall listen to music. Try to study. Get bored.'

I decided on the safe flat. There would be food in the fridge, I told myself. Give her a meal, a drink, get her talking. Then either drive her to the farmhouse or send her by cab.

We entered the city. I parked two streets away from the safe flat and took her arm as we walked along the tree-lined pavement. I would have done the same for any woman in a dark street, but there was something disturbing about feeling her bare arm inside Brandt's sleeve. The city was unfamiliar to me. In the lighted windows of the houses, people talked and laughed as if we didn't exist. She clasped my arm and drew my hand against her breast – to be precise, the underside of it, I could feel its shape precisely through the layers of clothing. I was remembering the Circus bar-room jokes about certain officers who picked up their best intelligence in bed. I was remembering Haydon asking me whether she had good tits. I felt ashamed, and took back my hand.

There was a man-door to one side of the cemetery gates. As I unlocked it and ushered her ahead of me, she turned and kissed me on the eyes, one after the other, while she held my face in both her hands. I gripped her waist and she seemed weightless. She was very happy. I could see her smile by the yellow cemetery lights.

'Everyone is dead,' she whispered excitedly. 'But we are alive.'

I went ahead of her up the stairs. Halfway, I looked back to make sure she was following me. I was scared that she might have changed her mind. I was scared altogether – not because I was without experience – thanks to Mabel I was not – but because I knew already that I was encountering a different category of woman from any I had known before. She was standing right behind me, holding her shoes in her hands, still smiling.

I opened the door for her. She stepped through and kissed me again, laughing in merriment, just as if I had lifted her up and carried her across the threshold on our wedding day. I remembered stupidly that Russians never shake hands in doorways, and perhaps Latvians didn't either, and perhaps her kisses were some kind of ceremony of exorcism. I would have asked her, except that, near enough, I had lost my voice. I closed the door, then crossed the room to turn up the fire, an electric convector affair which, as long as the room was cold, blew out warm air with enormous vigour, but afterwards only fitfully, like an old dog dreaming.

I went to the kitchen to fetch some wine. When I returned she had disappeared and the light was on under the bathroom door. I set the table carefully with knives and forks and spoons and cheese and cold meat and glasses and paper napkins and anything else that I could possibly think of, because I was taking refuge in the distancing formalities of hospitality.

The bathroom door opened and she emerged wearing Brandt's coat wrapped round her as a dressing-gown and, to judge by her bare legs, little else. Her hair was brushed. In our safe flats, we always keep a brush and comb for hospitality.

And I remember thinking that if she was as bad as Haydon seemed to think she was, it was a pretty terrible thing for her to be wearing Brandt's coat in order to deceive the man she was already betraying; and a pretty terrible thing for me to be the man she had selected, while my agents were heading for high danger with lethal pills in their coat pockets. But I had no sense of guilt. I mention this in order to try to explain that my mind was zigzagging in any number of directions in its effort to still my desire for her.

I kissed her and took off her coat, and I never saw before

or since anyone so beautiful. And the truth is that, at that moment and at that age, I had not yet acquired the power to distinguish between truth and beauty. They were one and the same to me, and I could only feel awe for her. If I had ever suspected her of anything, the sight of her naked body convinced me of her innocence.

After that, the images of my memory must tell you their own tale. Even today I see us as two other people, never as ourselves.

Bella naked by the half light of the fire, lying on her side as I had first seen her by the fire in the farmhouse. I had fetched the duvet from the bedroom.

'You're so beautiful,' she whispered.

It had not occurred to me that I could fill her with a comparable wonder.

Bella at the window, the light from the cemetery making a perfect statue of her body, gilding her fleece and drawing light patterns on her breasts.

Bella kissing Ned's face, hundreds of small kisses as she brings him back to life. Bella laughing at the limitless beauty of herself, and of the two of us together. Bella taking laughter into love, a thing that had never happened to me before, until every part of each of us was a matter for celebration, to be kissed and suckled and admired in its own way.

Bella turning away from Ned to offer herself, thrusting back to accept him as she continues whispering to him. Her whispering stops. She begins her ascent, arching backward until she is upright. And suddenly she is crying out, crying to me and the dead, and she is the most living thing on earth.

Ned and Bella calm at last, standing at the window and gazing down into the graveyard.

There is Mabel, I say, but it seems too early to get married.

'It is always too early,' she replies as we start to make love again.

Bella in the bath and myself crammed happily against the taps the other end while she lazily fondles me under the water and talks about her childhood.

Bella on the duvet, drawing my head between her legs.

Bella above me, riding me.

Bella kneeling over me, her secret garden open to my face as she transports me to places I have never imagined, not even lying in my wretched single bed, dreaming over and over of this moment and trying with far too little knowledge to ward off the unknown.

And betweenwhiles you may see Ned dozing on Bella's breast, our untouched food still on the table that I had set so formally in self-protection. With a mind made lucid by our lovemaking, I ask whatever else I can think of that will satisfy Bill Haydon's curiosity, and my own.

I drove her home and reached my flat around seven in the morning. In no mood to sleep for the second night running, I sat down and wrote my encounter report instead, my pen flying because I was still in paradise. There was no message from the *Daisy* but I expected none. Come evening, I received an interim report on her progress. She had passed Kiel and was heading for the Kieler Förde. She would be hitting open sea in a couple of hours. I had a tame German journalist to see that night and a consular meeting in the morning, but I passed the news in veiled terms to Bella on the telephone and promised to come to her soon, for she was determined I should visit her at the farmhouse. When Brandt returned, she said, she wanted to be able to look at all the places in the house where we had made love, and think of me. I suppose it testifies to the power of love's illusion that I found nothing underhand in this, or paradoxical. We had created a world together and she wished to have it round her when I was taken away from her. That was all. She was Brandt's girl. She expected nothing of me but my love.

When I arrived, we made straight for the long drawing room, where this time it was she who had laid the table. We sat at it quite naked, which was what she wanted. She wanted to see me among the familiar furniture. Afterwards we made love in their bed. I suppose I should have been ashamed, but I felt only the excitement of being appointed to the most secret places of their lives. 'These are his hairbrushes,' she said. 'These are his clothes, you are on his side of the bed.' One day I will understand what this means, I thought. And then, more grimly: or is this the pleasure that she takes in betrayal?

Next evening I had arranged to visit an old Pole in Lübeck who had established a clandestine correspondence with a distant nephew in Warsaw. The boy was being trained for cypher work in the Polish diplomatic service, and wanted to spy for us in exchange for resettlement in Australia. London Station was considering a direct approach to him. I returned to Hamburg and slept like the dead. Next morning, while I was still writing my report, a signal from London announced that the *Daisy* had successfully refuelled in Sundre and was on course for the Finnish Gulf with passenger Volodia aboard. I phoned Bella and told her all was still well, and she said, 'Please come to me.'

I spent the morning in the Reeperbahn police station extricating a pair of drunk British merchant sailors who had broken up a brothel, and the afternoon at a ghastly consular wives' tea party to rally support for the Week of the Political Prisoner. I wished the merchant sailors had broken up that brothel too. I arrived at the farmhouse at eight in the evening and we went straight to bed. At two in the morning the phone rang and Bella answered it. It was my cypher clerk calling me from the shipping office: a decypher yourself, flash priority; I was required at once. I drove like the wind and made the office in forty minutes. As I sat down to the code-books, I realised that Bella's smells were on my face and hands.

The signal had been transmitted over Haydon's symbol, personal to Head of Station, Hamburg. The *Daisy*'s landing party had come under heavy fire from prepared positions, it said. The dinghy was unaccounted for, and so was everyone aboard it, which meant Antons Durba and his passenger, and very likely whoever was waiting on the beach. There was no word of the Estonian patriots. The *Daisy* had sighted ultraviolet-light signals from the shore, but only one completed series of the agreed pattern, and the assumption was that the Estonian team had been taken captive as soon as they had lured the landing party to its fate. It was a familiar story, even if it was five years old. The fallback radio in Tallinn was not replying.

I was to pass this information to nobody and return to London on the first flight of the morning. A seat had been reserved for me. Toby Esterhase would meet me at Heathrow. I drafted an acknowledgement and handed it to my clerk, who accepted it without comment. He knows, I thought. How could he not? He had telephoned me at the farmhouse and spoken to Bella. The rest he could see in my face and, for all I knew, he could smell it too.

This time there was no joss burning in Haydon's room and he was sitting at his desk. Roy Bland, his Head of Eastern Europe, sat one side of him, Toby Esterhase the other. Toby's jobs were never easily defined, for he liked to keep them vague in the hope that they would multiply. But in practice he was Haydon's poodle, a role which later cost him dear. And I was surprised to see George Smiley sitting unhappily apart from them on the edge of Haydon's chaise longue, even if the symbolism of his posture did not dawn on me till three years later.

'It's an inside job,' Haydon said without preliminaries. 'The mission was blown sky high in advance. If Durba hasn't gone down with the ship, he's already swinging by his thumbs, telling his all. Volodia doesn't know a lot, but that may be his tough luck, because his interrogators aren't going to believe him and he's got a hamper full of explosives to explain. Maybe he took the pill, but I doubt it – he's a ninny.'

'Where's Brandt?' I said.

'Sitting under a bright light in the Sarratt interrogation wing and roaring like a bull. Somewhere somebody blundered. We're asking Brandt whether it might possibly be him. If not, who? It's a carbon-copy fuck-up from the last time round. Each member of the crew is being grilled separately.'

'Where's the *Daisy*?'

'In Helsinki. We've put a navy crew aboard and they're under orders to get her out tonight. The Finns don't fancy being seen providing safe harbour for people teasing the Bear. If the press don't get to hear about it, it'll be a bloody miracle.'

'I see,' I said stupidly.

'Good. I don't. What do we do? You tell me. You've got thirty Baltic agents waiting on your every word. What do you say? Abort? Apologise? Act natural and look busy? All suggestions gratefully acknowledged.'

'The Durbas weren't conscious to the Estonian network,' I objected. 'Antons can't blow what he doesn't know.'

'So who blew Antons, pray? Who blew the landing party, the coordinates, the beach, the time? Who set us up? We asked Brandt the same question, funnily enough. We thought he might suggest Bella, the Baltic strumpet. He suggested it was one of us lot instead, the cheeky bastard.'

He was furious and his fury was directed at me. I would never have imagined that lethargy could convert to such violent anger. Yet he still spoke quietly, in the nasal, upper-class drawl he had. He still managed to remain offhand. Even in passion he conveyed a deadly casualness, which made him all the more formidable.

'So what do *you* say?' he demanded of me.

'What about?'

'About *her,* sweetheart. Pouting Miss Latvia.' He was holding up the encounter report that I had written after our first night together. 'Christ Almighty, I asked for an assessment, not a bloody aria.'

'I think she's innocent,' I said. 'I think she's a simple peasant kid. That's my assessment. I expect it's Brandt's too. She answered my questions, she gave a plausible account of herself.'

Haydon had found his charm again. He could do that at the drop of a hat. He drew you and he repelled you. I remember that exactly. He danced all ways for you, playing your emotions against each other, because he had none of his own.

'Most spies *do* give a plausible account of themselves,' he retorted as he turned the pages of my report. 'The better ones do, anyway. Don't they, Tobe?' – favouring Esterhase.

'Absolutely, Bill. All the way, I would say,' said Esterhase the pleaser.

The others had a copy too. Silence settled while they studied it, pausing at the passages Haydon had sidelined. Roy

Bland lifted his head and peered at me. Bland had lectured to us at Sarratt. He was a North Countryman and former don who had spent years behind the Curtain under academic cover. His accent was broad and very flat.

'Bella admits her father's not her father, right, Ned? Her mother was raped by the Germans and got pregnant from it, so she's half German by origin. Right, Ned?'

'Yes. Right, Roy. That's what she told me.'

'So when her father, as she calls him, when Feliks comes back from prisoner-of-war camp, and hears what's happened, he adopts the child. Her. Bella. Nice of him. She volunteered that to you. She made no secret of it. Right, Ned?'

'Yes. Right, Roy.'

'Then why the fuck doesn't she tell Brandt the same tale as she tells you?'

I had asked her this myself, and so was able to answer him at once. 'When he brought her to the West, she was afraid he wouldn't take her in if he knew she wasn't his best friend's natural daughter. They weren't lovers then. He was offering protection and a life. She was scared. She took it. She'd been living in the forest. It was her first time in the West. Her own father was dead, so she needed another father figure.'

'Brandt, you mean?' said Bland slyly.

'Yes, of course.'

'Well, don't you think it's pretty bloody odd then, Ned, that Brandt didn't know the truth about her *anyway*?' he demanded triumphantly. 'If Brandt was her father's close buddy like he says he was, wouldn't he be bound to know all that? Come on, Ned!'

Smiley cut in, I thought in order to help me: 'Brandt very probably *does* know, Roy. Would *you* tell your best friend's daughter that she was the illegitimate child of a German soldier if you thought she wasn't aware of it? I'm sure *I* wouldn't. *I'd* go to quite some lengths to protect her. Specially if the father was dead and I was in love with the daughter.'

'Bugger love,' said Haydon, turning another page of my report. 'Brandt's a randy old goat. Who's this Tadeo she keeps talking about? "Tadeo saw the bodies being loaded into the truck. Tadeo says he saw my father's body go in last. They'd shot most of the men in the face, but my father was shot in the chest and stomach, a machine gun had nearly cut him in two." I mean, Christ, for a wilting violet she's bloody explicit when it helps her story, I will say.'

'Tadeo was her first lover,' I said.

'Jealous, are we?' Haydon asked me, drawing laughter from the satraps either side of him.

But not from Smiley. And not from me.

'Tadeo was a boy at her school,' I said. 'He'd been ordered to keep guard outside the house while the meeting took place, but he was making love with Bella in a field nearby. That's how she managed to escape. Tadeo told her to run for it, and who to ask for when she reached the partisans. Then he hid in a nearby house and watched what happened before joining her. It's in my report.'

Toby Esterhase added his own kind of sneer, in his own kind of Austro-Hungarian English. 'And Tadeo is most conveniently dead, of course, Ned. Being a witness in Bella's story is actually quite a risky business, I would say.'

'He was shot by a frontier guard,' I said. 'He wasn't even trying to cross. He was making a reconnaissance. She has the feeling everyone she touches dies,' I added, thinking involuntarily of Ben.

'She could be right, at that,' said Haydon.

Perversely, it seemed to me, Roy Bland now joined in my

defence – for increasingly I had the feeling I was in the dock. 'Mind you, Tadeo could be kosher *and* wrong about Feliks's death. Maybe the police faked his death. After all, he did go into the truck last. He'd have been covered with blood any-way in that slaughterhouse. They wouldn't have needed to splash the tomato ketchup on him, would they? It would have been done for them already.'

Smiley took up Bland's cudgels. I was beginning to regret I had lobbied so hard to be posted out of his care.

'Is the father *really* so important to us, Bill?' he objected. 'Feliks can be the Judas of all time, and still have a perfectly honest daughter, can't he?'

'I believe that too,' I said. 'She admires her father. She has no problem talking about him. She honours him. She's still in mourning for him.'

I was remembering how she had looked down into the graveyard. I was remembering her determination to celebrate the gift of life. I refused to believe she had been pretending.

'All right,' said Haydon impatiently, shoving a full-plate photograph at me across the desk. 'We'll stretch a point and trust you. What the hell are we supposed to make of this lot?'

It was a much enlarged photograph and out of register. I guessed it was a photograph of a photograph. It was stamped in red along the top left corner with the one word 'Witch-craft', which I had heard on the grapevine was London Station's most secret source.

Toby Esterhase's warning to me confirmed this: 'You never saw this photograph actually, Ned,' he told me over Haydon's shoulder, with the kind of smarminess people reserve for the young. 'Also you never saw the word "Witchcraft". When you leave this room, your mind will be a blank, totally.'

It was a group photograph of young men and women

arranged against a background of what could have been a barracks, or the campus of a university. They were about sixty strong, and in civilian uniform, the men in suits and ties, the women in high white blouses and long skirts. A group of older men and an evil-looking woman stood to one side of them. The mood, like the clothes and the building and the background, was sullen.

'Second row of the chorus, third from the right,' said Haydon, handing me a magnifying glass. 'Good tits, same as the young man said.'

It was Bella, there was no doubt of it. Bella three or four years younger it was true, and Bella with her hair swept back in what I guessed to be a bun. But Bella's broad, fair eyes and Bella's irrepressible smile, and the high, firm cheeks I adored.

'Did Bella ever whisper in your tiny shell-like that she'd been at language school in Kiev?' Haydon asked me.

'No.'

'Did she give any account of her education at all, apart from how she'd had it off with Tadeo in the hay?'

'No.'

'Of course Kiev is more of a holiday school than a school. Not a place many chaps talk about afterwards much. Unless they're confessing. Theoretically it's a school for tomorrow's interpreters but I'm afraid that in practice it's more a spawning ground for Moscow Centre hopefuls. Centre owns it, Centre staffs it, Centre skims the cream. The slops go to their Foreign Office, same as here.'

'Has Brandt seen this?' I asked.

His levity fell from him. 'You're joking, aren't you? Brandt's a hostile witness, so are they all.'

'Can I see Brandt?'

'I wouldn't recommend it.'

'Does that mean no?'

'Yes. It means no.'

'Was Witchcraft also the source of the report against Bella's father?'

'Mind your own bloody business,' he said, but I had caught Toby's startled eye and sensed that I was right.

'Does Moscow Centre always take class photographs of its white hopes?' I asked, emboldened as Smiley's head lifted to me in what I again took to be support.

'We take 'em at Sarratt,' Haydon retorted. 'Why shouldn't Moscow Centre?'

I could feel the sweat running down my back, and I knew my voice was slipping. But I floundered on. 'Has anyone else in this photograph been identified?'

'As a matter of fact, yes.'

'What as?'

'Never mind.'

'What languages did she learn?'

Haydon had had enough of me. He lifted his eyes to heaven as if appealing for the gift of patience. 'Well, they *all* learn English, darling, if *that's* what you're asking,' he drawled and, putting his chin in his hand, gave Smiley a long look.

I am not clairvoyant and I had no way of knowing what was passing between the two men, or what had passed already. But even allowing for the advantages of hindsight, I am sure I had the sensation of being caught between hostile camps. Even somebody as remote from Head Office politics as I was could not help hearing the rumble of the battle that was raging: how the great X had walked clean past the great Y in the corridor without so much as a 'Good morning'; how A had refused to sit at the same table with B in the canteen.

And how Haydon's London Station was becoming a service within a service, gobbling up the regional directorates, taking over the special sections, the watchers, the listeners, right the way down to such humble beings as our postmen, who sat in dripping sorting offices, loyally steaming open mail with gas kettles permanently on the boil. It was even hinted that the true clash of Titans was between Bill Haydon and the reigning Chief, the last to call himself Control, and that Smiley as Control's cupbearer was more on his master's side than Haydon's.

But then it was also hinted that Smiley himself was under sentence – or, put more tactfully – contemplating an academic appointment so that he could take more care of his marriage.

Haydon looked jauntily at Smiley, but the jaunty look became a chill stare as he waited for Smiley to return it. The rest of us waited too. The embarrassment was that Smiley didn't return it. He was like a man declining to acknowledge a salute. He sat on the chaise longue with his eyebrows lifted, and his long eyelids turned down, and his round head tilted, seeming to study the Persian prayer mat that was another eccentric feature of Bill's room. And he simply went on studying it as if he were unaware of Haydon's interest in him, though we all knew – even I knew – that he wasn't. Then he puffed out his cheeks and pulled a frown of disapproval. And finally he stood – not dramatically, for George never had that far to go – and gathered up his papers.

'Well, I think we've had the meat of this, don't you, Bill?' he said. 'Control will see indoctrinated officers in one hour, please, if that's convenient, and we'll try to take a view. Ned, you and I have a small piece of Zurich history to clear up. Perhaps you'd drop by when Bill has done with you.'

Twenty minutes later I was sitting in Smiley's office.

'Do you believe that photograph?' he asked, with no pretence of talking about Zurich.

'I suppose I have to.'

'Why do you suppose that? Photographs can be faked. There is such a thing as disinformation. Moscow Centre has been known to go in for it now and then. They've even stooped to discrediting innocent people, I'm told. They have an entire department, as a matter of fact, devoted to little else. It runs to about five hundred officers.'

'Then why frame Bella? Why not go for Brandt or one of the crew?'

'What's Bill told you to do?'

'Nothing. He says I'll get my orders in due course.'

'You never answered his question. Do you think we should abort the network?'

'It's hard for me to say. I'm just the local link. The network's run direct from London Station.'

'Nevertheless.'

'We can't exfiltrate thirty agents. We'd start a war. If the supply lines are blown and the escape routes are closed, I don't see there's anything we can do for them at all.'

'So they're dead anyway,' he suggested, more in confirmation than question. A phone was ringing on his desk but he didn't pick it up. He continued to look at me with a merciful concern. 'Well, if they *are* dead, will you please remember it's not your fault, Ned?' he added kindly. 'Nobody expects you to take on Moscow Centre single-handed. It may be the Fifth Floor's fault, it may be mine. It certainly isn't yours.'

He nodded me to the door. I closed it after me and heard his phone stop ringing.

*

I returned to Hamburg the same night. Bella sounded excited when I rang, and sad that I wasn't rushing round to her at once.

'Where's Brandt?' she asked. She had no notion of telephone security. I said Brandt was fine, just fine. I felt guilty talking to her when I knew so much and she so little. I was to be natural towards her, Haydon had said: 'Whatever you did before, keep doing it or do it better. I don't want her guessing anything.' I should tell her that Brandt loved her, which he was apparently insisting on. I guessed that in his travail he was asking to see me. I hoped so, because I trusted him and he was my responsibility.

I tried not to feel upset for myself when there were so many larger tragedies round me, but it was hard. Until a few days ago, Brandt and the crew had been mine to care for. I had been their spokesman and champion. Now one of them was dead or worse, and the rest had been taken out of my hands. The network, though it had worked to London, had been my proxy family. Now it was like the remnants of a ghostly army, out of touch, floating between life and death.

Worst of all was my sense of dislocation, of holding a dozen conflicting theories in my head at once, and favouring each in turn. One minute I was insisting to myself that Bella was innocent, just as I had maintained to Haydon. The next I was asking myself how she could have communicated with her masters. The answer was, only too easily. She shopped, she went to cinemas, she went to school. She could meet couriers, fill and empty dead-letter boxes to her heart's content.

But no sooner had I gone this far than I ran to her defence. Bella was not *bad*. The photograph was a plant and the story about her father amounted to nothing. Smiley had said as much. There were a hundred ways in which the mission could have been blown without Bella having the least thing to do with it. Our operational security was tight, but not as tight as I would have wished. My predecessor had turned out to be corrupt. Might he not, in addition to inventing agents, have sold a few as well? And even if he hadn't, was it really so unreasonable of Brandt to suggest that the leak could have come from our side of the fence, not his?

Now I would not have you think that, alone in his cot that night, the young Ned unravelled single-handed the skein of treachery that later took all George Smiley's powers to expose. A source can be a plant, a plant can be ignored, an experienced intelligence officer can take a wrong decision – all without the assistance of a traitor within the Fifth Floor's gates. I knew that. I was not a child, and not one of your grey-cheeked Circus conspiracy-theorists either.

Nevertheless I did ponder, as any of us might when he is stretched to the limits of his allegiance to his Service. I pieced together from my worm's-eye view all the rumours that had reached me on the Circus grapevine. Stories of unaccountable failure and repeated scandal, of the mounting anger of our American Cousins. Of meaningless reorganisations, wasteful rivalries between men who were today immortals and tomorrow had resigned. Horror stories of incompetence being taken as proof of grand betrayal – and unnerving evidence of betrayal dismissed as incompetence.

If there is such a thing as growing up, you may say that sometime that night I made one of those leaps into maturity. I realised that the Circus was much the same as any other British institution, except that it was more so, since it played its games in the safety of sealed rooms, with other people's lives for counters. Yet I was pleased to have made my recognition. It gave me back the responsibility for my actions, which hitherto I had been a little too willing to lay at other people's feet. If my career till now had been a constant battle between submission and identity, then you might say that submission had maintained the upper hand. But that night I crossed some sort of border. I decided that from then on, I would pay more heed to my own instincts and desires, and less to the harness that I seemed unable to dispense with.

We met at the safe flat. If there was neutral ground to be found anywhere, it was there. She still knew nothing of the catastrophe. I had told her only that Brandt had been summoned to England. We made love at once, blindly and hungrily; then I waited for the clarity of after-love to begin my interrogation.

I began playfully stroking her hair, smoothing it against her head. Then I swept it back with both my hands, and scooped it into a rough bun.

'This way you look *very* stern,' I said, and kissed her, still holding it in place. 'Have you ever worn it like this?' I kissed her again.

'When I was a girl.'

'When was that?' I said, between our joined lips. 'You mean before Tadeo? When?'

'Until I went to the forest. Then I cut it off. Another woman did it with a knife.'

'Have you got a photograph of yourself like this?'

'In the forest we did not take photographs.'

'I mean before. When you wore it like a stern lady.'

She sat up. 'Why?'

'Just tell me.'

She was watching me with her almost colourless eyes. 'At school, they took our photographs. Why?'

'In groups? In classes? What sort of photographs?'

'Why?'

'Just tell me, Bella. I need to know.'

'They took photographs of us in our class, and they took photographs for our documents.'

'What documents?'

'For identity. For our passports.'

She did not mean a passport as we understand it. She meant a passport for moving about inside the Soviet Union. No free citizen could cross the road without one.

'A full-face photograph? Not smiling?'

'Yes.'

'What did you do with your old passport, Bella?'

She didn't remember.

'What did you wear for it – for the photograph?' I kissed her breasts. 'Not these. What did you wear?'

'A blouse and tie. What nonsense are you talking?'

'Bella, listen to me. Is there anyone you can think of, back at home, a schoolfriend, an old boyfriend, a relation, who would have a photograph of you with your hair back? Someone you could write to, perhaps, who could be contacted?'

She considered for a moment, staring at me. 'My aunt,' she said grumpily.

'What's her name?'

She told me.

'Where does she live?'

In Riga, she said. With Uncle Janek. I seized an envelope, sat her still naked at a table and made her write out their full address. Then I put a piece of plain writing paper before her and dictated a letter which she translated as she wrote.

'Bella.' I lifted her to her feet and kissed her tenderly. 'Bella, tell me something else. Did you ever go to any school, of any kind, except the schools in your own town?'

She shook her head.

'No holiday schools? Special schools? Language schools?'

'No.'

'Did you learn English at school?'

'Of course not. Otherwise I would speak English. What's happening to you, Ned? Why are you asking me these stupid questions?'

'The *Daisy* sailed into trouble,' I said, still face to face with her. 'There was shooting. Brandt wasn't hurt but others were. That's all I'm allowed to tell you. We're to fly back to London tomorrow, you and I together. They need to ask us some questions and find out what went wrong.'

She closed her eyes and began shaking. She opened her mouth and made a silent scream.

'I believe in you,' I said. 'I want to help you. And Brandt. That's the truth.'

Gradually she came back to me and put her head on my chest while she wept. She was a child again. Perhaps she had always been one. Perhaps, by helping me to grow up, she had increased the distance between us. I had brought a British passport for her. She had no nationality of her own. I made her stay the night with me and she clutched me like a drowning girl. Neither of us slept.

On the plane she held my hand but we were already continents apart. Then she spoke in a voice that I had not heard from her before. A firm, adult voice of sadness and disillusionment that reminded me of Stefanie's when she had delivered her Sibyl's warning to me on the island.

'*Es ist ein reiner Unsinn,*' she said. It is a pure nonsense.

'What is?'

She had taken away her hand. Not in anger, but in a kind of worldly despair. 'You tell them to put their feet into the water and you wait to see what happens. If they are not shot, they are heroes. If they are shot, they are martyrs. You gain nothing that is worth having and you encourage my people to kill themselves. What do you want us to do? Rise up and kill the Russian oppressor? Will you come and help us if we try? I don't think so. I think you are doing something because you cannot do nothing. I think you are not useful to us at all.'

I could never forget what Bella said, for it was also a dismissal of my love. And today I think of her each morning as I listen to the news before walking my dog. I wonder what we thought we were promising to those brave Balts in those days, and whether it was the same promise which we are now so diligently breaking.

This time it was Peter Guillam who was waiting at the airport, which was a relief to me, because his good looks and breezy manners seemed to give her confidence. For a chaperone he had brought Nancy from the watchers, and Nancy had made herself motherly for the occasion. Between them they led Bella through immigration to a grey van which belonged to the Sarratt inquisitors. I wished that someone could have thought to send a less formidable vehicle, because when she saw the van she stopped and looked back to me in accusation before Nancy grabbed her by the arm and shoved her in.

In the turbulent life of a case officer, I was learning, there was not always such a thing as an elegant goodbye.

I can only tell you what I next did, and what I later heard. I made for Smiley's office, and spent most of my day trying to catch him between meetings. Circus protocol required me to go first to Haydon, but I had already exceeded Haydon's brief by the questions I had put to Bella, and I suspected Smiley would give me a more sympathetic hearing. He listened to me; he took charge of Bella's letter and examined it.

'If we have it posted in Moscow and give a Finnish safe address for them to write back to, it might just work,' I urged him.

But, as so often with Smiley, I had the impression that he was thinking beyond me into realms from which I was excluded. He dropped the letter in a drawer and closed it.

'I rather think it won't be necessary,' he said. 'Let us hope not anyway.'

I asked him what they would do with Bella.

'I suppose much the same as they have done with Brandt,' he replied, waking sufficiently from his absorption to give me a sad smile. 'Take her through every detail of her life. Try to trip her up. Wear her down. They won't hurt her. Not physically. They won't tell her what they have against her. They'll just hope to break her cover. It seems that most of the men who looked after her in the forest were rounded up recently. That won't speak well for her, naturally.'

'What will they do with her afterwards?'

'Well, I think we can still prevent the worst, even if we can't prevent much else these days,' he replied, returning to his papers. 'Time you went on to Bill, isn't it? He'll be wondering what you're up to.'

And I remember the expression on his face as he dismissed me: the pain and frustration in it, and the anger.

Did Smiley have the letter posted as I suggested? Did the letter produce a photograph and did the photograph turn out to be the very one that Moscow Centre's forgers had dropped into their group photograph? I wish it were so neat, but in reality it never is, though I like to believe that my efforts on Bella's behalf had some influence on her release and resettlement in Canada, which occurred a few months later in circumstances that are a puzzle to me.

For Brandt refused to take her back, let alone go with her. Had Bella told him of our affair? Had someone else? I hardly think it possible, unless Haydon himself did it out of mischief. Bill hated all women and most men too, and liked nothing better than to turn people's affections inside out.

Brandt too was given a clean ticket and, after some resistance from the Fifth Floor, a gratuity to start him in a respectable walk of life. That is to say, he was able to buy a boat and take himself to the West Indies, where he resumed his old trade of smuggling, except that this time he chose arms to Cuba.

And the betrayal? The Brandt network had simply been too efficient for Haydon's stomach, Smiley told me later, so Bill had betrayed it as he had betrayed its predecessor, and tried to fix the blame on Bella. He had arranged for Moscow Centre to fake the evidence against her, which he then presented as coming from his spurious source Merlin, the provider of the Witchcraft material. Hard on the mole's tracks by then, Smiley had voiced his suspicions in high places, only to be sent into exile for being right. It took another two years for him to be brought back to clean the stable.

And there the story stood until our own internal *perestroika* began in earnest – in the winter of '89 – when Toby Esterhase, the ubiquitous survivor, conducted a middle-ranking Circus delegation to Moscow Centre as a first step to what our blessed Foreign Office insisted on calling a 'normalisation of the relationship between the two services'.

Toby's team was welcomed at Dzerzhinsky Square and shown many of the appointments, though not, one gathers, the torture chambers of the old Lubyanka, or the roof on which certain careless prisoners had occasionally lost their footing. Toby and his men were wined and dined. They were shown, as the Americans say, a time. They bought fur hats and pinned facetious badges on them and had themselves photographed in Dzerzhinsky Square.

And on the last day, as a special gesture of goodwill, they were escorted to the gallery of Centre's huge communications hall, where reports from all sources are received and processed. And it was here, as they were leaving the gallery, says Toby, that he and Peter Guillam in the same moment spotted a tall, flaxen, thickset fellow in half silhouette at the further end of the corridor, emerging from what was apparently the men's lavatory, for there was only one other door in that part of the corridor, and it was marked for women.

He was a man of some age, yet he strode out of the doorway like a bull. He paused, and for a long beat stared straight at them, as if in two minds whether to come towards them and greet them or retreat. Then he lowered his head and, as it seemed to them, with a smile, swung away from them and disappeared into another corridor. But not before they had ample opportunity to remark his seamanly roll and wrestler's shoulders.

Nothing goes away in the secret world; nothing goes away in the real one. If Toby and Peter are right – and there are those who still maintain that Russian hospitality had got the better of them – then Haydon had an even stronger reason to point the finger of suspicion at Bella, and away from Sea Captain Brandt.

Was Brandt bad from the beginning? If so, I had unwittingly furthered his recruitment and our agents' deaths. It is a dreadful thought and sometimes in the cold grey hours as I lie at Mabel's side, it comes home to haunt me.

And Bella? I think of her as my last love, as the right turning I never took. If Stefanie had unlocked the door of doubt in me, Bella pointed me towards the open world while there was still time. When I think of my women since, they are aftercare. And when I think of Mabel, I can only explain her as the lure of domesticity to a man returned from the front line. But the memory of Bella remains as fresh for me as on our first night in the safe flat overlooking the cemetery – though in my dreams she is always walking away from me, and there is reproach even in her back.

5

'Are you saying we could be housing another Haydon *now?*' a student named Maggs called out amid the groans of his colleagues. 'What's his motivation, Mr Smiley? Who's paying him? What's his bag?'

I had had my doubts about Maggs ever since he had joined. He was earmarked for a cover career in journalism, and already had the worst characteristics of his future trade. But Smiley was unruffled.

'Oh well, I'm sure that in retrospect we owe Bill a great debt of thanks,' he replied calmly. 'He administered the needle to a Service that had been far too long a-dying.' He made a fussy little frown of perplexity. 'As to *new* traitors, I'm sure our present leader will have sown her discontents, won't she? Perhaps I'm one. I do find I become a great deal more radical in my old age.'

But believe me, we didn't thank Bill at the time.

There was Before the Fall and there was After the Fall and the Fall was Haydon, and suddenly there was not a man or woman in the Circus who could not tell you where he was and what he was doing when he heard the dreadful news. Old hands tell each other to this day of the silence in the corridors, the numbed, averted faces in the canteen, the unanswered telephones.

The greatest casualty was trust. Only gradually, like dazed people after an air attack, did we step shyly, one by one, from our shattered houses, and set to work to reconstruct the citadel. A fundamental reform was deemed necessary, so the Circus abandoned its ancient nickname and the warren of Dickensian corridors and crooked staircases in Cambridge Circus that had housed its shame, and built itself instead a vile steel-and-glass affair not far from Victoria, where the windows still blow out in a gale and the corridors reek of stale cabbage from the canteen, and typewriter-cleaning fluid. Only the English punish themselves with quite such dreadful prisons. Overnight we became, in formal parlance, the Service, though the name 'Circus' still occasionally crosses our lips in the same way as we speak of pounds, shillings and pence long after decimalisation.

The trust was broken because Haydon had been part of it. Bill was no upstart with a chip on his shoulder and a pistol in his pocket. He was exactly who he had always sneeringly described himself to be: Church and Spy Establishment, with uncles who sat on Tory Party committees, and a run-down estate in Norfolk with tenant farmers who called him 'Mr William'. He was a strand of the finely spun web of English influence of which we had perceived ourselves the centre. And he had caught us in it.

In my own case – I still claim a certain distinction for this – I actually succeeded in hearing the news of Bill's arrest twenty-four hours after it had reached the rest of the Circus, for I was incarcerated in a windowless mediaeval cell at the back of a run of grand apartments in the Vatican. I was commanding a team of Circus eavesdroppers under the guidance of a hollow-eyed friar supplied to us by the Vatican's own secret service, who would rather have gone to the Russians themselves than seek the assistance of their secular colleagues a mile up the road in Rome. And our mission was to winkle a probe microphone into the audience room of a corrupt Catholic bishop who had got himself involved in a drugs-for-arms deal with one of our disintegrating colonies – well, why be coy? It was Malta.

With Monty and his boys flown in for the occasion, we had tiptoed through vaulted dungeons, up underground staircases, until we had reached this vantage point, from which we proposed to drill a fine hole through a course of old cement that ran between the blocks of a three-foot party wall. The hole by agreement was to be no more than two centimetres in diameter, wide enough for us to insert the elongated plastic drinking straw that would conduct the sound from the target room to our microphone, small enough to spare the hallowed masonry of the Papal palace. Today we would use more sophisticated equipment, but the seventies were the last of the steam age and probes were still the fashion. Besides, with the best will in the world, you don't show off your prize gadgets to official Vatican liaison, let alone to a friar in a black habit who looks as though he has stepped straight out of the Inquisition.

We drilled, Monty drilled, the friar watched. We poured water on to red-hot drill-heads, and on to our sweating hands and faces. We muffled the drone of our drills with liquid foam, and every few minutes we took readings to make sure we hadn't drilled our way into the holy man's apartment by mistake. For the aim was to stop the drill-head a centimetre short of entry, and listen from inside the membrane of the wallpaper or surface plaster.

Suddenly we were through, but worse than through. We

were in thin air. A hasty sampling by vacuum produced only exotic threads of silk. A bemused silence descended on us. Had we struck furniture? Drapes? A bed? Or the hem of some unsuspecting prelate's robe? Had the audience room been altered since we had taken the reconnaissance photographs?

At which low point the friar was inspired to remember, in an appalled whisper, that the good bishop was a collector of priceless needlework, and we realised that the shreds of cloth we were staring at were not pieces of sofa or curtain, or even some priest's finery, but fragments of Gobelin tapestry. Excusing himself, the friar fled.

Now the scene changes to the old Kentish town of Rye, where two sisters named the Misses Quayle ran a tapestry restoration business, and by a mercy – or, you may say, by the ineluctable laws of English social connection – their brother Henry was a retired member of the Service. Henry was run to earth, the sisters were roused from their beds, an RAF jet plane wafted them to Rome's military airport, from where a car sped them to our side. Then Monty calmly returned to the front of the building and ignited a smoke bomb which cleared half the Vatican and gave our augmented team four desperate hours in the target room. By mid-afternoon of the same day, the Gobelin was passably patched and our probe microphone snugly in place.

The scene changes yet again to the grand dinner given by our Vatican hosts. Swiss Guards stand menacingly at the doors. Monty, a white napkin at his throat, is seated between the sedate Misses Quayle and wiping the last of his cannelloni from his plate with a piece of bread while he regales them with accounts of his daughter's latest accomplishments at her riding school.

'Now you won't know this, Rosie, and there's no reason

why you should, but my Beckie has the best pair of hands for her age in the whole of South Croydon—'

Then Monty stops dead in his tracks. He is reading the note I have passed him, delivered to me by hand of a messenger from our Rome Station: *Bill Haydon, Director of Circus Clandestine Operations, has confessed to being a Moscow Centre spy.*

Sometimes I wonder whether that was the greatest of all Bill's crimes: to steal for good the lightness we had shared.

I returned to London to be told that when there was more to tell me I would be told. A few mornings later Personnel informed me that I had been classified 'Tailor Halftone', which was Circus jargon for 'unpostable to all but friendly countries'. It was like being told I would spend the rest of my life in a wheelchair. I had done nothing wrong, I was in no disgrace, quite the contrary. But in the trade, cover is virtue, and mine was blown.

I packed up my desk and gave myself the rest of the day off. I drove into the country and I still don't remember the drive, but there is a walk I do on the Sussex Downs, over whaleback chalk hills with cliffs five hundred feet high.

It took another month before I heard my sentence. 'You'll be back with the émigrés, I'm afraid,' Personnel said, with his customary distaste. 'And it's Germany again. Still, the allowances are quite decent, and the skiing isn't bad either, if you go high enough.'

6

It was approaching midnight but Smiley's good spirits had increased with every fresh heresy. He's like a jolly Father Christmas, I thought, who hands round seditious leaflets with his gifts.

'Sometimes I think the most *vulgar* thing about the Cold War was the way we learned to gobble up our own propaganda,' he said, with the most benign of smiles. 'I don't *mean* to sound didactic, and of course in a way we'd done it all through our history. But in the Cold War, when our enemies lied, they lied to conceal the wretchedness of their system. Whereas when *we* lied, we concealed our virtues. Even from ourselves. We concealed the very things that made us right. Our respect for the individual, our love of variety and argument, our belief that you can only govern fairly with the consent of the governed, our capacity to see the other fellows' view – most notably in the countries we exploited, almost to death, for our own ends. In our supposed ideological rectitude, we sacrificed our compassion to the great god of indifference. We protected the strong against the weak, and we preferred the art of the public lie. We made enemies of decent reformers and friends of the most disgusting potentates. And we scarcely paused to ask ourselves how much longer we could defend our society by these means and remain a society worth defending.' A glance to me again. 'So it wasn't much wonder, was it, Ned, if we opened our gates to every con-man and charlatan in the anti-Communist racket? We got the villains we deserved. Ned knows. Ask Ned.'

At which Smiley, to the general delight, burst out laughing – and I, after a moment's hesitation, joined in and assured my students that I would tell them about it some day.

Perhaps you caught the show, as they say in the States. Perhaps you were part of the appreciative audience at one of the many rousing performances they gave on their tireless trail through the American mid-West, as they pressed the flesh and worked the rubber-chicken luncheons of the lecture circuit, a hundred dollars a plate and every plate a sell-out. We called it the Teodor–Latzi show. Teodor was the Professor's first name.

Perhaps you joined in one of the numberless standing ovations as our two heroes humbly took centre stage, the Professor tall and resplendent in one of several costly new suits purchased for his tour, and the diminutive Latzi his chubby mute, his shallow eyes brimming with ideals. There were ovations before they started speaking and ovations when they had finished. No applause was loud enough for 'two great American Hungarians who, single-handed, kicked themselves a hole in the Iron Curtain'. I am quoting the Tulsa *Herald*.

Perhaps your all-American daughter dressed herself in the becoming costume of a Hungarian peasant girl and put flowers in her hair for the occasion – such things happened too. Perhaps you sent a donation to the League for the Liberation, Post Box something or other, Wilmington. Or did you read about our heroes in the *Reader's Digest* in your dentist's waiting room?

Or perhaps, like Peter Guillam, who was based in Washington at the time, you were honoured to be present at their grand world *première*, jointly stage-managed by our American Cousins, the Washington city police and the FBI, at no less a shrine of right-thinking than the austere and panelled Hay-Adams Hotel, just across the square from the White House. If so, you must have been rated a serious influence-maker. You had to be a front-line journalist or lobbyist at least to be admitted to the hushed conference room where every understated word had the authority of an engraved tablet, and men in bulging blazers watched tautly over your comfort and convenience. For who knew when the Kremlin would strike back? It was still that kind of time.

Or maybe you read their book, slipped by the Cousins to an obedient publisher on Madison Avenue and launched to a fanfare of docile critical acclaim before occupying the lower end of the non-fiction bestseller list for a spectacular two weeks. I hope you did, for though it appeared over their joint names, the fact is I wrote a slice of it myself, even if the Cousins took exception to my original title. The title of record was *The Kremlin's Killer*. I'll tell you what mine was later.

As usual, Personnel had got it wrong. For anybody who has lived in Hamburg, Munich is not Germany at all. It is another country. I never felt the remotest connection between the two cities, but when it came to spying, Munich like Hamburg was one of the unsung capitals of Europe. Even Berlin ran a poor second when it came to the size and visibility of Munich's invisible community. The largest and nastiest of our organisations was a body known best by the place that housed it, Pullach, where much too soon after 1945 the Americans had installed an unlovely assembly of old Nazi officers under a former general of Hitler's military intelligence. Their brief was to pay court to other old Nazis in East Germany and, by bribery, blackmail or an appeal to comradely sentiment, procure them for the West. It never seemed to occur to the Americans that the East Germans might be doing the same thing in reverse, though they did more of it and better.

So the German Service sat in Pullach, and the Americans sat with them, egging them on, then getting cold feet and egging them off. And where the Americans sat, there sat everybody else. And now and then frightful scandals broke, usually when one or other of this company of clowns literally forgot which side he was working for, or made a tearful confession in his cups, or shot his mistress or his boyfriend or himself, or popped up drunk on the other side of the Curtain to declare his loyalty to whomever he had not been loyal to so far. I never in my life knew such an intelligence bordello.

After Pullach came the codebreakers and security artists, and after these came Radio Liberty, Radio Free Europe and Radio Free Everywhere Else, and inevitably, since they were largely the same people, the émigré conspirators, who by now were feeling a little down on their luck but dared not say it. And much time was spent among these exiled bodies arguing out niceties about who would be Master of the Royal Horse when the monarchy was restored; and who would be awarded the Order of Saint Peter and the Hedgehog; or succeed to the Grand Duke's summer palace once the Communist chickens had been removed from its drawing rooms; or who would recover the crock of gold that had been sunk to the bottom of the Whatnotsee, always forgetting that the said lake had been drained thirty years ago by the Bolshevik usurpers, who had built a six-acre hydroelectric plant on the site before running out of water.

As if this were not enough, Munich played host to the wildest sort of All German aspiration, whose adherents regarded even the 1939 borders as a mere prelude to Greater German needs. East Prussians, Saxons, Pomeranians, Silesians, Balts and Sudeten Germans all protested the terrible injustice done to them, and drew fat pay-packets from Bonn for their grief. There were nights, as I trudged home to Mabel through the beery streets, when I fancied I could hear them singing their anthems behind Hitler's marching ghost.

Are they still in business as I write? Oh, I fear they are, and looking a lot less mad than in the days when it was my job to move among them. Smiley once quoted Horace Walpole to me, not a name that would otherwise have sprung naturally to my mind: This world is a comedy to those that think, said Walpole, a tragedy to those that feel. Well, for comedy Munich has her Bavarians. And for tragedy, she has her past.

My memory is patchy nearly twenty years later regarding the Professor's political antecedents. At the time, I fancied I understood them – indeed, I must have done, for most of my evenings with him were spent listening to his recitations of Hungarian history between the wars. And I am sure we put them into the book too – a chapter's worth, at least, if I could only lay my hands on a copy.

The problem was, he was so much happier evoking Hungary's past than her present. Perhaps he had learned, in a life of continual adjustment, that it is wise to limit one's concerns to issues safely consigned to history. There were the Legitimists, I remember, and they supported King Charles, who made a sudden return to Hungary in 1921, much to the consternation of the Allies, who ordered him smartly from the stage. I don't think the Professor could have been a day above five years old when this moving event occurred, but he spoke of it with tears in his enlightened eyes, and there was much in his bearing to suggest the transitory touch of monarchy. And when he mentioned the Treaty of Trianon, the refined white hand that held his wine glass trembled in restrained outrage.

'It was a *Diktat*, Herr Ned,' he protested to me in courtly reproof. 'Imposed upon us by you victors. You robbed us of two-thirds of our land under the Crown! You gave it to Czechoslovakia, Romania, Yugoslavia. Such scum you gave it to, Herr Ned! And we Hungarians were cultivated people! Why did you do it to us? For what?'

I could only apologise for my country's bad behaviour, just as I could only apologise for the League of Nations, which destroyed the Hungarian economy in 1931. Quite how the League achieved this reckless act I never understood, but I remember it had something to do with the wheat market, and the League's rigid policy of orthodox deflation.

Yet when we approached more contemporary matters, the Professor became strangely reticent in his opinions.

'It is another catastrophe,' was all he would say. 'It is all a consequence of Trianon and the Jews.'

Shafts of evening sunlight sloped through the garden window on to Teodor's superb white head. He was a lion of a fellow, believe me, wide-browed and Socratic, like a grand conductor close to genius all the time, with sculpted hands and flowing locks, and a stoop of intellectual profundity. Nobody who looked so venerable could be shallow – not even when the learned eyes appeared a mite too small for their sockets, or slipped furtively to one side in the manner of a diner in a restaurant who catches sight of a better meal passing by.

No, no, he was a great, good man, and fifteen years our

joe. If a man is tall, then clearly he has authority. If he has a golden voice, then his words are also golden. If he looks like Schiller, he must feel like Schiller. If the smile is remote and spiritual, then so for sure is the man within. Thus the visual society.

Except that just occasionally, as I think now, God amuses Himself by dealing us an entirely different man inside the shell. Some founder and are rumbled. Others expand until they meet the challenge of their looks. And a few do neither, but wear their splendours like a favour granted from above, blandly accepting the homage that is not their due.

The Professor's operational history is quickly told. Too quickly, for it was a mite banal. He was born in Debrecen, close to the Romanian border, an only son of indulgent parents of the small nobility who trimmed their sails to every wind. Through them, he inherited money and connections, a thing that happened more often in the so-called Socialist countries, even in those days, than you would suppose. He was a man of letters, a writer of articles for learned journals, a bit of a poet and a lover several times married. He wore his jackets like capes, the sleeves loose. All these luxuries he could well afford, on account of his privileges and discreet wealth.

In Budapest, where he taught a languid version of philosophy, he had acquired a modest following among his students, who discerned more fire in Teodor's words than he intended, for he was never cut out to be an orator, rhetoric being something for the rabble. Nevertheless, he had risen a certain distance to their needs. He had observed their passion, and as a natural conciliator he had responded by giving it a voice – moderate enough in all conscience, but a voice for all that, and one they respected, along with his beautiful manners and air of representing an older, better order. He was of an age, by then, to be warmed by youthful adulation, and he was always vain. And through vanity he allowed himself to be carried on the counter-revolutionary tide. So that when the Soviet tanks turned back from the border and surrounded Budapest on the terrible night of November 3, 1956, he had no choice but to run for his life, which he did, into the arms of British Intelligence.

The Professor's first act on arriving in Vienna was to telephone a Hungarian friend at Oxford, pressing him in his peremptory way for money, introductions and letters testifying to his excellence. This friend happened also to be a friend of the Circus, and it was the high season for recruitment.

Within months, the Professor was on the payroll. There was little courtship, no arch approach, no customary fan dance. The offer was made, and accepted as a due. Within a year, with generous American assistance, Professor Teodor had been set up in Munich, in a comfortable house beside the river, with a car and his devoted if distraught wife Helena, who had escaped with him – one suspected, somewhat to his regret. Henceforth, and for an extraordinary length of time, Professor Teodor had been the unlikely spearhead of our Hungarian attack, and not even Haydon had unseated him.

His cover job was Radio Free Europe's patrician-at-large on the subject of Hungarian history and culture, and it fitted him like a glove. He had never been much else. In addition, he lectured a little and gave private tuition – mainly, I noticed, to girls. His clandestine job, for which, thanks to the Americans, he was remarkably well paid, was to foster his links with the friends and former students he had left behind, to be a focus for them and a rallying point and, under guidance, to shape them into an operational network, though none, to my knowledge, had ever quite emerged. It was a visionary operation, and better on the page perhaps than on the ground. Yet it ran and ran. It ran for five years, and then another five and by the time I took up the great man's file, it had completed an extraordinary fifteen years. Some operations are like that, and stagnation favours them. They are not expensive, they are not conclusive, they don't necessarily lead anywhere – but then neither does political stalemate – they are free of scandal. And each year when the annual audit is taken, they are waved through without a vote, until their longevity becomes their justification.

Now I won't say the Professor had achieved nothing for us in all that time. To say so would not only be unfair, it would be derogatory to Toby Esterhase, himself of Hungarian origin, who on his reinstatement After the Fall had become the desk officer handling the Professor's case. Toby had paid a heavy price for his blind support of Haydon, and when he was given the Hungary desk – never the most exalted of Iron Curtain slots – the Professor promptly became the most important player in Toby's personal rehabilitation programme.

'Teodor, I would say, Ned – Teodor is our absolutely total star,' he had assured me before I left London, over a lunch he nearly paid for. 'Old school, total discretion, lot of years in the saddle, loyal like a leech. Teodor is our ace, totally.'

And certainly one of the Professor's more striking accomplishments had been to escape the Haydon axe – either because he had been lucky or, less charitably, because the Professor had never produced enough intelligence to merit the interest of a busy traitor. For I could not help noticing as I prepared myself for the takeover – my predecessor having dropped dead of a stroke while on leave in Ibiza – that whereas

Teodor's personal file ran to several volumes, his product file was unusually slender. Partly this could be explained by the fact that his main function had been to spot talent rather than exploit it, partly that the few sources he had guided into our net over the long period he had been working for us were still relatively unproductive.

'Hungary, Ned, that's actually a damned hard target, I would say,' Toby assured me when I delicately pointed this out to him. 'It's too open. An open target, you get a lot of crap you know already. If you don't get the Crown Jewels, you get the common knowledge – who needs it? What Teodor produces for the Americans, it's fantastic.'

This seemed to be the nub. 'So what *does* he produce for them actually?' I asked. 'Apart from hearts and minds on the radio, and articles no one reads?'

Toby's smile became unpleasantly superior. 'Sorry, Ned, old boy. "Need to know," I'm afraid. You're not on the list for this one.'

A few days later, as protocol required, I called on Russell Sheriton in Grosvenor Square to say my goodbyes. Sheriton was the Cousins' Head of Station in London, but he was also responsible for their Western European operations. I bided my time, then dropped the name of Teodor.

'Ah now, that's for Munich to say, Ned,' Sheriton said quickly. 'You know me. Never trespass on another man's preserves.'

'But is he doing you any good? That's all I want to know. I mean joes do burn out, don't they? Fifteen years.'

'Well now, we thought he was doing *you* some good, Ned. To hear Toby speak, you'd think Teodor was propping up the free world single-handed.'

No, I thought. To hear Toby speak, you'd think Teodor was propping up Toby single-handed. But I was not cynical.

In spying, as in much of life, it is always easier to say no than yes. I arrived in Munich prepared to believe that Teodor was the star Toby had cracked him up to be. All I wanted was to be assured.

And I was. At first I was. He was magnificent. I thought my marriage to Mabel had ridded me of such swift enthusiasms, and in a way it had, until the evening when he opened the door to me and I decided I had walked in on one of those perfectly preserved relics of mid-European history, and that all I could decently do was sit at his feet like the rest of his disciples and drink in his wisdom. This is what the Service is for! I thought. Such a man is worth saving on his own account! The culture, I thought. The breadth. The years and years of service.

He received me warmly but with a certain distance, as became his age and distinction. He offered me a glass of fine Tokay and treated me to a discourse on its provenance. No, I confessed, I knew little about Hungarian wines, but I was keen to learn. He talked music, of which I am also sadly ignorant, and played a few bars for me on his treasured violin, the very one he had brought with him when he escaped from Hungary, he explained, and made not by Stradivarius but someone infinitely better, whose name has long escaped me. I thought it a wonderful privilege to be running an agent who had fled with his violin. He talked theatre. A Hungarian theatrical company was presently on tour in Munich with an extraordinary *Othello*, and though Mabel and I had yet to see the production, his opinion of it enchanted me. He was dressed in what Germans call a *Hausjacke*, black trousers and a pair of splendidly polished boots. We talked of God and the world, we ate the best *gulyás* of my life, served by the distraught Helena, who whispered her excuses and left us. She was a tall woman and must once have been beautiful, but she preferred to wear the signs of her neglect. We rounded off the meal with an apricot *palinká*.

'Herr Ned, if I may call you so,' said the Professor, 'there is one matter which weighs heavily on my mind, and which you will permit me to raise with you at the outset of our professional relationship.'

'Please do,' I said generously.

'Unfortunately, your most recent predecessor – a good man, of course' – he broke off, evidently unable to speak ill of the recent dead – 'and, like yourself, a man of culture—'

'Please,' I repeated.

'It concerns my British passport.'

'I didn't know you had one!' I exclaimed in surprise.

'That is the point. I haven't. One understands there are problems. It is so with all bureaucracies. Bureaucracies are the most evil of man's institutions, Herr Ned. They enshrine the worst of us and bring low the best of us. An exiled Hungarian living in Munich in the employment of an American organisation is not naturally eligible for British citizenship. I understand that. Nevertheless, after my many years of collaboration with your department, I am owed this passport. A temporary travel document is not a dignified alternative.'

'But I understood the Americans were giving you a passport! Wasn't that the deal right from the beginning? The Americans to be responsible for your citizenship and resettlement? That includes a passport, surely. It must!'

I was upset that a man who had given us so much of his life should have been denied this simple dignity. But the Professor had learned a more philosophical attitude.

'The Americans, Herr Ned, are a young people and a mercenary people. Having used the best of me, they can scarcely regard me as a man of the future. For the Americans, I belong already to the garbage heap of obsolescence.'

'But didn't they promise – subject to satisfactory service? I'm sure they did!'

He made a gesture I shall never forget. He lifted his hands from the table as if he were raising a prodigiously heavy rock. He brought them almost to the level of his shoulders, before letting them crash at full force back on to the table, the imaginary rock between them. And I remember his eyes, indignant from the exertion, accusing me in the silence. So much for your promises, he was saying. Yours and the Americans, both.

'Just get me my passport, Herr Ned.'

As a loyal case officer, concerned to do the best for my joe, I threw myself upon the problem. Knowing Toby of old, I decided to take an official tone from the beginning: no half promises, no vaporous reassurances for me. I informed Toby of Teodor's request and asked for guidance. He was my desk officer after all, my London anchor. If it was true that the Americans were sliding out of their undertaking to give the Professor citizenship, the matter would have to be dealt with in London or Washington, I said, not Munich. And if, for reasons outside my knowledge, a British passport was to be granted after all, this too would require the energetic endorsement of the Fifth Floor. The days were gone for good when the Home Office handed out free British citizenship to every ex-Circus Tom, Dick and Teodor. The Fall had seen to that.

I did not signal my request, but sent it by bag, which in Circus lore gives greater formality. I wrote a fighting letter and a couple of weeks later followed it with a reminder. But when the Professor asked for a progress report, I was noncommittal.

It's in the pipeline, I assured him; London does not take kindly to being hustled. But I still wondered why Toby took so long to answer.

Meanwhile, at my meetings with Teodor, I strove to unravel what precisely he was doing for us that made him the star of Toby's underpopulated firmament. My investigations were not made easier by the Professor's prickliness, and at first I wondered whether he was withholding his cooperation until the question of his passport was settled. Gradually I realised that where our secret work was concerned, this was his normal demeanour.

One of his more humdrum jobs was maintaining a one-roomed student flat in the Schwabing district, which he used as a safe address for receiving mail from certain of his Hungarian contacts. I persuaded him to take me there. He unlocked the door and there must have been a dozen envelopes lying on the mat, all with Hungarian stamps.

'My goodness, when did you last come here, Professor?' I asked him as I watched him gather them laboriously together.

He shrugged, I thought gracelessly.

'How many letters do you normally reckon to receive in a week, Professor?'

I took the envelopes from him and went through the postmarks. The oldest had been posted three weeks ago, the most recent, one. We moved to the tiny desk, which was covered in dust. With a sigh he settled himself in the chair, opened a drawer and withdrew a couple of bottles of chemicals and a paintbrush from a concealed recess. Taking up the first envelope, he examined it gloomily, then slit it open with a pocket knife.

'Who's it from?' I asked, with more curiosity than he appeared to consider warranted.

'Pali,' he replied gloomily.

'Pali at the Agriculture Ministry?'

'Pali from Debrecen. He has been visiting Romania.'

'What for? Not the toxic-weapons conference? That could be a scoop!'

'We shall see. An academic conference of some kind. His field is cybernetics. He is undistinguished.'

I watched him dip the brush into the first bottle and paint the back of the handwritten letter with it. He rinsed the brush in water and applied the second chemical. And it seemed to me he was determined to demonstrate his disdain for such menial employment. He repeated the process for every letter, sometimes varying the routine by spreading open the envelope and treating the inside of it, or by painting between the lines of the visible handwriting. In the same slow motion, he sat himself at an upright Remington and wearily tapped out in translation the texts that had emerged: anticipated mineral and power deficiencies in the new industries . . . bauxite quotas for mines in the Bakony Mountains . . . low metal content of iron ore recently extracted in the region of Miskolc . . . projected yield of maize and sugar-beet harvest in the region of somewhere else . . . rumours of five-year plan to revitalise State railway network . . . disruptive action against Party officials in Sopron . . . I could almost hear the yawns of the Third Floor analysts as they waded through such turgid stuff. I remembered Toby's boast that Teodor was only interested in the highest quality of intelligence. If this was the highest, what in heaven's name was the lowest? Patience, I told myself. Great agents have to be humoured.

The next day I received a reply to my letter about the passport. The problem, Toby explained, was that there had been a lot of changes among the Cousins' Hungarian Section in recent years. An effort was now being made, he said – making suspicious use of the passive voice – to establish the terms of any undertakings given by the Americans or ourselves. Meanwhile I should avoid discussing the matter with Teodor, he added – as if it were I, not the Professor, who was making the running.

The matter was still in the air three weeks later when I lunched with Milton Wagner at the Cosmo. Wagner was an old hand and my American opposite number. Now he was winding up his career as the Cousins' Chief of Eastern Operations, Munich. The Cosmo was the kind of place Americans make anywhere, with crisp potato skins and garlic dip, and club sandwiches impaled on enormous plastic hairpins.

'How are you getting along with our distinguished academic friend?' he asked, in his southern drawl, after we had despatched our other business.

'Splendidly,' I replied.

'Couple of our people seem to think Teodor's been having himself a free ride these how many years,' said Wagner lazily.

This time I said nothing.

'The boys back home have been holding a retrospective of his work. Not good, Ned. Not good at all. Some of the "Hullo, Hungary" stuff he's been pushing out on the radio. It's been said before. They've found one passage makes a perfect fit with an article published in *Der Monat* back in '48. The original writer recognised his own words soon as he heard them on the air and flipped.' He helped himself liberally to ketchup. 'Could be any day now we haul him in for a full and frank exchange.'

'Probably going through a bad patch,' I said.

'Fifteen years is a long bad patch, Ned.'

'Is he aware you're checking on him?'

'In Radio Free Europe, Ned? Among Hungarians? *Gossip?* You must be joking.'

I could no longer contain my anxiety. 'But why has nobody warned London? Why haven't *you?*'

'Understand we did, Ned. Understand the message fell on pretty deaf ears. Bad time for you boys. Don't we know it.'

By now the momentous force of his news had got through to me. If the Professor was cheating with his broadcasts, whom else might he not be cheating?

'Milt, can I ask you a silly question?'

'Be my guest, Ned.'

'Has Teodor *ever* done good work for you? In all his time? Secret work? Very secret work, even?'

Wagner pondered this, determined to give the Professor the benefit of the doubt. 'Can't say he has, Ned. We did consider using him as an intermediary for one of our big fish one time, but we kind of didn't like the old man's manners.'

'Can I believe that?'

'Would I ever lie to you, Ned?'

So much for the fantastic work he's doing for the Americans, I thought. So much for the years of loyal service nobody can quite recall.

I signalled Toby straight away. I wasted time drafting different texts because my anger kept getting in the way. I understood only too well now why the Americans were refusing to give the Professor his passport, and why he had turned to us for one instead. I understood his air of last things, his listlessness, his lack of urgency: he was waiting to be sacked. I repeated Wagner's information and asked whether it was known to Head Office. If not, the Cousins were in default of their sharing agreement with us. If, on the other hand, the Cousins *had* warned us, why hadn't I been warned too?

Next morning I had Toby's slippery reply. It took a regal tone. I suspected he had got somebody to write it for him, for it was accent-free. The Cousins had given London a 'non-specific warning', he explained, that the Professor might be facing 'disciplinary enquiries at some future date on the subject of his broadcasts'. Head Office – by which I suspected he meant himself – had 'adopted the view' that the Professor's relationship with his American employers was not of direct concern to the Circus. Head Office also 'took the point' – who but Toby could have made it? – that with so much operational work to occupy him, the Professor could be excused for any 'small defects' in his cover work. If another cover job had to be found for the Professor, Head Office would 'take steps at the appropriate time'. One solution would be to place him with one of the tame magazines to which he was already an occasional contributor. But that was for the future. The Professor had fallen foul of his employers before, Toby reminded me, and he had ridden out the storm. This was true. A woman secretary had complained of his advances, and elements of the Hungarian community had taken exception to his anti-Semitic views.

For the rest, Toby advised me to cool down, bide my time, and – always a maxim of Toby's – act as if nothing had happened. Which was how matters stood one week and twelve hours later when the Professor telephoned me at ten at night, using the emergency wordcode and asking me in a strangled but imperious voice to come round to his house immediately, entering by way of the garden door.

My first thought was that he had killed someone, possibly his wife. I could not have been more wrong.

*

The Professor opened the back door, and closed it swiftly after me. The lights inside the house were dimmed. Somewhere in the gloom, a Biedermeier grandfather clock ticked like a big old bomb. At the entrance to the living room stood Helena, her hands to her mouth, smothering a scream. Twenty minutes had passed since Teodor's call, but the scream still seemed to be on the point of coming out of her.

Two armchairs stood before a dying fire. One was empty. I took it to be the Professor's. In the other, somewhat obscured from my line of sight, sat a silky, rounded man of forty, with a cap of soft black hair, and twinkling round eyes that said we were all friends, weren't we? His winged chair was high-backed and he had fitted himself into the angle of it like an aircraft passenger prepared for landing. His rather circular shoes stopped short of the floor, and it occurred to me they were East European shoes: marbled, of an uncertain leather, with moulded, heavy-treaded soles. His hairy brown suit was like a remodelled military uniform. Before him stood a table with a pot of mauve hyacinths on it, and beside the hyacinths lay a display of objects which I recognised as the instruments of silent killing: two garottes made of wooden toggles and lengths of piano wire; a screwdriver so sharpened that it was a stiletto; a Charter Arms .38 Undercover revolver with a five-shot cylinder, together with two kinds of bullet, six soft-nosed, and six rifled, with congealed powder squashed into the grooves.

'It is cyanide,' the Professor explained, in answer to my silent perplexity. 'It is an invention of the Devil. The bullet has only to graze the victim to destroy him utterly.'

I found myself wondering how the poisonous powder was supposed to survive the intense heat of a gun barrel.

'This gentleman is named Ladislaus Kaldor,' the Professor

continued. 'He was sent by the Hungarian secret police to kill us. He is a friend. Kindly sit down, Herr Ned.'

With ceremony, Ladislaus Kaldor rose from his chair and pumped my hand as if we had concluded a profitable deal.

'Sir!' he cried happily, in English. 'Latzi. I am sorry, sir. Don't worry anything. Everybody call me Latzi. Herr Doktor. My friend. Please sit down. Yes.'

I remember how the scent of the hyacinths seemed to go so nicely with his smile. It was only slowly I began to realise I had no sense of danger. Some people convey danger all the time; others put it on when they are angry or threatened. But Latzi, when I was able to consult my instincts, conveyed only an enormous will to please. Which perhaps is all you need if you're a professional killer.

I did not sit down. A chorus of conflicting feelings was yelling in my head, but fatigue was not among them. The empty coffee cups, I was thinking. The empty plates with cake crumbs. Who eats cake and drinks coffee when his life is being threatened? Latzi was sitting again, smiling like a conjuror. The Professor and his wife were studying my face, but from different places in the room. They've quarrelled, I thought; crisis has driven them to their separate corners. An American revolver, I thought. But not the spare cylinder that serious players customarily carried. East European shoes, and with soles that leave a perfect print on every carpet or polished floor. Cyanide bullets that would burn off their cyanide in the barrel.

'How long's he been here?' I asked the Professor.

He shrugged. I hated his shrugs. 'One hour. Less.'

'More than one hour,' Helena contradicted him. Her indignant gaze was fixed upon me. Until tonight she had made a point of ignoring me, slipping past me like a ghost, smiling or scowling at the ground to show her disapproval. Suddenly she needed my support. 'He rang the bell at eight-forty-five exactly. I was listening to the radio. The programme changed.'

I glanced at Latzi. 'You speak German?'

'*Jawohl*, Herr Doktor!'

Back to Helena. 'Which programme?'

'The BBC World Service,' she said.

I went to the radio and switched it on. A reedy Oxford academic of unknown gender was bleating about Keats. Thank you, BBC. I switched it off.

'He rang the bell – who answered it?' I said.

'I did,' said the Professor.

'He did,' said Helena.

'Please,' said Latzi.

'And then?'

'He was standing on the doorstep, wearing a coat,' said the Professor.

'A raincoat,' Helena corrected him.

'He asked if I was Professor Teodor, I said yes. He gave his name, he said "Forgive me, Professor, I have come to kill you with a garotte or cyanide bullet but I do not wish to, I am your disciple and admirer. I wish to surrender to you and remain in the West."'

'He spoke Hungarian?' I asked.

'Naturally.'

'So you invited him in?'

'Naturally.'

Helena did not agree. 'No! First Teodor asked for *me*,' she insisted. I had not heard her correct her husband before tonight. Now she had done so twice in as many minutes. 'He

calls to me and says, "Helena, we have a guest." I say, "Good."
Then he asks Latzi into the house. I take his raincoat, I hang
it in the hall, I make coffee. That is how it happened exactly.'

'And cake,' I said. 'You made cake.'

'The cake was made already.'

'Were you afraid?' I asked – for fear, like danger, was something else that was missing.

'I was disgusted, I was shocked,' she replied. 'Now I am
afraid – yes, I am very afraid. We are all afraid.'

'And you?' I said to the Professor.

He shrugged again, as if to say I was the last man on earth
to whom he would confide his feelings.

'Why don't you take your wife to the study?' I said.

He was disposed to argue, then changed his mind. Strangers arm in arm, they marched from the room.

I was alone with Latzi. I stood, he sat. Munich can be a
very silent city. Even in repose his face smiled at me ingratiat-
ingly. His small eyes still twinkled, but there was nothing I
could read in them. He gave me a nod of encouragement, his
smile broadened. He said 'Please,' and eased himself more
comfortably into his chair. I made the gesture every Middle
European understands. I held out my hand, palm upward,
and passed my thumb across the tip of my forefinger. Still
smiling, he rummaged in his inside jacket pocket and handed
me his papers. They were in the name of Egon Braubach of
Passau, born 1933, occupation artist. I never saw anyone who
looked less like a Bavarian artist. They comprised one West
German passport, one driver's licence and one social security
document. None of them, it seemed to me, carried the least
conviction. Neither did his shoes.

'When did you enter Germany?'

'This afternoon, Herr Doktor, this afternoon at five. Please.'

'Where from?'

'Vienna, please. Vienna,' he repeated, in a breathless rush, as if making me a gift of the entire city, and gave another wriggling motion of his rump, apparently to achieve greater subservience. 'I caught the first train to Munich this morning, Herr Doktor.'

'At what time?'

'At eight o'clock, sir. The eight-o'clock train.'

'When did you enter Austria?'

'Yesterday, Herr Doktor. It was raining. Please.'

'Which papers did you present at the Austrian border?'

'My Hungarian passport, Your Excellency. In Vienna I was given German papers.'

Sweat was forming on his upper lip. His German was fluent but unmistakably Balkan. He had travelled by train, he said: Budapest, Gyôr, Vienna, Herr Doktor. His masters had given him a cold chicken and a bottle of wine for the journey. With best pickles, Your Honour, and paprika. More smiles. Arriving in Vienna, he had checked in at the Altes Kaiserreich Hotel, near the railway station, where a room had been reserved for him. A humble room, a humble hotel, Your Excellency, but I am a humble man. It was at the hotel, late at night, that he was visited by a Hungarian gentleman whom he had not seen before – 'But I suspect he was a diplomat, Herr Doktor. He was distinguished like yourself!' This gentleman gave him his money and documents, he explained – and the arsenal that lay before us on the table.

'Where are you staying in Munich?'

'It is a modest guesthouse on the edge of town, Herr

Doktor,' he replied, with an apologetic smile. 'More a brothel. Yes, a brothel. One sees many men there, coming and going all the time.' He told me its name, and I had half a notion he was going to recommend a girl as well.

'Did they tell you to stay there?'

'For the discretion, Herr Doktor. The anonymity. Please.'

'Do you have luggage there?'

He gave the poor man's shrug, quite unlike the Professor's. 'A toothbrush,' he said. 'Some clothes. A bag, sir. Modest materials.'

In Hungary he was by vocation an agricultural journalist, he said, but he had made himself a second living working for the secret police, first as an informer, and more recently, for the money, as assassin. He had performed certain duties inside Hungary but preferred – forgive him, Excellency – not to say what these were until he was assured he would not be prosecuted in the West. The Professor was his first 'foreign duty', but the thought of killing him had offended his sense of decorum.

'The Professor is a man of format, Herr Doktor! Of reputation! He is not some Jew or priest! Why should I kill this man? I'm a respectable human being, good heavens! I have my honour! Please!'

'Tell me your orders.'

They were not complicated. He was to ring the Herr Professor's doorbell, they had said – so he had rung it. The Professor was sure to be at home, since on Wednesdays he gave private tuition until nine, they had said. – The Professor was indeed at home. – He should describe himself as a friend of Pali from Debrecen. – He had taken the liberty not to describe himself in these terms. – Once inside the house, he should kill the Herr Professor by whatever means seemed appropriate, but preferably the garotte, since it was sure and silent, though there was always a regrettable danger of decapitation. He should kill Helena also, they said – perhaps kill her first, depending on who opened the door to him, they were not particular. It was for this contingency that he had brought a second garotte. With a garotte, Herr Doktor, he explained helpfully, one could never be sure of being able to disentangle the instrument after use. He should then telephone a number in Bonn, ask for Peter, and report that 'Susi will be staying with friends tonight' – Susi being the Professor's codename for the operation, Excellency. This was the signal for success, though in the present circumstance, Herr Doktor, it must be admitted that he had not been successful. Giggle.

'Telephone from here?' I asked.

'From this house, exactly. To Peter. Please. They are violent men, Herr Doktor. They threaten my family. I have no choice, naturally. I have a daughter. They gave me strict instructions: "From the Professor's house you will telephone Peter." '

This also surprised me. Since the Professor was identified to the Hungarian secret police as a Western asset – and had been for fifteen years – one might suppose they would be suspicious of his telephone.

'What do you do if you've failed?' I asked.

'If the duty cannot be fulfilled – if the Herr Professor has guests, or is for some reason not available – I am to ring from a phone box and say that Susi is on her way home.'

'From any particular phone box?'

'All phone boxes are suitable, Herr Doktor, in the event of a non-completion. Peter may then give further instructions, he may not. If not, I return at once to Budapest. Alternatively, Peter may say, "Try again tomorrow," or he may say, "Try in two days." It is all in the hands of Peter in this case.'

'What is the Bonn telephone number?'

He recited it.

'Turn out your pockets.'

A khaki handkerchief, some badly printed family snaps, including some of a young girl, presumably his daughter, three East European condoms, an open packet of Russian cigarettes, a wobbly tin penknife of obvious Eastern manufacture, a stub of unpainted pencil, 960 West German marks, some small change. The return half of a second-class rail ticket, Vienna–Munich–Vienna. I never in my life saw such miserably assembled pockets. Did the Hungarian Service have no despatchers? Checkers? What the Devil were they thinking of?

'And your raincoat,' I said, and watched him fetch it from the hall. It was brand-new. The pockets were empty. It was of Austrian manufacture and good quality. It must have cost serious Western money.

'Did you buy this in Vienna?'

'*Jawohl,* Herr Doktor. It was raining cats and dogs and I had no protection.'

'When?'

'Please?'

'What with?'

'Please?'

I discovered he could anger me quite quickly. 'You caught the first train this morning, right? It left Vienna before the shops opened, right? You didn't get your money till late last night when the Hungarian diplomat visited you. So when did you buy the coat and what did you use for money? Or did you steal it? Is that the answer?'

First he frowned; then he laughed indulgently at my

breach of good manners. It was clear that he forgave me. He opened his hands to me in generosity. 'But I bought it last night, Herr Doktor! When I arrived at the station! With my personal *Valuten* that I brought with me from Hungary for shopping, naturally! I am not a liar! Please!'

'Did you keep the receipt?'

He shook his head sagely, advice to a younger man. 'To keep receipts, Herr Doktor? I give you this advice. To keep receipts is to invite questions about where you get your money. A receipt – it's like a spy in the pocket. Please.'

Too many excuses, I thought, releasing myself from the brilliance of his smile. Too many answers in one paragraph. All my instincts told me to trust nobody and nothing about the story that was being told me. It was not so much the sloppiness of the assassination plan that strained my credulity – the implausible documents, the contents of the pockets, the shoes – not even the basic improbability of the mission. I had seen enough of low-level Soviet satellite operations to regard such amateurishness as the norm. What disturbed me about these people was the unreality of their behaviour in my company, the feeling there was one story for me and one for them; that I had been brought here to perform a function, and the collective will required me to shut up and get on with it.

Yet at the same time I was trapped. I had no choice, and no time, but to take everything they had told me at face value. I was in the position of a doctor who, while suspecting a patient of malingering, has no option but to treat his symptoms. By the laws of the game, Latzi was a prize. It was not every day that a Hungarian assassin offered to defect to the West, no matter how incompetent he was. By the same token, the man was in considerable danger, since it was unthinkable that an assassination operation of this consequence could be launched without separate surveillance.

When in doubt, says the handbook, take the operational line. Were they watching the house? It was necessary to assume so, though it was not an easy house to watch, which was what had commended it to Teodor's handlers fifteen years ago. It stood at the end of a leafy cul-de-sac and backed on to the river. The way into the garden led along a deserted tow-path. But the front porch was visible to anybody passing by, and Latzi could have already been observed entering it.

I went upstairs and from the landing window surveyed the road. The neighbouring houses were in darkness. I saw no sign of stray cars or people. My own car was parked in the next sidestreet, close to the river. I returned to the drawing room. The telephone was on the bookcase. I handed Latzi the receiver and watched him dial the number in Bonn. His hands were girlish and moist. Obligingly, he tilted the earpiece in my direction, and himself with it. He smelt of old blanket and Russian tobacco. The phone rang out, I heard a man's voice, very grumpy, speaking German. For somebody awaiting news of a killing, I thought, you're doing a good job of pretending you aren't.

A thick accent, presumably Hungarian: 'Hullo? Yes? Who is it?'

I nodded to Latzi to go ahead.

'Good evening, sir. I wish, please, to speak to Mr Peter.'

'What about?'

'Is this Mr Peter, please? It is a private matter.'

'What do you want?'

'Is this Peter?'

'My name is Peter!'

'It is regarding Susi, Mr Peter,' Latzi explained, with a side-ways wink at me. 'Susi will not be coming home tonight, Mr Peter. She will be staying with friends, I am afraid. Good friends. She will be looked after. Good night, Mr Peter.'

He was about to replace the receiver, but I stayed his hand long enough to hear a growl of contempt or incomprehension the other end before he rang off.

Latzi smiled at me, very pleased with himself. 'He plays it well, Herr Doktor. A true professional, I would say. A fine actor, you agree?'

'Did you recognise the voice?'

'No, Herr Doktor. Alas, the voice is not familiar to me.'

I shoved open the study door. The Professor sat at his desk, his fists in front of him. Helena sat on the tutorial sofa. I felt a need to acquaint the Professor with my scepticism. I stepped into the room, closing the door behind me.

'The man Latzi, as you call him, is a criminal,' I said. 'Either he's some kind of confidence trickster, or he's a self-confessed murderer who came to Germany on false papers in order to kill you and your wife. Either way, you're within your rights to turn him over to the West German police and be done with him. Do you want to do that? Or do you want to leave the decisions to us? Which?'

To my surprise, he appeared for the first time that evening genuinely alarmed. Perhaps he had not expected to be challenged. Perhaps the proximity of his own death had dawned on him. Either way, I had the impression he was attaching more importance to my question than I understood. Helena had turned her eyes away from me and was watching him also. Critically. A woman waiting to be paid.

'Do whatever you must do,' he muttered.

'Then you must do as I ask. Both of you.'

'We are cooperative. We shall be – yes, cooperative. We have been – cooperative – for many years. Too many.'

I glanced at Helena.

'It will be my husband's responsibility,' she said.

I had no time to ponder the mysteries of this ominous statement. 'Then please put together some night things and be ready at the garden door in five minutes,' I said, and returned to the drawing room and Latzi.

I think he had been standing at the door, for he stepped quickly back as I entered, then clasped his hands to his chin and beamed at me, asking what was *gefällig* – what was my pleasure?

'Have you ever seen the Professor before tonight?'

'No, sir. Only photographs. One would admire him anywhere. A true aristocrat.'

'And his wife?'

'She is known to me, sir. Naturally.'

'How?'

'She was once an actress, Herr Doktor, one of the best in Budapest.'

'And you saw her on the stage?'

Another pause. 'No, sir.'

'Then where did you see her?'

He was trying to read me. I had the impression he was wondering whether she might have told me something, and he was trimming his answers accordingly.

'Theatre bills, Your Excellency. When she was young, her famous face was on every street corner. All young men loved her – I was no exception.'

'Where else?'

He saw that I had nothing. And I saw that he saw. 'So sad

about a woman's looks, Herr Doktor. A man, he can remain impressive until he is eighty. A woman—' he sighed.

I let him pack together his weapons, then took possession of them. I loaded the soft-nosed bullets into the revolver. As I did so, a thought occurred to me.

'When I walked in here, the cylinder was empty and the bullets were spread on the table.'

'Correct, Excellency.'

'When did you take the bullets out of the cylinder?' I asked.

'Before entering the house. So that I could demonstrate my peaceful intentions. Naturally.'

'Naturally.'

As we moved to the hall, I shoved the revolver into my waist-band.

'If you take it into your head to run away, I shall shoot you in the back,' I explained to him, and had the satisfaction of seeing his little eyes swivel in alarm. Professional assassins, it seemed, did not take kindly to their own medicine.

I tossed him his raincoat and glanced round the room for other traces of him. There were none. I ordered silence and led the three of them into the garden and along the tow-path to my car. A famous actress, I thought, and not a word about it on the file. I put the Professor and Helena in the back, and Latzi in the front beside me. Then we sat still for five minutes while I waited for the slightest sign that we were being watched. Nothing. It was by now midnight and a new moon had risen among the stars. I circled the town, keeping a watch on my mirror, then took the autobahn south-west to the Starnbergersee, where we kept a safe house for briefing and debriefing joes in passage. It lay close to the lake's edge and was manned by two murderous long-haired wonders left over from London Station's Lamplighters Section. They were called Jeffrey and Arnold. Arnold was hovering in the doorway by the time we reached it. One hand was in the pocket of his kaftan. The other hung threateningly to his side.

'It's me, you buffoon,' I said softly.

Jeffrey showed the Professor and his wife to their bedroom while Arnold sat with Latzi in the drawing room. I went down the garden to the boat-house, where I was at last able to talk to Toby Esterhase on the safe telephone. He was amazingly composed. It was as if he had been expecting my call.

Toby arrived in Munich on the first flight from London next morning, wearing a beaver-lamb coat and a leather trilby hat, and looking more the impresario than the beleaguered spy.

'Nedike, my God!' he cried, embracing me like a prodigal father. 'Listen, you look fantastic, I would say. Congratulations, okay? Nothing like a little excitement to bring the blooms to your cheeks. How's Mabel, actually? A marriage, that's something you got to water, same as a flower.'

I drove slowly and spoke, as best I could, dispassionately, giving him the fruits of my researches throughout the long night. I wanted him to know everything I knew by the time we reached the lake house.

Neither the Americans nor the West Germans had any trace of Latzi, I said. Neither, I gathered from Toby, had London.

'Latzi, that's an unwritten page, Ned. Totally,' Toby agreed, surveying the passing landscape with every sign of approval.

There was also no trace of his Bavarian covername, or of any of the covernames that Latzi claimed to have used on his 'duties' inside Hungary, I said.

Toby lowered his window to enjoy the fragrance of the fields.

Latzi's West German passport was a fake, I continued with determination, one of a batch recently run up by a low-grade forger in Vienna and sold on the private market.

Toby was mildly indignant. 'I mean who buys that crap, for God's sake?' he protested, as we passed a pair of palomino horses grazing in a paddock. 'With passports, these days, you get what you pay for actually. What you get for crap like that, it's six months in a stinking gaol.' And he shook his head sadly like a man whose warnings go unheeded until it's too late.

I blundered on. The phone number in Bonn belonged to the Hungarian military attaché, I said, whose first name was indeed listed as Peter. He was an identified Hungarian Intelligence officer. I allowed myself a restrained irony:

'That's a new one for us, isn't it, Toby? A spy using his own name as a covername? I mean why bother any more? You're Toby, so we'll keep it a secret and call you Toby instead. Great.'

But Toby was too set on enjoying his day in Bavaria to be disturbed by the implications of my words. 'Nedike, believe me, those army guys, they're total idiots. Hungarian military intelligence, that's the same as Hungarian military music, know what I mean? They blow it out their arses actually.'

I continued my recitation. West German Security had a permanent tap running on the Hungarian attaché's telephone, I said. A cassette of Latzi's conversation with Peter was on its way to my office. From what I understood, it offered no surprises except to underline that Peter appeared genuinely unprepared for the call. Peter had neither made nor received further calls last night, I said, nor had there been any burst of diplomatic signals traffic from the roof of the Hungarian Embassy in Bonn. Peter had, however, complained to the Protocol Department of the West German Foreign Office about telephone harassment on his home line. This was not, I suggested, the act of a conspirator. Toby was less sure.

'Could be one thing, Ned, could be the other,' he said, leaning back in his seat and languidly tilting the flat of his hand both ways. 'A man thinks he's been compromised? So maybe it's not so stupid he makes a formal complaint once, brushes over his traces – why not?'

I gave him the rest. I was determined to. Latzi's description of the putative diplomat in Vienna tallied with that of one Leo Bakocs, Commercial Secretary and, like Peter, an identified Hungarian Intelligence officer, I said. Cousin Wagner was getting hold of a photograph for us to show to Latzi later in the day.

The name Bakocs brought a fond smile to Toby's lips. 'They drag *Leo* in on this? Listen, Leo's so vain he spies only on duchesses.' He laughed in jolly disbelief. 'Leo in some lousy hotel, handing over garottes to a smelly assassin? Tell me another, Ned. I mean.'

'It isn't me who's telling you,' I said. 'It's Latzi.'

Lastly, I said, I had despatched Jeffrey to the Munich whorehouse to pay Latzi's bill and collect his overnight bag. The only article of interest in his luggage was a set of pornographic photographs.

'It's the tension, Ned,' Toby explained magnanimously. 'In a foreign country, killing somebody you don't know, you need a little private company – know what I mean?'

In return, Toby had brought me nothing whatever, private or otherwise. I had imagined him on the phone all night, and perhaps he had been. But not in support of my enquiries.

'Maybe we have a party tonight,' he proposed. 'Harry Palfrey of Legal Department is coming over with a couple of guys from the Foreign Office. That's a nice fellow, Harry. Very English.'

I was bewildered. 'What branch of the Foreign Office?' I said. 'Who? Why Palfrey?'

But as Toby would say, questions are never dangerous until you answer them. We arrived at the lake house to find Arnold cooking eggs and bacon. The Professor and Latzi sat at one end of the table. Helena, a vegetarian, sat at the other, eating a nut bar from her handbag.

Arnold was blond and lank. His hair was done in a knot at the back. 'They had a bit of a dingdong, Ned,' he confided to me disapprovingly while Toby fell about the Professor's neck. 'The Professor and his missus, a real dogfight. I don't know who started it or what it was about, I wouldn't ask.'

'Did Latzi join in?'

'He was going to, Ned, but I told him to keep quiet. I don't like a man who comes between husband and wife, I never did.'

In retrospect, our discussions that day resemble an intricate minuet, beginning in our humble kitchen and ending in the courts of the Almighty Himself – more precisely in the be-flagged conference room of the American Consulate General, where the inspiring features of President Nixon and Vice President Agnew smiled favourably on our endeavours.

For Toby, as I soon realised, far from doing nothing, had laid on an entire programme for himself, which he advanced from stage to stage with the dexterity of a ringmaster. In the kitchen, he listened to the whole story over again from Latzi

and the Professor, while Helena chewed her nut bar. I had
never seen Toby in full Hungarian flight before and found
time to marvel at the transformation. With one sentence
he had flung aside the unnatural corset of his Anglo-Saxon
restraint and was back among his people. His eyes caught
fire. He preened, and his back arched as if he were sitting on
a parade horse.

'Ned, they say you have been quite fantastic actually,' he
called to me down the table in the midst of all this. 'A tower
of strength, they are saying, completely. I think maybe they
will recommend you a Nobel prize!'

'Tell them to make it an Oscar, I'll accept,' I said sourly,
and took myself for a walk down to the lakeside to recover
my temper.

I returned to the house to find Toby and the Professor
closeted in the drawing room, talking volubly. Toby's high
respect for the Professor seemed, if anything, to have
increased. Latzi was helping Arnold with the washing-up and
they were both sniggering. Latzi had evidently been telling a
dirty joke. Helena was nowhere to be seen. Next, it was Latzi's turn to sit alone with Toby, while the Professor and his
wife walked uneasily at the lakeside, pausing every few steps
to remonstrate with each other, until the Professor turned
on his heel and strode back to the house.

Seizing the moment, I slipped out and joined Helena. Her
lips were pursed and her face was sickly-white – whether from
fear, anger or fatigue, I couldn't tell. When she spoke, she had
to stop and begin again before the words would come.

'He is a *liar*,' she said. 'It is all lies! Lie, lie! He is a liar!'

'Who is?'

'They are *both* liars. From the day of birth, they *lie*. On
their deathbeds, they *lie*.'

'So what's the truth?' I said.

'*Wait* is the truth!'

'Wait for what?'

'I have warned him. "If you do this, I shall tell the English." So we wait. If he does it, I shall tell you. If he repents, I shall spare him. I am his wife.'

She walked to the house, a stately woman. As she entered it, a black limousine pulled up in the drive and Harry Palfrey, the Circus legal adviser, emerged, accompanied by two other members of the English governing classes. I recognised the taller of them as Alan Barnaby, luminary of the Foreign Office's misnomered Information and Research Department, which traded in Communist counter-propaganda at its sleaziest. Toby was shaking him warmly by the hand while with his other he beckoned me to join them. We went indoors and sat down.

At first I smouldered in silence. The players had been sent upstairs. Toby was doing the talking, the others listened to him with the special reverence their kind reserves for paupers or black men. I even found myself feeling a little protective of him – of Toby Esterhase, God help me, who protected no one but himself!

'What we are dealing with here, Alan, without talking out of turn actually, is a completely top source who is now expended,' Toby explained. 'A great joe, but his day is over.'

'You mean the Prof,' Barnaby said helpfully.

'They are on to him. They know his value too well. From certain clues I have obtained from Latzi, it's clear the Hungarians have a fat dossier on the Professor's operations. After all, I mean, why would they try to kill a fellow who is no use to us? A Hungarian assassination attempt – that's a *Good Housekeeping* certificate for the target, I would say.'

'We can't be responsible for the Professor's safety indefinitely,' Palfrey cautioned us with his loser's smile. 'We can give him protection for a bit, naturally. But we can't accept a life interest in him. He has to know that. We may have to get him to sign something just to make the point.'

The second Foreign Office man was round and shiny with a chain across his waistcoat. I had a childish urge to pull it and see if he squealed.

'Well, *I* think we may all be talking too much,' he said silkily. 'If the Americans agree to take the pair of 'em off our hands, the Prof and his missus, we shan't have to worry, shall we? Best keep our heads down and our powder dry, what?'

Palfrey demurred. 'He should still sign a release for us, Norman. He has rather been playing us off against the Cousins in the last few years.'

Ever the protector of his own, Toby gave a knowing smile. 'All the best joes do this, I would say, Harry. One hand washes the other, even at Teodor's level. The question is, now that he is no longer usable, what have we got to lose except trouble actually? I mean, I am not the expert here,' he added, with an ingratiating smile at Barnaby.

'What about the assassin fellow?' said the man called Norman. 'Will he play ball as well? Bloody dangerous, isn't it, sitting up there like a duck in a tree?'

'Latzi is flexible,' said Toby. 'He is scared, he is also a complete patriot.' I would not have backed him on either of these points, but I was too sickened to interrupt. 'These *apparatchiks*, when they step out of the system, they are in shock. Latzi is coping with it. He agonises over his family, but he is reconciled. If Teodor accepts, Latzi will accept also. With guarantees, naturally.'

'What *sort* of guarantees?' said the shiny Foreign Office

man, so quickly that not even Harry Palfrey got in ahead of him.

Toby did not falter. 'Well, naturally the usual. Latzi and Teodor don't want to be thrown on to the rubbish heap when this one's over, I would say. Nor does Helena. American passports, a good bit of money at the end of the road, assistance and protection – I mean, that's basic, so to speak.'

'The whole thing's a con,' I blurted. I had had enough.

Everybody was smiling at me. They would have smiled whatever I had said. They were that sort of crowd. If I had said I was a Hungarian double agent, they would have smiled. If I had said I was Adolf Hitler's reincarnated younger brother, they would have smiled. All but Toby, that is, whose face had acquired the lifelessness of someone who knows that all he can safely be at this moment is nobody at all.

'Now why on earth do you say that, Ned?' Barnaby was asking, awfully interested.

'Latzi's not a trained killer,' I said. 'I don't know what he is, but he isn't a killer. He was carrying an unloaded gun. No professional in his right mind does that. He's posing as a Bavarian artist, but he's wearing Hungarian clothes and half the junk in his pockets is Hungarian. I was standing over him when he made his phone call to Bonn. Fine, the attaché's first name is Peter. It's in the diplomatic list as Peter. Peter wasn't expecting that call in a month of Sundays. Latzi laid it on him. Listen to the German tape of their conversation.'

'Then what about the chap in Vienna, Ned?' said Barnaby, still determined to patronise me. 'The chap who gave him his money and his hardware? Eh? Eh?'

'They never met. We showed Latzi the photograph and he was delighted. "That's the man," he said. Oh sure: he'd seen a photograph somewhere else. Ask Helena, she knows. She's not telling at the moment, but if we put pressure on her, I'm sure she will.'

Toby came briefly alive. 'Pressure, Ned? Helena? Pressure, that's something you use when you know you can squeeze harder than the other fellow. That woman is crazy about her husband. She defends him to the grave actually.'

'The Professor's fallen foul of the Americans,' I said. 'They're rolling up his red carpet. He's desperate. If he didn't set up the assassination himself, Latzi did. The whole ploy is a device for him to cut his losses and make a new life.'

They waited for me to continue, all of them. It was as if they were waiting for the punchline. Finally Toby spoke. He had rediscovered his form.

'Nedike, how long since you slept actually?' he asked with an indulgent smile. 'Tell us, please.'

'What's that got to do with it?'

Toby was ostentatiously studying his watch. 'I think you have been now thirty hours without sleep, Ned. You took some pretty damn big decisions in that time – all good ones, I would say. I don't think we can blame you for having a bit of a reaction.'

It was as if I had never spoken. All heads had turned back to Toby.

'Well, *I* think it's rather important we take a peek at the cast,' Barnaby was saying as I headed for the door. 'Can we whistle them down, Toby? Question of how they'll shape up under the spotlights.'

'I think there's news value in doing this thing straight away, Barnaby,' Palfery was saying, as I headed for the garden and sanity. 'Strike while the iron is hot. With me?'

'With you all the way, Harry. Hundred per cent.'

★

I refused to be present for the first audition. I sulked in the kitchen and let Arnold minister to me while I pretended to listen to some story about his mother walking out on the fellow she'd been with for twenty years and shacking up with her childhood sweetheart. I watched Toby skip upstairs to fetch his champions, and scowled when the three men descended some minutes later, Latzi with his black hair slicked into a parting, the Professor with his jacket outside his shoulders, his seer's head struck forward in contemplation and his white mane flowing becomingly.

Then Helena came into the kitchen with tears streaming down her cheeks, so Arnold gave her a hug and fetched a blanket for her, because the spring morning was crisp and she was shivering. Then Arnold made her a camomile tea, and sat with his arm round her till Toby bustled in to say we were all expected at the American Consulate in two hours.

'Russell Sheriton is flying in from London, Pete de May from Bonn. They are mustard for it, Ned. Totally mustard. Washington throws its cap in the air, completely.' I do not recall whether Pete de May was grander than Sheriton or less grand. But grand enough. 'Ned, that Teodor's fantastic,' Toby assured me privately.

'Really? In what way?'

'You know what they told him? "What you are doing is damn risky, Professor. Do you think you can handle it?" You know what he replied? "Mr Ambassador, risks are what we all take to protect civilised society." He's quiet, he's dignified. Latzi too. Ned, after this you get some sleep, okay? I phone Mabel.'

We rode in two cars, Toby with the Hungarians, myself with Palfrey and the Foreign Office. Opening the car door for me, Palfrey touched my arm and offered me some steel-edged advice. 'I think from now on, it's all hands pulling together,

Ned. Tired is one thing. Talk about con-tricks is something else. Yes? Agreed?'

We must have numbered twenty head. The Consul General presided. He was a pallid mid-Westerner, an ex-lawyer like Palfrey, and kept talking anxiously about 'reprocussions'. Milton Wagner was seated between Sheriton and de May. It was clear to me that, whatever their private thoughts, Sheriton and Wagner had orders to keep their scepticism to themselves. Perhaps they too had recognised that there were worse ways of getting rid of useless agents than off-loading them on to the US Information Services, who were represented by a quartet of troubled believers whose names I never learned.

Pullach was spoken for, naturally. Though not involved, they had sent their own observer, so we could be confident that our determinations would be the gossip of Potsdam by afternoon. They also insisted on making a voluble complaint about Vienna. It seemed that Pullach had a running battle with the Austrian police about forged passports, and suspected them of selling them to the Hungarians. Quite a lot of the meeting was taken up by an Oberst von-und-zu somewhere or other moaning about Austrian duplicity.

The three champions did not, of course, attend our deliberations, but sat in the waiting room. When sandwiches were passed round, a generous plate was sent out to them. And when they were finally called in, several of the lay members of the meeting broke into applause, which must have been the first of many times from then on when they heard the roar of the greasepaint.

But it was Helena's tears that stole the show. The Professor said his few words, and his halting dignity worked its predictable magic. Latzi followed him, and a cold chill fell over the room as he explained why he had carried the two garottes, which were then passed gingerly round the table with the rest of the exhibits. But when Helena stepped forward on the Professor's arm, I felt a lump rise to my throat, and knew that everyone in the room was feeling the same.

'I support my husband,' was all the great actress could declaim.

But it was enough to bring the room to its feet.

It was late evening before I managed to speak to her alone. We were washed out by then; even the irrepressible Latzi was exhausted. The captains and the kings had departed, Toby had departed. I was sitting with Arnold in the drawing room of the lake house. An American van, with blackened windows and two plainclothes marines aboard, was waiting in the drive, but our stars were learning to keep their public waiting. The day had been spent preparing afternoon press announcements and signing Palfrey's releases, which he turned out to have brought with him in his briefcase.

She entered hesitantly, as if she expected me to strike her, but the anger had been drained out of me.

'We shall get our passports,' she said, sitting down. 'It is the new world.'

Arnold slipped tactfully from the room, closing the door behind him.

'Who's Latzi?' I said.

'He is a friend of Teodor.'

'What else is he?'

'He is an actor. A bad, oh a *bad* actor from Debrecen.'

'Did he ever work for the secret police?'

She made a gesture of deprecation. 'He had connections.

When Teodor needed to arrange himself with the authorities, Latzi was the go-between.'

'You mean, when Teodor needed to inform on his students?'

'Yes.'

'Did Latzi supply Teodor with his information while you were in Munich?'

'At first only a little. But when none came from other sources, more. Then much more. Latzi prepared the material for Teodor. Teodor sold it to the British and Americans. Otherwise we would have had no money.'

'Was Latzi getting help from the secret police to do this?'

'It was private. Things are changing in Hungary. It is no longer prudent to be involved with the authorities.'

I unlocked the door and watched her make her exit, head erect.

A few weeks later, back in London, I faced Toby with her story. He was neither surprised nor contrite.

'Women, Ned, that's a criminal class actually. Better we eat the soup, not stir it.'

A few weeks more and the Teodor–Latzi show was riding high. So was Toby. How much was he a part of it? How much did he know when? The whole of it? Did he dream up the entire piece of theatre in order to make the best of his imperilled agent and get him off his hands? I have often secretly suspected that the play was a three-hander, at the least, with Helena as the reluctant audience.

'Know what, Nedike?' Toby declared, throwing an affectionate arm around my shoulder. 'If you can't ride two horses at once, you better stay out of the Circus.'

You remember the pseudonymous Colonel Weatherby in the book? The master of disguises, at ease in seven European languages? Pimpernel leader of the East European resistance fighters? The man who 'flitted back and forth across the Iron Curtain as if it were of frailest gossamer'? That was me. Ned. I didn't write that part, thank God. It was the work of some venal sports journalist from Baltimore recruited by the Cousins. Mine was the introductory pen portrait of the great man, printed under the caption 'The Real Professor Teodor as I Knew Him', and gouged out of me by Toby and the Fifth Floor. My working title for the book was *Tricks of the Trade*, but the Fifth Floor said that might be misunderstood. They promoted me instead.

But not before I had taken my indignation to George Smiley, who had just given up his job as acting chief and was on the point of removing himself for the nearly last time to the shadows of academia. I was back in London on a mid-tour break. It was a Friday evening and I ran him to earth in Bywater Street, packing for the weekend. He heard me out, he gave a small chuckle, then a larger chuckle. He muttered, '*Oh Toby*' affectionately under his breath.

'But then they *do* assassinate, don't they, Ned,' he objected as he laboriously folded a tweed suit. 'The Hungarians, I mean. Even by East European standards, they're one of the foulest mobs there are, surely?'

Yes, I conceded, the Hungarians killed and tortured pretty much at will. But that didn't alter the fact that Latzi was a fake and Teodor was Latzi's accomplice, and as to Toby—

Smiley cut me short. 'Now, Ned, I think you're being a little bit prissy. Every church needs its saints. The anti-Communist church is no exception. And saints as a bunch are a pretty bogus lot, when you come down to it. But no one would pretend they don't have their uses, once they get the job. Do you think this shirt will do, or must I give it another iron?'

John le Carré

We sat in his drawing room sipping our Scotches and listening to the clamour of party-goers in Bywater Street.

'And did the ghost of Stefanie stalk the Munich pavements for you, Ned?' Smiley enquired tenderly, just when I was beginning to wonder whether he had dozed off.

I had long ceased to marvel at his capacity to put himself in my shoes.

'Now and then,' I replied.

'But not in the flesh? How sad.'

'I once rang one of her aunts,' I said. 'I'd had some silly row with Mabel and gone to a hotel. It was late. I expect I was a bit drunk.' I found myself wondering whether Smiley already knew, and decided I was being fanciful. 'Or I *think* it was an aunt. It could have been a servant. No, it was an aunt.'

'What did she say?'

'"Fräulein Stefanie is not at home."'

A long silence, but this time I did not make the mistake of thinking he had gone to sleep.

'Young voice?' he enquired thoughtfully.

'Quite.'

'Then perhaps it was Stefanie who answered.'

'Perhaps it was.'

We listened again to the raised voices in the street. A girl was laughing. A man was cross. Somebody hooted a horn and drove away. The sounds died. Stefanie's my Ann, I thought, as I walked back across the river to Battersea, where I had kept my little flat: the difference is, I never had the courage to let her disappoint me.

7

Smiley had interrupted himself – some tale of a Central American diplomat with a passion for British model railways of a certain generation, and how the Circus had bought the man's lifelong allegiance with a Hornby Double-O shunting engine stolen from a London toy museum by Monty Arbuck's team. Everyone was laughing until this sudden reflective silence, while Smiley's troubled gaze fixed itself upon some point outside the room.

'And just occasionally we meet the reality we've been playing with,' he said quietly. 'Until it happens, we're spectators. The joes live out our dreams for us, and we case officers sit safe and snug behind our one-way mirrors, telling ourselves that seeing is feeling. But when the moment of truth strikes – if it ever does for you – well, from then on we become a little more humble about what we ask people to do for us.'

He never once glanced at me as he said this. He gave no hint of who was in his mind. But I knew, and he knew. And each knew the other knew that it was Colonel Jerzy.

I saw him and I said nothing to Mabel. Perhaps I was too surprised. Or perhaps the old habits of dissembling die so hard that even today my first response at any unexpected event is to suppress the spontaneous reaction. We were watching the nine-o'clock news on television, which for Mabel and myself has become a kind of Evensong these days, don't ask me why. And suddenly I saw him. Colonel Jerzy. And instead of leaping from my chair and shouting, 'My God! Mabel! Look, that fellow in the back there! That's Jerzy!' – which would have been the healthy reaction of any ordinary man – I went on watching the screen and sipping my whisky and soda. Then, as soon as I was alone, I slipped a fresh tape into the video machine so that I could be sure of catching the repeat when it came round on 'Newsnight'. Since when – the incident is now six weeks old – I must have watched it a dozen more times, for there is always some extra nuance to be relished.

But I shall leave that part of the story to the end where it belongs. Better to give you the events in the order they occurred, for there was more to Munich than Professor Teodor, and there was more to spying in the wake of Bill Haydon's exposure than waiting for the wounds to heal.

Colonel Jerzy was a Pole and I have never understood why so many Poles have a soft spot for us. Our repeated betrayals of their country have always seemed to me so disgraceful that if I were Polish, I would spit on every passing British shadow, whether I had suffered under the Nazis or the Russians – the British in their time having abandoned the poor Poles to both. And I would certainly be tempted to plant a bomb under the so-called 'competent department' of the British Foreign Office. Dear heaven, what a phrase! As I write, the Poles are once more squeezed between the unpredictable Russian Bear and the rather more predictable German Ox. But you may be quite sure that if they should ever need a good friend to help them out, the same 'competent department' of the British Foreign Office will send its treacly regrets and plead a more enticing function up the road.

Nevertheless, the record of my Service boasts a disproportionate rate of success in Poland, and an almost embarrassing number of Polish men and women who, with reckless Polish courage, have risked their necks and those of their families in order to spy for 'England'.

No wonder then if, in the aftermath of Haydon, the casualty rate among our Polish networks was correspondingly high. Thanks to Haydon, the British had added yet another betrayal to their long list. As each new loss followed the previous one with sickening inevitability, the air of mourning in our Munich Station became almost palpable, and our sense of shame was compounded by our helplessness. None of us had any doubt of what had happened. Until the Fall, Polish Security – ably led by their Chief of Operations, Colonel Jerzy – had held Haydon's treachery close to their chests, contenting themselves with penetrating our existing networks and using them as channels of disinformation – or, where they succeeded in turning them, playing them back at us with skill.

But After the Fall, the Colonel felt no further need of delicacy, and in the course of a few days savagely silenced those of our loyal agents whom till then he had allowed to remain in place. 'Jerzy's hitlist', we called it as the tally rose almost daily, and in our frustration we developed a personal hatred of the man who had murdered our beloved joes, sometimes not bothering with the formalities of a trial, but letting his interrogators have their fun until the end.

It may seem odd to think of Munich as a springboard to Poland. Yet for decades Munich had been the command centre for a range of Polish operations. From the roof of our

Consular annexe in a leafy suburb, our antennae had listened night and day for our Polish agents' signals – often no more than a blip compressed between words spoken on the open radio. And in return, on pre-determined schedules, we had transmitted comfort and fresh orders to them. From Munich we had despatched our Polish letters, impregnated with secret writing. And if our sources managed to travel outside Poland, it was from Munich again that we flew off to debrief and feast them and listen to their worries.

It was from Munich also, when the need was great enough, that our Station officers would cross into Poland, always singly and usually in the guise of a visiting businessman bound for a trade fair or exhibition. And in some roadside picnic spot or backstreet café, our emissaries would come briefly face to face with our precious joes, transact their business and depart, knowing they had refilled the lamp. For nobody who has not led a joe's life can imagine what loneliness of faith it brings. A well-timed cup of bad coffee shared with a good case officer can raise a joe's morale for months.

Which is how it happened that, one winter's day soon after the beginning of the second half of my tour in Munich (and the welcome departure of Professor Teodor and his appendages to America), I found myself flying into Gdansk on a LOT Polish Airlines flight from Warsaw, with a Dutch passport in my pocket describing me as Franz Joost of Nijmegen, born forty years before. According to my businessman's visa application, my mission was to inspect prefabricated agricultural buildings on behalf of a West German farming consortium. For I have some basic grounding as an engineer, and certainly enough to exchange visiting cards with officials from their Ministry of Agriculture.

My other mission was more complicated. I was looking

for a joe named Oskar, who had returned to life six months after being given up for dead. Out of the blue, Oskar had sent us a letter to an old cover address, using his secret writing equipment and describing everything he had done and not done from the day he had first heard of the arrests till now. He had kept his nerve. He had remained at his job. He had anonymously denounced some blameless *apparatchik* in his Archives Section in order to divert suspicion. He had waited, and after a few weeks the *apparatchik* disappeared. Encouraged, he waited again. Rumour reached him that the *apparatchik* had confessed. Given Colonel Jerzy's tender ministrations, this was not surprising. As the weeks went by, he began to feel safe again. Now he was ready to resume work if someone would tell him what to do. In earnest of this, he had stuck microdots to the third, fifth and seventh full stops of the letter, which were the pre-arranged positions. Blown up, they amounted to sixteen pages of top secret orders from the Polish Defence Ministry to Colonel Jerzy's department. The Circus analysts declared them 'likely and presumed reliable', which, coming from them, was an ecstatic declaration of faith.

You must imagine now the excitement that Oskar's letter kindled in the Station, and even in myself, though I had never met him. Oskar! the believers cried. The old devil! Alive and kicking under the rubble! Trust Oskar to beat the rap! Oskar, our hardened Polish Admiralty clerk, based at Gdansk's coastal defence headquarters, one of the best the Station ever had!

Only the hardest-nosed, or those nearest to retirement, dismissed the letter as a lure. Saying 'no' in such cases is easy. Saying 'yes' takes nerve. Nevertheless, the nay-sayers are always heard the clearest, particularly after Haydon, and for a while there was a stalemate when no one had the nerve to jump either way. Buying time, we wrote to Oskar asking for more collateral. He wrote back angrily demanding to know whether he was trusted, and this time he insisted on a meeting. 'A meeting or nothing,' he said. And in Poland. Soon or never.

While Head Office continued to vacillate, I begged to be allowed to go to him. The unbelievers in my Station told me I was mad, the believers said it was the only decent thing to do. I was convinced by neither side, but I wanted clarity. Perhaps I also wanted it for myself, for Mabel had recently shown signs of withdrawing herself from our relationship and I was not disposed to rate myself too highly. Head Office sided with the nos. I reminded them of my naval background. Head Office dithered and said, 'No, but maybe.' I reminded them of my bilinguality and the tested strength of my Netherlands identity, which our Dutch liaison condoned in exchange for favours in another field. Head Office measured the risks and the alternatives, and finally said, 'Yes, but only for two days.' Perhaps they had concluded that, after Haydon, I hadn't that many secrets to give away anyway. Hastily I put together my cover and set off before they could change their minds again. It was six below as my plane touched down at Gdansk airport; thick snow was lying in the streets, more was falling and the quiet gave me a greater sense of safety than was prudent. But I was taking no risks, believe me. I might be looking for clarity, but I was nobody's innocent any more.

Gdansk hotels are of a uniform frightfulness and mine was no exception. The lobby stank like a disinfected urinal; checking-in was as complicated as adopting a baby and took longer. My room turned out to be someone else's and she spoke no known language. By the time I had found another room, and a maid to remove the grosser traces of its previous inhabitant, it was dusk and time for me to make my arrival known to Oskar.

Every joe has his handwriting. In summer, said the file, Oskar liked to fish, and my predecessor had held successful conversations with him along the river bank. They had even caught a couple of fish together, though the pollution had made them inedible. But this was deep-frozen winter, when only children and masochists fished. In winter Oskar's habits changed and he liked to play billiards at a club for small officials near the docks. And this club had a telephone. To initiate a meeting, my predecessor, who spoke Polish, had only to call him there and conduct a cheery conversation built round the fiction that he was an old naval friend named Lech. Then Oskar would say, 'All right, I'll meet you tomorrow at my sister's for a drink,' which meant 'Pick me up in your car on the corner of so-and-so street in one hour's time.'

But I spoke no Polish. And besides, the rules of post-Haydon tradecraft dictated that no agent should be reactivated by means of past procedures.

In his letter, Oskar had provided the telephone numbers of three cafés, and the times at which he would try to be available in each of them – three because there was always the likelihood that one of the phones would be out of order or occupied. If none of the phone calls worked, then we would resort to a car pick-up, and Oskar had told me which tram stop I should stand at, and at what time. He had provided the registration number of his new blue Trabant.

And if all of this seems to place me in a passive role, that is because the iron rule for such meetings is that the agent in the field is king, and it's the agent who decides what is the safest course for him, and the most natural to his lifestyle. What Oskar was suggesting was not what I would have suggested, nor did I understand why we had to speak on the telephone before we met. But perhaps Oskar understood. Perhaps he was afraid of a trap. Perhaps he wanted to sample the reassurance of my voice before he took the plunge.

Or perhaps there was some sidelight I had yet to learn of: he was bringing a friend with him; he wished to be evacuated at once; he had changed his mind. For there is a second rule of tradecraft as rigid as the first, which says that the outrageous is to be regarded at all times as the norm. The good case officer *expects* the entire Gdansk telephone system to fail the moment he begins his call. He *expects* the tram stop to be at the centre of a road works, or that Oskar will that morning have driven his car into a lamp-post or developed a temperature of a hundred and four, or that his wife will have persuaded him to demand a million dollars in gold before resuming contact with us, or that her baby will have decided to be premature. The whole art – as I told my students till they hated me for it – is to rely on Sod's Law and otherwise nothing.

It was with this maxim in mind that, having spent a fruitless hour telephoning the three cafés, I placed myself at the agreed tram stop at ten past nine that night, and waited for Oskar's Trabant to grope its way towards me down the street. For though the snow had by now ceased to fall, the street was still no more than a pair of black tracks at one side of the tramlines, and the few cars that passed had the wariness of survivors returning from the front.

There is old Danzig the stately Hanseatic port, and there is Gdansk the Polish industrial slum. The tram stop was in

Gdansk. To left and right of me as I waited, dour, low-lit concrete apartment houses hunched under the smouldering orange sky. Looking up and down the street, I saw not the smallest sign of human love or pleasure. Not a café, not a cinema, not a pretty light. Even the pair of drunks slumped in a doorway across the street seemed afraid to speak. One peak of laughter, one shout of goodfellowship or pleasure would have been a crime against the drabness of this outdoor prison. A car slipped by but it was not blue and it was not a Trabant. Its side windows were caked with snow, and even after it had passed I could not have told you how many people were inside. It stopped. Not at the side of the street, not on the pavement or in a turning or a layby, for mounds of snow blocked them all. It simply stopped in the twin black tracks of the road, and cut its engine, then its lights.

Lovers, I thought. If so, they were lovers blind to danger, for the road was two-way. A second car appeared, travelling in the same direction as the first. It too pulled up, but short of my tram stop. More lovers? Or merely a sensible driver allowing plenty of skidding distance between himself and the stationary car ahead of him? The effect was the same; there was one car to either side of me, and as I stood waiting, I saw that the two silent drunks were standing clear of their doorway and looking very sober. Then I heard the single footstep behind me, soft as a bedroom slipper in the snow, but close. And I knew that I must not make any sudden movement, certainly not a clever one. There was no springing free, there was no preemptive blow that would save me, because what I was beginning to fear in my imagination was either nothing or it was everything. And if it was everything, there was nothing I could do.

A man was standing to my left, close enough to touch me.

He wore a fur coat and a leather hat and carried a collapsed umbrella that could have been a lead pipe shoved into a nylon sheath. Very well, like myself he was waiting for the tram. A second man was standing to my right. He smelt of horse. And very well, like his companion and myself, he too was waiting for the tram, even if he had ridden here on horseback. Then a man's voice spoke to me in mournful Polish English, and it came neither from my left nor my right, but from directly behind me, where I had heard the slippered footstep.

'Oskar will not be coming tonight, I am afraid, sir. He has been dead for six months.'

But by then he had given me time to think. A whole age, in fact. I knew of no Oskar. Oskar who? Coming where? I was a Dutchman who spoke only a limited amount of English, with a thick Dutch accent like my uncles and aunts in Nijmegen. I paused while I let his words have their effect on me; then I turned – but slowly and incuriously.

'You are confusing me, sir, I think,' I protested, in the slow singsong voice I had learned at my mother's knee. 'My name is Franz Joost, from Holland, and I do not think that I am waiting for anyone except the tram.'

And that was when the men on either side of me grabbed hold of me like good professionals, pinning my arms and knocking me off balance at the same moment, then dragging and toppling me all the way to the second car. But not before I had time to recognise the squat man who had addressed me, his damp grey jowls and sodden night-clerk's eyes. It was our very own Colonel Jerzy, the much publicised hero of the Protection of the Polish People's Republic, whose expressionless photograph had graced the front pages of several illustrious

Polish newspapers around the time that he was gallantly arresting and torturing our agents.

There are deaths we unconsciously prepare for, depending on our choice of trades. An undertaker contemplates his funeral, the rich man his destitution, the gaoler his imprisonment, the debauchee his impotence. An actor's greatest terror, I am told, is to watch the theatre empty itself while he wrestles in a void for his lines, and what else is that but a premature vision of his dying? For the civil servant, it is the moment when his protective walls of privilege collapse around him and he finds himself no safer than the next man, exposed to the gaze of the overt world, answering like a lying husband for his laxities and evasions. And most of my intelligence colleagues, if I am honest, came into this category: their greatest fear was to wake up one morning to read their real names *en clair* in the newspapers; to hear themselves spoken of on the radio and television, joked and laughed about and, worse yet, questioned by the public they believed they served. They would have regarded such public scrutiny as a greater disaster than being outwitted by the opposition, or blown to every kindred service round the globe. It would have been their death.

And for myself, the worst death, and therefore the greatest test, the one for which I had prepared myself ever since I passed through the secret door, was the one that was upon me now: to have my uncertain courage tested on the rack; to be reduced mentally and physically to my last component of endurance, knowing I had within me the power to stop the dying with a word – that what was going on inside me was mortal combat between my spirit and my body, and that those who were applying the pain were merely the hired mercenaries in this secret war within myself.

So that from the first blinding explosion of pain, my response was recognition: Hullo, I thought, you've come at last – my name is Joost, what's yours?

There was no ceremony, you see. He didn't sit me at a desk in the tried tradition of the screen and say, 'Either talk to me or you'll be beaten. Here is your confession. Sign it.' He didn't have them lock me in a cell and leave me to cook for a few days while I decided that confession was the better part of courage. They simply dragged me out of the car and through the gateway of what could have been a private house, then into a courtyard where the only footprints were our own, so that they had to topple me through the thick snow, slewing me on my heels, all three of them, punching me from one to the other, now in the face, now in the groin and stomach, now back to the face again, this time with an elbow or a knee. Then, while I was still double, kicking me like a half-stunned pig across the slithery cobble as if they couldn't wait to get indoors before they had me.

Then, once indoors, they became more systematic, as if the elegance of the old bare room had instilled in them a sense of order. They took me in turns, like civilised men, two of them holding me and one hitting me, a proper democratic rota, except that when it was Colonel Jerzy's fifth or fiftieth turn, he hit me so regretfully and so hard that I actually did die for a while, and when I came round I was alone with him. He was seated at a folding desk, with his elbows on it, holding his unhappy head between his grazed hands as if he had a hangover, and reviewing with disappointment the answers I had given to the questions he had put to me between onslaughts, first lifting his head in order to study with disapproval my altered appearance, then shaking it painfully and sighing as if to say life really wasn't fair to him, he didn't know what more he could do to me to help me see the light. It dawned on me that more time had passed than I realised, perhaps several hours.

This was also the moment when the scene began to take on a resemblance to the one I had always imagined, with my tormentor sitting comfortably at a desk, brooding over me with a professional's concern, and myself spreadeagled against a scalding waterpipe, my arms handcuffed either side of a black concertina-style radiator, with corners that bit into the base of my spine like red-hot teeth. I had been bleeding from the mouth and nose and, I thought, from one ear as well, and my shirt front looked like a slaughterer's apron. But the blood had dried and I wasn't bleeding any more, which was another way of calculating the passage of time. How long does blood take to congeal in a big empty house in Gdansk when you are chained to a furnace and looking into the puppyish face of Colonel Jerzy?

It was terribly hard to hate him, and with the burning in my back it was becoming harder by the moment. He was my only saviour. His face stayed on me all the time now. Even when he turned his head downward to the table in private prayer, or got up and lit himself a filthy Polish cigarette and took a stretch around the room, his lugubrious gaze seemed to stay on me without reference to where the rest of him had gone. He turned his squat back to me. He gave me a view of his thick bald head and the pitted nape of his neck. Yet his eyes – treating with me, reasoning with me and sometimes, as it seemed, imploring me to ease his anguish – never left me for a second. And there was a part of me that really wanted to help him and it was becoming more and more strident with the burning. Because the burning was not a burning any more, it was pure pain, a pain indivisible and absolute, mounting like a scale that had no upper limit. So that I would have given almost anything to make him feel better – except myself. Except the part of me that made me separate from him, and was therefore my survival.

'What's your name?' he asked me, still in his Polish English.

'Joost.' He had to bend over me to hear me. 'Franz Joost.'

'From Munich,' he suggested, using my shoulder as a prop while he put his ear closer to my mouth.

'Born Nijmegen. Working for farmers in the Taunus, by Frankfurt.'

'You've forgotten your Dutch accent.' He shook me a little to wake me.

'You just don't hear it. You're a Pole. I want to see the Dutch Consul.'

'You mean British Consul.'

'Dutch.' And then I think I repeated the same word 'Dutch' several times, and went on repeating it till he threw cold water over me, then poured a little of it into my mouth to let me rinse and spit. I realised I was missing a tooth. Lower jaw, front left. Two teeth perhaps. It was hard to tell.

'Do you believe in God?' he asked me.

When he stared down at me like this, his cheeks fell forward like a baby's and his lips formed themselves in a kiss, so that he looked like a puzzled cherub.

'Not at the moment,' I said.

'Why not?'

'Get me the Dutch Consul. You've got the wrong man.'

I saw that he didn't like being told this. He wasn't used to being given orders or contradicted. He passed the back of his right hand across his lips, a thing he sometimes did before he hit me, and I waited for the blow. He began patting his pockets, I assumed for some instrument.

'No,' he remarked, with a sigh. 'You are mistaken. I have got the right man.'

He knelt to me and I thought he was preparing to kill me, because I had noticed that he was at his most murderous when he appeared most unhappy. But he was unlocking my handcuffs. When he had done so, he shoved his clenched fists under my armpits and hauled me – I almost thought helped me – to a spacious bathroom with an old, freestanding bath filled with warm water.

'Strip,' he said, and watched me dejectedly while I dragged off what remained of my clothes, too exhausted to care about what he would do to me once I was in the water: drown me, or cook me or freeze me, or drop in an electric wire.

He had my suitcase from the hotel. While I lay in the bath, he picked out clean clothes and tossed them on to a chair.

'You leave on tomorrow's plane for Frankfurt via Warsaw. There has been a mistake,' he said. 'We apologise. We shall cancel your business appointments and say you were the victim of a hit-and-run car.'

'I'll need more than an apology,' I said.

The bath was doing me no good. I was afraid that if I lay flat any longer, I would die again. I hauled myself into a crouch. Jerzy held out his forearm. I clutched it and stood upright, swaying dangerously. Jerzy helped me out of the bath, then handed me a towel and watched me gloomily while I dried myself and pulled on the clean clothes he had laid out for me.

He led me from the house and across the courtyard, carrying

my case in one hand and bearing my weight with the other, because the bath had weakened me as well as easing the pain. I peered round for the henchmen but saw none.

'The cold air will be good for you,' he said, with the confidence of an expert.

He led me to a parked car, and it did not resemble either of the cars that had taken part in my arrest. A toy steering wheel lay on the back seat. We drove down empty streets. Sometimes I dozed. We reached a pair of white iron gates guarded by militia.

'Don't look at them,' he ordered me, and showed them his papers while I dozed again.

We got out of the car and stood on a grass clifftop. An inshore wind froze our faces. Mine felt big as two footballs. My mouth had moved into my left cheek. One eye had closed. There was no moon and the sea was a growl behind the salt mist. The only light came from the city behind us. Occasionally phosphorous sparks slipped past us, or puffs of white spume spun away into the blackness. This is where I'm supposed to die, I thought as I stood beside him; first he beats me, then he gives me a warm bath, now he shoots me and shoves me over the cliff. But his hands were hanging glumly at his sides and there was no gun in them, and his eyes – what I could make out of them – were fixed on the starless darkness, not on me; so perhaps someone else was going to shoot me, someone already waiting in the dark. If I had had the energy, I could have killed Jerzy first. But I hadn't, and I didn't feel the need. I thought of Mabel, but without any sense of loss or gain. I wondered how she'd manage living on a pension, whom she'd find. *Fräulein Stefanie is not at home*, I remembered ... *Then perhaps it was Stefanie who answered*, Smiley was saying ... So many unanswered prayers, I was thinking. But so many never offered, either. I was feeling very drowsy.

At last Jerzy spoke, his voice no less despondent than before. 'I have brought you here because there isn't a microphone on earth can hear us. I wish to spy for your country. I need a good professional to act as intermediary. I have decided to choose you.'

Once more I lost my sense of time and place. But perhaps he had lost his too, for he had turned his back on the sea and, with his hand clutched to his leather hat to hold it against the wind, he had undertaken a mournful study of the inland lights, scowling at things that needed no scowling at, sometimes punching the wind-tears from his cheeks with his big fists.

'Why should anyone spy for Holland?' I asked him.

'Very well, I propose to spy for Holland,' he replied wearily, indulging a pedant. 'Therefore I need a good professional *Dutchman* who can keep his mouth shut. Knowing what fools you *Dutchmen* have employed against us in the past, I am understandably selective. However, you have passed the test. Congratulations. I select you.'

I thought it best to say nothing. Probably I didn't believe him.

'In the false compartment of your suitcase you will find a wad of Polish secret documents,' he continued, in a tone of dejection. 'At Gdansk airport you will have no Customs problems, naturally. I have given orders for them not to examine your luggage. For all they know, you are by now my agent. In Frankfurt, you are on home ground. I shall work to you and nobody else. Our next meeting will be in Berlin on May 5th. I shall be attending the May Day celebrations to mark the glorious victory of the proletariat.'

He was trying to light a fresh cigarette, but the wind kept putting out his matches. So he took his hat off and lit the cigarette inside the crown, lowering his fat face to it as if he were drinking water from a stream.

'Your people will wish to know my motive,' he continued when he had taken a deep draught of cigarette smoke. 'Tell them—' Suddenly at a loss, he sank his head into his shoulders and peered round at me as if pleading for advice on how to deal with idiots. 'Tell them I'm bored. Tell them I'm sick of the work. Tell them the Party's a bunch of crooks. They know that anyway, but tell them. I'm a Catholic. I'm a Jew. I'm a Tartar. Tell them whatever the hell they want to hear.'

'They may want to know why you have chosen to come to the *Dutch*,' I said. 'Rather than to the Americans, or the French or whoever.'

He thought about that too, puffing at his cigarette in the darkness. 'You Dutch had some good joes,' he said ruminatively. 'I got to know some of them pretty well. They did a good job till that bastard Haydon came along.' An idea occurred to him. 'Tell them my father was a Battle of Britain pilot,' he suggested. 'Got himself shot down over Kent. That should please them. You know Kent?'

'Why should a Dutchman know Kent?' I said.

If I had weakened, I could have told him that, before our so-called 'friendly' separation, Mabel and I had bought a house in Tunbridge Wells. But I didn't, which was as well, because when Head Office came to check the story out, there was no record of Jerzy's father having flown anything larger than a paper kite. And when I put this to Jerzy several years later – long after his loyalty to the perfidious British had been demonstrated beyond all doubt – he just laughed, and said his father was an old fool who cared for nothing but vodka and potatoes.

So why?

For five years Jerzy was my secret university of espionage, but his contempt for motive – his own particularly – never relaxed. First we idiots do what we want to do, he said; then we look round for justifications for having done it. All men were idiots to him, he told me, and we spies were the biggest idiots of all.

At first I suspected that he was spying for vengeance, and drew him out on the people above him in the hierarchy who might have slighted him. He hated them all, himself the most.

Then I decided he was spying for ideological reasons, and that his cynicism was a disguise for the finer yearnings he had discovered in his middle age. But when I attempted to use my wiles to break his cynicism down – 'Your family, Jerzy, your mother, Jerzy. Admit you're proud to have become a grandfather' – I found only more cynicism beneath. He felt nothing for any of them, he retorted, but so icily that I concluded that he did indeed, as he maintained, hate the entire human race, and that his savagery, and perhaps his betrayal too, were the simple expression of this hatred.

As to the West, it was run by the same idiots who ran everything in the world, so what's the difference? And when I told him this simply was not so, he became as defensive of his nihilist creed as any other zealot, and I had to rein myself in for fear of angering him seriously.

So why? Why risk his neck, his life, his livelihood and the family he hated, to do something for a world he despised?

The Church? I asked him that too, and significantly, as I think now, he bridled. Christ was a manic depressive, he retorted. Christ needed to commit suicide in public, so he provoked the authorities until they did him the favour. 'Those God-thumper guys are all the same,' he said with contempt. 'I've tortured them. I know.'

Like most cynics, he was a Puritan, and this paradox repeated itself in him in several ways. When we offered to drop money for him, open a Swiss bank account, the usual, he flew into a rage and declared he was not some 'cheap informant'. When I picked a moment – on the instruction of Head Office – to assure him that if ever things went wrong, we would spare no effort to get him out and provide him with a new identity in the West, his contempt was absolute: 'I'm a Polish creep, but I would rather face a firing squad of my fellow creeps than die a traitor in some capitalist pigsty.'

As to life's other comforts, we could offer him nothing he had not got. His wife was a scold, he said, and going home after a heavy day at the office bored him. His mistress was a young fool, and after an hour with her he preferred a game of billiards to her conversation.

Then why? I kept asking myself when I had exhausted my checklist of the Service's standard-issue motives.

Meanwhile, Jerzy continued to fill our coffers. He was turning his Service inside out as neatly as Haydon had ever done with ours. When Moscow Centre gave him orders, we knew of them before he passed them to his underlings. He photographed everything that came within his reach; he took risks I begged him not to take. He was so heedless that sometimes he left me wondering whether, like the Christ he was so determined to deny, he was looking for a public death. It was only the unflagging efficiency of what we were pleased to call his cover work that protected him from suspicion. For that was the dark side of his balancing act: God help the Western agent, real or imagined, who was invited to make his voluntary confession at Jerzy's hands.

Only once in the five years that I ran him did he seem to let slip the clue I was searching for. He was tired to death. He had been attending a conference of Warsaw Pact Intelligence chiefs in Bucharest, in the midst of fighting off charges of brutality and corruption against his Service at home. We met in West Berlin, in a *pension* on the Kurfürstendamm which catered to the better type of representative. He was a really tired torturer. He sat on my bed, smoking and answering my follow-up questions about his last batch of material. He was red-eyed. When we had finished, he asked for a whisky, then another.

'No danger is no life,' he said, tossing three more rolls of film on the counterpane. 'No danger is dead.' He took out a grimy brown handkerchief and carefully wiped his heavy face with it. 'No danger, you do better stay home, look after the baby.'

I preferred not to believe it was danger he was talking about. What he was talking about, I decided, was feeling, and his terror that by ceasing to feel he was ceasing to exist – which perhaps was why he was so devoted to instilling feeling in others. For that moment, I thought I caught a glimpse of why he was sitting with me in the room breaking every rule in his book. He was keeping his spirit alive at a time of his life when it was beginning to look like dying.

The same night I dined with Stefanie at an American restaurant ten minutes' walk from the *pension* where Jerzy and I had met. I had wangled her telephone number from a sister in

Munich. She was as tall and beautiful as I remembered her, and determined to convince me she was happy. Oh, life was *perfect*, Ned, she declared. She was living with this *terribly* distinguished academic, not in his first youth any more – but look here, nor are we – and completely adorable and wise. She told me his name. It meant nothing to me. She said she was pregnant by him. It didn't show.

'And *you*, Ned, how did it go for *you*?' she asked, as if we were two generals reporting to each other from successful, but separate, campaigns.

I gave her my most confident smile, the one that had earned me the trust of my joes and colleagues in the years since I had seen her.

'Oh, I think it worked out pretty well actually, thanks, yes,' I said, with seeming British understatement. 'After all, you can't expect one person to be everything you need, can you? It's a pretty good partnership, I'd say. Good parallel living.'

'And you still do that work?' she said. 'Ben's work?'

'Yes.'

It was the first time either of us had mentioned him. He was living in Ireland, she said. A cousin of his had bought a tumbledown estate in County Cork. Ben sort of caretook for him while he wasn't there, stocking the river and looking after the farm and so on.

I asked whether she ever saw him.

'No,' she said. 'He won't.'

I would have driven her home, but she preferred a cab. We waited in the street till it came, and it seemed to take a terribly long time. As I closed the door on her, her head tipped forward as if she had dropped something on the floor. I waved her out of sight but she didn't wave back.

*

The nine-o'clock news was showing us an outdoor meeting of Solidarity in Gdansk, where a Polish Cardinal was exhorting an enormous crowd to moderation. Losing interest, Mabel settled the *Daily Telegraph* on her lap and resumed her crossword. At first the crowd heard the Cardinal noisily. Then, with the devotion Poles are famous for, they fell silent. After his address, the Cardinal moved among his flock, bestowing blessings and accepting homage. And as one dignitary after another was brought to him, I picked out Jerzy hovering in the background, like the ugly boy excluded from the feast. He had lost a lot of weight since he had retired, and I guessed that the social changes had not been kind to him. His jacket hung on him like someone else's; his once-formidable fists were hardly visible inside the sleeves.

Suddenly the Cardinal has spotted him, just as I had.

The Cardinal freezes as if in doubt of his own feelings, and for a moment makes himself neater somehow, almost in obedience, pressing in his elbows and drawing back his shoulders to attention. Then slowly his arms lift again and he gives an order to one of his attendants, a young priest who seems reluctant to obey it. The Cardinal repeats the order, the priest clears a path to Jerzy; the two men face each other, the secret policeman and the Cardinal. Jerzy winces, as if he has digestion pains. The Cardinal leans forward and speaks in Jerzy's ear. Awkwardly, Jerzy kneels to receive the Cardinal's blessing.

And each time I replay this moment I see Jerzy's eyes close apparently in pain. But what is he repenting? His brutality? His loyalty to a vanished cause? Or his betrayal of it? Or is squeezing the eyes shut merely the instinctive response of a torturer receiving the forgiveness of a victim?

*

I fish. I drop into my little reveries. My love of English land-scape has, if possible, increased. I think of Stefanie and Bella, and my other half-had women. I lobby our Member of Parliament about the filthy river. He's a Conservative, but what on earth does he imagine he's conserving? I've joined one of the sounder environmentalist groups; I collect signatures on petitions. The petitions are ignored. I won't play golf, I never would. But I'll walk round with Mabel on a Wednesday afternoon, provided she's playing alone. I encourage her. The dog enjoys himself. Retirement is no time to be wandering lost, or puzzling how to reinvent mankind.

8

My students had decided to give Smiley a rough ride, just as they'd done to me from time to time. We'd be running along perfectly smoothly – a double session on natural cover, say, in the late afternoon – when one of them would start hectoring me, usually by adopting an anarchic stance which nobody in his right mind could sustain. Then a second would chime in, then all of them, so that if I didn't have any sense of humour shining-ready – and I'm only human – they'd be trampling me till the bell rang for close of play. And next day all would be forgotten: they'd have fed whatever little demon had got hold of them, and now they'd like to go back to learning, please, so where were we? At first I used to brood over these occasions, suspect conspiracy, hunt for ringleaders. Then cautiously I came to recognise them as spontaneous expressions of resistance to the unnatural harness that these children had chosen to put on.

But when they started in on Smiley, their guest of honour and mine, even questioning the entire purpose of his life's work, my tolerance ended with a snap. And this time the offender was not Maggs, either, but the demure Clare, his girlfriend, who had sat so adoringly opposite Smiley throughout dinner.

'No, no, Ned,' Smiley protested, as I leapt angrily to my

feet. 'Clare has a valid point. Nine times out of ten a good journalist *can* tell us quite as much about a situation as the spies can. Very often they're sharing the same sources anyway. So why not scrap the spies and subsidise the newspapers? It's a point that should be answered in these changeable times. Why not?'

Reluctantly I resumed my seat, while Clare, snuggling close against Maggs, continued to gaze angelically at her victim, while her colleagues smothered their grins.

But where I would have taken refuge in humour, Smiley elected to treat her sally seriously:

'It is perfectly true,' he agreed, 'that most of our work is either useless, or duplicated by overt sources. The trouble is, the spies aren't there to enlighten the public, but governments.'

And slowly I felt his spell reunite them. They had moved their chairs to him in a disordered half-circle. Some of the girls were sprawled becomingly on the floor.

'And governments, like anyone else, trust what they pay for, and are suspicious of what they don't,' he said. Thus delicately passing beyond Clare's provocative question, he addressed a larger one: 'Spying is eternal,' he announced simply. 'If governments *could* do without it, they never would. They adore it. If the day ever comes when there are no enemies left in the world, governments will invent them for us, so don't worry. Besides – who says we only spy on enemies? All history teaches us that today's allies are tomorrow's rivals. Fashion may dictate priorities, but foresight doesn't. For as long as rogues become leaders, we shall spy. For as long as there are bullies and liars and madmen in the world, we shall spy. For as long as nations compete, and politicians deceive, and tyrants launch conquests, and consumers need resources, and the homeless look for land, and the hungry for food, and the rich for excess, your chosen profession is perfectly secure, I can assure you.'

And with the topic thus neatly turned back to their own future, he once more warned them of its perils:

'There's no career on earth more cockeyed than the one you've picked,' he assured them, with every sign of satisfaction. 'You'll be at your most postable while you're least experienced, and by the time you've learned the ropes, no one will be able to send you anywhere without a trade description round your necks. Old athletes know they've played their best games when they were in their prime. But spies in their prime are on the shelf, which is why they take so ungraciously to middle age, and start counting the cost of living how they've lived.'

Though his hooded gaze to all appearance remained fixed upon his brandy, I saw him cast a sideways glance at me. 'And then, at a certain age, you want the answer,' he continued. 'You want the rolled-up parchment in the inmost room that tells you who runs your lives and why. The trouble is that by then you're the very people who know best that the inmost room is bare. Ned, you're not drinking. You're a brandy traitor. Fill him up, someone.'

It is an uncomfortable truth of the period of my life that follows that I recall it as a single search, the object of which was unclear to me. And that the object, when I found him, turned out to be the lapsed spy Hansen.

And that, although in reality I was pursuing quite other goals and people among my eastward journey, all of them in retrospect seem to have been stages on my journey to him. I can put it no other way. Hansen in his Cambodian jungle

was my Kurtz at the heart of darkness. And everything that
happened to me on the way was a preparation for our meeting. Hansen's was the voice I was waiting to hear. Hansen
held the answer to the questions I did not know I was asking.
Outwardly, I was my stolid, moderate, pipesmoking, decent
self, a shoulder for weaker souls to rest their heads on. Inside,
I felt a rampant incomprehension of my uselessness; a sense
that, for all my striving, I had failed to come to grips with life;
that in struggling to give freedom to others, I had found none
for myself. At my lowest ebb, I saw myself as ridiculous, a
hero in the style not of Buchan but of Quixote.

I took to writing down sardonic versions of my life, so that
when, for instance, I reviewed the episodes I have described
to you this far, I gave them picaresque titles that emphasised
their futility: the Panda – I safeguard our Middle Eastern
interests! Ben – I run to earth a British defector! Bella – I make
the ultimate sacrifice! Teodor – I take part in a grand deception! Jerzy – I play the game to the end! Though with Jerzy, I
had to admit, a positive purpose had been served, even if it
was as shortlived as most intelligence, and as irrelevant to the
human forces that have now engulfed his nation.

Like Quixote, I had set out in life vowing to check the flow
of evil. Yet in my lowest moments I was beginning to wonder whether I had become a contributor to it. But I still
looked to the world to provide me with the chance to make
my contribution – and I blamed it for not knowing how to
use me.

To understand this, you should know what had happened
to me after Munich. Jerzy, whatever else he did to me, brought
me a sort of prestige, and the Fifth Floor decided to invent a
job for me as roving operational fixer, sent out on short
assignments 'to appraise, and where possible exploit oppor--

tunities outside the remit of the local station' – thus my brief, signed and returned to maker.

Looking back, I realise that the constant travel this entailed – Central America one week, Northern Ireland the next, Africa, the Middle East, Africa again – soothed the restlessness that was stalking me, and that Personnel in all likelihood knew this, for I had recently embarked on a senseless love affair with a girl called Monica, who worked in the Service's Industrial Liaison Section. I had decided I needed an affair; I saw her in the canteen and cast her in the part. It was as banal as that. One night it was raining, and as I started to drive home, I saw her standing at a number 23 bus stop. Banality made flesh. I took her to her flat, I took her to her bed, I took her to dinner and we tried to work out what we had done, and came up with the convenient solution that we had fallen in love. It served us well for several months, until tragedy abruptly called me to my senses. By a mercy, I was back in London briefing myself for my next mission when word came that my mother was failing. By an act of divine ill taste, I was in bed with Monica when I took the call. But at least I was able to be present for the event, which was lengthy, but unexpectedly serene.

Nevertheless, I found myself entirely unprepared for it. Somehow I had taken for granted that, in the same way that I had managed to negotiate myself round awkward hurdles in the past, I would do the same in the case of my mother's death. I could not have been more mistaken. Very few conspiracies, Smiley once remarked, survive contact with reality. And so it was with the conspiracy that I had made with myself to let my mother's death slip past me as a timely and necessary release from pain. I had not taken into my calculations that the pain could be my own.

I was orphaned and elated both at once. I can describe it no other way. My father had long been dead. Without my realising it, my mother had done duty for both parents. In her death I saw the loss, not only of my childhood, but of most of my adulthood as well. At last I stood unencumbered before life's challenges, yet many of them were already behind me – fudged, missed or botched. I was free to love at last, but whom? Not, I am afraid, Monica, however much I might protest the contrary and expect the reality to follow. Neither Monica nor my marriage offered me the magic it was henceforth my duty as a survivor to pursue. And when I looked at myself in the mirror of the undertaker's rose-tinted lavatory after my night's vigil, I was horrified by what I saw. It was the face of a spy branded by his own deception.

Have you seen it too, around you? On you? That face? In my case it was so much my everyday companion that I had ceased to notice it until the shock of death brought it home to me. We smile, but our withholding makes our smile false. When we are exhilarated, or drunk – or even, as I am told, make love – the reserve does not dissolve, the gyroscope stays vertical, the monitory voice reminds us of our calling. Until gradually our very withholding becomes so strident it is almost a security risk by itself. So that today – if I go to a reunion, say, or we have a Sarratt old-boys' night – I can actually look round the room and see how the secret stain has come out in every one of us. I see the overbright face or the underlit one, but inside each I see the remnants of a life withheld. I hear the hoot of supposedly abandoned laughter and I don't have to mark down the source of it to know that nothing has been abandoned – not its owner, nor its interior restrictions, nothing. In my younger days, I used to think it was just the inhibited British ruling classes who became that person. 'They were born into captivity and had no option from then on,' I would tell myself as I listened to their unconvincing courtesies, and returned their good-chap smiles. But, as only half a Briton, I had exempted myself from their misfortune – until that day in the undertaker's pink-tiled lavatory when I saw that the same shadow that falls across us all had fallen across me.

From that day on, I now believe, I saw only the horizon. I am starting so late! I thought. And from so far back! Life was to be a search, or nothing! But it was the fear that it was nothing that drove me forward. That's how I see it now. And so, please, must you see it, in the fragmented recollections that belong to this surreal passage of my life. In the eyes of the man I had become, every encounter was an encounter with myself. Every stranger's confession was my own, and Hansen's the most accusing – and therefore, ultimately, the most consoling. I buried my mother, I said goodbye to Monica and Mabel. The next day I departed for Beirut. Yet even that simple departure was attended by a disconcerting episode.

To brief myself for my mission, I had been sharing a room with a rather clever man called Giles Latimer, who had made a corner for himself in what was known as 'the Mad Mullah department', studying the intricate and seemingly indecipherable web of Muslim fundamentalist groups operating out of Lebanon. The notion so beloved of the amateur terror industry that these bodies are all part of a super plot is nonsense. If only it were so – for then there might be some way to get at them! As it is, they slip about, grouping and regrouping like drops of water on a wet wall, and they are about as easy to pin down.

But Giles, who was an Arabist and a distinguished bridge

player, had come as near to achieving the impossible as anyone was likely to, and my job was to sit at his feet in order to prepare myself for my mission. He was tall, angular and woolly. He was of my intake. His boyish manner was given extra youthfulness by the redness of his cheeks, though this was actually the consequence of clusters of tiny broken blood vessels. He was indefatigably, painfully gentlemanly, forever opening doors and leaping to his feet for women. In the spring weather I twice saw him get drenched to the skin on account of his habit of lending his umbrella to whoever was proposing to venture out of doors without one. He was rich but frugal, and a thoroughly good man, with a thoroughly good wife, who organised Service bridge drives and remembered the names of the junior staff and their families. Which made it all the more bizarre when his files started disappearing.

It was I, inadvertently, who first noticed the phenomenon. I was tracking a German girl called Britta on her odyssey through the terrorist training camps in the Shuf Mountains, and I requested a contingent file which contained sensitive intercept material about her. The material was American and limited by a subscription list, but when I had gone through the rigmarole of signing myself in, nobody could find it. Nominally it was marked to Giles, but so was almost everything, because Giles was Giles and his name was on every list around.

But Giles knew nothing of it. He remembered reading it, he could quote from it; he thought he had passed it on to me. It must have gone to the Fifth Floor, he said, or back to Registry. Or somewhere.

So the file was posted missing and the Registry bloodhounds were informed, and everything ran along normally for a couple of days until the same thing happened again, though this time it was Giles's own secretary who started the hunt when Registry called in all three volumes on a misty group called the Brothers of the Prophet, supposedly based in Damour.

Once again, Giles knew nothing: he had neither seen nor touched them. The Registry bloodhounds showed him his signature on the receipt. He flatly disowned it. And when Giles denied something, you didn't feel like challenging him. As I say, he was a man of transparent rectitude.

By now, the hunt was up in earnest and inventories were being taken left and right. Registry was in its last days before computerisation, and could still find what it was looking for, or know for sure that it was lost. Today somebody would shake his head and phone for an engineer.

· What Registry discovered was that thirty-two files marked out to Giles were missing. Twenty-one of them were standard top secret, five had higher gradings, and six were of a category called RETAIN, which meant, I am afraid, that nobody of strong pro-Jewish sentiments should be admitted as a signatory. Parse that how you will. It was a squalid limitation and there were few of us who were not embarrassed by it. But this was the Middle East.

My first intimation of the scale of the crisis came from Personnel. It was a Friday morning. Personnel always liked the shelter of the weekend when he was about to wield his axe.

'Has Giles been *well* lately, Ned?' he asked me, with old-boy intimacy.

'Perfectly,' I said.

'He's a Christian, isn't he? Christian sort of chap. Pious.'

'I believe so.'

'Well, I mean we all are in a way, but he is a *heavy* sort of Christian, would you say, Ned? What's your opinion?'

'We've never discussed it.'

'Are you?'

'No.'

'Would you say, for example, he could be sympathetic to something like – say – the British-Israelite sect, or one of those sort of things, at all? Nothing against them, mind. Every man to his convictions, me.'

'Giles is very orthodox, very down the middle, I am sure. He's some sort of lay dignitary at his parish church. I believe he gives the odd Lenten Address, and that's about it.'

'That's what I've got down here,' Personnel complained, tapping his knuckles on a closed file. 'That's the picture I've got of him exactly, Ned. So what's up? Not always easy, my job, you know. Not always pleasant at all.'

'Why don't you ask him yourself?'

'Oh I know, I know, I must. Unless you would, of course. You could take him out to lunch – my expense, obviously. Feel his bones. Tell me what you think.'

'No,' I said.

His old-boy manner gave way to something a lot harder. 'I thought you'd say that. I worry about you sometimes, Ned. You're putting yourself about with the women and you're a touch stubborn for your health. It's the Dutch blood in you. Well, keep your mouth shut. That's an order.'

In the end it was Giles who took me out to lunch. Probably Personnel had played the game both ways, pitching some tale to Giles in reverse. Whether he had or not, at twelve-thirty Giles sprang suddenly to his feet and said, 'To hell with it, Ned. It's Friday. Come on, I'll give you lunch. Haven't had a pissy lunch for years.'

So we went to the Travellers', and sat at a table by the window and we drank a bottle of Sancerre very fast. And suddenly

Giles began talking about a liaison trip he'd made recently to the FBI in New York. He kicked off quite normally; then his voice seemed to get stuck on one note, and his eyes got fixed on something only he could see. I put it down to the wine at first. Giles didn't look like a drinker and didn't drink like one. Yet there was great conviction in the way he spoke and – as he continued – a visionary intensity.

'Peculiar chaps actually, the Americans, Ned, you want to watch out for them. One doesn't think they're after one at first. One's hotel, for instance. You can always read the clues in a hotel. Too much smiling when you sign in. Too much interest in your luggage. They're watching you. Damned great highrise greenhouse. Swimming pool on the top floor. You can look down on the helicopters going up the river. "Welcome, Mr Lambert, and have a nice day, sir." I was using Lambert. I always do for America. The fourteenth floor they'd put me on. I'm a methodical chap. Always have been. Shoe-trees and that kind of thing. Can't help it. My father was the same. Shoes here, shirts there. Socks there. Suits in a certain order. We never have lightweight suits, do we, the English? You think they're lightweight. You choose lightweight. Your tailor tells you they're lightweight. "Lightest we've got, sir. We don't go any lighter." You'd think they'd have learned by now, the amount of American business they do. But they haven't. Cheers.'

He drank and I drank with him. I poured him some mineral water. He was sweating.

'Next day I come back to the hotel. Meetings all day long. Lot of trying to like each other. And I do, I mean they're nice chaps. Just – well, different. Different attitudes. Carry guns. Want results. There can't be any, though, can there? We all know that. The more fanatics you kill, the more there are of

them. I know that, they don't. My father was an Arabist too,
you know.'

I said I didn't. I said, 'Tell me about him.' I wanted to
deflect him. I felt I would feel much better if he talked about
his father instead of the hotel.

'So I walk in and they hand me the key. "Hey, hang on," I
say. "This isn't floor fourteen. This is floor twenty-one. Mistake." I smile, naturally. Anyone can make a mistake. It's a
woman this time. Very strong-looking woman. "It is not a
mistake, Mr Lambert. You're on the twenty-first floor. Your
room is 2109." "No, no," I say. "It's 1409. Look here." I had this
identity card they give you somewhere and I looked for it.
Turned out my pockets while she watched, but couldn't find
it. "Look," I said. "Believe me. I have that kind of memory.
My room is 1409." She gets out the guest list, shows it to me.
Lambert, 2109. I go up in the lift, unlock the room, it's all
there. Shoes here. Shirts there. Socks there. Suits in the same
order. Everything where I'd put it in the other room, down
on the fourteenth floor. Know what they'd done?'

Again I said I didn't.

'Photographed it. Polaroid.'

'Why would they do that?'

'They wanted to mike me – 2109 was miked, 1409 was
clean. No good to them, so they moved me up. They thought
I was an Arab spy.'

'Why would they think that?'

'Because of my father. He was a Lawrence man. They
knew that. They'd decided. That's what they do. Photograph
your room.'

I scarcely remember the rest of lunch. I don't remember
what we ate or what else we drank or anything at all. I have a
recollection of Giles extolling Mabel at great length as the

perfect Service wife, but perhaps that was my conscience. All I really remember is the two of us side by side in Giles's room back at Head Office, and Personnel standing in front of Giles's steel cupboard with the door removed, and the thirty-two missing files crammed higgledy-piggledy into the shelves – all the files Giles hadn't been able to cope with while he was having what Smiley called his 'Force Twelve nervous breakdown' in place.

And the reason for it, as I learned later? Giles too had found his Monica. What had unhinged him, ostensibly, was his passion for a twenty-year-old girl in his village. His love for her, his guilt and despair had dictated that he could no longer function. He had continued going through the day's motions – naturally, he was a soldier – but his mind wouldn't play any more. It had acquired its own preoccupations, even if he wouldn't own to them.

What else had unhinged him, I leave that to you, and to our in-house shrinks who seem to be daily gaining ground. Something to do, perhaps, with the gap between our dreams and our realities. Something to do with the gap between what Giles longed for when he was young, and what he'd got now that he was nearly old. And the hard truth was, Giles had frightened me. I felt he had gone ahead of me down the road I myself was treading. I felt it as I drove to the airport; I felt it on the plane while I thought about my mother. And downed several in-flight whiskies in order not to feel it more.

I was still feeling it as I set out my own meagre wardrobe in Room 607 at the Commodore Hotel, Beirut, and the telephone began ringing a few inches from my head. As I picked up the receiver, I had a wayward fancy I was going to hear Ahmed at the front desk telling me I had been allocated a new room on floor twenty-one. I was wrong. Surreal episode number two had just announced itself.

Shooting had started, semi-automatic on the move. Most likely a bunch of kids in a Japanese pick-up hosing down the neighbourhood with AK 47s. It was one of those seasons in Beirut when you could set your watch by the first excitements of the evening. But I had never minded too much about the shooting. Shooting has a logic, if a haphazard one. It's directed at you, or away from you. My personal phobia was car bombs – never knowing, as you hurried along a pavement or dawdled in the sweating, crawling traffic, whether a parked car was going to take out the entire block with one huge heave, and leave you in such tiny shreds that there was nothing worth a body bag, let alone a burial. The thing you noticed about car bombs – I mean afterwards – was shoes. People blown clean out of them, but the shoes intact. So that even after the bits of body had been picked out and taken away, there was still the odd pair or two of wearable shoes among the broken glass and smashed false teeth and shreds of someone's suit. A little machine-gun fire, like now, or the odd hand-held rocket, didn't trouble me as much as it did some people.

I lifted the receiver and when I heard a woman's voice I quickened, not only because of my domestic ambiguities but because my errand was to trace a German woman – the same Britta who had been taking lessons in terror in the Shuf Mountains.

But it was not Britta. It was not Monica and not Mabel. The voice was middle-American and scared. And I was Peter, remember – Peter Carter, from a great British newspaper, even if its local correspondent had never heard of me. I was reminding myself of this as I listened to her.

'Peter, for Christ's sake, I need to be with you,' she said in a single rush of breath. 'Peter, where the fuck have you been?'

A rattle of heavy machine-gun fire broke out, to be promptly silenced by the smack of a rocket-propelled grenade. The voice on the phone resumed in greater agitation.

'Jesus, Peter, why don't you call me? Okay, I said some shitty things. I spoilt your copy. I'm sorry. I mean, Jesus, what are we? Children? You know how I hate this stuff.'

A frenzy of rifle fire. Sometimes the kids just shot into the sky for effect.

Her voice rose steeply. 'Talk to me, Peter! Tell me something funny, will you, please? Something funny must be happening *somewhere* in the world! Peter, will you please answer me? You're not dead are you? You're not lying on the floor with your head blown off? Just nod for no. I don't want to die alone, Peter. I'm sociable. I love sociably, I die sociably. Peter, answer me. Please.'

'What room are you calling?' I said.

Dead silence. The really dead silence that gathers between bursts of gunfire.

'Who is this?' she demanded.

'This is Peter, but I don't think I'm your Peter. What room are you calling?'

'This room.'

'What number?'

'Room 607.'

'I'm afraid he must have checked out. I arrived in Beirut this afternoon. This is the room they gave me.'

A grenade exploded, answered by another. Out in the street, perhaps three blocks away, somebody screamed seriously. The scream ended.

'Is he dead?' she whispered.

I didn't answer.

'Could have been a woman,' she said.

'Could have been,' I agreed.

'Who are you? You British?'

'Yes.' Peter is too, I thought, without knowing why.

'What do you do?'

'For a living?'

'Just talk to me. Keep talking.'

'I'm a journalist,' I said.

'Like Peter?'

'I don't know what kind of journalist he is.'

'He's tough. The danger school. Are you tough?'

'Some things scare me, some don't.'

'Mice?'

'Mice scare me stiff.'

'Are you good?'

'As good as the news, I suppose. I don't write much any more. I'm editorial these days.'

'Married?'

'Are you?'

'Yes.'

'To Peter?'

'No, not Peter.'

'How long have you known him?'

'My husband?'

'No. Peter,' I said. I did not ask myself why I was more interested in her adultery than her marriage.

'You don't time things like that out here,' she said. 'A year, a couple of years – you don't talk that way. Not in Beirut. You're married too, aren't you? You didn't want to tell me till I told you first.'

'Yes, I am.'

'So tell me about her.'

'My wife?'

'Sure. Do you love her? Is she tall? Great skin? Very British, stiff upper lip?'

I told her some harmless things about Mabel and invented some others, hating myself.

'I mean, who on earth can believe in sex after fifteen years of the same person?' she said.

I laughed but didn't answer.

'Are you faithful to her, Peter?'

'Infallibly,' I said, after a delay.

'Okay, let's do work. Go back to work. What are you doing out here? Something special? Tell me what you're doing.'

The spy in me dodged the question: 'I think it's time you told me what *you* do,' I said. 'Are you a journalist too?'

A stream of tracer tore into the sky. The firing followed.

Her voice turned weary, as if the fear had worn her out. 'I file copy, sure.'

'Who for?'

'A lousy wire service, what else? Fifty cents a line, till some big prick steals it and makes two grand in an afternoon. What's new?'

'What's your name?' I asked.

'I don't know. Maybe Annie. Call me Annie. Listen, you're real nice, know that? What do you do if a Doberman humps your leg?'

'Bark?'

'Fake an orgasm. I'm scared, Peter. Maybe I didn't make that clear. I need a drink.'

'Where are you?'

'Right here.'

'Where's here?'

'In the hotel, for Christ's sake. The Commodore. Standing in the lobby, smelling Ahmed's garlic and getting eyeballed by the Greek.'

'Who's the Greek?'

'Stavros. He pushes hard drugs and swears up and down they're soft. He's serious sleaze.'

I listened, and for the first time made out the babble of voices in the background. The shooting was over.

'Peter?'

'Yes.'

'Peter, put that light out.'

She must have known there was only one light working in the room, a rickety bedside light with a tilted parchment shade. It lay on a locker between the two divans. I turned it off. There were stars again.

'Unlock your door and leave it ajar. One inch. Got booze?'

'A bottle of Scotch,' I said.

'Vodka?'

'No.'

'Ice?'

'No.'

'I'll bring some. Peter?'

'Yes?'

'You're a good man. Anybody ever told you that?'

'Not for a long time.'

'Watch this space,' she said, and rang off.

She never came to me.

You may imagine it any way you like, as I did, all ways, while I sat on the divan, watching the door in the darkness and watching my life go by while I waited to hear her tread in the corridor.

After an hour I went downstairs. I sat in the bar and listened to every female American voice I could find. None fitted. I looked for someone who might call herself Annie and proposition a man she had only talked to on the telephone. I bribed Ahmed to tell me who had used the house phone from the lobby at nine o'clock that night, but his memory, for whatever reason, did not stretch to an emotional American woman.

I went so far as to try to establish the identity of the previous occupant of my room, and whether his first name was Peter, but Ahmed became mysteriously vague and said he had been in Tripoli visiting his old mother, and the hotel kept no lists.

Did the real Peter return in the nick of time and sweep her off? Did Stavros the Greek? Was she a whore? Was I? Was Ahmed pimping her? Was the phone call some kind of elaborate trick she played on newcomers to the hotel, to hook them on their first nervous night alone?

Or was she, as I prefer to think, simply a frightened woman missing her boyfriend and craving a body to hold on to when the nightly thunder of the city started driving her mad?

Whatever mystery she presented, I had learned something about myself even if it disconcerted me. I had learned how perilous was my solitude, how available I was, how much I needed to give love and receive it; and how fickle in me was that virtue which the Service called 'personal security', compared with my growing hunger for connection. I thought of Monica and my hollow protestations of love which so failed to move the gods they were addressed to. I thought of Giles Latimer and his hopeless passion. And somehow the woman who called herself Annie seemed to belong to the same line of anguished messengers, all speaking from inside myself.

After the faceless girl came the faceless boy. That happened the next evening.

Exhausted, I had settled myself in the hotel lobby and I was drinking my Scotch alone. I had been visiting the camps round Sidon and my hand was still shaking from just another day in southern Lebanon. Now it was the magic hour of dusk, when Beirut's human animal kingdom agreed to put aside its feuds and assemble at the common watering hole. I have seen the same thing happen in the jungle. Perhaps you have too. At a single command, elephants, wart-hogs, gazelles, lions and giraffes tiptoe from the protective darkness of the trees and, mostly in silence, arrange themselves on the muddy flats. You could observe the Commodore lobby at the same hour, when the journalists came back from their day's excursions. As the electric glass doors, always a little too slow on their feet, sighed and grunted from their exertions, so the dark of the early Beirut night disgorged its motley: a Swedish television unit, fronted by a grey-faced blonde in designer denims; a photographer and correspondent from an American weekly; the wire men always in pairs; an elderly and utterly mysterious East German with his Japanese mistress. All had the same self-consciously undramatic way of entering, and pausing, and setting down the day's burden.

Not that their day was over. For the real journalists, there were films to be despatched, stories to be written and telexed and telephoned. Someone was missing and must be accounted for. So-and-so had taken a bad bullet, did his wife know? Nevertheless, with the closing of the glass doors behind them, their day was won back from the enemy. The hack-pack was battening down the hatches for the night.

And as I watched, I waited – to meet a man who knew a

man who knew another man who just might know the woman I had been sent to find. My day till then had yielded nothing, except another tour of the wretched of the earth.

Elsewhere in the lobby, other species were gathering, less glamorous but frequently more interesting to the observer: carpetbaggers and arms dealers and drug dealers and dark-suited minor diplomats, the pedlars in influence and information, switching at their worry-beads as their restless eyes darted from face to face about the room. And the spies – everyone's spies – trading openly, because in Beirut their trade was everyone's. There was not a man or woman in the place who had not got his source of inside information, if it was only Ahmed behind the counter, who for a few dollars and a smile would tell you the secrets of the universe.

But the figure who had caught my eye was exotic even by the standards of the Commodore's menagerie. I did not see him enter. He must have come in behind a group. I saw him inside the lobby, framed against the darkness of the glass doors, dressed in a striped football shirt and a clean white nurse's scarf tied lightly round his head. If he had not been slender and flat-chested, I would not have been certain, at first sight, whether he was a woman pretending to be a man, or a man pretending to be a woman.

The security man had noticed him too. So had Ahmed the concierge behind his formidable counter. His two Kalashnikovs were propped against the wall behind him, just below the pigeon-holes where the room keys hung, and I saw Ahmed ease a half-step backward so that he had one within reach. A small hand-grenade in that lobby at that hour could have wiped out half the better rackets in the city.

But the apparition kept moving forward, either unaware or unheeding of the curiosity he was arousing. He was tall and young and agile, but rigid. He was like a person without will, summoned forward by his controller's voice. I saw him better now. He had dark glasses, black stubble and moustache. That was why his face had seemed so black. And the white nurse's scarf over his head. But it was the automaton's stiffness of his walk that set my skin tingling and made me wonder what kind of believer we might have on our hands.

He had reached the centre of the lobby. A few people made way for him. Some looked at him and looked away, others turned their backs in abstention, as if they knew and did not like him. Suddenly, under the brightness of the centre light, he seemed to be ascending. With his shrouded head forward and his arms barely moving, he was mounting his own scaffold on orders from above. I saw now that he was American. I saw it in the dipping knees and hanging wrists and slightly girlish hips. An all-American boy. His dark glasses were not dark enough, apparently, for a cloth eyeshade dangled from one long hand. It was of the kind that gamblers are supposed to wear, and night editors in forties films. He was six feet tall, at least. He wore sneakers, vestal white like his headscarf, and soundless.

An Arab freak? I wondered.

A crazed Zionist? There had been a few of those.

Stoned?

A high-school war tourist on the hippy trail, searching for kicks in the city of the damned?

Changing direction, he had begun talking to the receptionist, but at an angle facing into the lobby, already searching for the person he was enquiring for. Which was when I saw the red spots scattered over his cheeks and forehead, like hives or chicken pox, but more vivid. The bedbugs had eaten him in some stinking hostel, I decided. He had stuck his head through the windscreen of a clapped-out car. He started walking towards me. Stiffly again, without expression. Purposefully, a man used to being looked at. Angrily, the eyeshade dangling from his hand. Glowering at me blindly through his black glasses as I sat drinking. A woman had taken his arm. She wore a skirt and could have been the nurse who had given him his headscarf. They stood before me. Me and no one else.

'Sir? This is Sol, sir,' she said – or Mort, or Syd, or whatever. 'He's asking whether you're the journalist, sir.'

I said I was a journalist.

'From London, sir, visiting? Are you the editor, sir? Are you influential, sir?'

Influential I doubted, I said with a deprecating smile. I was on the managerial side, here on a brief swing.

'And going back to London, sir? Soon?'

In Beirut you learn not to talk in advance about your movements. 'Pretty soon,' I conceded, though the truth was I was planning to return south again next day.

'Can Sol speak with you a moment, sir, just speak? Sol needs very much to speak with a person who has influence with the major Western newspapers. The journalists here, he feels they've seen it all, they're jaded. Sol needs a voice from outside.'

I made space and she sat beside me while Sol very slowly lowered himself into a chair – this covered, silent, very clean man in his long football sleeves and headscarf. Seated finally, he laid his wrists over his knees, holding the eyeshade in both hands. Then he gave a long sigh and began to murmur to me.

'There's this thing I've written, sir. I'd like, please, to have it printed in your newspaper.'

His voice, though soft, was educated and polite. But it was lifeless and, like his movements, economical, as if each word hurt him to produce. Inside the lenses of his very dark glasses, I saw that his left eye was smaller than his right. Narrower. Not swollen, not closed by a punch, just altogether smaller than its partner, taken from a different face. And the spots were not bites, not hives, not cuts. They were craters, like the pock-marks of small-arms fire on a Beirut wall, stamped with heat and speed. Like craters also, the skin around them had risen but not closed.

His story followed without my asking for it. He was a relief volunteer, sir, a third-year medical student from Omaha. He believed in peace, sir. And he had been in this bombing, sir, down by the Corniche, in this restaurant that had been one of the worst-hit places, just wiped out, you should go down there and take a look, a place called Akhbar's, sir, where a lot of Americans went, there was this car bomb and car bombs are the worst. You can't get worse than car bombs for surprise.

I said I knew that.

Almost everyone in the restaurant had died except himself, sir, the people nearest the wall just blew apart, he continued, unaware that he had painted my own worst nightmare for me. And now he had this thing he had written, he felt he had to say it, sir, a sort of mild statement about peace, which he needed to print in my newspaper, maybe it would do some good, he was thinking of like this weekend or maybe Monday. He'd like to donate the fee to charity. He guessed it could be like a couple of hundred dollars, maybe more. In the Beirut hospitals, that still bought people a piece of hope.

'We need a pause, sir,' he explained, in his dead voice as the woman fished a wad of typescript from his pocket for him. 'A pause for moderation. Just a break between wars to find the middle way.'

Only in the Commodore in Beirut could it have seemed natural that a bomb-shocked peace-seeker should be pleading a hopeless cause to a journalist who wasn't one. Nevertheless I promised to do what I could. When I had done my business with the man I was waiting for – who knew nothing, of course, had heard nothing, but perhaps, sir, if I spoke to Colonel Asme in Tyre? – I settled in my room and with a glass at my elbow began to read his offering, determined that, if it had any reasonable chance of publication, I would twist the arm of one of our numberless Fleet Street friendlies when I returned to London, and see it done.

It was a tragic piece, and quickly it became unreadable: a rambling, emotional appeal to Jews, Christians and Muslims alike to remember their own mothers and children, and live together in love. It urged the middle ground of compromise and gave inaccurate examples from history. It proposed a new religion 'like Joan of Arc would have given us only the English wouldn't let her, so they burned her alive, disregarding her screams and the will of the ordinary people.' This great new movement, he said, would 'bind the Semitic races in a spiritual brotherhood of love and tolerance'. Then it lost its way completely, and resorted to capital letters, underlining, and rows of exclamation marks. So that by the time I reached the end, it had ceased to be what it set out to be at all, and was talking about 'this whole family, kids and grandparents, that was sitting up beside the wall nearest to the epicentre'. And how they had all been blown to pieces, not once, but over and over again, each time Sol allowed himself to look into his anguished memory.

Suddenly I was writing the piece for him. To her. To Annie. First in my mind, then in the margin of his pages, then on a fresh sheet of A4 paper from my briefcase, which was quickly covered so I took another. I was sweating, the sweat was pouring off me like rain; it was that kind of Beirut night, quiet till now but with a damp, itchy heat rolling off the mountains and an evil grey smog like gunsmoke draping itself across the sea. I was writing, and wondering if she would ring again. I was writing as the bombed boy, to a girl I didn't know. I was writing – as I saw to my dismay when I awoke next morning – pretentious junk. I was proclaiming maverick affections, mouthing great sentiments, pontificating about the unbreakable cycle of human evil, about man's endless search for reasons to do the wrong thing.

A pause, the boy had said. A pause for moderation, a break between wars. I put him right on that. I put Annie right on it too. I told them that the only pauses in the history of human conflict had been pauses not for moderation but excess, pauses for the world to redivide itself, for the thugs and the victims to find each other, for greed and deprival to regroup. I wrote like an adolescent bleeding heart, and when the morning came and I saw the pages of my handwriting strewn over the floor around the empty whisky bottle, I could not believe this was the work of anyone I knew.

So I did the only thing I could think of. I put them in the handbasin and cremated them, then broke up the ash and scattered it in the lavatory and flushed it into the body-blocked sewers of Beirut. And when I had done that, I took myself for a punishing pelt along the waterfront, running as hard as I could go from whatever was coming after me.

I was running towards Hansen, away from myself, but I had one more stop to make along the way.

My German girl, Britta, turned out to be in Israel, in the middle of the Negev Desert, in a compound of stark grey huts near a village called Revivim. The huts had a ploughed strip round them, and a double perimeter of barbed-wire fencing with a manned watchtower at each corner. If there were other European prisoners in the compound apart from her, I was not introduced to them. Her only companions that I saw were young Arab girls, mainly from poor villages in the West Bank or the Gaza, who had been talked or bullied by their Palestinian comrades into committing acts of savagery against the hated Zionist occupiers, most often planting bombs in marketplaces or tossing them into civilian buses.

I arrived there by jeep from Beersheeba, driven by a hardy young Colonel of Intelligence whose father, while still a boy, had been trained as a Night Raider by the eccentric General Wingate during the British Mandate. The Colonel's father remembered Wingate squatting naked in his tent by candle-light, drawing out the battle plan in the sand. Every Israeli soldier seems to talk about his father and a good few talk about the British. After the Mandate, they think they know us for what we probably still are: anti-Semitic, ignorant and imperial-ist, with just enough exceptions to redeem us. Dimona, where the Israelis store their nuclear arsenal, was up the road.

My sense of unreality had not left me. To the contrary, it had intensified. It was as if I had lost the distance from the human condition that is essential to our trade. My feelings and the feelings of others seemed to count more with me than my observations. It is quite easy in the Lebanon, if you drop your guard, to develop an unreasoning hatred of Israel. But I had succumbed to a serious dose of the disease. Trudging through the mud and stench of the shattered camps, crouching in the sandbagged hovels, I convinced myself that the Israeli thirst for vengeance would not be stilled until the accusing eyes of the last Palestinian child had been closed for good.

Perhaps my young Colonel got a hint of this, for though I had flown in from Cyprus it was still only a few hours since I had left Beirut, and something of what I felt may still have been legible in my face.

'You get to see Arafat?' he asked, with a moody smile as we drove along the straight road.

'No, I didn't.'

'Why not? He's a nice guy.'

I let that go.

'Why do you want to see Britta?'

I told him. There was no point in not doing so. It had taken all London's powers of persuasion to get me the interview with her at all, and my hosts were certainly not going to let me speak to her alone.

'We think she may be willing to talk to us about an old boy-friend,' I said.

'Why would she do that?'

'He jilted her. She was angry with him.'

'Who's the boyfriend?' – as if he didn't know.

'He's Irish. He has the rank of adjutant in the IRA. He briefs bombers, reconnoitres targets, supplies the equipment. She lived underground with him in Amsterdam and Paris.'

'Like George Orwell, huh? *Down and Out*?'

'Like George Orwell.'

'How long ago he jilted her?'

'Six months.'

'Maybe she's not angry any more. Maybe she'll tell you go suck. For a girl like Britta, six months is a hell of a long time.'

I asked whether she had talked much in her captivity. It was a delicate question, since the Israelis were still not saying how long they had been holding her, or how they had obtained her in the first place. The Colonel was broad-faced and brown-skinned. His family came originally from Russia. He wore parachute wings on his short-sleeved khaki shirt. He was twenty-eight, a Sabra, born in Tel Aviv, engaged to a Sephardi from Morocco. His father, the Night Raider, was now a dentist. All this he had told me in the first few minutes of our acquaintance, in a guttural English he had captured single-handed.

'Talked?' he repeated with a grim smile, in answer to my question. 'Britta? That lady didn't stop talking since she became a resident.'

Knowing a little of Israeli methods, I was not surprised, and I shuddered inwardly at the prospect of questioning a woman who had been subjected to them. It had happened to me in Ireland: a man buttoned to the neck who had stared at me like a dead man and confessed to everything.

'Do you interrogate her yourself?' I asked, noticing afresh his thick brown forearms and the uncompromising set of his jaw. And thinking, perhaps, of Colonel Jerzy.

He shook his head. 'Impossible.'

'Why?'

He seemed about to tell me something, then changed his mind. 'We got experts,' he said. 'Shin Bet guys, smart like Britta. Take their time with her. Family.'

I had heard about this loving family too, though I didn't say so. The Zionists had lured her into a trap, a bloodshot-eyed informant had whispered to me in Tyre. She had left the camps and gone to Athens with her new boyfriend, Said, and three of Said's friends, he said. Good boys. All able. The plan had been to shoot down an El Al plane as it made its approach to Athens airport. The boys had got themselves a hand-held rocket launcher and a rented house on the flight-path. Britta's job, as an unsuspicious-looking European, was to stand in a phone box at the airport with a thirty-dollar shortwave receiver and relay the control tower's instructions to the boys on the roof as the plane came in. Everything had been set fair, said my bone-weary informant. The rehearsals had gone like a dream. But on the day, the operation had fouled up.

Listening to him, I had filled in the rest of the story for myself, imagining how the Service would have done the job if we'd had the foreknowledge: two teams to assault the roof and the phone box simultaneously; the target plane, forewarned and empty, landing safely at Athens airport; the plane's homeward journey to Tel Aviv with the terrorists chained in their seats. I wondered what they would do with her. Whether they would put her on trial or trade her for favours in return.

'What happened to the boys she was with in Athens?' I asked the Colonel, ignoring London's injunction to show no curiosity in such matters.

'Boys? She knows nothing from boys. Athens? Where's Athens already? She's an innocent German tourist on vacation in Eilat. We kidnapped her, we drugged her, we imprisoned her, now we're framing her for propaganda. She invites us to prove the contrary because she knows we can't. You want any more information? Ask Britta, be our guest.'

His mood mystified me, the more so when, as we got out of the jeep, he laid a hand on my shoulder and wished me a sort of luck. 'She's all yours,' he said. '*Mazel tov.*'

I was beginning to dread what I might find.

A dumpy little woman in army uniform received us in her clean office. Prison staff never go short of cleaners, I thought. She was Captain Levi and she was Britta's unlikely gaoler. She spoke English the way a small-town American schoolmistress might speak it, but more slowly, with greater care. She had twinkly eyes and short grey hair and a look of kindly res-ignation. She had the dusty complexion of prison life, but when she put her hands together you felt she ought to be knitting for her grandchildren.

'Britta is very intelligent,' she said apologetically. 'For an intelligent man to question an intelligent woman, that's sometimes difficult. Do you have a daughter, sir?'

I was not about to fill in my character profile for her so I said no, which happened also to be the truth.

'A pity. Never mind. Maybe you still get one. A man like you, you have time. You speak German?'

'Yes.'

'Then you are lucky. You can communicate with her in her language. That way you get to know her better. Britta and I, we can speak only English together. I speak it like my late hus-band, who was American. Britta speaks it like her late lover, who was Irish. Tel Aviv says we are to allow you two hours. Will you be happy with two hours? If you need more, we shall ask them – maybe they say yes. Maybe two hours will be too much. We shall see.'

'You are very kind,' I said.

'Kind, I don't know. Maybe we should be less kind. Maybe we are making kind too much. You will see.'

And with this, she sent for coffee and for Britta, while the Colonel and myself took up our places along one side of the plain wood table.

But Captain Levi did not sit at the table, I supposed because she was not part of the interview. She sat beside the door on a straight kitchen chair, her eyes lowered as if in preparation for a concert. Even when Britta walked in between two young wardresses, she only lifted her eyes as far as was neces-sary to watch the three women's feet pass her to the centre of the room and halt. One wardress pulled back a chair for Britta, the second unlocked her handcuffs. The wardresses left, and we settled to the table.

And I would like to paint for you the scene exactly as I saw it from where I sat: with the Colonel to my right, and Britta opposite us across the table, and the bowed grey head of Captain Levi almost directly behind her, but slightly to the left, wearing a reminiscent expression that was half a smile. Throughout our discussion she stayed like that, still as a wax-work. Her part-smile of familiarity never altered and never went away. There was concentration in her pose, and some-thing of effort, so that I wondered whether she was straining to pick out phrases and words she could identify, perhaps from a combined knowledge of Yiddish and English, for Britta, being a Bremen girl, spoke a clear and authoritarian German, which makes comprehension easier.

And Britta, without a doubt, was a fine sample of her breed. She was 'blonde as a bread roll', as they say up there, tall and deep-shouldered and well-grown, with wide rather insolent blue eyes and a strong, attractive jaw. She had Moni-ca's youth and Monica's height as well; and, as I could not avoid speculating, Monica's sensuality. My suspicion that they had been maltreating her vanished as soon as she walked in. She held herself like a ballerina, but with more intelli-gence and more of life's reality than is to be found in most dancers. She would have looked well in tennis gear or in a *dirndl* dress, and I suspected that in her time she had worn both. Even her prison tunic did not diminish her, for she had made herself a cloth belt out of something, and tied it at the waist, and she had brushed her fair hair over her shoulders in a cape. Her first gesture when her hands were freed was to offer me one, at the same time dropping a schoolgirl bob, whether out of irony or respect it was too soon to tell. Her grasp was like a boy's, but lingering. She wore no make-up but needed none.

'*Und mit wem hab' ich die Ehre?*' she enquired, either courteously or impishly. And whom do I have the honour to address?

'I'm a British official,' I said.

'Your name, please?'

'It's unimportant.'

'But you are very important!'

Prisoners when they are brought up from their cells often say silly things in their first flush, so I answered her with consideration.

'I'm working with the Israelis on aspects of your case. That's all you need to know.'

'Case? I am a case? How amusing. I thought I was a human being. Please sit down, Mr Nobody,' she said, doing so herself.

So we sit as I have described, with Captain Levi's face behind her, a little out of focus like its expression. The Colonel had not stood up to greet Britta, and he barely bothered to look at her now she was sitting before him. He seemed suddenly to be without expectation. He glanced at his watch. It was of dull steel and like a weapon on his brown wrist. Britta's wrists were white and smooth like Monica's, but chafed with red rings from the handcuffs.

Suddenly she was lecturing me.

She began at once, as if she were resuming a tutorial, and in a sense she was, for I soon realised she lectured everyone this way, or everyone whom she had dismissed as bourgeois. She said she had a statement to make which she would like me to relay to my 'colleagues', as she called them, since she felt that her position was not being sufficiently appreciated by the authorities. She was a prisoner of war, just as any Israeli soldier in Palestinian hands was a prisoner of war, and entitled to the treatment and privileges set out in the Geneva Convention. She was a tourist here, she had committed no crime against Israel; she had been arrested solely on the strength of her trumped-up record in other countries, as a deliberate act of provocation against the world proletariat.

I gave a quick laugh, and she faltered. She was not expecting laughter.

'But look here,' I objected. 'Either you're a prisoner of war or you're an innocent tourist. You can't be both.'

'The struggle is between the innocent and the guilty,' she retorted without hesitation, and resumed her lecture. Her enemies were not limited to Zionism, she said, but what she called the dynamic of bourgeois domination, the repression of natural instincts, and the maintenance of despotic authority disguised as 'democracy'.

Again I tried to interrupt her, but this time she talked straight through me. She quoted Marcuse at me and Freud. She referred to the rebellion of sons in puberty against their fathers, and the disavowal of this rebellion in later years as the sons themselves became the fathers.

I glanced at the Colonel, but he seemed to be dozing.

The purpose of her 'actions', she said, and those of her comrades, was to arrest this instinctual cycle of repression in all its forms – in the enslavement of labour to materialism, in the repressive principle of 'progress' itself – and to allow the real forces of society to surge, like erotic energy, into new, unfettered forms of cultural creation.

'None of this is faintly interesting to me,' I protested. 'Just stop, please, and listen to my questions.'

Acts of so-called 'terrorism' had therefore two clear purposes, she continued, as if I had never spoken, of which the first was to disconcert the armies of the bourgeois-materialist conspiracy, and the second to instruct, by example, the pit-ponies of the earth, who had lost all knowledge of the light. In other words, to introduce ferment and awaken conscious-ness at the most repressed human levels.

She wished to add that though she was not an adherent of Communism, she preferred its teachings to those of cap-italism, since Communism provided a powerful negation of the ego-ideal which used property to construct the human prison.

She favoured free sexual expression and – for those who needed them – the use of drugs as a means of discovering the free self as contrasted with the unfree self that is castrated by aggressive tolerance.

I turned to the Colonel. There is an etiquette of interroga-tion as there is about everything else. 'Do we have to go on listening to this nonsense? The lady is your prisoner, not mine,' I said. For I could hardly lay the law down to her across his table.

The Colonel lifted his head high enough to glance at her with indifference. 'You want to go back down, Britta?' he asked her. 'You want bread and water for a couple of weeks?' His German was as bizarre as his English. He seemed sud-denly a lot older than his age, and wiser.

'I have more to say, thank you.'

'If you're going to stay up here, you answer his questions and you shut up,' said the Colonel. 'It's your choice. You want to leave now, it's fine by us.' He added something in Hebrew to Captain Levi, who nodded distantly. An Arab pris-oner entered with a tray of coffee – four cups and a plate of sugar biscuits – and handed them round meekly, a coffee cup for each of us and one for Captain Levi, the biscuits at the centre of the table. An air of lassitude had settled over us. Britta stretched out her long arm for a biscuit, lazily, as if she were in her own home. The Colonel's hand crashed on the table just ahead of her as he removed the plate from her reach.

'So what do you wish to ask me, please?' Britta enquired of me, as if nothing at all had happened. 'Do you wish me to deliver the Irish to you? What other aspects of my case could interest the English, Mr Nobody?'

'If you deliver us one particular Irishman, that will be fine,' I said. 'You lived with a man named Seamus for a year.'

She was amused. I had provided her with an opening. She studied me, and seemed to see something in my face she recognised. '*Lived* with him? That is an exaggeration. I slept with him. Seamus was only for sex,' she explained, with a mischievous smile. 'He was a convenience, an instrument. A *good* instrument, I would say. I was the same for him. You like sex? Sometimes another boy would join us, maybe sometimes a girl. We make combinations. It was irrelevant but we had fun.'

'Irrelevant to what?' I asked.

'To our work.'

'What work?'

'I have already described our work to you, Mr Nobody. I have told you of its aims, and of our motivations. Humanitarianism is not to be equated with non-violence. We must fight to be free. Sometimes even the highest causes can only be served by violent methods. Do you know that? Sex also can be violent.'

'What kind of violent methods was Seamus involved in?' I asked.

'We are speaking not of wanton acts but of the people's right of resistance against acts committed by the forces of repression. Are you a member of those forces or are you in favour of spontaneity, Mr Nobody? Perhaps you should free yourself and join us.'

'He's a bomber,' I said. 'He blows up innocent people. His most recent target was a public house in southern England. He killed one elderly couple, the barman and the pianist, and I give you my word he didn't liberate a single deluded worker.'

'Is that a question or a statement, Mr Nobody?'

'It's an invitation to you to tell me about his activities.'

'The public house was close to a British military camp,' she replied. 'It was providing infrastructure and comfort to Fascistic forces of oppression.'

Again her cool eyes held me in their playful gaze. Did I say she was attractive? What is attraction in such circumstances? She was wearing a calico tunic. She was an enforced penitent of crimes that she did not repent. She was alert in every part of herself, I could feel it, and she knew I felt it, and the divide between us enticed her.

'My department is considering offering you a sum of money on your release, payable, if you prefer, to somebody you nominate in the meantime,' I said. 'They want information that would lead to the arrest and conviction of your friend Seamus. They are interested in his past crimes, others he has yet to commit, safe addresses, contacts, habits and weaknesses.' She waited for me to go on, so, perhaps unwisely, I did. 'Seamus is not a hero. He's a pig. Not what you call a pig. A real pig. Nobody did bad things to him when he was young; his parents are decent people who run a tobacco shop in County Down. His grandfather was a policeman, a good one. Seamus is blowing people up for kicks because he's inadequate. That's why he treated you badly. He only exists when he's inflicting pain. The rest of the time he's a spoilt little boy.'

I had not scratched the surface of her steady stare.

'Are you inadequate, Mr Nobody? I think perhaps you are. In your occupation, that is normal. You should join us, Mr Nobody. You should take lessons with us, and we shall convert you to our cause. Then you will be adequate.'

You must understand that she did not raise her voice while she said this, or indulge in dramatics of any kind. She remained condescending and composed, even hospitable. The mischief in her lay deep and well disguised. She had a healthy natural smile and it stayed with her all the time she spoke, while Captain Levi behind her continued to gaze into her own memories, perhaps because she did not understand what was being said.

The Colonel glanced at me in question. Not trusting myself to speak, I lifted my hands from the table, asking what's the point? The Colonel said something to Captain Levi, who in the disappointed manner of someone who has prepared a meal only to see it taken away uneaten, pressed a bell for the escort. Britta rose to her feet, smoothed her prison tunic over her breasts and hips and held out her hands for the handcuffs.

'How much money were they thinking of offering me, Mr Nobody?' she enquired.

'None,' I said.

She dropped me another bob and walked between her guards towards the door, her hips flowing inside her calico tunic, reminding me of Monica's inside her dressing-gown. I was afraid she would speak again but she didn't. Perhaps she knew she had won the day, and anything more would spoil the effect. The Colonel followed her out and I was alone with Captain Levi. The half smile had not left her face.

'There,' she said. 'Now you know a little what it feels like to hear Britta's music.'

'I suppose I do.'

'Sometimes we communicate too much. Perhaps you should have spoken English to her. So long as she speaks English, I can care for her. She is a human being, she is a woman, she is in prison. And you may be sure she is in agony. She is courageous, and so long as she speaks English to me I can do my duty for her.'

'And when she speaks German to you?'

'What would be the point, since she knows I cannot understand her?'

'But if she did – and if you could understand her? What then?'

Her smile twisted and became slightly shameful. 'Then I think I would be frightened,' she replied in her slow American. 'I think if she ordered something of me, I would be tempted to obey her. But I do not let her order me. Why should I? I do not give her the power over me. I speak English and I stay the boss. I was for two years in concentration camp in Buchenwald, you see.' Still smiling at me, she delivered the rest in German, in the clenched, hushed whisper of the campnik: *'Man hört so scheussliche Echos in ihrer Stimme, wissen Sie.'* One hears such dreadful echoes in her voice, you see.

The Colonel was standing in the doorway waiting for me. As we walked downstairs, he put his hand once more on my shoulder. This time I knew why.

'Is she like that with all the boys?' I asked him.

'Captain Levi?'

'Britta.'

'Sure. With you a bit more, that's all. Maybe that's because you're English.'

Maybe it is, I thought, and maybe it's because she saw more in me than just my Englishness. Maybe she read my unconscious signals of availability. But whatever she saw in me, or didn't, Britta had provided the summation of my confusion until now. She had articulated my sense of trying to hold on to a world that was slipping away from me, my susceptibility to every stray argument and desire.

The summons to find Hansen arrived the same night, in the middle of a jolly diplomatic party given by my British Embassy host in Herzliyya.

9

Earnest Perigrew was quizzing Smiley about colonialism. Sooner or later, Perigrew quizzed everyone who came to Sarratt about colonialism, and his questions always hovered at the edge of outrage. He was a troubled boy, the son of British missionaries to West Africa, and one of those people the Service is almost bound to employ, on account of their rare knowledge and linguistic qualifications. He was sitting as usual alone, amid the shadows at the back of the library, his gaunt face thrust forward and one long hand held up as if to fend off ridicule. The question had started reasonably, then degenerated into a tirade against Britain's indifference towards her former enslaved subjects.

'Yes, well, I think I rather agree with you,' said Smiley courteously, to the general surprise, when he had heard Perigrew to the end. 'The sad answer is, I'm afraid, that the Cold War produced in us a kind of *vicarious* colonialism. On the one hand we abandoned practically every article of our national identity to American foreign policy. On the other we bought ourselves a stay of execution for our vision of our colonial selves. Worse still, we encouraged the Americans to behave in the same way. Not that they needed our encouragement, but they were pleased to have it, naturally.'

Hansen had said much the same. And in much the same

language. But where Smiley had lost little of his urbanity, Hansen had glared into my face with eyes lit by the red hells from which he had returned.

I flew from Israel to Bangkok because Smiley said Hansen had gone mad and knew too many secrets: a decypher your-self signal, care of the Head of Station, Tel Aviv. Smiley had charge of Service security at the time, with the courtesy rank of deputy chief. Whenever I heard of him, he seemed to be scuttling round plugging another leak or another scandal. I spent the weekend in a heatwave sweating my way through the stack of hand-delivered files and an hour on the tele-phone placating Mabel, who had fallen at the last fence of her annual race to become ladies' captain of our local golf club and was scenting intrigue.

I don't know why they're so hard on Mabel. Perhaps it's her way of plain talking that puts them off. I did what I could. I told her that nothing I had come upon in the Service could compare with the skulduggery of those Kent wives. I prom-ised her a splendid holiday when I returned. I forget where the holiday was going to be because we never took it.

Hansen's file gave me a portrait of a type I had grown familiar with because we used a good few of them. I was one myself and Ben was another: the crossbred Englishman who adopts the Service as his country and endows it with a bunch of qualities it hasn't really got.

Like myself, Hansen was half a Dutchman. Perhaps that was why Smiley had chosen me. He was born in the long night of the German Occupation of Holland and raised in the shadow of Delft Cathedral. His mother, a counter clerk at Thomas Cook's, was of English parents who urged her to go back to London with them when the war broke out. She refused, choosing instead to marry a Delft curate, who a year afterwards got himself shot by a German firing squad, leaving his pregnant wife to fend for herself. Undaunted, she joined a British escape line and, by the time the war ended, had charge of a fully fledged network, with its own communications, informants, safe houses and the usual appointments. My mother's work with the Service had not been so different.

By what route the infant Hansen found his way to the Jesuits, the file did not relate. Perhaps the mother converted. Those were dark years still, and if expediency required it, she may have swallowed her Protestant convictions to buy the boy a decent education. Give the Jesuits his soul, she may have reasoned, and they will give him a brain. Or perhaps she sensed in her son from early on the mercurial nature that later ruled his life, and she determined to subordinate him to a stronger religious discipline than was offered by the easy-going Protestants. If so, she was wise. Hansen embraced the faith as he embraced everything else, with passion. The nuns had him, the brothers had him, the priests had him, the scholars had him. Till at twenty-one, schooled and devout but still a novice, he was packed off to a seminary in Indonesia to learn the ways of the heathen: Sumatra, Molucca, Java.

The Orient seems to have been an instinctive love of Hansen's as it is for many Dutchmen. The good Dutch, like Heine's proverbial pine tree, can stand on the shores of their flat little country and sniff the Asian scents of lemon grass and cooking pots on the chill sea air. Hansen arrived, he saw, he was conquered. Buddhism, Islam, the rites and superstitions of the remotest savages – he flung himself on all of them with a fervour that only intensified the deeper he penetrated into the jungle.

Languages also came naturally to him. To his native Dutch and English he had effortlessly added French and German. Now he acquired Tamil, Khmer, Thai, Sanskrit and more than a smattering of Cantonese, often hiking hundreds of miles of hill country in his quest for a missing dialect or ritualistic link. He wrote papers on philology, marriage rites, illumination and monkeys. He discovered lost temples in the depths of the jungle, and won prizes the Society forbade him to accept. After six years of fearless exploring and enquiring, he was not only the kind of academic showpiece Jesuits are famous for; he was also a full priest.

But few secrets can survive six years. Gradually the stories about him began to acquire a seamy edge. Hansen the skin artist. Hansen's appetites. Don't look now but here comes one of Hansen's girls.

It was the scale as well as the duration that did for him: the fact that once they started probing, they found no corner to his life that was immune, no journey that did not have its detour. A woman here or there – a boy or two – well, from what I have seen of priesthood round the globe, such peccadilloes are to be found more in the observance than the breach.

But this wholesale indulgence, in every kampong, in every tawdry sidestreet, this indefatigable debauchery, flaunted, as they now discovered, beneath their noses for more than a decade, with girls who by Western standards were barely eligible for their First Communion, let alone the marriage bed – and many of them under the Church's own protection – made Hansen suddenly and dramatically untenable. Faced with the evidence of such prolonged and dedicated sinning, his Superior responded more in grief than indignation. He ordered Hansen to return to Rome, and sent a letter ahead of him to the General of the Society. From Rome, he told Hansen sadly, he would most likely go to Loyola in Spain, where qualified Jesuit psychotherapists would help him come to terms with his regrettable weakness. After Loyola – well, a new beginning, perhaps a different hemisphere, a different decade.

But Hansen, like his mother before him, stubbornly declined to leave the place of his adoption.

At a loss, the Father Guardian packed him off to a distant mission in the hills run by a traditionalist of the sterner school. There Hansen suffered the barbarities of house arrest. He was watched over like a madman. He was forbidden to pass beyond the precincts of the house, denied books, paper, company, laughter. Men take to confinement in different ways, as they take differently to heights or cold or dying. Hansen took to it terribly, and after three months could bear no more. As his brother guardians escorted him to Mass, he hurled one of them down a staircase while the other fled. Then he headed back to Djakarta and, with neither money nor passport, went to ground in the brothels he knew well. The girls took him into their care, and in return he worked as pimp and bouncer. He gave out beer, washed glasses, ejected the unruly, heard confessions, gave succour, played with the children in the back room. I see him, as I know him now, doing all those things without fuss or complication. He was barely thirty and his desires burned bright as ever. Until one day, yielding as so often to an impulse, Hansen shaved, put on a clean shirt, and presented himself to the British Consul to claim his British soul.

And the Consul, being neither deaf nor blind, but a long-standing member of the Service, listened to Hansen's story, asked a humdrum question or two and, from behind a mask of apathy, sprang to action. For years he had been looking for a man of Hansen's gifts. Hansen's waywardness did not deter the Consul in the least. He liked it. He signalled London for background; he lent Hansen cautious sums of cash against receipts in triplicate, for he did not wish to show undue enthusiasm. When London came back with a white trace on Hansen's mother, indicating she was a former agent of the Service, the Consul's cup brimmed over.

Another month and Hansen was semi-conscious, which means he knew, but only half knew, but then again might not know, that he just could be half in touch with what one might loosely refer to as British Intelligence. Another two months and, restless as ever, he was taking a swing through southern Java ostensibly in search of ancient scrolls, in reality to report back to the Consul the strength of Communist subversion, which was his newly adopted anti-Christ. By the end of the year he was headed for London with the brand-new British passport he had wanted in his pocket, though not in his own name.

I turned to his potted training record, all six months of it. Clive Bellamy, a gangly, mischievous Etonian, was in charge of Sarratt. 'Excellent at all things practical,' he wrote in Hansen's end-of-course report. 'Has a first-rate memory, fast reactions, is self-sufficient. Needs to be ridden hard. If there's ever a mutiny on my ship, Hansen will be the first man I'll flog. Needs a big canvas and a first-rate controller.'

I turned to the operational record. No madness there either. Since Hansen was still Dutch, Head Office decided to keep him that way and play down his Englishness. Hansen bridled but they overruled him. At a time when the British abroad were being seen by everyone except themselves as Americans without the clout, Head Office would kill for a Swede and steal for a West German. Even Canadians, though more easily manufactured, were smiled on. Back in Holland, Hansen formalised his severance from the Jesuits and set about looking for new employment back East. A score of Oriental academic bodies were spread around the capitals of Western Europe in those days. Hansen did his rounds of them, gaining a promise here and a commitment there. A French Oriental news agency took him on as a stringer. A London weekly, nudged by Head Office, made a berth for him on condition they got him free. Till bit by bit his cover was complete – wide enough for him to have a reason to go anywhere and ask what questions he wanted, varied enough to be financially inscrutable, since no one would ever be able to tell which of his several employers were paying him how much for what. He was ready to be launched. British interests in South-East Asia might have dwindled with her Empire, but the Americans were in there knee-deep with an official war running in Vietnam, an unofficial one in Cambodia and a secret one in Laos. In our unlovely role as camp follower, we were delighted to offer them Hansen's precious talents.

Espionage technology can do a lot. It can photograph crops and trenches, tanks and rocket sites and tyre-marks and the migration of the reindeer. It can flinch at the sound of a Russian fighter pilot breaking wind at forty thousand feet or a Chinese general belching in his sleep. But it can't replace human understanding. It can't tell you what's in the heart of a Cambodian farmer whose hill crops have been blown to smithereens by Dr Kissinger's unmarked bombers, whose daughters have been sold into prostitution in the city, and whose sons have been lured into leaving the fields and fighting for an American puppet army, or urged, by way of family insurance, into the ranks of the Khmer Rouge. It can't read the lips of jungle fighters in black pyjamas whose most powerful weapon is the perverted Marxism of a blood-hungry Sorbonne-educated Cambodian psychopath. It can't sniff the exhaust fumes of an army that is unmechanised. Or break the codes of an army without radio. Or calculate the supplies of men who can nourish themselves on ground beetles and wood bark; or the morale of those who, having lost all they possess, have only the future to win.

But Hansen could. Hansen, the adopted Asian, could trek without food for a week, squat in the kampongs and listen to the murmur of the villagers, and Hansen could read the rising wind of their resistance long before it stirred the Stars and Stripes on the Embassy roofs of Phnom Penh and Saigon. And he could tell the bombers – and, to his later remorse, he did – he could tell the American bombers which villages were playing host to the Vietcong. He was a fisher of men, too. He could recruit helpers from every walk of life and instruct them how to see and hear and remember and report. He knew how little to tell them and how much, how to reward them and when not to.

For months, then years, Hansen functioned that way in the so-called 'liberated areas' of northern Cambodia where the Khmer Rouge nominally held sway, until the day he vanished from the village he had made his home. Vanished soundlessly, taking the inhabitants with him. Soon to be given up for dead, another jungle disappearance.

And remained dead until a short time ago, when he had come alive in a brothel in Bangkok.

'Take your time, Ned,' Smiley had urged me on the telephone to Tel Aviv. 'If you want to add a couple of days for jet-lag, it's quite all right by me.'

Which was Smiley-speak for 'Get to him as fast as you can

and tell me I haven't got another king-sized scandal on my hands.'

Our Station Head in Bangkok was a bald, rude, moustachi-oed little tyrant called Rumbelow, whom I had never warmed to. The Service offers precious few prospects for men of fifty. Most are blown; many are too tired and disenchanted to care whether they are or not. Others head for private banking or big business, but the marriage seldom lasts. Something has happened to their way of thinking that unsuits them to the overt life. But a very few, of whom Toby Esterhase was one and Rumbelow another, pull off the trick of holding the Service hostage to their supposed assets.

Exactly what Rumbelow's were I never knew. Seedy, I am sure, for if he specialised in anything, it was human baseness. One rumour said he owned a couple of corrupt Thai generals who would work to him and to no one else. Another that he had managed to perform a grimy favour for a member of the royal household that was not transferable. Whatever his hold on them, the barons of the Fifth Floor would hear no ill of him. 'And for God's sake, don't rub up Rumbelow the wrong way, Ned,' Smiley had begged me. 'I'm sure he's a pain in the neck, but we do need him.'

I met him in my hotel room. To the overt world I was Mark Seymour, occupation accountant, and had no wish to parade myself at the Embassy or his house. I had been flying twenty hours. It was early evening. Rumbelow spoke like an Etonian bookmaker. Come to think of it, he looked like one as well.

'It was *sheerest* bloody coincidence we bumped into the bastard at all,' he told me huffily. 'One puts out one's feelers, naturally. One keeps one's ear to the proverbial ground. One

knows the score. One's heard of other cases. One isn't insensi-
tive. One doesn't like to think of one's joe trussed to a stick,
being carted through the jungle for weeks on end, while the
Khmer Rouge torture the hell out of him, naturally. Not an
ostrich. Know the score. Your brown man doesn't obey the
Queensberry Rules, you know,' he assured me, as if I had
implied the opposite. And, plucking a handkerchief from the
sleeve of his sweat-patched suit, he pummelled his stupid
moustache with it. 'Your *average* joe would be yelling for a
quick bullet after one night of it.'

'Are you sure that's what happened to him?'

'Not sure of anything, thank you, old boy. Rumour, that's
all. How *can* I be sure, if the bastard won't even talk to us?
Threatens violence if we try! For all *I* know, the KR never
had sight nor sound of him. Never did trust a Dutchman, not
out here – they think they own the bloody place. Hansen
wouldn't be the first joe to lie doggo when things got too hot
for him, then come bouncing back when it's all over, asking
for his gong and his pension, not by any means. Still in possession of all his fingers and thumbs, by all accounts. Not
missing any other part of his anatomy either, to judge by
where he's holed out. Duffy Marchbanks spotted him. Remember Duffy? Good chap.'

With a sinking heart, yes, I remembered Duffy. I had
remembered him when I saw his name in the file. He was a
flamboyant crook based in Hong Kong, with a taste for fast
deals in anything from opium to shellcases. For a few mis-
guided years we had financed his office.

'Purest chance, it was, on Duffy's part. He'd popped up
here on a flying visit. One day, that's all. One day, one night,
then back to the missus and a book. Offshore leisure consortium wanted him to buy a hundred acres of prime coastland

for them. Did his business, then off they go to this girlie restaurant, Duffy and a bunch of his traders – Duffy's not averse to a bit of the other, never has been. Place called The Sea of Happiness, slap in the middle of the red-light quarter. Upmarket sort of establishment, as they go, I'm told. Private rooms, decent food if you like Hunanese, a straight deal and the girls leave you alone unless you tell 'em not to.'

At girlie restaurants, he explained, somehow contriving to suggest he had never personally been to one, young hostesses, dressed or undressed, sat between the guests and fed them food and drink while the men talked high matters of business. In addition, The Sea of Happiness offered a massage parlour, a discothèque and a live theatre on the ground floor.

'Duffy clinches the deal with the consortium, a cheque is passed, he's feeling his oats. So he decides to do himself a favour with one of the girls. Terms agreed, off they go to a cubicle. Girl says she's thirsty, how about a bottle of champagne to get her going? She's on commission, naturally – they all are. Never mind. Duffy's feeling expansive, so he says why not? Girl presses a bell, squawks into the intercom, next thing Duffy knows, in marches this bloody great European chap with an ice bucket and a tray. Sets it down, Duffy gives him twenty baht for himself, fellow says "Thank you" in English, polite enough but no smiles, clears out. It's Hansen. Jungle Hansen. Not a portrait . . . himself!'

'How does Duffy know that?'

'Seen his photograph, hasn't he?'

'Why?'

'Because we showed Duffy the bloody photograph, for heaven's sake, when Hansen went missing! We showed it to everyone we knew, all over the bloody hemisphere! We didn't say why – we just said if you spot this man, holler. Head Office's orders, thank you, not *my* idea. *I* thought it was bloody insecure.'

To calm himself, Rumbelow poured us both another whisky. 'Duffy roars back to his hotel, phones me at home straight away. Three in the morning. "It's your fellow," he tells me. "What fellow?" I say. "Fellow you sent me that pretty picture of, back in Hongkers a year ago or more. He's potboy at a whorehouse called The Sea of Happiness." You know how old Duffy talks. Loose. I sent Henry round next day. Bloody fool made a hash of it. You heard about that, I hope? Typical.'

'Did Duffy speak to Hansen? Ask him who he was? Anything?'

'Not a dickie bird. Looked clean through him. Duffy's a trouper. Salt of the earth. Always was.'

'Where's Henry?'

'Sitting downstairs in the lobby.'

'Call him up.'

Henry was Chinese, the son of a Kuomintang warlord in the Shan States and our resident chief agent, though I suspect he had long ago taken out reinsurance with the Thai police and was earning a quiet living playing both ends against the middle.

He was a podgy, over-eager, shiny fellow and he smiled too much. He wore a gold chain round his neck and carried a smart leather notebook with a gold pen in it. His cover work was translator. No translator I had ever met sported a Gucci notebook, but Henry was different.

'Tell Mark how you made a bloody fool of yourself at The Sea of Happiness last Thursday evening,' Rumbelow ordered menacingly.

'Sure, Mike.'

'Mark,' I said.

'Sure, Mark.'

'His orders were to take a look. That's *all* he was to do,' Rumbelow barged in before Henry could tell anything at all. 'Take a look, sniff, get out, call me. Right, Henry? He was to spin the tale, sniff, *see* if he could spot Hansen anywhere, *not* approach him, report back to me. A discreet, no-contact reconnaissance. Sniff and tell. Now tell Mark what you did.'

First Henry had had a drink at the bar, he said; then he had watched the show. Then he had sent for the Mama San, who hurried over assuming he had a special wish. The Mama San was a Chinese lady from the same province as Henry's father, so they had an immediate bond.

He had shown the Mama San his translator's card and said he was writing an article about her establishment – the superb food, the romantic girls, the high standards of sensitivity and hygiene, particularly the hygiene. He said he had a commission from a German travel magazine that recommended only the best places.

The Mama San took the bait and offered him the run of the house. She showed him the private dining rooms, the kitchens, cubicles, toilets. She introduced him to the girls – and offered him one on the house, which he declined – to the head chef, the doorman and the bouncers, but not, as it happened, to the enormous round-eye whom Henry had by then spotted three times, once as he carried a tray of glasses from the private dining rooms to the kitchens, once crossing a corridor pushing a trolley of bottles and once emerging from an open steel doorway which apparently led to the drinks store.

'But who is your *farang* who carries the bottles for you?'

Henry had cried out with amusement to the Mama San. 'Must he stay behind and work because he cannot pay his bill?'

The Mama San laughed also. Against *farangs*, or Westerners, all Asians feel naturally united. 'The *farang* lives with one of our Cambodian girls,' she replied with contempt, for Cambodians are rated even lower than *farangs* and Vietnamese in the Thai zoology. 'He met her here and fell in love with her, so he tried to buy her and make a lady out of her. But she refused to leave us. So he brings her to work every day, and stays until she is free to go home again.'

'What kind of *farang* is he? German? English? Dutch?'

The Mama San shrugged. What was the difference? Henry pressed her. But a *farang* who brings his woman to the brothel and pushes drinks about while she goes with other men, he insisted, and then takes her home again to his bed? This must be quite some girl!

'She is number nineteen,' said the Mama San, with a shrug. 'Her house name is Amanda. Would you like her?'

But Henry was too excited by his journalistic *coup* to be sidetracked. 'But the *farang*, what is his name? What is his history?' he cried in great amusement.

'He is called Ham Sin. He speaks Thai with us and Khmer with the girl but you must not put him in your magazine, because he is illegal.'

'I can disguise him. I can make it all disguised. Does the girl love him in return?'

'She prefers to be here at The Sea of Happiness with her friends,' the Mama San said primly.

Henry could not resist taking a look. The girls who were not with clients lounged on plush benches behind a glass wall, wearing numbers round their necks and nothing else, while they chatted to each other or tended their fingernails or stared vacuously at an ill-tuned television set. As Henry watched, number 19 stood up in response to a summons, picked up her little handbag and a wrap and walked from the room. She was very young. Many girls lied about their age in order to defeat the regulations – penniless Cambodians particularly. But this girl, said Henry, had looked no more than fifteen.

It was here that Henry's excess of zeal began to lead him astray. He said his goodbyes to the Mama San and drove his car into an alley opposite the rear entrance, where he settled down to wait. Soon after one o'clock the staff began leaving, among them Hansen, twice the height of anyone else, leading number 19 on his arm. In the square, Hansen and the girl looked round for a cab and Henry had the temerity to pull up his car beside them. Pimps and illegal cab drivers thrive at that hour of night, and Henry in his time had been both, so perhaps the move came naturally to him.

'Where you want to go, sir?' he called to Hansen in English. 'You want me to drive you?'

Hansen gave an address in a poor suburb five miles north. A price was agreed, Hansen and his girl got into the back of the car; they set off.

Now Henry began to lose his head in earnest. Flushed by his success, he decided for no reason he could afterwards explain that his best course of action would be to deliver his quarry and the girl to Rumbelow's house, which lay not north but west. He had not of course prepared Rumbelow for this bold manoeuvre; he had hardly prepared himself for it. He had no assurance that Rumbelow was at home, or in any condition, at one-thirty in the morning, to conduct a conversation with a former spy who had disappeared off the map for eighteen months. But reason, at that moment, did not predominate in Henry's mind. He was a joe, and there is not a joe in the world who does not, at one time or another in his life, do something totally daft.

'You like Bangkok?' Henry asked Hansen gaily, hoping to distract his passengers from the route he was taking.

No answer.

'You been here long?'

No answer.

'That's a nice girl. Very young. Very pretty. She your regular girl?'

The girl had her head on Hansen's shoulder. From what Henry could see in the mirror, she was already asleep. For some reason, this knowledge excited Henry further.

'You want a tailor, sir? All-night tailor, very good? I take you there. Good tailor.'

And he drove wildly into a sidestreet, pretending to look for his wretched tailor while he hurried towards Rumbelow's house.

'Why are you going west?' said Hansen, speaking for the first time. 'I don't want to go this way. I don't want a tailor. Get back on the main road.'

The last of Henry's common sense deserted him. He was suddenly terrified by Hansen's size and Hansen's tactical advantage in sitting behind him. What if Hansen was armed? Henry jammed on the brakes and stopped the car.

'Mr Hansen, sir, I am your friend!' he cried in Thai, much as he might plead for mercy. 'Mr Rumbelow is your friend too. He's proud of you! He wants to give you a lot of money. You come with me, please. No problem. Mr Rumbelow will be very happy to see you!'

That was the last speech Henry made that night, for the

next thing he knew, Hansen had pushed the back of Henry's driving seat so hard that Henry's head nearly went through the windscreen. Hansen got out of the car and hauled Henry into the street. After that, Hansen lifted Henry to his feet and flung him across the road, to the dismay of a group of sleeping beggars, who began whimpering and clamouring while Hansen strode to where Henry lay and glared down at him.

'You tell Rumbelow, if he comes for me, I'll kill him,' he said in Thai.

Then he led the girl up the road in search of a better cab, one arm round her waist while she dozed.

By the time I had heard the two men's story to the end, I was suddenly dreadfully tired.

I sent them away, telling Rumbelow to call me next morning. I said that before I did anything else I was going to sleep off my jet-lag. I lay down and was at once wide awake. An hour later, I was presenting myself at The Sea of Happiness and buying a ticket for fifty dollars. I removed my shoes, as custom required, and moments later I was standing in a neon-lit cubicle in my stockinged feet, staring into the passive, much painted features of girl number 19.

She wore a cheap silk wrap with tigers on it, but it was open from the neck down. Underneath it she was naked. A heavy Japanese-style make-up covered her complexion. She smiled at me and thrust her hand swiftly towards my groin, but I replaced it at her side. She was so slight it seemed a mystery that she was equal to the work. She was longer-legged than most Asian girls and her skin was unusually pale. She threw off her wrap and, before I could stop her, sprang on to the frayed chaise longue, where she arranged herself in what she imagined to be an erotic pose, caressing herself and uttering sighs of desire. She rolled on to her side with her rump thrust out, draping her black hair across her shoulder so that her tiny breasts poked through it. When I did not advance on her, she lay on her back and opened her thighs to me and bucked her pelvis, calling me 'darling' and saying 'please'. She flung herself away from me so that I could admire her back view, keeping her legs apart in invitation.

'Sit up,' I said, so she sat up and again waited for me to come to her.

'Put on your wrap,' I said.

When she appeared not to understand, I helped her into it. Henry had written the message for me in Khmer. 'I want to speak to Hansen,' it read. 'I am in a position to obtain Thai papers for yourself and your family.' I handed it to her and watched her study it. Could she read? I had no way of telling. I held out a plain white envelope addressed to Hansen. She took it and opened it. The letter was typed and its tone was not gentle. It contained two thousand baht.

'As an old friend of Father Vernon,' I had written, using the wordcode familiar to him, 'I must advise you that you are in breach of your contract with our company. You have assaulted a Thai citizen and your girlfriend is an illegal Cambodian immigrant. We may have no alternative but to pass this information to the authorities. My car is parked across the street. Give the enclosed money to the Mama San as payment to release you for the night, and join me in ten minutes.'

She left the cubicle, taking the letter with her. I had not realised till then how much noise there was in the corridor: the jangling music, the tinny laughter, the grumbles of desire, the swish of water down the ramshackle pipes.

*

I had left the car unlocked and he was sitting in the back, the girl beside him. Somehow I had not doubted he would bring the girl. He was big and powerful, which I knew already, and haggard. In the half darkness, with his black beard and hollowed eyes and his flattened hands curled tensely over the back of the passenger seat, he resembled one of the saints he had once worshipped, rather than the photographs on his file. The girl sat slumped and close to him, sheltering against his body. We had not gone a hundred metres before a rain-burst crashed on us like a waterfall. I pulled into the kerb while each of us stared through the drenched windscreen, watching the torrents of water swarm over the gutters and potholes.

'How did you get to Thailand?' I yelled in Dutch. The rain was thundering on the roof.

'I walked,' Hansen replied in English.

'Where did you come over?' I yelled, in English also.

He mentioned a town. It sounded like 'Orania Prathet'. The downpour ended and I drove for three hours while the girl dozed and Hansen sat guard over her, alert as a cat, and as silent. I had selected a beach hotel advertised in the Bangkok *Nation*. I wanted to get him out of his own setting, into one that I controlled. I drew the key and paid a night's lodging in advance. Hansen and the girl followed me down a concrete path to the beach. The bungalows stood in a half ring facing the sea. Mine was at one end. I unlocked the door and went ahead of them. Hansen followed, after him the girl. I switched on the light and the air-conditioning. The girl hovered near the door, but Hansen kicked off his shoes and placed himself at the centre of the room, casting round him with his hollowed eyes.

'Sit down,' I said. I pulled open the refrigerator door. 'Does she want a drink?' I asked.

'Give her a Coca-Cola,' said Hansen. 'Ice. Got any limes in there?'

'No.'

He watched me on my knees in front of the refrigerator.

'How about you?' I asked.

'Water.'

I searched again: glasses, mineral water, ice. As I did so, I heard Hansen say something tender to the girl in Khmer. She protested and he overrode her. I heard him go into the bedroom and come out again. Climbing to my feet, I saw the girl curled on the daybed that ran along one wall of the room, and Hansen bending over her with a blanket, tucking her up. When he had finished, he switched out the lamp above her and touched her cheek with his fingertips before striding to the french window to stare at the sea. A full red moon hung above the horizon. The rainclouds made black mountains across the sky.

'What's your name?' he asked me.

'Mark,' I said.

'Is that your real name? Mark?'

The surest knowledge we have of one another comes from instinct. As I watched Hansen's figure framed in the window and gazing out to sea, and the moonlight picking out the lines and hollows of his ravaged face, I knew that the lapsed priest had appointed me his confessor.

'Call me whatever you like,' I said.

You must think of a strong but uneasy English voice, the tone rich, the manner shocked, as if its owner never expected it to say the things he is hearing. The slight accent is East Indian Dutch. The bungalow is unlit, designed for fornication, and gives on to a tiny illuminated swimming pool and concrete rockery. Beyond this nonsense lies a superb and placid Asian sea, with a wide moon-path, and stars sparkling in the water like sunspots. A couple of fishermen stand upright in their sampans, tossing their round nets into the water and drawing them slowly out again.

In the foreground you must set the jagged, towering figure of Hansen as he prowls the room in his bare feet, now pausing at the french window, now perching himself on the arm of a chair before slipping soundlessly away to another corner. And always the voice, now fierce, now ruminative, now shaken, and now, like his body, resting itself for minutes on end while it gathers strength for the next ordeal.

Stretched on her daybed, the Cambodian girl lies wrapped in a blanket, her forearm crooked Asian style beneath her head. Was she awake? Did she understand what he was saying? Did she care? Hansen cared. He could not pass her without stopping to gaze down at her, or fiddle with the blanket at her neck. Once, dropping to the floor beside her, he stared ardently into her closed eyes while he laid his palm on her brow as if to test her temperature.

'She needs limes,' he murmured. 'Coca-Cola is nothing for her. Limes.'

I had sent out for them already. They arrived, by hand of a boy from the front desk. There was business while Hansen squeezed them for her, then held her upright while she drank.

His first questions were a vague catechism about my standing in the Service. He wished to know with what authority I had been sent, with what instructions.

'I want no thanks for what I have done,' he warned me. 'There are no thanks for bombing villages.'

'But you may need help,' I said.

His response was to tell me formally that he would never again, in any circumstance, work for the Service. I could have told him that too, but I refrained. He had thought he was working for the British, he said, but he had been working for murderers. He had been another man when he did the things he did. He hoped the American pilots had been other men as well.

He asked after his sub-agents – the farmer so-and-so, the rice trader so-and-so. He asked about the stay-behind network he had painstakingly built up against the certain day when the Khmer Rouge would break out of the jungle and help themselves to the cities, a thing that neither we nor the Americans, despite all the warnings, had ever quite believed would happen. But Hansen had believed it. Hansen was one of the warners. Hansen had told us time and again that Kissinger's bombs were dragon's teeth, even though Hansen had helped direct them to their targets.

'May I believe you?' he asked me when I assured him there had been no pattern of arrests among his sources.

'It's the truth,' I said, responding to the supplication in his voice.

'Then I didn't betray them,' he muttered in marvel. For a moment he sat and cupped his head in his hands, as if holding it together.

'If you were captured by the Khmer Rouge, nobody could expect you to stay silent, anyway,' I said.

'Silent! My God.' He almost laughed. 'Silent!' And, standing sharply, he swung away to the window again.

By the moonlight I saw tears of sweat clinging to his great bearded face. I started to say something about the Service wishing to acquit itself honourably by him, but halfway through my speech he flung out his arms to their fullest

extent, as if testing the limits of his confinement. Finding
nothing to obstruct them, they fell back to his sides.

'The Service to hell,' he said softly. 'The West to bloody,
bloody hell. We have no business making our wars here, ped-
dling our religious recipes. We have sinned against Asia: the
French, the British, the Dutch, now the Americans. We have
sinned against the children of Eden. God forgive us.'

My tape recorder lay on the table.

We are in Asia. Hansen's Asia. The Asia sinned against. Listen
to the frenetic chatter of the insects. Thais and Cambodians
alike have been known to bet large sums on the number of
times a bullfrog will burp. The room is twilit, the hour forgotten, the room forgotten also; the moon has risen out of
sight. The Vietnam War is back with us, and we are in the
Cambodian jungle with Hansen, and modern comforts are
few, unless we include the American bombers that circle
miles above us, like patient hawks, waiting for the computers
to tell them what to destroy next: for instance, a team of
oxen whose urine has been misread by secret sensors as the
exhaust fumes of a military convoy; for instance, children
whose chatter has been mistaken for military commands.
The sensors have been hidden by American commandos
along the supply routes Hansen has indicated to them –
but unfortunately the sensors are not as well informed as
Hansen is.

We are in what the American pilots call badland, though
in the jungle definitions of good and bad are fluid. We are in
a Khmer Rouge 'liberated area' that provides sanctuary for
Vietcong troops who wish to attack the Americans in the
flank rather than head-on from the north. Yet despite these
appearances of war, we are among people with no collective

perception of their enemies, in a region unmapped except by fighters. To hear Hansen speak, the region is as close to paradise as makes no difference, whether he speaks as priest, sinner, scholar or spy.

A few miles up the trail by jeep is an ancient Buddhist temple which, with the help of villagers, Hansen has excavated from the depths of vegetation, and which is the apparent reason for his being there, and for the notes he takes, and for the wireless messages he sends, and for the trickle of visitors who arrive usually just before nightfall, and depart at first light. The kampong where he lives is built on stilts in a clearing at the edge of a good river, in a plain of fertile fields that climb in steps to a rain forest. A blue mist is frequent. Hansen's house is set high up the slope in order to improve his radio reception and give a view of whatever enters and leaves the valley. In the wet season, it is his habit to leave the jeep in the village and trudge up to his house on foot. In the dry season, he drives into his compound, most often taking half the village children with him. As many as a dozen of them will be waiting to clamber over the tailboard for the five-minute ride from the village to his compound.

'Sometimes my daughter was among them,' Hansen said.

Neither Rumbelow nor the file had mentioned that Hansen had a daughter. If he had hidden her from us, he was gravely in breach of Service rules – though heaven knows, Service rules were about the last thing that mattered to either of us by then. Nevertheless he stopped speaking and glared at me in the darkness as if waiting for my reproof. But I preserved my silence, wishing to be the ear he had been waiting for, perhaps for years.

'While I was still a priest, I visited the temples of Cambodia,' he said. 'While I was there, I fell in love with a village woman and made her pregnant. In Cambodia it was the best time still. Sihanouk ruled. I remained with her until the child was born. A girl. I christened her Marie. I gave the mother money and returned to Djakarta, but I missed my child terribly. I sent more money. I sent money to the headman to look after them. I sent letters. I prayed for the child and her mother, and swore that one day I would care for them properly. As soon as I returned to Cambodia, I put the mother in my house, even though in the intervening years she had lost her beauty. My daughter had a Khmer name, but from the day she came to me I called her Marie. She liked that. She was proud to have me as her father.'

He seemed concerned to make clear to me that Marie was at ease with her European name. It was not an American name, he said. It was European.

'I had other women in my household, but Marie was my only child and I loved her. She was more beautiful than I had imagined her. But if she had been ugly and ungracious I would have loved her no less.' His voice acquired sudden strength and, as I heard it, warning. 'No woman, no man, no child, ever claimed my love in such a way. You may say that Marie is the only woman I have loved purely except for my mother.' He was staring at me in the darkness, challenging me to doubt his passion. But under Hansen's spell, I doubted nothing and had forgotten everything about myself, even my own mother's death. He was assuming me, occupying me.

'Once you have embarked upon the impossible concept of God, you will know that real love permits no rejection. Perhaps that is something only a sinner can properly understand. Only a sinner knows the scale of God's forgiveness.'

I think I nodded wisely. I thought of Colonel Jerzy. I was wondering why Hansen needed to explain that he could not reject his daughter. Or why his sinfulness was a concern to him when he spoke of her.

'That evening when I drove home from the temple, there were no children waiting for me in the kampong, though it was the dry season. I was disappointed because we had made a good find that day and I wanted to tell Marie about it. They must be having a school festival, I thought, but I could not think which one. I drove up the hill to the compound and called her name. The compound was empty. The gatehouse empty. The women's cookpots empty under the stilts. I called Marie again, then my wife. Then anybody. No one came. I drove back to the village. I went into the house of one of Marie's friends, then another and another, calling Marie. Even the pigs and chickens had disappeared. I looked for blood, for traces of fighting. There were none. But I found footprints leading into the jungle. I drove back to the compound. I took a spade and cached my radio in the forest, halfway between two tall trees that made a line due west, close to an old ant-hill shaped like a man. I hated all my work for you, all my lies, for you and for the Americans. I still do. I walked back to the house, uncached my codepads and equipment and destroyed them. I was glad to. I hated them also. I put on boots and filled a rucksack with food for a week. With my revolver I sent three bullets through the jeep's engine to immobilise it; then I followed the footprints into the jungle. The jeep was an insult to me, because you had bought it.'

Alone, Hansen had set off in pursuit of the Khmer Rouge. Other men – even men who were not Western spies – might have thought twice and a third time, even with their wife and daughter taken hostage. Not Hansen. Hansen had one thought and, absolutist that he was, he acted on it.

'I could not allow myself to be separated from God's

grace,' he said. He was telling me, in case I did not know, that beyond the girl's survival lay the survival of his immortal soul.

I asked him how long he had marched for. He didn't know. To begin with he had marched only at night and lain up by day. But the daylight gnawed at him and gradually, against all jungle sense, it drew him forward. As he marched, he recalled every event of Marie's life from the night when he had lifted her from her mother's womb and, with a ritual bamboo stave, cut the cord and ordered the women in attendance to give him water so that he could wash her; and with the water, by his authority as priest and father, had christened her Marie after his own mother and the mother of Christ.

He remembered the nights when she had lain sleeping in his arms or in the rush crib at his feet. He saw her at her mother's breast in the firelight. He flailed himself for the dreadful years of separation in Djakarta and on his training course in England. He flailed himself for all the falsity of his work for the Service, and for his weakness, as he described it, his treachery against Asia. He was referring to his work of directing the American bombers.

He relived the hours he had spent telling her stories and singing her to sleep with English and Dutch songs. He cared only for his love for her, and his need of her, and for her need of him.

He was following the tracks because he had nothing else to follow. He knew now what had happened. It had happened to other kampongs, though none in Hansen's region. The fighters had surrounded the kampong at night and waited till dawn, when the able-bodied left for the fields. They had taken the able-bodied, then crept into the village and taken the elderly and the children, afterwards the livestock. They were provisioning themselves but they were also adding to their ranks. They were in a hurry or they would have ransacked the houses, but they wanted to return to the jungle before they were discovered. Soon, by the light of a full moon, Hansen came upon the first grisly proofs of his theory: the naked bodies of an old storekeeper and his wife, their hands bound behind their backs. Had they been unable to keep up? Were they too ugly? Had they argued?

Hansen marched faster. He was thanking God that Marie looked like a full Asian. In most children of mixed blood, the European strain would have been there for every Asian to see, but Hansen, though a giant, was dark-skinned and slim-bodied, and somehow with his Asian soul he had succeeded in engendering an Asian girl.

Next night another corpse lay beside the trail and Hansen approached it fearfully. It was Ong Sai, the argumentative schoolmistress. Her mouth was wide open. Shot while protesting, Hansen diagnosed, and pressed anxiously forward. In search of Marie, his pure love, the earth mother who was his daughter, the only keeper of his grace.

He wondered which sort of unit he was following. The shy boys who banged on your door at night to ask a little rice for the fighters? The grim-jawed cadres who regarded the Asian smile as an emblem of Western decadence? And there were the zombies, he remembered: freebooting packs of homeless who had clubbed together from necessity, more outlaws than guerrillas. But already in the group ahead of him he had an intimation of discipline. A less organised gang would have stayed to loot the village. They would have made camp to eat a meal and congratulate themselves. On the morning after he found Ong Sai, Hansen took special care to conceal himself while he slept.

'I had a premonition,' he said.

In the jungle you ignored premonition at your peril. He buried himself deep in the undergrowth and smeared himself with mud. He slept with his revolver in his hand. He woke at evening to the smell of woodsmoke and the shrill sound of shouting, and when he opened his eyes he found himself looking straight into the barrels of several automatic rifles.

He was talking about the chains. Jungle fighters, trained to travel light, humping a dozen sets of manacles for hundreds of kilometres – how had it happened? He was still mystified. Yet somebody had carried them, somebody had made a clearing and driven a stake into the centre of the clearing, and dropped the iron rings round the stake, and attached the twelve sets of chains to the twelve iron rings in order to tether twelve special prisoners to the rain and heat and cold and dark. Hansen described the pattern of the chains. To do so, he broke into French. I assumed he needed the protection of a different language. '*…une tringle collective sur laquelle étaient enfilés des étriers . . . nous étions fixés par un pied . . . j'avais été mis au bout de la chaîne parce que ma cheville trop grosse ne passait pas . . .*'

I glanced at the girl. She lay, if it were possible, more inert than before. She could have been dead or in a trance. I realised Hansen was sparing her something he did not want her to hear.

By day, he said, still in French, our ankles were released, enabling us to kneel and even crawl, though never far, because we were tethered to the stake and had each other's bodies to contend with. Only by night, when our foot irons were fixed to heavy poles that made up the circumference of the enclosure, were we able to stretch full length. The availability of chains determined the number of special prisoners, who were drawn exclusively from the village bourgeoisie, he said. He recognised two village elders, and a stringy forty-year-old widow called Ra who had a reputation for prophecy. And the three rice-dealing brothers Liu, who were famous misers, one of whom looked already dead, for he lay curled round his chains like a hairless hedgehog. Only the sound of his sobbing proved he was alive.

And Hansen, with his horror of captivity? How had he responded to his chains?

'*Je les ai portées pour Marie,*' he answered in the swift, warning French I was learning to respect.

The prisoners who were not special were confined to a stockade at the clearing's edge, from which at intervals one of them was led or dragged to headquarters, a place out of sight behind a hillock. Questioning was brief. After a few hours' screaming, a single pistol shot would ring out and the uneasy quiet of the jungle would return. Nobody came back from questioning. The children, including Marie, were allowed to roam provided they did not approach the prisoners or venture up the hillock which hid the headquarters. The boldest of them had already struck up an acquaintance with the young fighters during the march, and were scurrying around them trying to perform errands or touch their guns.

But Marie had stayed apart from everyone. She sat in the dust of the clearing on the other side of the poles, watching over her father from dawn till night. Even when they hauled her mother from the stockade and her screams for Hansen rang out from behind the hillock, changing to screams for mercy and ending with the usual pistol shot, Marie's eyes never flinched from Hansen's face.

'Did she know?' I asked in French.

'The whole camp knew,' he replied.

'Had she been fond of her mother?'

Was it my imagination or had Hansen closed his eyes in the darkness?

'I was the father of Marie,' he replied. 'I was not the father of their relationship.'

How had I known that the mother and daughter had hated each other? Was it because I sensed that Hansen's love for Marie had been a jealous and demanding one – absolute, like all his loves, excluding rivals?

'I was not allowed to speak to her, nor she to me,' he was saying. 'Prisoners spoke to nobody on pain of death.'

Even a groan was enough, as one of the luckless Liu brothers learned when the guards reduced him to permanent silence with their rifle butts, and replaced him next morning with a cringing leftover from the stockade. But between Marie and her father no words were necessary. The stoicism Hansen saw in his daughter's face was the impassioned determination of his own heart as he lay bound and helpless in his chains. With Marie to support him, he could bear anything. Each would be the salvation of the other. Her love for him was as fierce and single-minded as his for her. He did not doubt it. For all his loathing of captivity, he thanked God he had followed her.

A day passed and another, but Hansen remained chained to the stake, burning in the sun, shaking in the evening cold, stinking in his own filth, his gaze and spirit fixed always upon Marie.

In his head, meanwhile, he was wrestling with the tactics of his situation.

From the start it had been clear to him that he was a celebrity. If they had been planning to capture a European, they would have made their attack before Hansen left his house, and searched the house afterwards. He was unexpected treasure, and they were waiting to hear what should be done with him. Others on the stake were fetched and disappeared, all but the one surviving Liu brother and the woman fortune teller, who after days of noisy questioning reappeared as camp trusties, abusing their former companions and trying by every means to ingratiate themselves with the soldiers.

An indoctrination class was formed, and each evening the children and selected survivors sat in a circle in the shade to be harangued by a young commissar with a red headband. While Hansen burned and froze, he could hear the commissar's shrill squawk, hour by hour, as he ranted against the hated imperialists. At first he resented these classes because they took Marie away from him. But when he made the effort, he could still lift his head high enough to see her straight body seated strictly at the far side of the circle, staring at him across the clearing. I will be your mother and your father and your friend, he told her. I will be your life, if I have to give up my own.

At other times he reproached himself with her spectacular beauty, regarding it as a punishment for his random lusts. Marie at twelve was without doubt the most beautiful in the camp, and though sex was forbidden to the cadres on the grounds that it was a bourgeois threat to their revolutionary will, Hansen could not help observe the effect that her thinly clothed figure had on the young fighters as they watched her pass; how their dulled eyes drank in her sprouting breasts and swinging haunches beneath the torn cotton frock, and their scowls darkened when they yelled at her. Worse still, he knew she was aware of their desire, and that her emerging womanhood responded to it.

Then a morning came when the routine of Hansen's captivity unaccountably improved, and his apprehensions deepened, for his benefactor was the young commissar in the red headband. Escorted by two soldiers, the commissar ordered Hansen to stand. When he was unable, the soldiers lifted him to his feet and, taking an arm each, let him stagger to a point along the river bank where an inlet made a natural pool.

'Wash,' the young commissar ordered.

For days – ever since they had bound him – Hansen had been vainly demanding the right to clean himself. On his first evening he had roared at them, 'Take me to the river!' They had beaten him. The next morning he had flung himself about on his chains, risking more beatings, yelling for a responsible comrade, all to assert his right to remain a person whom his captors could respect and consequently preserve.

Under the gaze of the soldiers, Hansen sufficiently rallied his racked limbs to bathe and – though it was a crucifixion – rub himself with the fine river mud before being led back to the stake. On each journey, he passed within a few feet of his beloved Marie in her habitual place beyond the ring of poles. Though his heart leapt at her nearness and the courage in her eyes, he could not suppress the suspicion that it was his own child who had purchased the rare comfort he was now enjoying. And when the commissar grunted a greeting to her, and Marie lifted her head and gave half a smile in return, the anguish of jealousy added itself to Hansen's pains.

After his bathe, they brought him rice – more than they

had given him in all the time he had been their prisoner. And instead of making him eat it from the bowl like a dog, they untied his hands and let him use his fingers, so that he was able to secrete a small amount in his palm, and drop it down the front of his tunic before they chained him again.

All day long he thought of nothing but the pellet of rice inside his shirt, making sure no movement of his body crushed it. I will win her back, he thought. I will supplant the commissar in her admiration. When evening came and they again led him to the river, he achieved the miracle he had been planning. Staggering more dramatically than was necessary, he succeeded in dropping a pellet of rice at Marie's feet, unnoticed by his guards. As he passed by her again on his way back, he saw to his secret ecstasy that it had vanished.

Yet her face told him nothing. Only her eyes, straight and sometimes lifeless in their devotion, told him she returned his absolute love. I was deluding myself, he decided as they refastened his chains. She is learning the prisoner's tricks. She is chaste and will survive. That evening he listened with a new tolerance to the commissar's indoctrination class. Lead him on, he urged her in the telepathic dialogue he conducted with her constantly; lull him, bewitch him, gain his trust but give him nothing. And Marie must have heard him, because as the class broke up he saw the commissar beckon her over to him and rebuke her while she remained cowed and silent. He saw her head fall forward. He saw her walk away from him, her head still lowered.

Next day and for a week, Hansen repeated his trick, convinced he was unobserved except by Marie. The pellet of rice, rolling lightly over his stomach each time he shifted his body, became a source of vital comfort to him. I am nourishing her from my own breast. I am her guardian, the protector of her chastity. I am her priest, giving her Christ's Sacrament.

The rice was all that mattered to him. His concern was to contrive new ways to smuggle it to her, waiting till he was past her and flicking the pellet backward, letting it fall down the inside of his tattered trouser leg.

'I was inordinate,' he said softly, in the tone of a penitent.

And because he had been inordinate, God took Marie from him. Suddenly one morning when they unchained him and led him to the pool, there was no Marie waiting to receive her Sacrament. At the evening indoctrination class, he saw that she had been elevated to the commissar's side, and he thought he heard her voice above the rest, intoning the liturgical responses with a new self-confidence. When night fell, he picked out her silhouette among the soldiers' fires – an accepted member of their company, sharing their rice like a comrade. Next day he did not see her at all, nor the day after.

'I wished to die,' he said.

But in the evening as he waited in despair, prone and motionless, for the guards to chain his feet, it was the young commissar who marched towards him, and Marie, dressed in a black tunic, who trotted at his side.

'Is this man your father?' the commissar asked as they reached Hansen.

Marie's stare did not falter, but she seemed to be searching her memory for her reply. 'Angka is my father,' she said finally. 'Angka is the father of all oppressed.'

'Angka was the Party,' Hansen explained for me, without my asking. 'Angka was the Organisation that the Khmer Rouge prayed to. In the Khmer Rouge's ladder of beings, Angka was God.'

'So who is your mother?' the commissar asked Marie.

'My mother is Angka. I have no mother but Angka.'

'Who is this man?'

'He is an American agent,' Marie replied. 'He drops bombs on our villages. He kills our workers.'

'Why does he pretend he is your father?'

'He wishes to trick us by claiming to be our comrade.'

'Test the spy's chains. See that they are tight enough,' the commissar commanded.

Marie knelt to Hansen's feet, exactly as he had taught her to kneel in prayer. For a moment, like the healing touch of Christ, her hand closed over his festering ankles.

'Can you insert your fingers between the chain and ankle?' the commissar asked.

In his panic, Hansen behaved as he always did when his feet were being chained. He flexed his ankle muscles, hoping to give himself more freedom when he relaxed. He felt her finger probe the chain.

'I can insert my little finger,' she replied, holding it up while she kept her body in the line of sight between the commissar and Hansen's feet.

'Can you insert it with difficulty or easily?'

'I can insert my finger only with difficulty,' she lied.

Watching them march away, Hansen noticed something that alarmed him. With her black tunic, Marie had put on the stealthy waddle of the jungle fighter. All the same, for the first time since his capture, Hansen slept soundly in his chains. She is joining them in order to deceive them, he assured himself. God is protecting us. Soon we shall escape.

The official interrogator arrived by boat, a smooth-cheeked student with an earnest, frowning manner. In Hansen's mind, that was how he named him: the student. A reception committee led by the commissar met him at the river bank and escorted him over the hillock to headquarters. Hansen knew he was the interrogator because he was the only one who did not turn his head to look at the last remaining prisoner rotting in the heat. But he looked at Marie. He stopped in front of her, obliging everybody to stop with him. He stood before her; he held his studious face close to her while he asked her questions Hansen could not hear. He kept it there while he listened to her parrot answers. My daughter is the camp whore, thought Hansen in despair. But was she? Nothing he had ever heard about the Khmer Rouge suggested they appointed or even tolerated prostitutes in their midst. Everything suggested the contrary. *'Angka hait le sexuel,'* a French anthropologist had said to him once.

Then they are ravishing her with their puritanism, he decided. They have locked her to them in a passion that is worse than a debauching. He lay with his face in the earth, praying to be allowed to take her sins of innocence upon himself.

I have no coherent picture of Hansen's interrogation for the reason he had little himself. I remembered my own treatment at the hands of Colonel Jerzy, and it was child's play by comparison. But Hansen's recollections had the same imprecision. That they tortured him goes without saying. They had built a wooden grid for the purpose. Yet they were also concerned to keep him alive, because between sessions they gave him food and even, if he remembered rightly, allowed him visits to the river bank, though it may have been a single visit broken by spells of unconsciousness.

There were also the sessions of writing, for in the literal mind of the student, no confession was real until it was written down. And the writing grew harder and harder and became a punishment in itself, even though they unstrapped him from the grid to make him do it.

As an interrogator, the student seems to have proceeded simultaneously on two intellectual fronts. When he was checked on the one, he shifted to the other.

You are an American spy, he said, and an agent of the counter-revolutionary puppet Lon Nol, also an enemy of the revolution. Hansen disagreed.

But you're also a Roman Catholic masquerading as a Buddhist, a prisoner of minds, a promoter of anti-Party superstitions, and a saboteur of the popular enlightenment, the student screamed at him.

In general, the student seems to have preferred making statements to asking questions: 'You will now please give all dates and places of your conspiratorial meetings with the counter-revolutionary puppet and American spy Lon Nol, naming all Americans present.'

Hansen insisted that no such meetings had occurred. But this gave the student no satisfaction. As the agony increased, Hansen recalled the names from an English folksong that his mother had used to sing him: Tom Pearce . . . Bill Brewer . . . Jan Stewer . . . Peter Gurney . . . Peter Davy . . . Dan'l Whidden . . . Harry Hawk . . .

'You will now please write down the ringleader of this rabble,' the student said, turning a page of his notebook. The student's eyes, said Hansen, were often nearly closed. I remembered that about Jerzy too.

'Cobbleigh,' Hansen whispered, lifting his head from the desk where they had sat him. *Thomas Cobbleigh,* he wrote. *Tom for short. Covername Uncle.*

The dates were important because Hansen was concerned

he would forget them once he had invented them, and be accused of inconsistency. He chose Marie's birthday and his mother's birthday and the date of his father's execution. He altered the year to suit Lon Nol's accession to power. For a conspiratorial place, he selected the walled gardens of Lon Nol's palace in Phnom Penh, which he had often admired on his way to a favourite *fumerie.*

His fear while he was confessing to this rubbish was that he would reveal true information by mistake, for it was by now clear to him that the student knew nothing about his real intelligence-gathering activities, and that the charges against him were based on the fact that he was a Westerner.

'You will please write down the name of each spy paid by you in the last five years, also each act of sabotage committed by you against the people.'

Not in all the days and nights that Hansen had passed anticipating his ordeal had he imagined he might fail on the score of creativity. He recited the names of martyrs whose agonies he had contemplated in order to prepare himself; of Oriental scholars safely dead; of authors of learned works on philology and linguistics. Spies, he said. All spies. And wrote them down, his hand jerking on the paper to the convulsions of the pain that continued to rack him long after they switched off the machine.

Writing desperately, he made a list of T. E. Lawrence's officers in the desert, which he remembered from his many readings of *Seven Pillars of Wisdom.* He described how on Lon Nol's personal orders he had organised the poisoning of crops and cattle by Buddhist priests. The student put him back on the grid and increased the pain.

He described the clandestine classes he had held in imperialism, and how he had encouraged the spread of bourgeois sentiment and family virtues. The student opened his eyes, offered his commiserations and again increased the pain.

He gave them nearly everything. He described how he had lit beacons to guide American bombers, and distributed rumours that the bombers were Chinese. He was on the brink of telling them who had helped him to lead American commandos to the supply trails, when mercifully he fainted.

But throughout his ordeal it was still Marie with whom he lived in his heart, to whom he cried out in his pain, whose hands drew him back to life when his body was begging to relinquish it, whose eyes watched over him in love and pity. It was Marie to whom he sacrificed his suffering and for whom he swore to survive. As he lay between life and death, he had an hallucination in which he saw himself stretched out in the well of the student's boat and Marie in her black tunic seated over him, paddling them upriver to heaven. But he still was not dead. They have not killed me. I have confessed to everything and they have not killed me.

But he had not confessed to everything. He had remained true to his helpers and he had not told them about his radio. And when they dragged him back next day and strapped him once more to the grid, he saw Marie sitting at the student's side, a copy of his confession lying before her on the table. Her hair was cropped, her expression closed.

'Are you familiar with the statements of this spy?' the student asked her.

'I am familiar with his statements,' she replied.

'Do the spy's statements accurately depict his lifestyle as you were able to observe it in his company?'

'No.'

'Why not?' the student asked, opening his notebook.

'They are not complete.'

'Explain why the spy Hansen's statements are not complete.'

'The spy Hansen kept a radio in his house which he used for signalling to the imperialist bombers. Also the names he has mentioned in his confession are fictitious. They are taken from a bourgeois English song which he sang to me when he was pretending to be my father. Also he received imperialist soldiers at our house at night and led them into the jungle. Also he has failed to mention that he has an English mother.'

The student appeared disappointed. 'What else has he failed to mention?' he asked, flattening a fresh page with the edge of his small hand.

'During his confinement, he has been guilty of many breaches of regulation. He has hoarded food and attempted to buy the collaboration of comrades in his plans to escape.'

The student sighed and made more notes. 'What else has he failed to mention?' he asked patiently.

'He has been wearing his foot chains improperly. When the chains were being fastened, he braced his feet illegally, leaving the chains loose for his escape.'

Until that moment Hansen had managed to persuade himself that Marie was playing a cunning game. No longer. The game was the reality.

'He is a whoremonger!' she screamed through her tears. 'He debauches our women by bringing them to his house and drugging them! He pretends to make a bourgeois marriage, then forces his wife to tolerate his decadent practices! He sleeps with girls of my own age! He pretends he is the father of our children and that our blood is not Khmer! He reads us bourgeois literature in Western languages in order to deprave us! He seduces us by taking us for rides in his jeep and singing imperialist songs to us!'

He had never heard her scream before. Nor evidently had the student, who appeared embarrassed. But she would not be checked. She persisted in denying him. She told them how he had forbidden her mother to love her. She was expressing a hatred for him that he knew was unfeigned, as absolute and inordinate as his love for her. Her body shook with the pent-up hatred of a misused woman, her features were crumpled with hatred and guilt. Her arm struck out and she pointed at him in the classic posture of accusation. Her voice belonged to someone he had never known.

'Kill him!' she screamed. 'Kill the despoiler of our people! Kill the corrupter of our Khmer blood! Kill the Western liar who tells us we are different from one another! Avenge the people!'

The student made a last note and ordered Marie to be led away.

'I prayed for her forgiveness,' Hansen said.

In the bungalow, I realised, it was dawn. Hansen was standing at the window, his eyes fixed on the misty plateau of the sea. The girl lay on the daybed where she had lain all night, her eyes closed, the empty Coca-Cola can beside her, her head still supported by her arm. Her hand, hanging down, looked worn and elderly. A terseness had entered Hansen's voice, and for a moment I feared that with morning he had decided to resent me. Then I realised it was not me he was at odds with but himself. He was remembering his anger as they carried him, bound but not chained, to the stockade to sleep – if sleep is what you do when your body is dying of pain, and the blood is filling your ears and nose. Anger against himself, that he had implanted in his child so much loathing.

'I was her father still,' he said in French. 'I blamed Marie for nothing, myself for everything. If only I had made my escape earlier, instead of counting on her to help me. If only I had fought my way out when I was strong, instead of placing my reliance in a child. I should never have worked for you. My secret work had endangered her. I cursed you all. I still do.'

Did I speak? My concern was to say nothing that would obstruct his flow.

'She was drawn to them,' he said, making her excuses for her. 'They were her own people, jungle fighters with a faith to die for. Why should she reject them?

'I was the last obstacle to her acceptance by her people,' he said, explaining her. 'I was an intruder, a corrupter. Why should she believe I was her father when they were telling her I was not?'

Still lying in the stockade, he remembered her on the day the young commissar dressed her in her bridal black. He remembered her expression of distaste as she stared down at him, fouled and beaten, a beggar at her feet, a cringing Western spy. And beside her, the handsome commissar with his red headband. 'I am wedded to the Angka,' she was saying to him. 'The Angka answers all my questions.'

'I was alone,' he said.

Darkness fell in the stockade, and he supposed that if they were going to shoot him they would wait for daylight. But the notion that Marie would go through life knowing she had ordered her father's death appalled him. He imagined her in middle age. Who would help her? Who would confess her? Who would give her release and absolution? The idea of his death became increasingly alarming to him. It will be her death too.

At some point he must have dozed, he said, for when dawn

came he found a bowl of rice on the floor of the stockade and he knew it had not been there the night before; even in his agony he would have smelt it. Not rolled into pellets, the rice, not hoarded against the naked skin, but a white mound of it, enough for five days. At first he was too tired to be surprised. Lying on his stomach to eat, he noticed the quiet. By this hour the clearing should have been alive with the sounds of soldiers waking for the day: singsong voices and washing noises from the river bank, the clatter of pans and rifles, the chant of slogans led by the commissar. Yet when he paused to listen, even the birds and monkeys seemed to have stopped their shrieking and he heard no human sounds at all.

'They had gone,' he said, from somewhere behind me. 'They had decamped in the night, taking Marie with them.'

He ate more rice and dozed again. Why have they not killed me? Marie has talked them out of it. Marie has bought me my life. Hansen set to work chafing his bonds against the wall of the stockade. By nightfall, covered in sores and flies, he was lying on the river bank, washing his wounds. He crawled back to the stockade to sleep, and next morning, with the remainder of his rice, he set off. This time, having no prisoners or livestock, they had left no tracks.

All the same, he went in search of her.

For months, Hansen thinks five or six, he remained in the jungle, moving from village to village, never settling, trusting no one – I suspect a little crazed. Wherever he could, he enquired after Marie's unit, but there was too little to describe it by and his quest became indiscriminate. He heard of units that had fighting girls. He heard of units that consisted of girls only. He heard of girls being sent into the towns as whores to gather information. He imagined Marie in all these situations. One night he crept back to his old house hoping she had taken refuge there. The village had been burned.

I asked him whether his cached wireless had been disturbed.

'I didn't look,' he replied. 'I didn't care. I hated you all.'

Another night he called on Marie's aunt, who lived in a remote village, but she hurled pans at him and he had to flee. Yet his determination to rescue his daughter was stronger than ever, for he knew now that he must rescue her from herself. She is cursed with my absolutism, he thought. She is violent and headstrong; it is I who am to blame. I have locked her in the prison of my own impulses. Only a father's love could ever have blinded him to this knowledge. Now his eyes were open. He saw her drawn to cruelty and inhumanity as a means of proving her devotion. He saw her reliving his own erratic quest, yet deprived of his intellectual and religious disciplines – vaguely believing, like himself, that her assumption into a great vision would bring her self-fulfilment.

Of his walk to the Thai border he said little. He headed southwest towards Pailin. He had heard there was a camp there for Khmer refugees. He crossed mountains and malarial marshes. Once arrived, he besieged the tracing centres and pinned her description on camp noticeboards. How he achieved this without papers, money or connections, yet kept his presence in Thailand secret, is a mystery to me still. But Hansen was a trained and hardened agent, even if he denied us. He was not disposed to let much stop him. I asked why he did not turn to Rumbelow for help, but he shook off the idea contemptuously.

'I was not an imperialist agent any more. I believed in nothing but my daughter.'

One day in the office of a relief organisation, he met an American woman who thought she remembered Marie.

'She left,' she said cautiously.

Hansen pressed her. Marie was one of a group of half a dozen girls, said the woman. They were whores but they had the assurance of fighters. When they were not entertaining men, they kept themselves apart from everyone and were tough to handle. One day they broke bounds. She had heard they were picked up by the Thai police. She never saw them again.

The woman who said this appeared unsure whether to say what else was on her mind, but Hansen gave her no choice.

'We were afraid for her,' she said. 'She gave different names for herself. She gave conflicting accounts of how she came to us. The doctors argued over whether she was mad. Somewhere along her journey, she had lost track of who she was.'

Hansen presented himself to the Thai police and, by threats or animal persuasion, traced Marie to a police hostel run for the enjoyment of the officers. They never asked him who he was, it seems, or what he had for papers. He was a round-eye, a *farang*, who spoke Khmer and Thai. Marie had stayed three months, then vanished, they said. She was strange, said a kindly sergeant.

'What is strange?' Hansen asked.

'She would speak only English,' the sergeant replied.

There was another girl, a friend of Marie's, who had stayed longer and married one of the corporals. Hansen obtained her name.

He had ceased speaking.

'And did you find her?' I asked after a long silence.

I knew the answer already, as I had known it from halfway

through his story, without knowing that I knew. He was sitting at the girl's head, which he was gently stroking. Slowly she sat upright and with her little, old hands rubbed her eyes, pretending she had been asleep. I think she had listened to us all night.

'It was all she understood any more,' Hansen explained in English, while he continued to stroke her head. He was speaking of the brothel where he had found her. 'She wanted no big choices, did you, Marie? No big words, no promises.' He pressed her to him. 'She wishes only to be admired. By her own people. By us. All of us must love Marie. That is what comforts her.'

I think he mistook my reticence for reproach, for his voice rose. 'She wishes to be harmless. Is that so bad? She wishes to be left alone, as all of them wish. It would be a good thing if more of us wished the same. Your bombers and your spies and your big talk are not for her. She is not the child of Dr Kissinger. She asks only for a small existence where she can give pleasure and hurt no one. Which is worse? Your brothel or hers? Get out of Asia. You should never have come, any of you. I am ashamed I ever helped you. Leave us alone.'

'I shall tell Rumbelow very little of this,' I said as I rose to leave.

'Tell him what you like.'

From the doorway, I took a last look at them. The girl was staring at me as I believe she had stared at Hansen from outside the circle of chains, her eyes unflinching, deep and still. I thought I knew what was in her mind. I had paid for her and not had her. She was wondering whether I wanted my money's worth.

Rumbelow drove me to the airport. Like Hansen, I would have preferred to do without him, but we had matters to discuss.

'You promised him *how* much?' he cried in horror.

'I told him he was entitled to a resettlement grant and all the protection we can give him. I told him you would be sending him a cashier's cheque for fifty thousand dollars.'

Rumbelow was furious. '*Me* give *him* fifty thousand dollars? My dear man, he'll be drunk for six months and spill his life story all over Bangkok. What about that Cambodian whore of his? She's in the know, I'll bet.'

'Don't worry,' I said. 'He turned me down.'

This news astonished Rumbelow so profoundly that he ran out of indignation altogether, preserving instead a wounded silence that lasted us the rest of the journey.

On the plane I drank too much and slept too little. Once, waking from a bad dream, I was guilty of a seditious thought about Rumbelow and the Fifth Floor. I wished I could pack off the whole tribe of them on Hansen's march into the jungle, Smiley included. I wished I could make them throw everything over for a flawed and impossible passion, only to see the object of it turn against them, proving there is no reward for love except the experience of loving, and nothing to be learned by it except humility.

Yet I was content, as I am content to this day whenever I think of Hansen. I had found what I was looking for – a man like myself, but one who in his search for meaning had discovered a worthwhile object for his life; who had paid every price and not counted it a sacrifice; who was paying it still and would pay it till he died; who cared nothing for compromise, nothing for his pride, nothing for ourselves or the opinion of others; who had reduced his life to the one thing that mattered to him, and was free. The slumbering subversive in me had met his champion. The would-be lover in me had found a scale by which to measure his own trivial preoccupations.

So that when a few years later I was appointed Head of the Russia House, only to watch my most valuable agent betray his country for his love, I could never quite muster the outrage required of me by my masters. Personnel was not all stupid when he packed me off to the Interrogators' Pool.

Maggs, my unpleasing crypto journalist, was trying to draw Smiley on the amoral nature of our work. He was wanting Smiley to admit that anything went, as long as you got away with it. I suspect he was actually wanting to hear this maxim applied to the whole of life, for he was ruthless as well as mannerless, and wished to see in our work some kind of licence to throw aside his few remaining scruples.

But Smiley would not give him this satisfaction. At first he appeared ready to be angry, which I hoped he would be. If so, he checked himself. He started to speak, but stopped again, and faltered, leaving me wondering whether it was time to call a halt to the proceedings. Until, to my relief, he rallied, and I knew he had merely been distracted by some private memory among the thousands that made up his secret self.

'You see,' he explained – replying, as so often, to the spirit rather than the letter of the question – 'it really is essential in a free society that the people who do our work should remain unreconciled. It's true that we are obliged to sup with the Devil, and not always with a very long spoon. And as everyone knows' – a sly glance at Maggs produced a gust of grateful laughter – 'the Devil is often far better company than the Godly, isn't he? All the same, our obsession with virtue won't go away. Self-interest is so *limiting.* So is expediency.' He paused again, still deep inside his own thoughts. 'All I'm really saying, I suppose, is that if the temptation to humanity does assail you now and then, I hope you won't take it as a weakness in yourselves, but give it a fair hearing.'

The cufflinks, I thought, in a flash of inspiration. George is remembering the old man.

For a long time I could not fathom why the story had continued to haunt me for so long. Then I realised I had happened upon it at a period when my relationship with my son Adrian had hit a low point. He was talking of not bothering with university, and getting himself a well-paid job instead. I mistook his restlessness for materialism and his dreams of independence for laziness, and one night I lost my temper and insulted him, and was duly ashamed of myself for weeks thereafter. It was during one of those weeks that I unearthed the story.

Then I remembered also that Smiley had had no children, and that perhaps his ambiguous part in the affair was to some extent explained by this. I was slightly chilled by the thought that he might have been filling an emptiness in himself by redressing a relationship he had never had.

Finally I remembered that just a few days after coming upon the papers, I had received the letter that anonymously denounced poor Frewin as a Russian spy. And that there were certain mystical affinities between Frewin and the old man, to do with dogged loyalty and lost worlds. All this for context, you understand, for I never knew a case yet that was not made up of a hundred others.

Finally there was the fact that, as so often in my life, Smiley turned out once again to have been my precursor, for

I had no sooner settled myself at my unfamiliar desk in the Interrogators' Pool than I found his traces everywhere: in our dusty archives, in back numbers of our duty officer's log and in the reminiscent smiles of our senior secretaries, who spoke of him with the old vestal's treacly awe, part as God, part as teddy bear and part – though they were always quick to gloss over this aspect of his nature – as killer shark. They would even show you the bone-china cup and saucer by Thomas Goode of South Audley Street – where else? – a present to George from Ann, they explained dotingly, which George had bequeathed to the Pool after his reprieve and rehabilitation to Head Office – and, of course, like the Grail itself, the Smiley cup could never possibly be *drunk* from by a mere mortal.

The Pool, if you have not already gathered as much, is by way of being the Service's Siberia, and Smiley, I was comforted to discover, had served out not one exile there but two: the first, for his gall in suggesting to the Fifth Floor that it might be nursing a Moscow Centre mole to its bosom; and the second, a few years later, for being right. And the Pool has not only the monotony of Siberia but its remoteness also, being situated not in the main building but in a run of cavernous offices on the ground floor of a gabled pile in Northumberland Avenue at the northern end of Whitehall.

And, like so much of the architecture around it, the Pool has seen great days. It was set up in the Second World War to receive the offerings of strangers, to listen to their suspicions and calm their fears or – if they had indeed stumbled on a larger truth – misguide or scare them into silence.

If you thought you had glimpsed your neighbour late at night, for instance, crouched over a radio transmitter; if you had seen strange lights winking from a window and were too shy or untrusting to inform your local police station; if the mysterious foreigner on the bus who questioned you about your work had reappeared at your elbow in your local pub; if your secret lover confessed to you – out of loneliness or bravado or a desperate need to make himself more interesting in your eyes – that he was working for the German Secret Service – why then, after a correspondence with some spurious assistant to some unheard-of Whitehall Under-Secretary, you would quite likely, of an early evening, be summoned to brave the blitz, and find yourself being guided heart-in-mouth down the flaking, sandbagged corridor, on your way to Room 909, where a Major Somebody or a Captain Somebody Else, both bogus as three-dollar bills, would courteously invite you to state your matter frankly without fear of repercussion.

And occasionally, as the covert history of the Pool records, great things were born, and are still occasionally born today, of these inauspicious beginnings, though business is not a patch on what it used to be, and much of the Pool's work is now given over to such chores as unsolicited offers of service, anonymous denunciations like the one levelled at poor Frewin and even – in support of the despised security services – positive vetting enquiries, which are the worst Siberias of all, and about as far as you can get from the high-wire operations of the Russia House without quitting the Service altogether.

All the same, there is more than mere humility to be learned from these chastisements. An intelligence officer is nothing if he has lost the will to listen, and George Smiley, plump, troubled, cuckolded, unassuming, indefatigable George, forever polishing his spectacles on the lining of his tie, puffing to himself and sighing in his perennial distraction, was the best listener of us all.

Smiley could listen with his hooded, sleepy eyes; he could listen by the very inclination of his tubby body, by his stillness and his understanding smile. He could listen because with one exception, which was Ann, his wife, he expected nothing of his fellow souls, criticised nothing, condoned the worst of you long before you had revealed it. He could listen better than a microphone because his mind lit at once upon essentials; he seemed able to spot them before he knew where they were leading.

And that was how George had come to be listening to Mr Arthur Wilfred Hawthorne of 12, The Dene, Ruislip, half a lifetime before me, in the very same Room 909 where I now sat, curiously turning the yellowed pages of a file marked 'Destruction Pending' which I had unearthed from the shelves of the Pool's strongroom.

I had begun my quest idly – you may even say frivolously – much as one might pick up an old copy of the *Tatler* in one's club. And suddenly I realised I had stumbled on page after page of Smiley's familiar, guarded handwriting, with its sharp little German t's and twisted Greek e's, and signed with his legendary symbol. Where he was forced to appear in the drama in person – and you could feel him seeking any means to escape this vulgar ordeal – he referred to himself merely as 'DO', short for Duty Officer. And since he was notorious for his hatred of initials, you are made once more aware of his reclusive, if not downright fugitive nature. If I had discovered a missing Shakespeare folio, I could not have been more excited. Everything was there: Hawthorne's original letter, transcripts of the microphoned interviews, initialled by Smiley himself, even Hawthorne's signed receipts for his travel money and out-of-pocket expenses.

My dull care was gone. My relegation no longer oppressed

me, neither did the silence of the great empty house to which I was condemned. I was sharing them with George, waiting for the clip of Arthur Hawthorne's loyal boots as he was marched down the corridor and into Smiley's presence.

'Dear Sir,' he had written to 'The Officer in Charge of Intelligence, Ministry of Defence'. And already, because we are British, his class is branded on the page – if only by the strangely imperious use of capitals so dear to uneducated people. I imagined much effort in the penning, and perhaps a dictionary at the elbow. 'I wish, Sir, to Request an Interview with your Staff regarding a Person who has done Special Work for British Intelligence at the highest Level, and whose Name is as Important to my Wife and myself as it may be to your good Selves, and which I am accordingly forbidden to Mention in this Letter.'

That was all. Signed 'Hawthorne, A. W., Warrant Officer Class II, retired.' Arthur Wilfred Hawthorne, in other words, as Smiley's researches revealed when he consulted the voters' list, and followed up his findings with an examination of the War Office files. Born 1915, Smiley painstakingly recorded on Hawthorne's personal particulars sheet. Enlisted 1939, served with the Eighth Army from Egypt to Italy. Ex-Sergeant Major Arthur Wilfred Hawthorne, twice wounded in battle, three commendations and one gallantry medal for his trouble, demobilised without a stain on his character, 'the best example of the best fighting man in the world,' wrote his commandant, in a glowing if hyperbolic commendation.

And I knew that Smiley, as a good professional, would have taken up his post well ahead of his client's arrival, just as I myself had done these last months: at the same scuffed yellow desk of wartime pine, singed brown along the leading edge – legend has it by the Hun; with the same mossy telephone, letters as well as numbers on the dial; the same hand-tinted photograph of the Queen, sitting on a horse when she was twenty. I see George frowning studiously at his watch, then pulling a sour face as he peered round him at the usual mess, for there had been a running battle for as long as anyone could remember about who was supposed to clean the place, the Ministry or ourselves. I see him tug a handkerchief from his sleeve – laboriously again, for no gesture ever came to George without a struggle – and wipe the grime off the seat of his wooden chair, then do the same in advance for Hawthorne on the other side of the desk. Then, as I had done myself a few times, perform a similar service for the Queen, setting her frame straight and bringing back the sparkle to her young, idealistic eyes.

For I imagined George already studying the feelings of his subject, as any good intelligence officer must. An ex-sergeant major would expect a certain order about him, after all. Then I see Hawthorne himself, punctual to the minute, as the janitor showed him in, his best suit buttoned like a battledress, the polished toecaps of his boots glistening like conkers in the gloom. Smiley's description of him on the encounter sheet was sparse but trenchant: height five seven, grey hair close cut, cleanshaven, groomed appearance, military bearing. Other characteristics: suppressed limp of the left leg, army boots.

'Hawthorne, sir,' he snapped, and held himself to attention till Smiley with difficulty persuaded him to sit.

Smiley was Major Nottingham that day and had an impressive card with his photograph to prove it. In my pocket as I read his account of the case lay a similar card in the name of Colonel Ned Ascot. Don't ask me why Ascot except to note that, in choosing a place-name for my alias, I was yet again unconsciously copying one of Smiley's little habits.

'What regiment are you from, sir, if you don't mind my asking?' Hawthorne enquired of Smiley as he sat.

'The General List, I'm afraid,' said Smiley, which is the only way we are allowed to answer.

But I am sure it came hard to Smiley, as it would to me, to have to describe himself as some kind of non-combatant.

As evidence of his loyalty, Hawthorne had brought his medals wrapped in a piece of gun cloth. Smiley obligingly went through them for him.

'It's about our son, sir,' the old man said. 'I've got to ask you. The wife – well, she won't hear of it any more, she says it's a load of his nonsense. But I told her I've got to ask you. Even if you refuse to answer, I told her, I won't have done my duty by my son if I didn't ask on his account.'

Smiley said nothing but I am sure his silence was sympathetic.

'Ken was our only boy, you see, Major, so it's natural,' said Hawthorne apologetically.

And still Smiley let him take his time. Did I not say he was a listener? Smiley could draw answers from you to questions he had never put, just by the sincerity of his listening.

'We're not asking for secrets, Major. We're not asking to know what can't be known. But Mrs Hawthorne is failing, sir, and she needs to know whether it's true before she goes.' He had prepared the question exactly. Now he put it. 'Was our boy, or was he not – was Ken – in the course of what appeared to be a criminal career, operating behind enemy lines in Russia?'

And here you might say that for once I was ahead of

Smiley, if only because after five years in the Russia House I had a pretty good idea of the operations we had conducted in the past. I felt a smile come to my face, and my interest in the story, if it was possible, increased.

But to Smiley's face, I am sure, came nothing at all. I imagine his features settling into a Mandarin immobility. Perhaps he fiddled with his spectacles, which always gave the impression of belonging to a larger man. Finally he asked Hawthorne – but earnestly, never a hint of scepticism – why he supposed this might be the case.

'Ken told me he was, sir, that's why.' And still nothing on Smiley's side, except an ever-open door. 'Mrs Hawthorne wouldn't visit Ken in prison, you see. I would. Every month. He was doing five years for grievous bodily harm, plus three more for being habitual. We had PD in those days, preventive detention. We're in the prison canteen there, me and Ken, sitting together at a table. And suddenly Ken puts his head close to mine, and he says to me in this low voice he's got, "Don't come here again, Dad. It's difficult for me. I'm not really locked up, you see. I'm in Russia. They had to bring me back special, just to show me to you. I'm working behind the lines, but don't tell Mum. Write to me – that's not a problem, they'll send it on. And I'll write back same as if I was a prisoner here, which is what I pretend to be, because you can't get better cover than a prison. But the truth is, Dad, I'm serving the old country just like you did when you was with the Desert Rats, which is why the best of us are put on earth." I didn't ask to see Ken after that. I felt I had to obey orders. I wrote to him, of course. In the prison. Hawthorne and then his number. And three months later he'd write back on prison paper like it was a different boy writing to me every time.

Sometimes the big heavy writing, like he was angry, some-times small and quick, like he hadn't had the time. Once or twice there was even the foreign words in there that I didn't understand, crossed out mainly, like he was having difficulty with his own language. Sometimes he'd drop me a clue. "I'm cold but safe," he'd say. "Last week I had a bit more exercise than I needed," he'd say. I didn't tell the wife because he said I wasn't to. Besides, she wouldn't have believed him. When I offered her his letters, she pushed them away – they hurt too much. But when Ken died we went and saw his body all cut to pieces in the prison morgue. Twenty stab wounds and nobody to blame. She didn't weep, she doesn't, but they might as well have stabbed her. And on the way home on the bus I couldn't help it. "Ken's a hero," I said to her. I was trying to wake her up because she'd gone all wooden. I got hold of her by the sleeve and gave her a bit of a shake to make her listen. "He's not a dirty convict," I said. "Not our Ken. He never was. And it wasn't convicts who done him in, either. It was the Red Russians." I told her about the cufflinks too. "Ken's romancing," she said. "Same as he always did. He doesn't know the difference, he never did, which has been his trouble all along." '

Interrogators, like priests and doctors, have a particular advantage when it comes to concealing their feelings. They can ask another question, which is what I would have done myself.

'What cufflinks, Sergeant Major?' Smiley said, and I see him lowering his long eyelids and sinking his head into his neck as he once more prepared himself to listen to the old man's tale.

' "There's no medals, Dad," Ken says to me. "Medals wouldn't be secure. You have to be gazetted to get a medal, there'd be too many in the know. Otherwise I'd have a medal same as you. Maybe an even better one, if I'm honest, like the Victoria Cross, because they stretch us as far as we can go and sometimes further. But if you do right in the job, you earn your cufflinks and they keep them for you in a special safe. Then once a year there's this big dinner at a certain place I'm not allowed to mention, with the champagne and butlers you wouldn't believe, and all us Russia boys go to it. And we put on our tuxedos and we wear the cufflinks, same as a uniform but secret. And we have this party, with the speeches and the handshakes, like a special investiture, same as you had for your medals, I expect, in this place I'm not allowed to mention. And when the party's over, we hand the cufflinks back. We have to, for the security. So if ever I go missing, or if something happens to me, just you write to them at the Secret Service and ask them for the Russia cufflinks for your Ken. Maybe they'll say they never heard of me, maybe they'll say, 'What cufflinks?' But maybe they'll make you a compassionate exception and let you have them, because they sometimes do. And *if* they do – you'll know that everything I ever did wrong was more right than you can imagine. Because I'm my dad's boy, right down the line, and the cufflinks will prove it to you. That's all I'm saying, and it's more than I'm allowed." '

Smiley asked first for the boy's full name. Then for the boy's date of birth. Then he asked about his schooling and qualifications, which were predictably dismal, both. I see him acting quiet and businesslike as he takes down the details: Kenneth Branham Hawthorne, the old soldier told him – Branham, that was his mother's maiden name, sir; he sometimes used it for what they called his crimes – born Folkestone, July 14, 1946, sir, twelve months after I came back from the war. I wouldn't have a child earlier, although the wife wanted it, sir, I didn't think it right. I wanted our boy brought up in peace, sir, with both his living parents to look after him, Major, which is the right of any child, I say, even if it's not as usual as it ought to be.

Smiley's next task was not half as easy as it might seem, whatever the improbabilities of Kenneth Hawthorne's story. Smiley was never one to deny a good man, or even a bad one, the benefit of the doubt. The Circus of those days possessed no such thing as a reliable central index of its resources, and what passed for one was shamefully and often deliberately incomplete, for rival outfits guarded their sources jealously and poached from their neighbours when they saw the chance.

True, the old man's story bristled with unlikelihoods. In purist terms it was grotesque, for example, to imagine a group of secret agents meeting once a year to dine, thus breaking the most elementary rule of 'need to know'. But worse things could happen in the lawless world of the irregulars, as Smiley was aware. And it took all his powers of ingenuity and persuasion to satisfy himself that Hawthorne was nowhere on their books: not as a runner, not as a lamplighter or a scalp-hunter, not as a signalman and not as any other of the beloved tradenames with which these seedy operators glamorised their ranks.

And when he had exhausted the irregulars he returned to the armed services, the security services and the Royal Ulster Constabulary, any one of which might conceivably have employed – if on some much more modest basis than the boy described – a violent criminal of Ken Hawthorne's character.

For one thing at least seemed certain: the boy's criminal record was a nightmare. It would have been hard to imagine a grimmer record of persistent and often bestial behaviour. As Smiley crossed and recrossed the boy's history, through childhood to adolescence, reform school to prison, there seemed to be no transgression, from pilfering to sadistic assault, that Kenneth Branham Hawthorne, born Folkestone 1946, had not stooped to.

Till at the end of a full week, Smiley appears reluctantly to have admitted to himself what in another part of his head he must have known all along. Kenneth Hawthorne, for whatever sad reasons, had been an unredeemable and habitual monster. The death he had suffered at the hands of his fellow prisoners was no more than he deserved. His past was written and complete, and his tales of heroism on behalf of some mythical British intelligence service were merely the last chapter in his lifelong effort to steal his father's glory.

It was mid-winter. It was a foul grey, sleet-driven evening on which to drag an old soldier back across London to a barren interviewing room in Whitehall. And Whitehall in the meagre lighting of those days was a citadel still at war, even if its guns were somewhere else. It was a place of military austerity, heartless and imperial; of lowered voices and blacked windows, of rare and hurried footsteps and averted eyes. Smiley was in the War too, remember, even if he was sitting behind German lines. I can hear the puttering of the paraffin Aladdin stove which the Circus had grudgingly approved to supplement the faulty ministerial radiators. It has the sound of a wireless transmitter operated by a freezing hand.

Hawthorne had not come alone to hear Major Nottingham's reply. The old soldier had brought his wife, and I can even tell you how she looked, for Smiley had written of her in his log and my imagination has long painted in the rest.

She had a buckled sick body wrapped in Sunday best. She wore a brooch in the design of her husband's regimental badge. Smiley invited her to sit, but she preferred her husband's arm. Smiley stood across the desk from them, the same burned, yellowed desk where I had sat in exile these last months. I see him standing almost to attention, with his rounded shoulders uncharacteristically straightened, his stubby fingers curled at the seams of his trousers in traditional army manner.

Ignoring Mrs Hawthorne, he addressed the old soldier, man to man. 'You understand I have absolutely nothing to say to you at all, Sergeant Major?'

'I do, sir.'

'I never heard of your son, you understand? Kenneth Hawthorne is not a name to me, nor to any of my colleagues.'

'Yes, sir.' The old man's gaze was fixed parade-ground style above Smiley's head. But his wife had her eyes fiercely turned on Smiley's all the time, even if she found it hard to fix on them through the thick lenses of his spectacles.

'He has never in his life worked for any British department of government, whether secret or otherwise. He was a common criminal all his life. Nothing more. Nothing at all.'

'Yes, sir.'

'I deny absolutely that he was ever a secret agent in the service of the Crown.'

'Yes, sir.'

'You understand also that I can answer no questions, give you no explanations, and that you will never see me again or be received at this building?'

'Yes, sir.'

'You understand finally that you may never speak of this moment to a living soul? However proud you may be of your son? That there are others still alive who must be protected?'

'Yes, sir. I understand, sir.'

Opening the drawer of our desk, Smiley took out a small red Cartier box, which he handed to the old man. 'I happened to find this in my safe,' he said.

The old man passed the box to his wife without looking at it. With firm fingers, she forced it open. Inside lay a pair of superb gold cufflinks with a tiny English rose set discreetly in a corner, hand-engraved, a marvel of fine work. Her husband still did not look. Perhaps he didn't have to; perhaps he didn't trust himself. Closing the box, she parted the clasp of her scuffed purse and popped it inside. Then snapped the purse shut again, so loudly you would think she was slamming down the lid on her son's tomb. I have listened to the tape; it too is waiting to be destroyed.

The old man still said nothing. They were too proud to bother with Smiley as they left.

And the cufflinks? you ask – where did Smiley get the cufflinks from? I had my answer not from the yellowing records of Room 909 but from Ann Smiley herself, quite by chance one evening in a splendid Cornish castle near Saltash where we both happened to be guests. Ann was on her own, and chastened. Mabel had a golf tournament. It was long after the Bill Haydon business, but Smiley still could not bear to have her near him. When dinner was over, the guests dispersed themselves in groups, but Ann stayed close to me, I supposed as a substitute for being close to George. And I asked her, half intuitively, whether she had ever given George a pair of cufflinks. Ann was always at her most beautiful when she was alone.

'Oh those,' she said, as if she scarcely remembered. 'You mean the ones he gave to the old man.'

Ann had given them to George on their first anniversary, she said. After her fling with Bill, he had decided they should be put to better use.

But *why*, exactly, did George decide that? I wondered.

At first it seemed perfectly clear to me. This was Smiley's soft centre. The old cold warrior was revealing his bleeding heart.

Like most things with George – maybe.

Or an act of vengeance against Ann perhaps? Or against his other faithless love, the Circus, at a time when the Fifth Floor was locking him out of the house?

Gradually I arrived at a slightly different theory, which I may as well pass on to you, since one thing is certain, and that is that George himself will not enlighten us.

Listening to the old soldier, Smiley recognised one of those rare moments when the Service could be of real value to real people. For once, the mythology of espionage would be used not to disguise yet another tale of incompetence or betrayal, but to leave an old couple with their dreams. For once, Smiley could look at an intelligence operation and say with absolute confidence that it had worked.

II

'And some interrogations,' said Smiley, gazing into the dancing flames of the log fire, 'are not interrogations at all, but communions between damaged souls.'

He had been talking about his debriefing of the Moscow Centre spymaster, codename Karla, whose defection he had secured. But for me, he was talking only of poor Frewin, of whom, so far as I know, he had never heard.

The letter denouncing Frewin as a Soviet spy arrived on my desk on a Monday evening, posted first class in the SW1 area of London on the Friday, opened by Head Office Registry on the Monday morning and marked by the Assistant Registrar on duty 'HIP to see', HIP being the unlikely acronym of the Head of the Interrogators' Pool; in other words, myself, and in the opinion of some the 'H' ought to be an 'R' – you Rest in Peace at the Interrogators' Pool. It was five o'clock by the time the Head Office green van unloaded its humble package at Northumberland Avenue, and in the Pool such late intrusions were customarily ignored until next morning. But I was trying to change all that and, having anyway nothing else to do, I opened the envelope at once.

Two pink trace slips were pinned to the letter, each bearing a pencilled note. Head Office's notes to the Pool always had the ring of instructions addressed to an idiot. The first read, 'FREWIN C presumed identical with FREWIN Cyril Arthur, Foreign Office cypher clerk,' followed by Frewin's positive vetting reference and white file number, which was a cumbersome way of telling me there was nothing recorded against him. The second said, 'MODRIAN S presumed identical with MODRIAN Sergei,' followed by a further string of references, but I didn't bother with them. After my five years in the Russia House, Sergei Modrian was plain Sergei to me, as he had been to the rest of us: old Sergei, the crafty Armenian, head boy of Moscow Centre's generously over-staffed residence at the Soviet Embassy in London.

If I had had any lingering wish to postpone my reading of the letter till tomorrow, Sergei's name dispelled it. The letter might be bunkum, but I was playing on home ground.

To the Director,
The Security Department,
The Foreign Office,
Downing Street, SW.

Dear Sir,

This is to inform you, that C. Frewin, a Foreign Office cypher clerk with constant and regular access to *Top Secret and Above*, has been keeping surreptitious company with S. Modrian, First Secretary at the Soviet Embassy in London, for the last four years, and has not revealed same in his annual vetting returns. Secret materials have been passed. Mr Modrian's whereabouts are no longer known, in view of the fact that he has recently been recalled to the Soviet Union. The said Frewin still resides at the Chestnuts, Beavor

Drive, Sutton, and Modrian has been present there at least on one occasion. C. Frewin is now living a *highly solitary life*.

Yours sincerely,

A. Patriot.

Electronically typed. Plain white A4 paper, no watermark. Dated, overpunctuated, accurately spelt and crisply folded. And no address of sender. There never is.

Having nothing much else to do that evening, I had a couple of Scotches at The Sherlock Holmes, then wandered round to Head Office, where I checked myself into the Registry reading room and drew the files. Next morning at the surgery hour of ten I took my place in Burr's waiting room, having first spelt my name to his glossy personal assistant, who seemed never to have heard of me. Brock, from Moscow Station, was ahead of me in the queue. We talked intently about cricket till his name was called, and managed not to refer to the fact that he had worked for me in the Russia House, most recently on the Blair case. A couple of minutes later, Peter Guillam drifted in clutching a bunch of files and looking hung-over. He had recently become Head of Secretariat for Burr.

'Don't mind if I squeeze ahead of you, do you, old boy? I've been sent for urgently. Bloody man seems to expect me to work in my sleep. What's your problem?'

'Leprosy,' I said.

There is nowhere quite like the Service – except possibly Moscow – for becoming an unperson overnight. In the upheavals that had followed Barley Blair's defection, not even Burr's predecessor, the nimble Clive, had kept his foothold on the slippery Fifth Floor deck. When last heard of, he was on his way to take up the salubrious post of Head of Station,

Guyana. Only our craven legal adviser, Harry Palfrey, seemed as usual to have weathered the changes, and as I entered Burr's shiny executive suite, Palfrey was slipping stealthily out of the other door – but not quite quickly enough, so he treated me to a rhapsodic smile instead. He had recently grown himself a moustache for greater integrity.

'Ned! Marvellous! We must do that lunch,' he breathed in an excited whisper, and disappeared below the waterline.

Like his office, Burr was all modern man. Where he came from was a mystery to me, but then I was no longer in the swim. Someone had told me advertising, someone else the City, someone else the Inns of Court. One wit in the Pool mailroom said he came from nowhere at all: that he had been born as found, smelling of aftershave and power, in his two-piece executive blue suit and his patent black shoes with side buckles. He was big and floating and absurdly young. Grasping his soft hand, you at once relaxed your grip for fear of denting it. He had Frewin's file in front of him on his executive desk, with my loose minute – written late last night – pinned to the cover.

'Where does the letter come from?' he demanded in his dry North Country cadence, before I had sat down.

'I don't know. It's well informed. Whoever wrote it did his homework.'

'Probably Frewin's best friend,' said Burr, as if that was what best friends were known for.

'He's got Modrian's dates right, he's got Frewin's access right,' I said. 'He knows the positive vetting routine.'

'Not a work of art, though, is it? Not if you're an insider? Most likely a colleague. Or his girl. What do you want to ask me?'

I had not expected this quickfire interrogation. After six months in the Pool, I wasn't used to being hurried.

'I suppose I need to know whether you want me to pursue the case,' I said.

'Why shouldn't I?'

'It's outside the Pool's normal league. Frewin's access is formidable. His section handles some of the most delicate signals traffic in Whitehall. I assumed you'd prefer to pass it to the Security Service.'

'Why?'

'It's their bailiwick. If it's anything at all, it's a straight security enquiry.'

'It's our information, our shout, our letter,' Burr retorted, with a bluntness that secretly warmed my heart. 'To hell with them. When we know what we've got, we'll decide where we go with it. All that those churchy buggers across the Park can think of is a judgeproof prosecution and a bunch of medals to hand around. I collect intelligence for the market-place. If Frewin's bad, maybe we can keep him going and turn him round. He might even get us alongside Brother Modrian back in Moscow. Who knows? The security artists don't, that's for sure.'

'Then presumably you'd prefer to hand the case to the Russia House,' I said doggedly.

'Why should I do that?'

I had assumed I would make an unappetising figure to him, for he was still of an age to find failure immoral. Yet he seemed to be asking me to tell him why he shouldn't count on me.

'The Pool has no charter to function operationally,' I explained. 'We run a front office and listen to the lonely hearts. We've no charter to conduct clandestine investigations or run agents, and no mandate to pursue suspects with Frewin's sort of access.'

'You can run a phone tap, can't you?'

'If you get me a warrant I can.'

'You can brief watchers, can't you? You've done that a few times, they say.'

'Not unless you authorise it personally.'

'Suppose I do? The Pool's also empowered to make vetting enquiries. You can play Mr Plod. You're good at it, by all accounts. This is a vetting matter, right? And Frewin's due for a vetting top-up, right? So vet him.'

'In positive vetting cases, the Pool is obliged to clear all enquiries with the Security Service in advance.'

'Assume it's done.'

'I can't do that unless I have it in writing.'

'Oh yes you can. You're not a Service hack. You're the great Ned. You've broken as many rules as you've stuck to, you have, I've read you up. You know Modrian, too.'

'Not well.'

'How well?'

'I had dinner with him once and played squash with him once. That's hardly knowing him.'

'Squash where?'

'At the Lansdowne.'

'How did that come about?'

'Modrian was formally declared to us as the Embassy's Moscow Centre link. I was trying to put together a deal with him on Barley Blair. A swap.'

'Why didn't you succeed?'

'Barley wouldn't go along with us. He'd done his own deal already. He wanted his girl, not us.'

'What's his game like?'

'Tricky.'

'Did you beat him?'

'Yes.'

He interrupted his own flow while he looked me over. It was like being studied by a baby. 'And you can handle it, can you? You're not under too much stress? You've done some good things in your time. You've a heart too, which is more than I can say for some of the capons in this outfit.'

'Why should I be under stress?'

No answer. Or not yet. He seemed to be chewing at something just behind his thick lips.

'Who believes in marriage these days, for Christ's sake?' he demanded. His regional drawl had thickened. It was as if he had abandoned restraint. 'If you want to live with your girl, live with her is my advice. We've cleared her, she's nobody's worry, she's not a bomb thrower or a secret sympathiser or a druggie, what's your bother? She's a nice girl in a nice way of life, and you're a lucky fellow. Do you want the case, or do you not?'

For a moment I was robbed of an answer. There was nothing surprising in Burr knowing of my affair with Sally. In our world you put those things on record before the record puts them on you, and I had already endured my obligatory confessional with Personnel. No, it was Burr's capacity for intimacy that had silenced me, the speed with which he had got under my skin.

'If you'll cover me and give me the resources, of course I'll take it,' I said.

'So get on with it, then. Keep me informed but not too much – don't bullshit me, always give me bad news straight. He's a man without qualities, our Cyril is. You've read Robert Musil, I dare say, haven't you?'

'I'm afraid I haven't.'

He was pulling open Frewin's file. I say 'pulling' because

his doughy hands gave no impression of having done anything before: now we are going to see how this file opens; now we are going to address ourselves to this strange object called a pencil.

'He's got no hobbies, no stated interests beyond music, no wife, no girl, no parents, no money worries, not even any bizarre sexual appetites, poor devil,' Burr complained, flipping to a different part of the file. When on earth had he found time to read it? I asked myself. I presumed the early hours. 'And how the hell a man of your experience, whose job is dealing with modern civilisation and its discontentments, can manage without the wisdom of Robert Musil is a question which at a calmer moment I shall require you to answer.' He licked his thumb and turned another page. 'He's one of five,' he said.

'I thought he was an only child.'

'Not his brothers and sisters, you mug, his work. There's five clerks in his dreary cyphers office and he's one of them. They all handle the same stuff; they're all the same rank, work the same hours, think the same dirty thoughts.' He looked straight at me, a thing he had not done before. 'If he did it, what's his motive? The writer doesn't say. Funny, that. They usually do. Boredom – how about that? Boredom and greed, they're the only motives left these days. Plus getting even, which is eternal.' He went back to the file. 'Cyril's the only one not married, notice that? He's a poofter. So am I. I'm a poofter, you're a poofter. We're all poofters. It's just a question which bit of yourself ends on top. He's no hair, see that?' I caught a flash of Frewin's photograph as he waved it past me and talked on. He had a daunting energy. 'Still that's no crime, I dare say, baldness, any more than marriage is. I should know, I've had three and I'm still not done. That's no normal denunciation, is it? That's why you're here. That letter knows what it's talking about. You don't think Modrian wrote it, do you?'

'Why should he have done?'

'I'm asking, Ned, don't fox with me. Wicked thoughts are what keep me going. Perhaps Modrian thought he'd leave a little confusion in his wake when he went back to Moscow. He's a scheming little monkey, Modrian, when he puts his mind to it. I've been reading him too.'

When? I thought again. When on earth did you find the time?

For another twenty minutes he zigzagged back and forth, tossing possibilities at me, seeing how they came back. And when I finally stepped exhausted into the anteroom, I walked straight into Peter Guillam again.

'Who the hell is Leonard Burr?' I asked him, still dazed.

Peter was astonished that I didn't know. 'Burr? My dear chap. Leonard was Smiley's Crown Prince for years. George rescued him from a fate worse than death at All Souls.'

Of Sally, my reigning extramarital girlfriend, what should I tell you? She was free, and spoke to the captive in me. Monica had been within my walls. Monica was a woman of the Service, bound and not bound to me by the same set of rules. But to Sally I was just a middle-aged civil servant who had forgotten to have any fun. She was a designer and sometime dancer whose passion was theatre, and she thought the rest of life unreal. She was tall and she was fair and rather wise, and sometimes I think she must have reminded me of Stefanie.

'Meet you, skipper?' Gorst cried over the telephone. 'Top up our Cyril? It'll be my pleasure, sir!'

We met the next day in a Foreign Office interviewing room. I was Captain York, another dreary vetting officer doing his rounds. Gorst was head of Frewin's Cypher Section, which was better known as the Tank: a lecher in a beadle's suit, a waddling, smirking man with prising elbows and a tiny mouth that wriggled like a worm. When he sat, he scooped up the skirts of his jacket as if he were exposing himself from behind. Then he kicked out a plump leg like a chorus girl, before laying it suggestively over the thigh of the other.

'Saint Cyril, that's what we call Mr Frewin,' he announced blithely. 'Doesn't drink, doesn't smoke, doesn't swear, certi-fied virgin. End of vetting interview.' Extracting a cigarette from a packet of ten, he tapped the tip of it on his thumb-nail, then moistened it with his busy tongue. 'Music's his only weakness. Loves the *operah*. Goes to the *operah* regular as clockwork. Never cared for it myself. Can't make out whether it's actors singing or singers acting.' He lit his cigar-ette. I could smell the lunchtime beer on his breath. 'I'm not too fond of fat women, either, to be frank. Specially when they scream at me.' He tipped his head back and blew out smoke rings, savouring them as if they were emblems of his authority.

'May I ask how Frewin gets on with the rest of the staff these days?' I said, playing the honest journeyman as I turned a page of my notebook.

'Swimmingly, Your Grace. Par-fectly.'

'The archivists, registrars, secretaries – no trouble on that front?'

'Not a finger. Not a mini-digit.'

'You all sit together?'

'In a big room and I'm the titular head of it. Very *tit-ular* indeed.'

'And I've had it said to me he's something of a misogynist,' I said, fishing.

Gorst gave a shrill laugh. 'Cyril? A *misogynist*? Bollocks. He just hates the girls. Won't speak to them, not apart from good morning. Won't come to the pre-Christmas party if he can help it, in case he has to kiss them under the mistletoe.' He recrossed his legs, indicating that he had decided to make a statement. 'Cyril Arthur Frewin – Saint Cyril – is a highly reliable, eminently conscientious, totally bald, incredibly boring clerk of the old school. Saint Cyril, though punctilious to a fault, has in my view reached his natural promotion ceiling in his line of country or profession. Saint Cyril is set in his ways. Saint Cyril does what he does, one hundred per cent. Amen.'

'Politics?'

'Not in my house, thank you.'

'And he's not workshy?'

'Did I say he was, squire?'

'No, to the contrary, I was quoting from the file. If there's extra work to be done, Cyril will always roll his sleeves up, stay on in the lunch hour, the evenings and so forth. That's still the case, is it? No slackening off of his enthusiasm?'

'Our Cyril is ready to oblige at all hours, to the pleasure of those who have families, wives or a nice piece of Significant Other to return to. He'll do the early mornings, he'll do lunch hours, he'll do evening watch, except for *operah* nights, of course. Cyril never counts the cost. Latterly, I will admit, he has been slightly less inclined to martyr himself, but that is no doubt a purely temporary suspension of service. Our Cyril does have his little moods. Who does not, Your Eminence?'

'So recently a slackening off, you would say?'

'Not of his work, never. Cyril is your total workslave,

always has been. Merely of his willingness to be put upon by his more human colleagues. Come five-thirty these days, Saint Cyril packs up his desk and goes home with the rest of us. He does not, for instance, offer to replace the late shift and remain solo incommunicado till nine o'clock and lock up, which was what he used to do.'

'You can't put a date to that change of habit, can you?' I enquired as boringly as I could manage, turning dutifully to a fresh page of my notebook.

Curiously enough, Gorst could. He pursed his lips. He frowned. He raised his girlish eyebrows and pressed his chins into his grimy shirt collar. He made a vast show of ruminating. And he finally remembered. 'The last time Cyril Frewin did young Burton's evening watch was Midsummer's Day. I keep a log, you see. Security. I also have quite an impressive memory, which I don't always care to reveal.'

I was secretly impressed, but not by Gorst. Three days after Modrian left London for Moscow, Cyril Frewin had ceased to work late, I was thinking. I had other questions that were clamouring to be asked. Did the Tank boast electronic typewriters? Did the cypher clerks have access to them? Did Gorst? But I was afraid of arousing his suspicions.

'You mentioned his love of opera,' I said. 'Could you tell me a little more about that?'

'No, I could not, since we do not get blow-by-blow accounts, and we do not ask for them. However, he does come in wearing a pressed dark suit on his *operah* days, if he doesn't bring his dinner jacket in a suitcase, and he does impart what I would refer to as a state of high if controlled excitement somewhat similar to other forms of anticipation, which I will not mention.'

'But he has a regular seat, for instance? A subscription seat?

It's only for the record. As you say, he's a bit short of relaxing pastimes otherwise.'

'As I think I told you, squire, alas, me and *operah* were not made for each other. Put down "opera buff" on his form and you're covered for your relaxing pastime is my advice.'

'Thank you. I will.' I turned another page. 'And really no enemies that you can think of?' I said, my pencil hovering over my notebook.

Gorst became serious. The beer was wearing off. 'Cyril is laughed at, Captain, I'll admit. But he takes it in good part. Cyril is not disliked.'

'No one who would speak ill of him, for instance?'

'I can think of no single reason whatever why anyone should speak ill of Cyril Arthur Frewin. The British civil servant, he may be sullen but he's not malicious. Cyril does his duty, as we all do. We're a happy ship. I wouldn't mind if you put that down, too.'

'I gather he went to Salzburg for Christmas this year. And previous years too, is that right?'

'That is correct. Cyril always takes his leave at Christmas. He goes to Salzburg, he hears the music. It's the one point on which he will make no concession to the rest of the Tank. There's some of the young ones try to complain about it, but I won't let them. "Cyril makes it up to you in other ways," I tell them. "Cyril's got his seniority, he loves his trip to Salzburg for the music, he has his little ways, and that's how it's going to stay." '

'Does he leave a holiday address behind when he goes?'

Gorst didn't know, but at my request he telephoned his personnel department and obtained it. The same hotel, the last four years running. He's been keeping company with Modrian for four years too, I thought, remembering the letter. Four years of Salzburg, four years of Modrian, ending in a *highly solitary life*.

'Does he take a friend, would you know?'

'Cyril never had a friend in his life, skipper.' Gorst yawned. 'Not one he'd take on holiday, that's for sure. Shall we do a lunch next time? They tell me you boys have very nifty expense accounts when you care to give them a tickle.'

'Does he talk about his Salzburg trips at all when he comes back? The fun he's had – the music he's heard – anything like that?' Thanks to Sally, I suppose, I had learned that people were expected to have fun.

Having made a brief show of thinking, Gorst shook his head. 'If Cyril has fun, squire, it's very, very private,' he said, with a last smirk.

That wasn't Sally's idea of fun at all.

From my office at the Pool I booked a secure line to Vienna and spoke to Toby Esterhase, who with his infinite talent for survival had recently been made Head of Station.

'I want you to shake out the Weisse Rose in Salzburg for me, Toby. Cyril Frewin, British subject. Stayed there every Christmas for the last four years. I want to know when he arrived, how long he stayed, whether he's stayed there before, who with, how much the bills come to and what he gets up to. Concert tickets, excursions, meals, women, boys, celebrations – anything you can get. But don't raise local eyebrows, whatever you do. Be a divorce agent or something.'

Toby was predictably appalled. 'Ned, listen to me. Ned, this is actually completely impossible. I'm in Vienna, okay? Salzburg, that's like the other side of the globe. This city is buzzing like a beehouse. I need more staff, Ned. You got to tell Burr. He doesn't understand the pressures here. Get me two more guys, we do anything you want, no problem. Sorry.'

He asked for a week. I said three days. He said he'd try his best and I believed him. He said he had heard a rumour that Mabel and I had broken up. I denied it.

Ever since I can remember, watchers have been most at home in condemned houses handy for bus routes and the airport. Monty's choice for his own headquarters was an unlikely Edwardian palazzo in Baron's Court. From the tiled hall, a stone staircase curled grandly through five pokey floors to a stained-glass skylight. As I climbed, doors flew open and shut like a French farce as his strange crew, in varying stages of undress, scurried between changing room, cafeteria and briefing room, their eyes averted from the stranger. I arrived in a garret once a painter's studio. Somewhere a women's foursome was playing noisy ping-pong. Closer at hand, two male voices were singing Blake's 'Jerusalem' under the shower.

I had not set eyes on Monty for a long time, but neither the years between nor his promotion to Head Watcher had aged him. A few grey hairs, a sharper edge to his hollow cheeks. He was not a natural conversationalist, and for a while we just sat and sipped our tea.

'Frewin, then,' he said finally.

'Frewin,' I said.

Like a marksman, Monty had a way of making his own particular area of quiet. 'Frewin's a funny one, Ned. He's not being normal. Now of course we don't know what normal is, do we, not really, not for Cyril, not apart from what you pick up from hearsay and that. Postman, milkman, neighbours, the usual. Everyone talks to a window cleaner, you'd be amazed. Or a Telecom engineer who's lost his way with a junction box. We've only been on him two days, all the same.'

With Monty, when he talked like this, you just pinned your ears back and bided your time.

'And nights, of course,' he added. 'If you count nights. Cyril's not sleeping, that's for sure. More prowling, judging by his windows and his teacups in the morning. And the music. One of his neighbours is thinking of complaining to him. She never has before, but she might this time. "Whatever's come over him?" she says. "Handel for breakfast is one thing, but Handel at three in the morning's a bit of another." She thinks he's having his change. She says men get like that at his age, same as women. We wouldn't know about that, would we?'

I grinned. And again bided my time. '*She* does, though,' Monty said reflectively. 'Her old man's gone off with a supply teacher from the comprehensive. She's not at all sure she'll have him back. Nearly raped our pretty boy who'd come to read the meter. Here – how's Mabel?' he demanded.

I wondered whether he too had heard the rumour; but I decided that if he had, he would not have asked me.

'Fine,' I said.

'Cyril used to take a newspaper on the train. The *Telegraph*, need you ask. Cyril doesn't hold with Labour – he says they're common. But he doesn't buy a paper any more. He sits. Sits and stares. That's all he does. Our bloke had to give him a nudge yesterday when they pulled up at Victoria. He'd gone off in a daydream. Going home last night, he tapped out the whole score of an opera on his briefcase. Nancy says it was Vivaldi. I suppose she knows. Remember Pauli Skordeno?'

I said I did. Diversions were part of Monty's way. Like, 'How's Mabel?' for instance.

'Pauli's doing seven years in Barbados for bothering a bank. What gets into them, Ned? He never put a foot wrong while he was watching. Never late, never naughty with his expenses, lovely memory, lovely eye, good nose. Burglaries galore we did. London, the Home Counties, the Midlands, the civil-rights boys, the disarmers, the Party, the naughty diplomats – we did the lot. Did Pauli ever get rumbled? Not once. The moment he goes private, he's all fingers and thumbs and boasting to the bloke next door to him in the bar. I think they *want* to be caught, that's my opinion. I think it's wanting recognition after all the years of being nobody.'

He sipped his tea. 'Cyril's other kick, apart from music, is his radio. He loves his radio. Only receiving, mind, as far as anybody knows. But he's got one of those fancy German sets with the fine tuning and big speakers for his concerts, and he didn't buy it locally because when it went on the blink the local shop had to send it off to Wiesbaden. Three months it took, and cost a fortune. He doesn't run a car, he doesn't hold with them. He shops by bus Saturday mornings, he's a stay-at-home except for his Christmases in Austria. No pets, he doesn't mix. Entertaining, forget it. No house-guests, lodgers, receives no mail except the bills, pays everything regular, doesn't vote, doesn't go to church, doesn't have a television. His cleaning lady says he reads a lot, mainly big books. She only comes once a week, usually when he's not there, and we didn't dare get close to her. A big book for her is anything bigger than a Bible-study pamphlet. His phone bills are modest, he's got six thousand in a building society, owns his house and maintains a well-managed bank account fluctuating between six and fourteen hundred, except Christmas times when it drops to around two hundred because of his holiday.'

Monty's sense of the proprieties again required us to make a detour, this time to discuss our children. My son Adrian had just won a modern languages scholarship to Cambridge, I said. Monty was hugely impressed. Monty's only son had just passed his law exam with flying colours. We agreed that kids were what made life worth living.

'Modrian,' I said when the formalities were once more over. 'Sergei.'

'I remember the gentleman well, Ned. We all do. We used to follow him round the clock some days. Except at Christmas, of course, when he took his home leave . . . Hullo! Are you thinking what I'm thinking? We all take leave at Christmas?'

'It had crossed my mind,' I said.

'We didn't even bother to pretend with Modrian, not after a while, you couldn't. *Oh*, he was a slippery eel, though. I could have walloped him sometimes, I really could. Pauli Skordeno got so angry with him once he let his tyres down outside the Victoria and Albert while he was inside sussing out a dead-letter box. I never reported it, I didn't have the heart.'

'Am I not right in thinking Modrian was also an opera buff, Monty?'

Monty's eyes became quite round, and I had the rare pleasure of seeing him surprised.

'Oh my Lord, Ned,' he exclaimed. 'Oh dear, oh dear. You're right. Sergei was a Covent Garden subscriber – of course he was, same as Cyril. We must have taken him there and fetched him – oh, a dozen times. He could have used a cab if he'd had any mercy, but he never did. He liked wearing us out in the traffic.'

'If we could know the performances he went to, and where he sat – if you could get them – we could try and match them up with Frewin's.'

Monty had fallen into a theatrical silence. He frowned, then scratched his head. 'You don't think this is all a touch too *easy* for us, do you, Ned?' he asked. 'I get suspicious when everything fits in a pretty pattern, don't you?'

'I won't be part of your pattern,' Sally had said to me the night before. 'Patterns are for breaking.'

'He *sings*, Ned,' Mary Lasselles murmured while she arranged my white tulips in a pickle jar. 'He sings *all* the time. Night and day, it doesn't matter. I think he missed his vocation.'

Mary was as pale as a nightnurse and as dedicated. A luminous virtue lit her unpowdered face and shone from her clear eyes. A shock of white, like the mark of early widowhood, capped her bobbed hair.

Of the many callings that comprise the over-world of intelligence, none requires as much devotion as that of the sisterhood of listeners. Men are no good at it. Only women are capable of such passionate espousal of the destiny of others. Condemned to windowless cellars, engulfed by tracks of grey-clad cable and banks of Russian-style tape recorders, they occupy a nether region populated by absent lives which they know more intimately than those of their closest friends or relations. They never see their quarries, never meet them, never touch them or sleep with them. Yet the whole force of their personalities is beamed upon these secret loves. On microphones and telephones they hear them blandish, weep, smoke, eat, argue and couple. They hear them cook, belch, snore and worry. They endure their children, in-laws and baby-sitters without complaint, as well as their tastes in television. These days, they even ride with them in cars, take them shopping, sit with them in cafés and bingo halls. They are the secret sharers of the trade.

Passing me a pair of earphones, Mary put on her own and, folding her hands beneath her chin, closed her eyes for better listening. So I heard Cyril Frewin's voice for the first time, singing himself a passage from *Turandot* while Mary Lasselles with her eyes shut smiled in her enchantment. His voice was mellow and, to my untutored ear, as pleasing as it clearly was to Mary.

I sat up straight. The singing had stopped. I heard a woman's voice in the background, then a man's, and they were speaking Russian.

'Mary, who the hell's that?'

'His teachers, darling. Radio Moscow's Olga and Boris, five days a week, 6 a.m. sharp. This is yesterday morning.'

'You mean he's teaching himself *Russian?*'

'Well, he listens to it, darling. How much of it is going into his little head is anybody's guess. Every morning, sharp at six, Cyril does his Olga and Boris. They're visiting the Kremlin today. Yesterday they were shopping at Gum.'

I heard Frewin mutter unintelligibly in the bath, I heard him call out 'Mother' in the night, while he tossed restlessly in bed. FREWIN Ella, I remembered, deceased, mother to FREWIN Cyril Arthur, q.v. I have never understood why Registry insists on opening personal files for the dead relatives of suspected spies.

I listened to him arguing with the British Telecom engineers' department after he had waited the statutory twenty minutes to be connected with them. His voice was edgy, full of unexpected emphases.

'Well, *next* time you elect to identify a *fault* on my line, I

would be *highly* grateful if you would kindly inform *me* as
the subscriber *prior* to barging into my house when my *clean-ing* woman happens to be in, and leaving particles of *wire* on
the carpets and *boot*marks on the kitchen *floor* . . .'

I listened to him phone the Covent Garden opera house to
say he would not be taking up his subscription ticket this Friday. This time his tone was self-pitying. He explained that he
was ill. The kind lady the other end said there was a lot of it
about.

I listened to him talking to the butcher in anticipation of
my visit, which Foreign Office Personnel had set for tomorrow morning at his house.

'Mr Steele, this is Mr Cyril Frewin. Good morning. I shall
not be able to come *in* to you on Saturday, owing to the fact
that I have a conference at my *house*. I would therefore be
grateful if you would kindly deliver four *good* lamb chops for
me on the Friday evening as you pass by on your way home.
Will that be convenient, Mr Steele? Also a jar of your
premixed mint *sauce*. No, I have redcurrant jelly already,
thank you. Will you attach your *bill*, please?'

To my over-acute ear, he sounded like a man preparing to
abandon ship.

'I'll take the engineers again, please, Mary,' I said. Having
twice more listened to Frewin's dogmatic tones of complaint
to British Telecom, I gave her a distracted kiss and stepped
into the evening air. Sally had said, 'Come round,' but I was
in no mood to spend an evening professing love to her and
listening to music I secretly detested.

I returned to the Pool. The Service laboratories had
completed their examination of the anonymous letter. A
Markus electronic, model number so-and-so, probably

Belgian manufacture, new or little used, was the best they could suggest. They believed they would be able to identify another document issuing from the same machine. Could I get one? End of report. The laboratories were still wrestling with the characteristics of the new generation of machines.

I rang Monty at his lair in Baron's Court. Frewin's complaint to the engineers was still ringing in my memory: his pauses, like unnatural commas, his use of the word *highly*, his habit of punching the unlikely word to achieve vindictive emphasis.

'Did your fellow notice a typewriter in Cyril's house, Monty, by any chance, while they were kindly mending his telephone?' I asked.

'No, Ned. There was no typewriter, Ned – not one they saw, put it that way.'

'Could they have missed it?'

'Easily, Ned. It was soft-pedalling only. No opening desks or cupboards, no photographing, not too much familiarity with his cleaning lady either, or she'll worry afterwards. It was "See what you can, get out fast, and be sure you leave a mess or he'll smell a rat."'

I thought of phoning Burr, but I didn't. My case officer's possessiveness was taking over, and I was damned if I was going to share Frewin with anyone, not even the man who had entrusted him to me. A hundred twisted threads were running through my head, from Modrian to Gorst to Boris and Olga to Christmas to Salzburg to Sally. In the end, I wrote Burr a minute setting out most of what I had discovered and confirming that I would 'make a first reconnaissance' of Frewin tomorrow morning when I interviewed him for his routine vetting clearance.

To go home? To go to Sally? Home was a hateful little

service flat in St James's, where I was supposed to be sorting myself out – though that's the last thing any man does when he sits alone with a bottle of Scotch and a reproduction painting of *The Laughing Cavalier*, dithering between his dreams of freedom and his addiction to what holds him prisoner. Sally was my Alternative Life, but I knew already I was too set to jump the wall and reach it.

Preferring to remain at my desk, therefore, I fetched myself a whisky from the safe and browsed through Modrian's file. It told me nothing I didn't already know, but I wanted him at the front of my head. Sergei Modrian, tried and tested Moscow Centre professional. A charmer, a bit of a dancer, a befriender, a smiling Armenian with a mercury tongue. I had liked him. He had liked me. In our profession, since we may like no one beyond a point, we can forgive a lot for charm.

My direct line was ringing. I thought for a moment it would be Sally, for contrary to regulations I had given her the number. It was Toby and he sounded pleased with himself. He usually did. He didn't mention Frewin by name. He didn't mention Salzburg. I guessed he was ringing from his flat, and I'd a shrewd notion he was in bed and not alone.

'Ned? Your man's a joke. Books himself a single room for two weeks, checks in, pays his two weeks in advance, gives the staff their Christmas box, pats the kids, makes nice to everybody. Next morning he disappears, does it every year. Ned, can you hear me? Listen, the guy's crazy. No phone calls out, one meal, two *Apfelsaft*, no explanations, taxi to the station. Keep my room, don't let it, maybe I'll be back tomorrow, maybe in a few days, I don't know. After twelve days, back he comes, no explanations, tips the staff some more, everybody happy like a heathen. They call him "the ghost". Ned, you got to talk nice to Burr for me. You owe me now. Toby works his fingers to the bone, tell him. Old star like you, a young fellow like Burr, he'll listen to you, costs you nothing. I need another man out here, maybe two. Tell him, Ned, hear me? Cheers.'

I stared at the wall, the one I couldn't scale; I stared at Modrian's file, I remembered Monty's dictum about too easy. I suddenly wanted Sally terribly, and had some cloudy notion that by solving the mystery of Frewin I would convert my recurring spurts for freedom into one bold leap. But as I reached for the phone to talk to her, it started to ring again.

'They fit,' said Monty in a flat voice. He had managed to check Frewin's opera attendance. 'It's Sergei and Cyril every time. When *he* goes, so does *he*. When *he* doesn't, neither does *he*. Maybe that's why *he* doesn't go any more. Got it?'

'And the seats?' I asked.

'Side by side, darling. What do you expect? Front to back?'

'Thanks, Monty,' I said.

Do I have to tell you how I spent that interminable night? Have you never telephoned your own son, listened to his unhappy jibes and had to remind yourself that he is yours? Talked frankly to an understanding wife about your inadequacies, not knowing what on earth they were? Have you never reached out for your mistress, cried 'I love you' and remained a mystified spectator to her untroubled fulfilment, before leaving her once more, to walk the London streets as if they were a foreign city? Have you never, from all the other sounds of dawn, picked out the wet chuckle of a magpie and fixed on it for your whole life long while you lie wide-eyed on your beastly single bed?

I arrived at Frewin's house at half past nine, having dressed myself as boringly as I could contrive, and that must have been boringly indeed, for I am not a natty dresser at the best of times, though Sally has appalling ideas about how she might improve my style. Frewin and I had agreed on ten but I told myself I wanted the element of surprise. Perhaps the truth was, I needed his company. A postman's van was parked up the street. A builder's truck with an aerial stood beyond it, telling me Monty's men were at their posts.

I forgot what month it was but I know it was autumn, both in my private life and in the prim cul-de-sac of steep brick houses. For I see a disc of white sun hanging behind the pollarded chestnut trees that had given the place its name, and I smell to this day the scent of bonfires and autumn air in my nostrils urging me to leave London, leave the Service, take to Sally and the world's real countryside. And I remember the whirr of small birds as they lifted from Frewin's telephone line on their way to somewhere better. And a cat in the next-door garden rising on its rear paws to box a drowsy butterfly.

I dropped the latch to the garden gate and crunched up the prim gravel path to the Seven Dwarfs semi-detached, with its bottle-glass windows and thatched porch. I reached out my hand for the bell, but the front door flew away from me. It was ribbed, and studded with fake coach bolts, and it shot back as if it had been blasted by a street bomb, almost sucking me after it into the dark tiled hall. Then the door stood still, and Frewin stood beside it, a bald centurion to his own endangered house.

He was taller than I had realised by a wrestler's head. His thick shoulders were braced to receive my attack, his eyes were fixed on me in scared hostility. Yet even at this first moment of encounter I sensed no contest in him, only a sort of heroic vulnerability made tragic by his bulk. I entered his house, and knew I was entering a madness. I had known it all night long. In desperation we find a natural kinship with the mad. I had known that for much longer.

'Captain York? Yes, well, welcome, sir. Welcome indeed. Personnel of their goodness *did* advise me you were coming. They don't always. But this time they did. Come in, please. You have your *duty* to do, Captain, as I have mine.' His vast, soggy hands were lifted for my coat but seemed unable to grapple with it. So they hovered above my neck as if to strangle or embrace me while he went on talking. 'We're all on the same side and no hard feelings, I say. I liken your job to airport security, personally, it's the same parameters. If they don't search *me*, they won't search the villains either, will they? It's the logical approach to the matter, in my view.'

Heaven knows what lost original he thought he was copying as he delivered these over-prepared words, but at least they freed him from his frozen state. His hands descended to my coat and helped me out of it, and I can feel now the reverence with which they did so, as if unveiling something exciting to us both.

'You fly a lot then, do you, Mr Frewin?' I asked.

He hung my coat on a hanger, and the hanger on a vile reproduction coat-tree. I waited for an answer but none came. I was thinking of his air travel to Salzburg, and I wondered whether he was too, and whether his conscience was speaking out of him in the tension of my arrival. He marched ahead of me to the drawing room, where by the light of the leaded bay window I was able to examine him at my ease, for he was already busy with the next article of his urgent hospitality: this time, an electric coffee percolator filled but not switched on – did I want the milk, or the sugar or the both, Captain? And the milk, Captain, was it hot or cold? And how about a home-made biscuit for you, Captain?

'You really made them yourself?' I asked as I fished one from the jar.

'Any fool who can read can cook,' said Frewin, with a chaotic grin of superiority, and I could see at once why Gorst would loathe him.

'Well, I can read, but I certainly can't cook,' I replied, with a rueful shake of my head.

'What's your first name, Captain?'

'Ned,' I replied.

'Well, that's because you're married, Ned, I expect. Your wife has robbed you of your self-sufficiency. I've seen it too often in life. In comes the wife, out goes the independence. I'm Cyril.'

And you're ducking my question about your air travel, I thought, refusing to allow him this attempted incursion into my private territory.

'If *I* ran this country,' Frewin announced over his shoulder to me while he poured, 'which I am *pleased* to say I shall never have the opportunity to *do*' – his voice was acquiring the didactic drum-beat of his conversation with the engineers – 'I would make an *absolute* law that *everyone*, regardless of colour, sex or creed, would take *cooking* as an obligatory subject *while* at school.'

'Good idea,' I said, accepting a mug of coffee, 'very sound,' and helped myself to sugar from the yellow beehive pot, which nestled like a missile in his damp paw. He had turned to me all at once, shoulders, waist and head together. His bare eyes, unfringed and unprotected, gazed down on me with a radiant and doting innocence.

'Play any games at all, Ned?' he enquired softly, tipping his head to one side for added confidentiality.

'A spot of golf, Cyril,' I lied. 'How about you?'

'Hobbies at all, Ned?'

'Well, I do like to do the odd watercolour when I'm on holiday,' I said, borrowing again from Mabel.

'Drive a car, do you, Ned? I expect you boys have to have all the skills at your fingertips, don't you?'

'Just an old Rover.'

'What year is it, then? What vintage, Ned? There's many a good tune played on an old fiddle, they say.'

His energy was not just in his person, I realised as I gave him the first date that occurred to me; it spilled into every object that came within his sphere. Into the reproduction horse-brasses that glistened like military cap-badges from his vigorous polishing. Into the polished fire grate and wood floor and the resplendent surface of his dining table. Into the very chair where I now sat and meekly sipped my coffee, for its arms were concealed in linen covers so pressed and spotless that I was reluctant to put hands on them. And I knew without his telling me that, cleaning woman or none, he tended all these things himself, that he was their servant and dictator, in the kingdom of his boundless wasted energy.

'Where do you live then, Ned?'

'Me? Oh well, London, really.'

'What part then, Ned? What district? Somewhere nice, or do you have to be slightly anonymous for your work?'

'Well, we're not really allowed to say, I'm afraid.'

'London born, are you? Hastings, me.'

'Sort of suburbs. You know. Pinner, say.'

'You must retain your discretion, Ned. Always. Your discretion is your dignity. Let nobody take it from you. It's your professional integrity, discretion is. Remember that. It could come in handy.'

'Thanks,' I said, affecting a sheepish laugh. 'I will.'

He was feeding on me with his eyes. He reminded me of my dog Lizzie when she watches me for a signal – unblinking, body ready to go. 'Shall we start, then?' he said. 'Want to sound the "off"? As soon as it's official, tell me. "Cyril. The red light's on." That's all you have to say.'

I laughed, shaking my head again, as if to say he was a card.

'It's only routine, Cyril,' I said. 'My goodness, you must know the questions by heart after all these years. Mind if I smoke?' I laboriously lit my pipe and dropped the match into the ashtray he was pressing on me. Then I resumed my study of his room. Along the walls, do-it-yourself shelves filled with do-it-yourself books, every one of them of global resonance: *The World's One Hundred Greatest Men*; *Gems of All the World's Literature*; *Music of the Great Ages in Three Volumes*. Next to them, his gramophone records in cases, all classical. And in the corner, the gramophone itself, a splendid teak affair with more control buttons than a simpleton like myself could master.

'Well now, if you like painting watercolours, Ned, why don't you try the music too?' he suggested, following my eye. 'It's the finest consolation in the world, good music is, properly played, if you choose right. I could put you on the right lines if you wanted.'

I puffed for a while. A pipe is a great weapon for playing slow against someone else's haste. 'I rather think I'm tone deaf, actually, Cyril. I have made the occasional effort, but I don't know, I sort of lose heart really . . .'

My heresy – drawn, I am afraid, from inconclusive debates

I had had with Sally – was already too much for him. He had sprung to his feet, his face a mask of horror and concern as he seized the biscuit jar and thrust it at me as if only food would save me.

'Now, Ned, that is not *right*, if I may say so! There is no such *thing* as a tone-deaf *person*! Take two, go on, there's plenty more in the kitchen.'

'I'll stick to my pipe if you don't mind.'

'Tone deafness, Ned, is merely a *term*, an expression, I will go so far as to say an *excuse*, designed to cover up, to disguise, a purely *temporary*, self-imposed *psychological* resistance to a certain world which your conscious mind is refusing you permission to enter! It is *merely* a fear of the unknown which is holding you *back*. Let me give you the example of certain acquaintances of mine . . .'

He ran on and I let him, while he dabbed at me with his forefinger, and with the other hand clutched the biscuit jar against his heart. I listened to him, I watched him, I expressed my admiration at the appropriate moments. I fished for my black notebook and removed the garter of black elastic from it as a signal to him that I was ready to begin, but he ignored me and ranted on. I imagined Mary Lasselles in her lair, smiling dreamily while her loved one lectured me. And Monty's boys and girls in their surveillance vans outside, cursing him and yawning while they waited to change shifts. For all I knew, Burr too – all of them hostages to Frewin's endless anecdote about a married couple he had had for neighbours when he lived in Surbiton, whom he had taught to share his musical appreciation.

'Anyway, I can tell my masters at PVHQ that music is still your great love,' I suggested with a smile when he had finished.

'PV' for Positive Vetting, you understand, and 'HQ' for Headquarters. My part as the downtrodden security work-horse required a higher authority than my own. Then, opening the notebook on my knee, I spread the pages, and with my unpainted government-issue pencil wrote the name FREWIN at the top of the left-hand page.

'Ah well, if you're talking about *love*, Ned – you *could* say music *was* my great love, yes. And music, to quote the bard, is the *food* of love. However, I'd *prefer* to say, it depends how you *define* love. What *is* love? That's your real question, Ned. *Define love.*'

God's coincidences are sometimes too vulgar to be borne. 'Well, I suppose *I* define it rather broadly,' I said doubtfully, my pencil poised. 'How do *you* define it?'

He shook his head and began energetically stirring his cof-fee, all his thick fingers gathered round the neck of one tiny Apostle spoon.

'Is this on the record?' he asked.

'It could be. Please yourself.'

'Commitment is how *I* define love. A great *number* of people speak of *love* as if it were some kind of *nirvana*. It isn't. I hap-pen to know that. Love is not *separate* from life. It's not *beyond* it or *superior* to it. Love is *within* life. Love is totally *integral* to life, and what you get *out* of it depends on the ways and means whereby you invest your *efforts* and your loyalty. Our Lord taught us that *perfectly* clearly, not that I'm a God-man per-sonally, I'm a rationalist. Love is *sacrifice* and love is hard work. Love is *also* sweat and tears, exactly as your great music has to be in order to qualify. By that token, yes, I'll grant you, Ned, *music* is my first love, if you follow me.'

I was following him only too well. I had made similar half-hearted representations to Sally, only to have them swept aside. I knew also that in his beleaguered state of mind there was no such thing to him as a casual question, let alone a casual answer – any more than there was to me, even if my systems of concealment were more sophisticated than his.

'I don't think I'll write that down,' I said. 'I think I'll regard it as what we call deep background.' In earnest of which, I pencilled a couple of words in the notebook, as a memo to myself and a sign to him that we were going on the record. 'All right, let's do the meat-and-potatoes work first,' I suggested, 'or PVHQ will say I'm dragging my feet as usual. Have you joined the Communist Party since you were last spoken to by one of our representatives, Cyril, or have you managed to restrain yourself?'

'I have not,' he said, with a smirk.

'Haven't joined or haven't restrained yourself?'

A broader smirk. 'The first. I like you, Ned. I cherish wit when I find it, I always have done. Not that we're overburdened with it at my place of work. Where wit's concerned, I'd be inclined to refer to the Tank as a total desert.'

'No friendship or peace groups?' I continued, affecting disappointment. 'Fellow-travelling organisations? Taken out membership to any homosexual or otherwise deviant-oriented clubs, formed a secret passion for any under-age choirboys lately?'

'No to the lot, thank you,' said Frewin, now smiling broadly.

'Run up vast debts, causing you to live beyond your means? Set up some tasteful redhead in the style to which she is not accustomed? Acquired a Ferrari motorcar on the hire purchase?'

'My needs remain as modest as they have always been, thank you. I am not of a materialist or self-indulgent nature, as you may have gathered. I rather abhor materialism, frankly. There's too much of it these days. Far.'

'And no to the rest?'

'All no.'

I was jotting all the time, making annotations against an imaginary checklist.

'So you wouldn't be flogging secrets for money then,' I commented, turning a page and adding a couple of ticks. 'And you have not launched yourself upon a course of foreign language instruction without first obtaining the consent of your employing department in writing, I take it?' My pencil was poised once more. 'Sanskrit? Hebrew? Urdu? Serbo-Croat?' I suggested. 'Russian?'

He was standing very still and staring at me, but I pretended to be unaware of this.

'Hottentot?' I continued facetiously. 'Estonian?'

'Since when's *that* been on the list?' Frewin demanded aggressively.

'Hottentot?'

I waited.

'Languages. A language isn't a defect. It's an attribute. An accomplishment! You don't have to list all your accomplishments, just to get cleared!'

I tilted back my head in reminiscence. 'Addendum to the Positive Vetting procedure, November 5, 1967,' I recited. 'I always remember that one. Fireworks Day. Special circular to all employing departments, yours included, requiring advance notice in writing of all intended language instruction courses. Recommended by Judicial Steering Committee, approved by Cabinet.'

He had turned his back to me. 'I regard this as a totally

out-of-court question and I refuse to answer it in any shape or form. Write that down.'

I puffed through my pipe smoke.

'I said write it down!'

'I wouldn't say that, Cyril, if I were you. They'll be cross with you.'

'Let them be.'

I drew on my pipe again. 'I'll put it to you the way HQ put it to me, shall I? "What's all this nonsense Cyril's been getting up to with his chums Boris and Olga?" they said. "Ask him that one – then see what he comes up with."'

Still turned away from me, he was scowling indignantly from place to place around the room, appealing to his polished world to witness my profanity. I waited for the explosion I was sure would come. But instead he peered at me in hurt reproach. *Us*, he was saying, *friends – and you do this to me*. And in the way that the brain in stress can handle a multitude of images at once, I saw before me, not Frewin, but a typist I had once interrogated in our Embassy in Ankara: how she had rolled back the sleeve of her cardigan and thrust out her arm at me and showed me the festering cigarette burns she had inflicted on herself the night before our interview. 'Don't you think you have made me suffer enough?' she asked. Yet it was not I who had made her suffer; it was the twenty-five-year-old Polish diplomat for whom she had sacrificed every secret she possessed.

I took my pipe from my mouth and gave him a reassuring laugh. 'Come on, Cyril. Aren't Boris and Olga two of the characters on this Russian course you're doing on the sly? Papering their house together? Going off to stay at Auntie Tanya's dacha, all that? You're doing the standard Radio

Moscow language course, five days a week, 6 a.m. sharp, that's what they told me. "Ask him about Boris and Olga," they say. "Ask him why he's learning Russian on the q.t." So I'm asking you. That's all.'

'They'd no business knowing I was doing that course,' he muttered, still grappling with the implications of my question. 'Bloody sniffer dogs. It was private. Privately selected, privately pursued. They can get lost. So can you.'

I laughed. But I was also put out. 'Now don't be like that, Cyril. You know the rules as well as I do. It's not your style to ignore a regulation. It's not mine either. Russian is Russian, and reporting is reporting. It's only a matter of getting it down in writing. I didn't make up the regulations. I get a brief, the same as anyone else.' I was talking to his back again. He had taken refuge at the bay window, and was gazing out at the rectangle that was his garden.

'What's their names?' he demanded.

'Olga and Boris,' I repeated patiently.

This enraged him. 'The people who brief you, idiot! I'm going to enter a complaint about them! Snooping, that's what it is. It's bloody brutal in this day and age. I'm holding you to blame too, frankly. What's their names?'

I still didn't answer him. I preferred to let the fury bank up in him.

'Number one,' he announced in a louder voice, still staring at his mud patch. 'Are you writing this down? Number one, I am not taking a language course within the meaning of the Act. A language course is going to a school or class, it is sitting on a bench with a bunch of snivelling typists with bad breath, it is submitting to the sneers of an uncouth instructor. Number two. I *do*, however, listen to *radio*, it being one of my *continuing* pleasures to scan the wavebands for examples of the quaint or esoteric. Write that down and I'll sign it. Finish, okay? Then take yourself off. I'm done with you, thank you, up to here. Nothing personal. It's them.'

'Which was how you stumbled on Boris and Olga,' I suggested helpfully, writing again. 'Got it. You scanned the wavebands and there they were. Boris and Olga. Nothing wrong in that, Cyril. Stick with it and you might even land yourself a language allowance, if you pass the test. It's only a few bob, I suppose, but it's better in your pocket than theirs, I always say.' I continued writing, but slowly, letting him hear the maddening scratch of my government-issue pencil. 'It's always the *not* reporting that bothers them most,' I confided, apologising for the foibles of my masters. ' "If he hasn't told us about Olga and Boris, what else hasn't he told us?" You can't blame them, I suppose. Their jobs are on the line, same as ours.'

Turn another page. Lick tip of pencil. Make another annotation. I was beginning to feel the excitement of the chase. Love as commitment, he had said, love as part of life, love as effort, love as sacrifice. But love for whom? I drew a heavy pencil line and turned a page.

'Can we pass on to your Iron Curtains, please, Cyril?' I asked in my weariest voice. 'HQ are devils for Iron Curtains. I wondered whether you'd any fresh names to add to the list of those you've already given us these past years. The last one' – I flipped to the back of the notebook – 'my goodness, that was aeons ago. A gentleman from East Germany, a member of a local choral society you joined. Is there no one you can think of since at all? They're a bit after you now, Cyril, I'll admit, now that they've caught you not reporting the language course.'

His disillusionment in me was again sliding into anger.

Once again he began punching the unlikely words. But this time it was as if he were punching me.

'You will find *all* my Iron Curtain contacts, past and present, *such* as they are, *duly* listed *and* submitted *to* my superiors, according to regulations. *If* you had troubled yourself to *obtain* this data from Foreign Office Personnel Department *prior* to this interview – and I mean why they send me a hack like you—'

I decided to cut him short. I did not think it useful that he should be allowed to reduce me to nothing. To insignificance, yes. But not to nothing, for I was the servant of a higher authority. I pulled a sheet of paper from the back of my notebook. 'Look, now, here you are, I've got them. All your Iron Curtains on one page. There's only been five ever, in your whole twenty years. HQ-cleared, I see, the lot. Well, so they would be, as long as you report them.' I put the sheet back in my notebook. 'Anyone to add, then? Who's to add? Think now, Cyril. Don't be hasty. They know an awful lot, my people. They shock me sometimes. Take your time.'

He took his time. And more time. And more. Finally he took the line of self-pity.

'I'm not a *diplomat*, Ned,' he complained in a small voice. 'I'm not out doing the gay hurrah every night, Belgravia, Kensington, St John's Wood, medals and white tie, rubbing shoulders with the great, am I? I'm a clerk. I'm not that man at all.'

'What man's that, Cyril?'

'I like a treat, that's different. I like a friend best.'

'I know you do, Cyril. HQ knows too.'

A fresh resort to anger to mask his rising panic. Deafening body language as he clenches his great fists and lifts his elbows. 'There is not a single *name* on that list that has *crossed* my path since I reported the *persons* concerned. The names in that list related *entirely* to the most *completely* casual encounters, which had no follow-up *whatsoever*.'

'But what about new people since?' I pleaded patiently. 'You'll not get past them, Cyril. I don't, so why should you?'

'If there *was* anyone to add, any contact at all, even a Christmas card from someone, you may *rest* assured I would have been the first to add him. Finish. Done. Over. Next question, thank you.'

Diplomat, I noted. *Him*, I noted. *Christmas*. Salzburg. I became if anything more laborious.

'That's not quite the answer they want, Cyril,' I said as I wrote in my notebook. 'That sounds a bit too much like flannel, frankly. They want a "yes" or a "no", or an "if yes, who?" They want a straight answer and they're not settling for flannel. "He didn't own up to his language, so why should we think he's owning up to his Iron Curtains?" That's what they're thinking, Cyril. That's what they're going to say to me too. It'll all come back on me in the end,' I warned him, still writing.

Once again I could feel that my ponderousness was a torture to him. He was pacing, snapping his fingers at his sides. He was muttering, working his jaw menacingly, growling again about getting names. But I was far too busy writing in my notebook to notice any of this. I was old Ned, Burr's Mr Plod, doing his duty by HQ.

'How's about this then, Cyril?' I said at last. And, holding up my notebook, I read aloud to him what I had written: ' "I, Cyril Frewin, solemnly declare that I have not made the acquaintance, however briefly, of any Soviet or Eastern Bloc citizen, other than those already listed by me, in the last twelve months. Dated and signed Cyril." '

I relit my pipe and studied the bowl in order to make quite sure it was drawing. I put the burned-out match in the matchbox, and the matchbox in my pocket. My voice, already slowed to a walking pace, now became a crawl.

'Alternatively, Cyril, and I say this advisedly, if there *is* anyone like that in your life, now's your chance to tell me. And them. I'll treat everything you say in confidence; so will they, depending what I tell them of it, which isn't always everything, not by any means. Nobody's a saint, after all. And HQ probably wouldn't clear them if they were.'

Intentionally or otherwise, I had touched the fuse in him. He had been waiting for an excuse and now I had delivered it.

'Saint? Who's talking *saint*? Don't *you* call me bloody saint, I won't have it! Saint Cyril, they call me, did you know that? Of course you did, you're taunting me!'

Taut-faced and rude. Battering me with words. Frewin against the ropes, slugging anything that came at him. 'If there *were* such a person – which there is not – I would *not* have told *you* or your snooping PV lot – I would have reported the matter *in writing*, according to regulations, to personnel department *at* the—'

For the second time, I allowed myself to cut him short. I didn't like him conducting the rhythm of our exchanges. 'But there really isn't anyone, is that right?' I said, as pressingly as my passive role allowed. 'There's no one? You haven't been to any functions – parties, get-togethers, meetings – official, unofficial – in London, outside London, abroad even – at which a citizen of an Iron Curtain country was remotely present?'

'Do I have to continue saying no?'

'Not if the answer's yes,' I replied, with a smile he didn't like.

'The answer is no. No, no, no. Repeat no. Got it?'

'Thank you. So I can put *none*, can I? That means no one, not even a Russian. And you can sign it. Yes?'

'Yes.'

'Meaning no?' I suggested, making another weak joke. 'I'm sorry, Cyril, but we do have to be crystal clear, otherwise HQ will fall on us from a great height. Look, I've written it down for you. Sign it.'

I handed him my pencil and he signed. I wanted to instil the habit in him. He handed back my notebook, smiling tragically at me. He had lied to me and he needed my comfort in his wretchedness. So I granted it to him – if only, I am afraid, because I wanted to take it away again very soon. I stowed the notebook in my inside pocket, stood up, and gave a big stretch as if announcing a break in our discussions, seeing that a tricky point was behind us. I rubbed my back a bit, an old man's ache.

'What's all that digging you've been doing out there, Cyril?' I said. 'Building your own deep shelter, are you? Hardly necessary these days, I'd have thought.'

Looking past him, my eye had fallen on a pile of new bricks stacked in a corner of the mud patch, with a tarpaulin tied over the top of them. An unfinished trench, about two feet deep, cut across the lawn towards them.

'I am *building* a *pond*,' Frewin retorted, seizing gratefully on my facetious diversion. 'I *happen* to be very fond of *water*.'

'A goldfish pond, Cyril?'

'An *ornamental* pond.' His good humour came sailing back. He relaxed, he smiled, and his smile was so warm and unaffected that I found myself smiling in return. 'What I intend to do, Ned,' he explained, drawing near to me in friendship, 'is construct three separate levels of water, beginning four feet above the existing ground, descending over eighteen-inch intervals to that trench. I shall then illuminate each pool from beneath with the aid of a concealed lamp. I shall then pump the water with an electric pump. And at night, instead of drawing the curtains, I shall be able to look out on to my own private display of illuminated pools and waterfalls!'

'And play your music!' I cried, responding in full measure to his enthusiasm. 'I think that's splendid, Cyril. Genius. I'm most impressed, I really am. I'd like my wife to see that. How was Salzburg, by the way?'

He actually reels, I thought, watching his head swing away from me. I hit him and he reels, and I wait till he recovers consciousness before I hit him again.

'You go to Salzburg for the music, they tell me. Quite a Mecca for you musicians, they tell me, Salzburg. Do they do opera at Christmas, or is it all carols and anthems you go for?'

They must have closed off the street, I thought, listening to the enormous silence. I wondered whether Frewin was thinking the same as he went on staring into the garden.

'Why should you care?' he answered. 'You're a musical ignoramus. You said so. As well as being a very considerable snooper.'

'Verdi? I've heard of Verdi. Mozart? He was Austrian, wasn't he? I saw the film. I'll bet they do you Mozart for Christmas. They'd have to. Which ones do they do?'

Silence again. I sat down and once again prepared myself to write to his dictation.

'Do you go alone?' I asked.

'Of course I do.'

'Do you always?'

'Of course I do.'

'Last time too?'

'Yes!'

'Do you stay alone?' I asked.

He laughed loudly. 'Me? Not for one minute. Not me. There's dancing girls waiting for me in my room when I arrive. They're changed every day.'

'But music night after night after night, the way you like it?'

'Who says what I like?'

'Fourteen nights of it. Twelve, I suppose, if you count the travel.'

'Could be twelve. Could be fourteen. Could be thirteen. What does it matter?' He was still concussed. He was talking from a long way off.

'Which is what you go for. To Salzburg. And what you pay for. Yes? Yes, Cyril? Give me a signal, please, Cyril. I keep thinking I'm losing you. And it was what you went for this Christmas too?'

He nodded.

'Concerts, night after night? Opera? Carols?'

'Yes.'

'Only the trouble is, you see, HQ says you only stayed the one night. You arrived on the first day as booked, they say, and you were off again next morning. You paid the full whack for your room, all two weeks, but the hotel never saw hide nor hair of you from your second day till you came back at the end of your holiday. So quite reasonably, really, HQ are asking where the bloody hell you went.' I took my boldest leap so far. 'And who with. They're asking whether you've got someone on the side. Like Boris and Olga, but real.'

I turned a couple more pages of my notebook, and in the deep silence the rustle was like falling bricks. His terror was infecting me. It was like a shared evil. The truth lay a membrane from us, yet the dread of it seemed to be as terrible to the man who was trying to keep it outside the door as to myself, who was trying to let it in.

'All we need to do is get it down on paper, Cyril,' I said. 'Then we can forget it. Nothing like writing something down for getting it out of the way, I say. It's no crime to have a friend. Even a foreign one isn't a crime, as long as he's written down. He is foreign, I take it? Only, I notice a certain hesitation in you here. He must be quite some friend, I will say, if you gave up all that music for him.'

'He's nowhere. He doesn't exist. He's gone. I was in his way.'

'Well, he hadn't gone at Christmas time, had he? Not if you were together with him. Was he Austrian, Cyril?'

Frewin was lifeless. He was dead with his eyes open. I had hit him once too often.

'All right, then, he's French,' I suggested more loudly, trying to jerk him from his introspection. 'Was he a Frenchie, Cyril, your chum? . . . They wouldn't mind about a Frenchie, even if they don't like them. Come on, Cyril, how about a Yank then? They can't object to a Yank!' No answer. 'Not Irish, was he? I hope not, for your sake!'

I did the laughing for him, but nothing stirred him from his melancholy. Still at the window, he had crooked his thumb and was boring the knuckle joint into his forehead, as if trying to make a bullet hole. Had he whispered something?

'I didn't catch you, Cyril!'

'He's above all that.'

'Above nationality?'

'He's above it.'

'You mean he's a diplomat?'

'He didn't *come* to Salzburg, can't you bloody listen?' He swung round at me and began screaming. 'You're bloody spastic, you know that? Never mind the answers, you can't even *ask* right! No wonder the country's in a mess! Where's your savvy gone? Where's your human understanding, for a change?'

I stood up again. Slowly. Keep him watching me. Give my back another rub. I wandered down the room. I shook my head as if to say this simply would not do.

'I'm trying to help you, Cyril. If you went to Salzburg and stayed there, that's one scenario. If you went on somewhere else – well, that's quite another. If your chum is Italian, say. And if you pretended to go to Salzburg but went – oh, I don't know – to Rome, say, or Milan, even Venice – well, that's another. I can't do it all for you. It's not fair and they wouldn't thank me if I did.'

He was wide-eyed. He was transferring his madness to me, appointing himself the sane one. I refilled my pipe, giving it my entire attention while I went on talking.

'You're a hard man to please, Cyril' – tamping the tobacco with my forefinger – 'you're a tease, if you want to know. "Don't touch me here, take your hand away from there, you can do this but only once." I mean, what *am* I allowed to talk about?'

I struck the match and held it to the bowl, and as I did so I saw that he had transferred his knuckles to his eyes in order not to be in the room. But I pretended not to notice. 'All right, we'll forget Salzburg. If Salzburg is hurtful, put Salzburg aside and let's go back to your Iron Curtains. Yes? Agreed?'

His hands slipped slowly from his face. No answer, but no

outright rejection either. I went on talking. He wanted me to. I could sense his reliance on my words as a bridge between the real world and the inner hell where he was living. He wanted me to do the talking for both of us. I felt I had to make his confession for him, which was why I decided to play my most perilous card.

'So suppose, for argument's sake, Cyril, we were to add the name of Sergei Modrian to this list and call it a day,' I suggested carelessly, almost covering over my words in my efforts to sound unthreatening. 'Just to be on the safe side,' I added cheerfully. 'What do you say?' His head was still hanging downward, his face cut off from me. Chatting cheerfully, I expanded on my latest helpful proposal for HQ. ' "All right," we say to them, "so take your wretched Mr Modrian. Don't play around with us any more, we'll come clean. Have him and go home. Ned and Cyril have got work to do." '

He was dangling, smiling like a hanged man. In the profound silence that had settled over the neighbourhood, I had the sensation of hearing my words resounding from the rooftops. But Frewin seemed barely to have heard them.

'Modrian's the one they want you to own up to, Cyril,' I continued reasonably. 'They told me. If you say yes to Modrian – and if I write him down, which I'm doing, and you allow me to, and I notice you're not stopping me, are you? – nobody can accuse either one of us of being less than frank with them. "Yes, I am a chum of Sergei Modrian and screw the lot of you" – how's that? "*And* I went with him to wherever we went, *and* we did this, we did that, we agreed to do certain other things, and we had a lovely time, or we didn't. And anyway, what's all the *glasnost* for, if I'm still being forbidden to associate with an extremely civilised Russian?" . . . How's that? Never mind the gaps for the moment, we can fill all those in later. Then, the way I see it, they can pack up the file for another year and we can all get on with our weekend.'

'Why?'

I affected not to understand.

'Why can they pack up the file then?' he demanded, as suspicions crowded in on him. 'When they've been who they are? They're not going to turn round and say, "What's the point?" Nobody does. Not when they've been one thing. They stay who they are. They don't become other people. They can't.'

'Come off it, Cyril!' He had sunk into his own thoughts and was becoming hard to reach. '*Cyril!*'

'What then? What's up? Don't shout.'

'So what's wrong with being Russian these days? HQ would be *far* more worried if Sergei was a Frenchie! I only suggested Frenchie as a trap. I regret that now, I apologise. But a Russian these days – for heaven's sake, we're not just talking friendly nations, we're talking partners! *You* know HQ. They're always behind the times. So's Gorst. Our job's to set the trend. Are you hearing me, Cyril?'

And that was where, for a moment, I thought I had lost the whole game – lost his complicity, lost his dependence, lost the willing suspension of his disbelief. He wandered past me like a sleep-walker. He stood himself at his bay window again, where he remained contemplating his half-dug pool and all the other half-built dreams of his life, which he must have known by now would never be completed.

Then, to my relief, he started talking. Not about what he had done. Not about who he had done it with. But why.

'You don't know what it means, do you, to be locked up all day with a bunch of morons?'

I thought at first he was complaining of his future, till I realised he was talking about the Tank.

'Listening to their filthy jokes all day, choking on their fags and their BO? Not *you*, you're privileged, however humble you make yourself out. Day after day of it, sniggers about tits and knickers and periods and little bits on the side? "Come on, Saint, tell us a naughty joke for a change! You're a deep one, I'll bet, Saint! What are you into – gym slips? Bit of the rough? What's the Saint's little fancy of a Saturday night?"' His energy had returned to him in full force, and with it, to my astonishment, an unexpected gift for mimicry. He was mincing at me, playing the music-hall queen, a ghastly soft grin twisting his hairless face. ' "Heard the one about the Boy Scouts and the Girl Guides, Saint? The excitement was in tents. Get *you!*" You wouldn't know about that, would you? "Do you pull it now and then, Saint? Give it a little jerk occasionally, just to make sure it's there? You'll go blind, you know. It'll drop off. I'll bet you've got a big one, haven't you? A real donkey knock, all the way down your leg and tucked into your garter." . . . You've never had that, have you, all day long, in the office, in the canteen? You're a gentleman. Know what they gave me April Fool's Day? A top secret incoming from Paris, Frewin's eyes only, decypher yourself, manual, ha ha. *Flash priority*, get the joke? I didn't. So I go into the cubicle and get out the books, don't I? And I decypher it, don't I? Manual. Everyone's got his head down. Nobody laughing or spoiling it. I do the first six groups and it's filth, some filthy joke all about a French letter. Gorst had done it. He'd had the boys at the Paris Embassy send it specially as a joke. "Steady on, Saint, keep your hair on, give us a smile. It was only a joke, Saint, can't you take a joke?" That's what Personnel said too, when I complained. Horseplay, they said. Pranks are good for morale. Think of it as a compliment, they said, show a little sporting instinct. If I hadn't had my music, I'd have killed myself long ago. I considered it, I don't mind telling you. Trouble was, I wouldn't see their faces when they found out what they'd done.'

A traitor needs two things, Smiley had once remarked bitterly to me at the time of Haydon's betrayal of the Circus: somebody to hate, and somebody to love. Frewin had told me whom he hated. Now he began to talk about whom he loved.

'I'd been all over the world that night – Puerto Rico, Cape Verde, Jo'burg – and there wasn't anything that took my fancy. I like the amateurs best, as a rule, the hacks. They've got more wit, which is what I like, I told you. I didn't even know it was morning. I've got these thick curtains up there, three hundred quids' worth, interlined. It's meat and drink to me after the Tank, the quiet is.'

A different smile had come up on him, a small boy's smile on his birthday.

'"Good morning to you, Boris, my friend," says Olga. "How are you feeling this morning?" Then she says it in Russian and Boris replies that he's feeling a bit low. He's often low, Boris is. He's prone to Slav depressions. Olga takes care of him, mind. She'll have a joke, but it's never cruelly meant. They have a fight now and then too – well, it's only natural, seeing they do everything together. But they always make it up in the same programme. They don't bear a grudge from day to day. Olga couldn't do that, to be frank. It's out with it and that's it, with Olga. Then they'll have a laugh together. That's how they are. Constructive. Friendly. Clean spoken. Musical too, naturally – well, they would be, being Russian. I wasn't that keen on Tchaikovsky till I heard them discussing him. But afterwards I came round to him straight away. Boris has got quite advanced tastes in music actually. Olga – well, she's a bit easy to please. Still, they're only actors, I suppose, reading their lines. But you forget that when you're listening to them, trying to learn the language. You believe in them.'

And you send your written work in, he was saying.

For free correction and advice, he was saying.

You don't even have to write to Moscow after the first time. They've got this box number in Luxembourg.

He had fallen quiet but not dangerously so. Nevertheless I was becoming scared that his trance might end too soon. I took myself out of his line of sight, and stood in a corner of the room behind him.

'What address did you give them, Cyril?'

'This one, of course. What else have I got to give them, then? A country house in Shropshire? A villa in Capri?'

'Did you give them your own name too?'

'Of course I didn't. Well, Cyril, yes. I mean anyone can be Cyril.'

'Good man,' I said approvingly. 'Cyril who?'

'Nemo,' he announced proudly. 'Mr C. Nemo. "Nemo" is Latin for "nobody", in case you didn't know.'

Mr C. Nemo. Like Mr A. Patriot, perhaps.

'Did you put your occupation?'

'Not my real one. You're being stupid again.'

'So what did you put?'

'Musician.'

'Did they ask for your age?'

'Of course they did. They had to. They had to know you were eligible, in case you won the prize. They can't give prizes to minors, can they? No one can.'

'And status – married or single – you told them that too?'

'I *had* to put my status, didn't I, with the prize being available to *couples*! They can't give a *prize* to *one* person and leave his wife out, it wouldn't be gracious.'

'What work did you send in – the first time round, for instance – do you remember?'

He decided to take further exception to my stupidity.

'Thickhead. What do you think I sent them? Bloody logarithms? You write in, you get the forms, you enrol, you get the Luxembourg box number, you get the book, you're one of them. After that you do what Boris and Olga tell you to do in the programme, don't you? "Complete the exercise on page 9. Answer the questions on page 12." Haven't you been to school, then?'

'And you were good. HQ says you've got a mind like an encyclopaedia when you use it. They told me.' I was beginning to learn how much he relished flattery.

'I was *more* than good, as a matter of fact, thank you, HQ. If you *wish* to know, I was in the nature of being their *top pupil*. Certain *notes* were sent to me by certain *tutors*, and some of them had a highly congratulatory *tone*,' he added, with the wild grin that came over him when he was praised. 'It gave me quite a fillip, if you wish to know, walking into the Tank of a Monday morning with one of their little *notes* in my pocket and not saying anything. I thought, I could tell some of *you* a tale if I wanted. I didn't, though. I preferred my privacy. I preferred my friendships. I wasn't going to have those animals making filthy comments about Olga and Boris, thank you.'

'And you wrote back to these tutors?'

'Only as Nemo.'

'But you didn't fool with them otherwise?' I asked, trying

to fathom what restraints, if any, were in his mind as he embarked on this first illicit love affair. 'I mean, if they asked you a plain question, you'd give them a plain answer. You weren't coy.'

'I was *not* coy! I had no *cause* to be! I took great care to be courteous, the same as my tutors were. They were high professors, some of them, academicians. I was *grateful* and I was *diligent*. That was the least they deserved, considering there was no fee and it was voluntary and in the interests of human understanding.'

The hunter in me again. I was calculating the moves they would have made as they played him along. I was working out how I would have played him myself, if the Circus had dreamed up anything so perfect.

'And I suppose, as you improved, they passed you on from plain printed exercises to the more ambitious stuff – composition, essays?'

'When it was deemed by the Board of Tutors in Moscow that I was ripe for it, yes, they moved me up to freestyle.'

'Do you remember the subjects they set you?'

He laughed his superior laugh. 'You think I'd forget them? Five nights at each one of them with the dictionary? Two hours' sleep if I'm lucky? Wake up, will you, Ned!'

I gave a rueful little laugh as I wrote to his dictation.

' "My Life" was the first one. I told them about the Tank, not mentioning names, of course, or the nature of our work, naturally. Nevertheless, a certain element of social comment was present, I won't deny it. I thought the Board had a right to know, specially with the *glasnost* in the pipeline and everything easing up for the benefit of all mankind.'

'What was the next one?'

' "My Home." I told them about my plans for the pond.'

They liked that. And my cooking. One of them was quite a major cook. After that they gave me "My Favourite Pastime", which could have been redundant but wasn't.'

'You described your love of music, I suppose?'

'Wrong.'

The rest of his answer rings in my ears today: as an accusation, as a cry of sympathy from a fellow sufferer; as a blind prayer flung into the ether by a man who, like myself, was desperate for love before it was too late.

'I elected "Good Company" as my favourite pastime, if you really wish to know,' he said as the wild smile came racing back to his cheeks. 'The fact that I had not *had* much good company in my life hitherto did not *deter* me from relishing the few occasions when it *had* come my way.' He seemed to forget that he had spoken, for he began again, in words I might have used of Sally: 'I had a feeling I had *renounced* something in my life which I *now* wished to reclaim,' he said.

'And did they admire your advanced work too? Were they impressed by it?' I asked as I diligently wrote this down.

He was smirking again. 'Moderately, I assume. Marginally. Here and there. With reservations, naturally.'

'Why do you assume that?'

'Because, unlike some, they had the grace and generosity to show their appreciation. That's why.'

And they showed it, said Frewin – I scarcely needed to press him further – they showed it in the person of one Sergei Modrian, First Secretary Cultural, of the Soviet Embassy in London, in his capacity as Radio Moscow's devoted local emissary despatched to answer Frewin's prayer.

Like all good angels, Modrian arrived without warning, on Frewin's doorstep one dank November Saturday, bearing with him the gifts of his high office: one bottle of Moskov-skaya vodka, one tin of Sevruga caviar, and one foully printed art-book about the Bolshoi Ballet. And one grandly typed letter appointing Mr C. Nemo to be an Honorary Student of Moscow State University, in recognition of his unique progress in the Russian language.

But the greatest gift of all was Modrian's own magical person, custom-trained to provide the good company Frewin had so loudly craved in his prize-winning essay for the Board.

We had arrived at our destination. Frewin was calm, Frewin was in triumph; Frewin, for however long, was fulfilled. His voice had broken free of its confinements; his plain face was lit with the smile of a man who had known true love and was longing to impart his luck. If there had been anyone in the world for whom I could ever have smiled in the same way, I would have been a different man.

'*Modrian*, Ned? Sergei Modrian? Oh, Ned, I mean we're talking the total top league here. One look at him, I knew. None of your half measures here, I thought. This one's the whole hog. We had the same sense of humour, of course, straight off. Acid. No wool across the eyes. The same interests too, right down to composers.' He attempted a more detached tone, but in vain. 'It is very *rare* in life, in my experience, for two human beings to be naturally compatible in each and every respect – bar women, where I have to admit that Sergei's experience far outran my own. Sergei's attitude to women' – he was trying hard to be disapproving – 'I'll put it this way: if it had been anyone else behaving in that manner, I would have been hard put to it to approve.'

'Did he introduce you to women, Cyril?'

His expression switched to one of adamant rejection. 'He assuredly did not, thank you. Nor would I have permitted him to. Nor would he have regarded such introductions as coming within the ambit of our relationship.'

'Not even on your trips to Russia together?' I ventured, taking another leap for him.

'Nowhere, thank you. It would have ruined them, as a matter of fact. Killed them stone dead.'

'So it's all hearsay, what they say about his women?'

'No, it's not. It's what Sergei told me himself. Sergei Modrian had a totally ruthless attitude to women. His colleagues confirmed this to me privately. Ruthless.'

I found time to marvel at Modrian's psychological dexterity – or was it the dexterity of his masters? Between Modrian the ruthless pursuer of women, and Frewin the ruthless rejecter of them, there was indeed a natural bond.

'So you met his colleagues too,' I said. 'In Moscow, presumably. At Christmas.'

'Only the ones he trusted. Their respect for him was incredible. Or Leningrad. I wasn't fussy, I'd no right to be. I was an honoured guest. I went along with whatever they'd arranged for me.'

I kept my eyes on my notebook. God knows what I was writing by then. Gobbledygook. Afterwards, there were whole tracts I couldn't read a word of. I selected my absolutely dullest tone.

'And was all this in honour of your remarkable linguistic abilities, Cyril? Or were you already providing informal services for Modrian by then? Like giving him information or whatever. Translating and so on. A lot do it, I'm told. They're not supposed to, of course. But you can't blame people – can you? – wanting to help the *glasnost* along, now it's come.

We've waited long enough. Only, I've got to put the proper history to this, Cyril. They'll skin me otherwise.'

I did not dare look up. I simply kept writing. I turned a page and wrote: *keep talking, keep talking, keep talking.* And still I did not look up.

I heard him whisper something I couldn't understand. I heard him mutter, 'It's *not*. I didn't. I never bloody did.' I heard him complain more loudly: 'Don't *say* that, do you mind? Don't you ever say that again, you and your HQ. "Giving him information" – what's all that about? They're wrong words. *I'm talking to you, Ned!'*

I looked up, sucking on my pipe and smiling. 'Are you, Cyril? Of course you are. I'm sorry. You're my sixth in a week, to be honest. They're all doing the *glasnost* these days. It's the fashion. I'm beginning to feel my age.'

He decided to comfort me. He sat down. Not in the chair, but on its arm. He put on an avuncular, friend-to-friend manner that reminded me of my preparatory-school head-master.

'You're by way of being a liberal yourself, aren't you, Ned? You've got the face for it anyway, even if you are a bit of a toady for HQ.'

'I suppose I'm a sort of free thinker in my way, yes,' I con-ceded. 'Though I do have my pension to consider, naturally.'

'Of course you are! You favour a mixed economy, don't you? You don't like public poverty and private wealth any more than I do. Humanity above ideology, you believe in that? Stop the derailed train of capitalism destroying all before it in its path? Of course you do! You've got a sensible concern for the environment, I dare say. Badgers, whales, fur coats, power stations. Even a vision of sharing, where it doesn't impinge. Brothers and sisters marching together towards common goals, culture and music for all! Freedom of movement and choice of allegiance! Peace! Well, then.'

'Makes good sense to me,' I said.

'You're not old enough to have done the thirties; neither am I. I wouldn't have held with them if I had been. We're *good men*, that's all we are. *Reasonable men*. That's what Sergei was too. You and Sergei – I can see it in your face, Ned, it's no good your trying to hide it, you're birds of a feather. So don't go painting me black and you white, because we're like minds, same as me and Sergei were. On the same side against the wickedness, the lack of culture, the filth. "We're 'the un-recognised aristocracy'" – that's what Sergei called us. He was right. You're one too, that's all I'm saying. I mean, who else is there? Who's the alternative to what we see around us every day, the degradation, the waste, the disrespect? Who are we going to listen to, up there in the attic at night, twiddling the dials? Not the yuppies, that's for sure. Not the pigs-in-clover lot – what have they got to say? Not the make-more spend-more be-more school, they're no help. Not the knickers-and-tits brigade, either. And we're not going to convert to Islam in a hurry, are we, not while they go round pinching countries off each other and doing the poison gas. So I mean what's the alternative for a feeling man, a man of conscience, now the Russians are abandoning their responsibilities right and left and putting on the hair shirt? Who's out there for us? Where's the vision any more? Where's the relief? The friendship? Someone's got to fill the gap. I can't be left in the air. I can't be without. Not after Sergei, Ned – I'd die. Sergei was the most important man on earth to me. Drink, meat and laughter, Sergei was. He was my total meaning.

What's going to happen? That's what I want to know. There's some heads could roll, in my view. Sergei had the ideology. I don't see it in you – I don't think I do anyway. I get a glimpse of it, a longing here and there, then I'm not at all sure. I don't know you've got the quality.'

'Try me,' I said.

'I don't know you've got the wit. The dance. I thought that as you came in. I compared you with Sergei in my mind, and I'm afraid I found you seriously wanting. Sergei didn't shuffle in like a deadbeat; he took me by storm. Rings the bell, marches in as if he's bought the place, sits down where you're sitting, but more awake – not that he ever sat anywhere long, Sergei didn't, he was a shocking fidget, even at the opera. Then he grins like an elf and lifts up a glass of his own vodka. "Congratulations, Mr Nemo," he says. "Or may I call you C? You've won the competition and I'm the first prize." '

He passed the back of his hand across his mouth, and I realised that he was wiping away a grin. 'He was a real flyer, Sergei was.'

He was laughing, so I laughed with him. Modrian was his false freedom, I was thinking. As Sally is mine.

'He hadn't even taken his coat off,' he continued. 'He went straight into his pitch. "Now the first thing we've got to talk about is the ceremony," he says. "Nothing flashy, Mr Nemo, just a couple of friends of mine, who happen to be Boris and Olga, plus one or two high dignitaries from the Board, and a small reception for a few of your many admirers in Moscow."

' "At your Embassy?" I said. "I'm not coming there. My office would kill me – you don't know Gorst."

' "No, no, Mr Nemo," he says. "No, no, Mr C. *I'm* not talking about the Embassy – who cares about the Embassy?

I'm talking about Moscow State University foreign language school and the official inauguration of your honorary studentship with full civilian honours."

'I thought I was dead at first. My heart had stopped beating. I could feel it. I'd never been beyond Dover in my life, let alone Russia, although I was Foreign Office. "Come to Moscow?" I said. "You're off your head," I said. "I'm a cypher clerk, not a trade union leader with an ulcer. I can't come to Moscow at the drop of a hat," I said. "Even if there is a prize at the end of it, and Olga and Boris waiting to shake my hand, and studentships and I don't know what. You don't seem to understand the position at all. I'm in highly sensitive work," I said. "The people aren't that sensitive, but the work is. I've got constant and regular access to top secret and above. I'm not just anybody off the street, into your plane to Moscow and nobody's the wiser. I thought I put that in my essays, some of them."

' "Then come to Salzburg," he says. "Who's counting? Take a plane to Salzburg, say you're doing the music there, slip up to Vienna, I'll have the air tickets ready – all right, it's Aeroflot but it's only two hours – no nonsense with the passports when we arrive, we'll keep the ceremony family, who's the wiser?" Then he hands me this document like a scroll, all with the burned edges and that, the full formal invitation, signed by the whole Board, English one side, Russian the other. I read the English, I don't mind telling you. I wasn't going to sit in front of him with a dictionary for an hour, was I? I'd have looked a total idiot, me a top language student.' He paused – a little shamefully, I thought. 'Then I told him my name,' he said. 'I shouldn't have done, really, but I'd had enough of being Nemo. I wanted to be me.'

*

Now you must lose me for a minute, as I lost Cyril. Until now, I had managed to stay abreast of his references. Where I had dared, I had even led them. Now suddenly he was running free and I was struggling to keep up with him. He was in Russia, but I wasn't. He'd given me no warning that we'd gone there. He was talking about Boris and Olga, not how they sounded any more, but how they looked; and how Boris had flung his arms round him, and how Olga had given him a demure but heartfelt Russian kiss – he didn't hold with kissing as a rule, Ned, but with the Russians it wasn't Gorst's kind of kissing at all, so you didn't mind. You even got to expect it, Ned, it being all part of what Russians regard as comradely. Frewin was looking twenty years younger and talking about being made a fuss of, all the birthdays that he'd never had. Olga and Boris in the flesh, Ned, no side to them, just natural, same as they were in their lessons.

' "Congratulations, Cyril," she says to me, "on your completely phenomenal progress in the Russian language." Well, through interpreters, naturally, I wasn't *that* far on, as I told her. Then Boris puts his arm round me. "We're proud to be of assistance, Cyril," he says. "There's a lot of our students fall by the wayside, to be truthful, but those as don't make up for all the rest." '

And by then at last I had pieced together the scene that he was painting for me in such broad, unpredicated strokes: his first Christmas in Russia, and for Frewin, I had no doubt, his first good Christmas anywhere, and Sergei Modrian playing ringmaster at his side. They are in a great room somewhere in Moscow, with chandeliers and speeches and a presentation, and fifty handpicked extras from Moscow Central Casting, and Frewin in paradise, which is exactly where Modrian wishes him to be.

Then, as abruptly as Frewin had treated me to this memory, he abandoned it. The light went out of his eyes, his head tipped to one side, and he beetled his eyebrows as if in judgment at his own behaviour.

Prudently, I returned him to time present. 'So where is it?' I said. 'The scroll he gave you. Here? The scroll, Cyril. Appointing you. Where?'

He stared at me, slowly waking. 'I had to give it back to Sergei. "When we're in Moscow, Cyril," he said, "you shall have it hanging on your wall and framed in gold. Not here. I wouldn't put you in the danger." He'd thought of everything, Sergei had, and he was quite right, what with you and your HQ snooping on me night and day.'

I allowed no pause, no alteration in my voice, not even in the direction of casualness. I lowered my eyes again and dug once more in my inside pocket. I was his candidate as Sergei's replacement, and he was courting me. He was showing me his tricks and asking me to take him on. Instinct told me to make him work harder for me. I addressed myself to the notebook again, and I spoke exactly as if I were asking him the name of his maternal grandfather.

'So when did you start giving Sergei all these great British secrets?' I said. 'Well, what we *call* secrets, anyway. Obviously what was secret a few years ago is not going to be the same as what's secret today, is it? We didn't win the Cold War by secrecy, did we? We won it with the openness. The *glasnost.*'

It was the second time I had mentioned passing over secrets, but on this occasion, when I crossed the Rubicon for him, he came with me. Yet he seemed not even to notice he was on the other side.

'Correct. That's how we won it. And Sergei didn't even want the secrets at first, either. "Secrets, Cyril, they're unimportant to me," he said. "Secrets, Cyril, in the changing world in which we live, I'm pleased to say, they're a drug on the market," he said. "I'd rather keep our friendship on a non official basis. However, if I *do* require something in that line, you may count on me to let you know." In the meantime, he said, it would be quite sufficient if I wrote him a few unofficial reports on the quality of Radio Moscow's programmes just to keep his bosses happy. Whether the reception was good enough, for example. You'd think they'd know that, really, but they don't. You never know with Russians where you're going to strike the ignorance in them, to be frank. That's not a criticism, it's a fact. He'd like my opinion of the course as well, he said, for standards of instruction generally, any suggestions I might have for Boris and Olga in the future, me being somewhat of an unusual pupil in my own right.'

'So what changed it?'

'Changed what? Be lucid, please, Ned. I'm not nobody, you know. I'm not Mr Nemo. I'm Cyril.'

'What changed Sergei's reluctance to take secrets from you?' I said.

'His Embassy did. The diehards. The barbarians. They always do. They prevailed on him. They declined to recognise the course of history; they preferred to remain total troglodytes in their caves and continue with their ridiculous Cold War.'

I said I did not understand him. I said he was a bit above my head.

'Yes, well, I'm not surprised. I'll put it this way. There was a lot of them in that Embassy didn't like the time given over to cultural friendship, for a start. There was this internal rivalry going on between the camps. I was an impotent spectator. The *doves*, they were in favour of the culture, naturally, and above all they were in favour of the *glasnost*. They saw culture filling the vacuum left behind by the withdrawal of hostilities. Sergei explained that to me. But the hawks – *including* the Ambassador, I regret to say – wanted Sergei concentrating more on the continuation of old attitudes, what's left of them, gathering intelligence and generally act-ing in an aggressive and conspiratorial manner regardless of the changes in the world climate. The Embassy diehards didn't care about Sergei being an idealist, not at all. Well, they wouldn't, would they, any more than what Gorst does. Sergei had to tread a highly precarious path, frankly, a bit for one side, then a bit for the other. So did I, it was duty. We'd do our culture together, a bit of language, a bit of art or music; then we'd do some secrets to satisfy the hawks. We had to justify ourselves to all parties, same as you with your HQ and me with the Tank.'

He was fading, I was losing him. I had to use the whip. 'So *when*?' I asked impatiently.

'When what?'

'Don't be clever with me, Cyril, do you mind? I've got to get this down. Look at the time. *When* did you start giving Sergei Modrian information, *what* did you give him, what for, how *much* for, when did it stop, and why, when it could perfectly well have continued? I'd like a weekend, Cyril, if you don't mind. So would my wife. I'd like to put my feet up in front of the telly. I'm not paid overtime, you know. It's strictly piecework, what they offer. One candidate's the same as another, when it comes to payday. We're living in a time of cost effectiveness, in case you haven't noticed. They tell me we could be privatised if we're not careful.'

He didn't hear me. He didn't want to. He was wander-ing, in his body and in his mind, looking for distraction, for

somewhere to hide. My anger was not all simulated. I was
beginning to hate Modrian. I was angry about how much we
depended on the credulity of the innocent in order to survive. It was sickening me that a trickster like Modrian had
contrived to turn Frewin's loneliness to treachery. I felt threatened by the notion of love as the antithesis of duty.

I stood up smartly, anger still my ally. Frewin was perched
listlessly on the edge of a carved Arthurian stool with the
Royal Navy's ensign stitched into the seat.

'Show me your toys,' I ordered him.

'What toys? I'm a man, if you don't mind, not an infant.
It's my house. Don't tell me what to do.'

I was remembering Modrian's tradecraft, the stuff he
used, the way he equipped his agents. I was remembering
my own tradecraft, from the days when I had run Frewin's
counterparts against the Soviet target, even if they were not
quite as mad as Frewin. I was imagining how I would have
handled a high-access walk-in like Frewin, living on borrowed
sanity.

'I want to see your camera, don't I?' I said petulantly. 'Your
high-speed transmitter, right, Cyril? Your signals plan. Your
one-time code-pads. Your crystals. Your white carbons for
your secret writing. Your concealment devices. I want to see
them, Cyril, I want to put them in my briefcase for Monday;
then I want to go home and watch Arsenal against United.
That may not be your taste, but it happens to be mine. So can
we move this along a bit and cut out the bullshit, *please?*'

The madness was running out, I could feel it. He was
drained and so was I. He sat head down and knees spread,
staring dully at his hands. I could sense the end beginning in
him – the moment when the penitent grows tired of his confession and of the emotions that compelled it.

'Cyril, I'm getting a bit edgy,' I said.

And when he still didn't respond, I strode to his telephone, the same one that Monty's fake engineer had made permanently live. I dialled Burr's direct line and heard his fancy secretary the other end, the same one who hadn't known my name.

'Darling?' I said. 'I'm going to be about another hour, if I'm lucky. I've got a slow one. Yes, all right, I know, I'm sorry. Well, I said I'm sorry. Yes, of course.'

I rang off and stared at him accusingly. He climbed slowly to his feet and led me upstairs. His attic was a spare bedroom, roof high. His radio receiver stood on a table in the corner – German, just as Monty had said. I switched it on while he watched me, and we heard an accented female Russian voice talking indignantly about Moscow's criminal mafia.

'Why do they *do* that?' Frewin burst out at me, as if I were responsible. 'The Russians. Why do they run down their own country all the time? They never used to. They were proud. I was proud too. All the cornfields, the classlessness, the chess, the cosmonauts, and ballet, the athletes. It was paradise till they started running it down. They've forgotten the good in themselves. It's bloody disgraceful. That's what I told Sergei.'

'Then why do you still listen to them?' I said.

He was almost weeping, but I pretended not to notice.

'For the message, don't I?'

'Make it snappy, will you, Cyril!'

'Telling me I'm reactivated. That I'm wanted again. "Come back, Cyril. All is forgiven, love, Sergei." That's all I need to hear.'

'How would they say that?'

'White paint.'

'Go on.'

' "There's white paint on the dog, Olga." . . . "We need a spot of white paint on the bookshelf, Boris." . . . "Oh dear, oh dear, Olga, look at the cat, someone has dipped her tail in white paint. I hate cruelty," says Boris. Why don't they say it when I'm listening?'

'Let's just stick to the method, can we? All right, you hear the message. On the radio. Olga or Boris says "white paint". Or they both do. *Then* what do you do?'

'Look in my signals plan.'

I held out my hand, commanding him with my snapping fingers. 'Hurry!' I said.

He hurried. He found a wooden hairbrush. Pulling the bristles from the casing, he shoved his big fingers into the gap and hauled out a piece of soft, flammable paper with times of the day and wavebands printed in parallel. He offered it to me, hoping it would satisfy. I took it from him without pleasure and snapped it into my notebook, glancing at my watch at the same moment.

'Thanks,' I said curtly. 'More, please, Cyril. I need a codebook and a transmitter. Don't tell me you haven't got them, I'm not in the mood.'

He was grappling with a tin of talcum powder, tugging at the base, trying desperately to please me. He talked nervously while he shook the powder into the handbasin.

'I was respected, you see, Ned, you don't get that a lot. There's three of these. Olga and Boris tell me which to use, like with the white paint except it was the composers. Tchaikovsky was number three, Beethoven was number two, Bach was one. They did them alphabetical to help me remember. You get the glimpses but you don't get the friends, not normally, do you? Not unless you meet Sergei or one of his lot.'

The powder was all poured away. Three radio crystals lay in his palm, together with a tiny code-pad and an eye-glass to enlarge it.

'He had all I'd got, Sergei did. I gave it to him. He'd tell me a thing, I'd add it to my life. I'd have a mood, he'd get me straight again. He understood. He could see right into me. It gave me a feeling of being known, which I liked. It's gone now. It's been posted back to Moscow.'

His rambling was scaring me. So was his feverish desire to pacify me. If I had been his hangman, he would have been gratefully loosening his tie.

'Your transmitter,' I snapped. 'What the hell's the good of a crystal and a code-pad if you can't send!'

At the same terrible pace, he bent his swelled body to the floor and rolled back a corner of the tufted Wilton carpet.

'I haven't got a knife actually, Ned,' he confessed.

Neither had I, but I dared not leave him, I dared not break my command over him. I crouched beside him. He was peering vaguely at a loose floorboard, trying to raise it with his thick fingertips. Clenching my fist, I punched one end of the board, and had the satisfaction of seeing the other end lift.

'Help yourself,' I said.

It was old stuff, I could have guessed, nothing they cared about any more – a rig of grey boxes, a squash transmitter, a lash-up to be fitted to his receiver. Yet he handed it to me proudly, in its tangled mess.

A terrible anxiety had entered his eyes. 'All I am now, you see, Ned, I'm a hole,' he explained. 'I don't mean to be morbid, do I, but I don't exist. This house isn't anything either. I used to love it. It looked after me, same as I looked after it. We'd have been nothing without each other, this house and me. It's hard for you to understand that, I dare say, if you have a wife, what a house is. She'd come between you. You and the house, I mean. Your wife. You and him. Modrian. I loved him, Ned. I was infatuated. "You're too much, Cyril," he used to say. "Cool down. Relax. Take a holiday. You're hallucinating." I couldn't. Sergei was my holiday.'

'Camera,' I ordered.

He didn't read me at once. He was obsessed with Modrian. He looked at me, but it was Modrian he saw.

'Don't be like that,' he said, not understanding.

'Camera!' I yelled. 'For Christ's sake, Cyril, don't you *ever* have a weekend?'

He stood at his wardrobe. Camelot sword blades carved on oak doors.

'Camera!' I shouted louder as he still hesitated. 'How can you slip film to a good friend at the opera if you haven't photographed your files in the first place?'

'Take it easy, Ned. Cool down, will you? Please.' Grinning in a superior way, he reached a hand into the wardrobe. But his eyes were ogling me, saying, 'Now watch this.' He groped in the wardrobe, smiling at me mysteriously. He pulled out a pair of opera glasses and trained them on me, first the right way, then back to front. Then he handed them to me so that I could do the same to him. I took them in my hands and felt their unnatural weight at once. I turned the central dial until it clicked. He was nodding at me, encouraging me, saying, 'Yes, Ned, that's the way.' He grabbed a book from the bookshelf and opened it at the centre, *All the World's Dancers*, illustrated. A young girl was doing a *pas de chat*. Sally too had been at ballet school. He unbuckled the neck strap and I saw that the short end did duty as a measuring chain. He took the binoculars from me and trained them on the book, measured the distance and turned the dial till it clicked.

'See?' he said proudly. '*Comprenez*, do you? They made it specially. For me. For opera nights. Sergei designed it personally. There's a lot of idleness in Russia, but Sergei had to have the best. I'd stay in late at the Tank. I'd photograph the whole weekly float for him if I felt like it, then give him the film while we were sitting in the stalls. I'd give it to him in one of the arias, usually – it was a sort of joke between us.' He handed the binoculars back to me and drifted down the room, scrabbling his fingertips on his bare scalp as if he had a full head of hair. Then he held out his hands like someone testing the atmosphere for rain.

'Sergei had the best of me, Ned, and he's gone. *C'est la vie*, I say. Now it's up to you. Have you got the courage? Have you got the wit? That's why I wrote to you. I had to. I was empty. I didn't know you, but I needed you. I wanted a good man who understood me. A man I could trust again. It's up to you, Ned. Now's your chance. Jump out of yourself and live, I say, while there is yet time. That wife of yours is a bit of a bully, by the sound of her. You'd be well advised to tell her to live her own life instead of yours. I should have advertised, shouldn't I?' A terrible smile, which he turned full upon me. 'Single man, non-smoker, fond of music and wit. I peruse those columns sometimes – who doesn't? I contemplate replying sometimes, except I'd never know how to break it off if I wasn't suited. So I wrote you a letter, didn't I? It was like writing to God in a way, till you came along in your shabby coat and asked a lot of spotty questions, no doubt drafted by HQ. It's time you stood on your own feet, Ned, same as me. You're cowed, that's your trouble. Your wife is partly to blame, in my opinion. I listened to your voice while you were apologising and I was not impressed. You won't reach out to take. Still, I reckon I could make something of you, and you could make something of me, too. You could help me dig my pool. I could show you music. That's evens, right? Nobody's impervious to music. I only did it because of Gorst.' His voice leapt in horror. '*Ned!* Leave that alone, do you mind! Take your thieving hands off my property, Ned. *Now!*'

I was fingering his Markus typewriter. It was in the wardrobe where he kept his opera glasses, stowed under a few shirts. Signed A. Patriot, I thought. '*A*' standing for *Anyone's*, I thought. Anyone who loved him. I'd guessed already and he'd told me already, but the sight of it had excited both of us with a sense of ending.

'So why did you break it off with Sergei?' I asked him, still fingering the keys.

But this time he didn't rise to my flattery. '*I* didn't break it off. *He* did. I haven't ended it now, not if you're stepping into his shoes. Put that away. Cover it over the way you found it, thank you.'

I did as he asked. I hid the evidence of the typewriter.

'What did he say?' I asked carelessly. 'How did he break it to you? Or did he write and run?' I was thinking of Sally again.

'Not a lot. You don't need a lot of words when someone's stuck in London and you're in Moscow. The silence speaks for itself.'

He wandered over to his radio and sat before it. I followed close on his heels, ready to restrain him.

'Let's plug her in, shall we, have a nice listen. I could still get a "Come back, Cyril," you never know.'

I watched him set up his transmitter, then fling open the leaded window and toss out the hairline-aerial, which was like a fishing line with a lead sinker but no hook. I watched him peer at his signals plan and type out SOS and his callsign on his squash recorder. Then he linked the recorder to the transmitter and, with a *whizz*, sent it into the ether. He did this several times before he switched over to receive, but nothing came and he didn't expect it to; he was showing me that it never would again.

'He did *tell* me it was over,' he said, staring at the dials. 'I'm not accusing him. He did *say.*'

'*What* was over? Spying?'

'Oh no, not spying, that'll go on for ever, won't it? Communism, really. He said Communism was just another minority religion these days, but we hadn't woken up to the fact. "Time to hang up your boots, Cyril. Better not come to Russia if you're rumbled, Cyril. You'd be a bit of an embarrassment to the new climate. We might have to give you back as a gesture. We're out of date, you see, you and me. Moscow Centre's decided. It's hard currency that talks to Moscow these days. They need all the pounds and dollars they can get. So I'm afraid we're on the shelf, you and me, we're *de trop* and slightly *déjà vu*, not to say a rather large embarrassment to all concerned. Moscow can't afford to be seen running Foreign Office cypher clerks with access to top secret and above, and they rather regard you and me as more of a liability than an asset, which is the reason why they're calling me home. My advice to you, Cyril, therefore, is to take a nice long holiday, see a doctor and get some sun and rest, because between you and me you're showing signs of being slightly barking. We'd like to do right by you but we're a bit strapped for hard currency, to be frank. If you'd like a modest couple of thousand, I'm sure we can do you a small something in a

Swiss bank, but the larger sums are unavailable till further notice." He was like a different person talking to me, to be honest, Ned,' he continued, in a tone of valiant incomprehension. 'We'd been these great friends and he didn't want me any more. "Don't take life so hard, Cyril," he says. He keeps telling me I'm under strain, too many people inside my head. He's right really, I suppose. I lived the wrong life, that's all. You don't know till it's too late, though, do you, sometimes? You think you're one person, you turn out to be another, same as opera. Still, not to worry, I say. Fight another day. Say not the struggle naught availeth. All grist to the mill. Yes.'

He had pulled back his soft shoulders and inflated himself somehow, seeing himself as a person superior to events. 'Right, then,' he said, and we returned spryly to the drawing room.

We had finished. All that remained was to mop up the missing answers and obtain an inventory of what he had betrayed.

We had finished, but it was I, not Frewin, who was resisting the final step. Sitting on the arm of the sofa, he turned his head away from me, smiling over-brightly and offering me his long neck for the knife. But he was waiting for a strike that I was refusing to deliver. His round bald head was craned tensely upward while he leaned away from me as if saying, 'Do it now, hit me here.' But I couldn't do it. I made no move towards him. I had the notebook in my hand, and enough written down for him to sign and destroy himself. But I didn't move. I was on his stupid side, not theirs. Yet what side was that? Was love an ideology? Was loyalty a political party? Or had we, in our rush to divide the world, divided it the wrong way, failing to notice that the real battle lay between those who were still searching, and those who, in order to prevail, had reduced their vulnerability to the lowest common factor of indifference? I was on the brink of destroying a man for love. I had led him to the steps of his own scaffold, pretending we were taking a Sunday stroll together.

'Cyril?'

I had to repeat his name.

'What is it?'

'I'm supposed to take a signed statement from you.'

'You can tell HQ that I was furthering understanding between great nations,' he said helpfully. I had the feeling that if he had been able, he would have told them for me. 'Tell them I was putting an end to the mindless and incredible hostility I had observed for many years in the Tank. That should keep them quiet.'

'Well, they did guess it would be something like that,' I said. 'It's just that there's a bit more to it than you understand.'

'Also, put in that I wish for a posting. I should like to leave the Tank forthwith and earn out my retirement in a non-classified appointment. I'll accept demotion, I've decided. I'm not short of a bob or two. I'm not proud. A change of work is better than a holiday, I say. Where are you going, Ned? The facilities are the other way.'

I was heading for the door. I was heading for sanity and escape. It was as if my world had reduced itself to this dreadful room. 'Just back to the office, Cyril. For an hour or so. I can't produce your statement out of a hat for you, you know. It's got to be properly drawn up on the right forms and so forth. Never mind about the weekend. I never like weekends anyway, to be truthful. Holes in the universe, if you want my secret opinion, weekends are.' Why was I speaking with his cadences? 'Not to worry, Cyril. I'll see myself out. You get some rest.'

I wanted to escape before they came. Looking past Frewin's head to the window, I could see Monty and two of his boys climbing out of their van, and a black police car pulling up outside the house – for the Service, thank God, has no powers of arrest.

But Frewin was talking again, the way the dying go on talking after you think they're dead.

'I can't be left alone, Ned, you see. Not any more. I can't explain it to a stranger, Ned, what I've done, not all over again, no one can.'

I heard a footfall on the gravel, then the ring of the doorbell. Frewin's head came up and his eyes found mine and I watched the knowledge dawn in them, and fade in disbelief, and dawn again. I kept my gaze on him while I opened the front door. Palfrey was standing at Monty's shoulder. Behind them stood two uniformed police officers and a man called Redman, better known as Bedlam, from the Service's team of shrinks.

'Marvellous, Ned,' Palfrey murmured, in a hasty aside to me as the others brushed past us into the drawing room. 'An absolute *coup*. You'll get a medal, I'll see to it.'

They had put handcuffs on him. It had not occurred to me that they would do that. They had handcuffed his hands behind his back, which made him lift his chin. I walked with him to the van and helped him into it, but by then he had found some kind of dignity of his own, and was no longer bothering whose hand was on his elbow.

★

'It's not everyone can crack a Modrian-trained spook between breakfast and lunchtime,' said Burr with dour satisfaction. We were eating a muted dinner at Cecconi's, where he had insisted on taking me the same evening. 'Our dear brethren across the Park are beside themselves with rage, anger, indignation and envy, which is never bad either.' But he was speaking to me from a world I had temporarily taken leave of.

'He cracked himself,' I said.

Burr looked sharply at me. 'I won't have that, Ned. I've not seen a hand played better. You were a whore. You had to be. We're all whores. Whores who pay. I've had enough of your melancholy, come to think of it – sitting over there in Northumberland Avenue, sulking like a stormcloud, caught between your women. If you can't take a decision, that's a decision. Leave your little love and go back to Mabel, if you want my advice, which you don't. I went back to mine last week and it's bloody murder.'

Despite myself I discovered I was laughing.

'So what I've decided is this,' Burr continued when he had generously consented to another enormous plate of pasta. 'You're to abandon sulking as a way of life, and you're to abandon the Interrogators' Pool, in which, in my humble opinion, you have been studying your own narcissistic reflection for somewhat too long. And you're to unroll your mat on the Fifth Floor and replace Peter Guillam as my Head of Secretariat, which will suit your Calvinist disposition and rid me of a thoroughly idle officer.'

I did what he suggested – all of it. Not because he had suggested it, but because he had spoken into my mind. I told Sally of my decision the next night and, if nothing else, the wretchedness of the occasion served to ease my memories of Frewin. For a few months, at her request, I continued writing to her from Tunbridge Wells, but it became as difficult as writing home from school. Sally was the last of what Burr had called my little loves. Perhaps I had had a notion that, added together, they could make up one big one.

12

'So it's over,' said Smiley. The glow of the dying fire lit the panelled library, gilding its gappy shelves of dusty books on travel and adventure, and the old, cracked leather of its arm-chairs, and the foxed photographs of its vanished battalions of uniformed officers with walking sticks; and finally our own assorted faces, turned to Smiley on his throne of hon-our. Four generations of the Service lounged about the room, but Smiley's quiet voice and the haze of cigar smoke seemed to bind us in a single family.

I did not remember ever quite inviting Toby to join us, but certainly the staff had been expecting him and the mess wait-ers had scurried out to greet him as he arrived. In his wide, watered-silk lapels and waistcoat with its Balkan frogging, he looked every inch the *Rittmeister*.

Burr had hastened directly from Heathrow, changing into his dinner jacket in the back of his chauffeur-driven Rover in deference to George. He had entered almost unremarked, with that soundless dancer's walk of his that big men seem to manage naturally. Then Monty Arbuck spotted him and at once gave up his seat. Burr had recently become the first man to make Coordinator before the age of thirty-five.

And at Smiley's feet lounged my last intake of students, the girls like cut flowers in their evening dresses, the boys keen and fresh-faced after their end-of-course exertions in Argyll.

'It's over,' Smiley repeated.

Was it his sudden stillness that alerted us? His altered voice? Or some almost priestly gesture that he made, a stiffening of his tubby body in piety or resolution? I couldn't have told you then, I can't tell you now. But I know I caught no one's eye, yet with his words I felt at once a kind of tensing among us, as if Smiley were calling us to arms – yet what he was talking about had as much to do with laying them down as taking them up.

'It's over, and so am I. Absolutely over. Time you rang down the curtain on yesterday's cold warrior. And please don't ask me back, ever again. The new time needs new people. The worst thing you can do is imitate us.'

I think he had intended to end there, but with George you do better not to guess. For all I know, he had committed his entire closing speech to memory before he came, worked on it, rehearsed it word for word. In either case our silence now commanded him, as did our need of ceremony. Indeed, so thorough was our dependence on him at that moment that if he had turned and walked from the room without offering us another word, our disappointment would have turned our love to gall.

'I only ever cared about the *man*,' Smiley announced. And it was typical of his artfulness that he should have opened with a riddle, then waited a moment before setting out to explain it. 'I never gave a fig for the ideologies, unless they were mad or evil, I never saw institutions as being worthy of their parts, or policies as much other than excuses for not feeling. *Man*, not the mass, is what our calling is about. It was *man* who ended the Cold War in case you didn't notice. It wasn't weaponry, or technology, or armies or campaigns. It was just *man*. Not even Western man either, as it happened, but our sworn enemy in the East, who went into the streets, faced the bullets and the batons and said: we've had enough. It was *their* emperor, not ours, who had the nerve to mount the rostrum and declare he had no clothes. And the ideologies trailed after these impossible events like condemned prisoners, as ideologies do when they've had their day. Because they have no heart of their own. They're the whores and angels of our striving selves. One day, history may tell us who really won. If a democratic Russia emerges – why then, Russia will have been the winner. And if the West chokes on its own materialism, then the West may still turn out to have been the loser. History keeps her secrets longer than most of us. But she has one secret that I will reveal to you tonight in the greatest confidence. Sometimes there are no winners at all. And sometimes nobody needs to lose. You asked me how we should think of Russia today.'

Was that really what we had asked him? What else explained his change of direction? We had talked loosely of the crumbling Soviet Empire, it was true; we had pondered the rise and rise of Japan and the historical shifts of economic power. And in the to-and-fro after dinner, yes, there had been a few passing references to my time in the Russia House, and a few questions touching on the Middle East and Smiley's work with the Fishing Rights Committee, which, thanks to Toby, had become common knowledge. But I don't think that was the question George was choosing to answer now.

'You ask,' he went on, 'can we ever trust the Bear? You seem to be amused, yet a bit unseated, by the notion that we can talk to the Russians like human beings and find common cause with them in many fields. I will give you several answers at once.

'The first is no, we can never trust the Bear. For one reason, the Bear doesn't trust himself. The Bear is threatened and the Bear is frightened and the Bear is falling apart. The Bear is disgusted with his past, sick of his present and scared stiff of his future. He often was. The Bear is broke, lazy, volatile, incompetent, slippery, dangerously proud, dangerously armed, sometimes brilliant, often ignorant. Without his claws, he'd be just another chaotic member of the Third World. But he isn't without his claws, not by any means. And he can't pull his soldiers back from foreign parts overnight, for the good reason that he can't house them or feed them or employ them, and he doesn't trust them either. And since this Service is the hired keeper of our national mistrust, we'd be neglecting our duty if we relaxed for one second our watch on the Bear, or on any of his unruly cubs. That's the first answer.

'The second answer is yes, we can trust the Bear completely. The Bear has never been so trustworthy. The Bear is begging to be part of us, to submerge his problems in us, to have his own bank account with us, to shop in our High Street and be accepted as a dignified member of our forest as well as his – all the more so because his society and economy are in tatters, his natural resources are pillaged and his managers incompetent beyond belief. The Bear needs us so desperately that we may safely trust him to need us. The Bear longs to wind back his dreadful history and emerge from the dark of the last seventy or seven hundred years. We are his daylight.

'The problem is, we Westerners do not find it in us naturally to trust the Bear, whether he's a White Bear or a Red Bear, or both kinds of bear at once, which is what he is at the moment. The Bear may be in perdition without us, but there are lots of us who believe that's exactly where he belongs.

Just as there were people in 1945 who argued that a defeated Germany should remain a rubble desert for the rest of human history.'

Smiley paused and seemed to wonder whether he had said enough. He glanced towards me but I refused to catch his eye. The waiting silence must have convinced him to go on.

'The Bear of the future will be whatever we make of him, and the reasons for making something of him are several. The first is common decency. When you've helped a man to escape from wrongful imprisonment, the least you can do is provide him with a bowl of soup and the means to take his place in a free world. The second is so obvious it makes me a little intemperate to have to mention it at all. Russia – even Russia alone, shorn of all her conquests and possessions – is a vast country with a vast population in a crucial part of the globe. Do we leave the Bear to rot? – encourage him to become resentful, backward, an over-armed nation outside our camp? Or make a partner of him in a world that's changing its shape every day?'

He picked up his balloon glass and peered thoughtfully into it while he swirled the last of his brandy. And I sensed that he was finding it harder to take his leave than he had expected.

'Yes. Well,' he muttered, as if somehow defending himself against his own assertions. 'It's not only our minds we're going to have to reconstruct, either. It's the over-mighty modern State we've built for ourselves as a bastion against something that isn't there any more. We've given up far too many freedoms in order to be free. Now we've got to take them back.'

He gave a shy grin, and I knew that he was trying to break his own spell upon us.

'So while you're out there striving loyally for the State, perhaps you'll do me a small favour and lean on its pillars from time to time. It's got a lot too big for its boots of late. It would be nice if you would cut it down to size. Ned, I'm a bore. Time you sent me home.'

He stood up abruptly, as if shaking himself free of something that threatened to hold him too tight. Then, very deliberately, he treated himself to a last slow look round the room – not at the students any more, but at the old photographs and trophies of his time, apparently committing them to memory. He was taking leave of his house after he had bequeathed it to his heirs. Then, with a great flurry, he launched a search for his spectacles, before he discovered he was wearing them. Then he drew back his shoulders and marched purposefully to the door as two students hastened to open it for him.

'Yes. Well. Goodnight. And thanks. Oh, and tell them to spy on the ozone layer, will you, Ned? It's dreadfully hot in St Agnes for the time of year.'

He left without looking back.

13

The rituals of retirement from the Service are probably no more harrowing than any other professional leavetaking, but they have their own poignancy. There are the ceremonies of remembering – lunches with old contacts, office parties, brave handshakes with tearful senior secretaries, courtesy visits to friendly services. And there are the ceremonies of forgetting, where snip by snip you sever yourself from the special knowledge not given to other mortals. For someone who has spent a lifetime in the Service, including three years in Burr's inmost Secretariat, these can be lengthy and repetitive affairs, even if the secrets themselves have retired long before you. Closeted in Palfrey's musty lawyer's office, mercifully quite often in the glow of a good lunch, I signed away one piece after another of my past, obediently mumbling after him the same shy little English oath, and listening each time to his insincere warnings of retribution should I be tempted by vanity or money to transgress.

And I would be deceiving us both if I pretended that the cumulative burden of these ceremonies did not slowly weigh me down, and make me wish that my day of execution could be brought forward – or, better still, regarded as accomplished. For day by day I began to feel like the man who is reconciled to death but has to spend the last of his energies consoling those who will survive him.

It was a considerable relief to me, therefore, when seated once more in Palfrey's wretched lair with three days still to go before my final freedom or imprisonment, I received a peremptory summons to Burr's presence.

'I've got a job for you. You'll hate it,' he assured me, and slammed down the phone.

He was still fuming when I reached his gaudy modern office. 'You're to read his file, then drive into the country and reason with him. You're not to offend him, but if you should happen to break his neck by accident you'll not find me over-critical.'

'Who is he?'

'Some leftover relic of Percy Alleline's. One of those beer-bellied tycoons from the City that Percy liked to play his golf with.'

I glanced at the cover of the top volume. 'BRADSHAW,' I read, 'Sir Anthony Joyston.' And in small letters underneath: 'asset index,' meaning that the file holder was perceived as an ally of the Service.

'You're to crawl to him, that's an order. Appeal to his better nature,' said Burr in the same acid tone. 'Strike the elder statesman's note. Bring him back into the fold.'

'Who says I am?'

'The sainted Foreign Office. Who do you think?'

'Why don't they do their own crawling?' I said, peering curiously at the career synopsis on page 1. 'I thought that was what they were paid for.'

'They tried. They sent a Junior Minister, cap in hand. Sir Anthony is crawlproof. He also knows too much. He can name names and point fingers. Sir Anthony Bradshaw' – Burr announced, raising his voice in a North Country salvo of indignation – 'Sir Anthony *Joyston* Bradshaw,' he corrected himself, 'is one of England's natural shits, who in the course of affecting to be of service to his country has picked up more knowledge of the disreputable activities of Her Majesty's Government than HMG ever picked up from Sir Anthony in regard to her adversaries. He accordingly has HMG by the balls. Your brief is to invite him, very courteously, to relax his grip. Your weapons for this task are your grey locks and your palpable good nature, which I have observed that you are not above putting to perfidious use. He's expecting you at five this evening and he likes punctuality. Kitty's cleared a desk for you in the anteroom.'

It was not long before Burr's outrage was explained to me. There are few things more riling in our trade than having to cope with the unappetising leftovers of one's predecessors, and Sir Anthony Joyston Bradshaw, self-styled merchant venturer and City magnate, was a gruesome example of the type. Alleline had befriended him – at his club, where else? Alleline had recruited him. Alleline had sponsored him through a string of shady transactions of dubious value to anybody but Sir Anthony, and there were uncomfortable suggestions that Alleline might have taken a cut. Where scandal had threatened, Alleline had sheltered Sir Anthony under the Circus's compendious umbrella. Worse still, many of the doors that Alleline had opened for Bradshaw appeared to have stayed open, for the reason that nobody had thought to close them. And it was through one of these that Bradshaw had now walked, to the shrill outrage of the Foreign Office and half of Whitehall.

I drew an Ordnance Survey map from Library and a Ford Granada from the car pool. At half past two, with the file pretty much in my head, I set off. Sometimes you forget how beautiful England is. I passed through Newbury and climbed a winding hill lined with beech trees whose long shadows were cut like trenches into the golden stubble. A smell of cricket fields filled the car. I mounted a crest, castles of white cloud waited to receive me. I must have been thinking of my childhood, I suppose, for I had a sudden urge to drive straight into them, a thing I had often dreamed of as a boy. The car dipped again and fell free, and suddenly a whole valley opened below me, strewn with hamlets, churches, folding fields and forests.

I passed a pub, and soon a great pair of closed and gilded gates appeared between stone gateposts capped by carved lions. Beside them stood a neat white gatehouse newly thatched. A fit young man lowered his face to my open window and studied me with sniper's eyes.

'To see Sir Anthony,' I said.

'Name, sir?'

'Carlisle,' I replied, using an alias for the last time.

The boy disappeared into the lodge; the gates opened, then closed as soon as I was through them. The park was bordered by a high brick wall – there must have been a couple of miles of it. Fallow deer lay in the shade of chestnut trees. The drive lifted and the house appeared before me. It was golden and immaculate and very large. The centre section was William and Mary. The wings looked later, but not much. A lake lay before it, vegetable gardens and greenhouses behind. The old stables had been converted to offices, with clever outside staircases and glazed external corridors. A gardener was watering the orangerie.

The drive skirted the lake and brought me to the front sweep. Two Arab mares and a llama eyed me over the fence of a lunging ring. A young butler came down the steps, dressed in black trousers and a linen jacket.

'Shall I park your car round the back, Mr Carlisle, once you've been introduced?' he asked. 'Sir Anthony does like a clear façade, when he can get one, sir.'

I gave him the keys and followed him up the wide steps. There were nine, though I can't imagine why I counted, except that it was something we had taught on the Sarratt awareness course, and in recent weeks my life seemed to have become less a continuation than a mosaic of past ages and experiences. If Ben had come striding up to me and grasped my hand, I don't think I would have been particularly surprised. If Monica or Sally had appeared to accuse me, I would have had my answers ready.

I entered a huge hall. A splendid double staircase rose to an open landing. Portraits of noble ancestors, all men, stared down at me, but somehow I didn't believe they were of one family, or could have lived here long without their women. I passed through a billiards room and noticed that the table and cues were new. I suppose I saw everything so clearly because I was treating each experience as my last. I followed the butler through a stately drawing room and traversed a second room that was got up as a hall of mirrors, and a third that was supposed to be informal, with a television set the size of one of those old ice-cream tricycles that used to call at my preparatory school on sunny evenings just like this. I arrived at a pair of majestic doors and waited while the butler knocked. Then waited again for a response. If Bradshaw were an Arab, he would keep me standing here for hours, I thought, remembering Beirut.

Finally I heard a male voice drawl 'Come,' and the butler took a pace into the room and announced, 'A Mr Carlisle, Sir Anthony, from London.'

I had not told him I had come from London.

The butler stepped aside and gave me a first view of my host, though it took a little longer before my host had his first view of Mr Carlisle.

He was sitting at a twelve-foot desk with brass inlay and cabriole legs. Modern oil paintings of spoilt children hung behind him. His correspondence was stacked in trays of thick stitched hide. He was a big, well-nourished man, and clearly a big worker also, for he had stripped to his shirt, which was blue with a midwife's white collar, and he was working in his braces, which were red. Also he was too busy to acknowledge me. First he read, using a gold pen to guide his eye. Then he signed, using the gold pen to write. Then he meditated, still in a downward direction, using the tip of the gold pen as a focus for his great thoughts. His gold cufflinks were as big as old pennies. Then at last he laid the pen down and, with a wounded – even accusatory – air, he raised his head, first to discover me, then to measure me by standards I had yet to ascertain.

At the same moment, by a happy chance of nature, a shaft of low sunlight from the french windows landed on his face, and I was able to measure him in return: the self-sadness of his pouchy eyes, as if he should be pitied for his wealth, the straight small mouth set tense and crooked in the puckered chins, the air of resolution formed of weakness, of boyhood suspicions in a grown-up world. At forty-five, this fattened child was unappeased, blaming some absent parent for his comforts.

Suddenly, Bradshaw was walking towards me. Stalking? Wading? There is an English walk these days peculiar to men of power, and it is a confection of several things at once. Self-confidence is one, lazy sportiveness another. But there is also menace in it, and impatience, and a leisured arrogance, which comes with the crablike splaying of elbows that give way to nobody, and the boxer's slouch of the shoulders, and the playful springiness in the knees. You knew long before you shook his hand that he had no truck with a whole category of life that ranged from art to public transport. You were silently forewarned to keep your distance if you were that kind of fool.

'You're one of Percy's boys,' he told me, in case I didn't know, while he sampled my hand, and was duly disappointed. 'Well, well. Long time no see. Must be ten years. More. Have a drink. Have champagne. Have what you like.' An order: 'Summers. Get us a bottle of shampoo, bucket of ice, two glasses, then bugger off. And nuts!' he shouted after him. 'Cashews. Brazils. Masses of fucking nuts – like nuts?' he enquired of me, with a sudden and disarming intimacy.

I said I did.

'Good. Me too. Love 'em. You've come to read me the riot act. Right? Go on. Not made of glass.'

He was flinging open the french windows so that I could have a better view of what he owned. He had chosen a different walk for this manoeuvre, more march, more swinging of the arms to the rhythm of unheard martial music. When he had opened the doors, he gave me his back to look at, and kept his arms up, palms propped against the door posts, like a martyr waiting for the arrow. And the City haircut, I thought: thick at the collar and little horns above the ears. In golds and browns and greens, the valley faded softly into eternity. A nanny and a small child were walking among the deer. She wore a brown hat with the brim up all the way round and a brown uniform like a Girl Guide's. The lawn was set for croquet.

'We're just appealing to you, that's all, Sir Anthony,' I said. 'Asking you another favour, like the ones you did for Percy.

After all, it was Percy who got you your knighthood, wasn't it?'

'Fuck Percy. Dead, isn't he? Nobody gives me anything, thank you. Help myself to it. What do you want? Spit it out, will you? I've had one sermon already. Portly Savoury from the Foreign Office. Used to flog him when he was my fag at school. Wimp then, wimp now.'

The arms stayed up there, the back was braced and aggressive. I might have spoken, but I felt strangely off key. Three days before my retirement, I was beginning to feel I hardly knew the real world at all. Summers brought champagne, uncorked it and filled two glasses, which he handed to us on a silver tray. Bradshaw snatched one and strode into the garden. I trailed after him to the centre of a grass alley. Azaleas and rhododendrons grew high to either side of us. At the farther end, a fountain played in a stone pond.

'Did you get a lordship of the manor when you bought this house?' I asked, thinking a little small talk might give me time to collect myself.

'Suppose I did?' Bradshaw retorted, and I realised he did not wish to be reminded that he had bought his house rather than inherited it.

'Sir Anthony,' I said.

'Well?'

'It's concerning your relationship with a Belgian company called Astrasteel.'

'Never heard of 'em.'

'But you are associated with them, aren't you?' I said, with a smile.

'Aren't now, never was. Told Savoury the same.'

'But you have holdings in Astrasteel, Sir Anthony,' I protested patiently.

'Zilch. Absolutely buggerall. Different bloke, wrong address. Told him.'

'But you do have a one hundred per cent holding in a company called Allmetal of Birmingham Limited, Sir Anthony. And Allmetal of Birmingham does own a company called Eurotech Funding & Imports Limited of Bermuda, doesn't it? And Eurotech of Bermuda does own Astrasteel of Belgium, Sir Anthony. So we may take it that a certain loose association might be said to exist between yourself on the one hand, and the company that is owned by the company you own on the other.' I was still smiling, still reasoning with him, joking him along.

'No holdings, no dividends, no influence over Astrasteel's affairs. Arm's length, whole thing. Told Savoury, tell the same to you.'

'Nevertheless, when you were invited by Alleline – back in the old days, I know, but not *so* long ago, was it? – to make deliveries of certain commodities to certain countries not strictly on the official shopping list for those commodities, Astrasteel *was* the company you used. And Astrasteel did what you told them to do. Because if they hadn't done, Percy would not have come to you – would he? You'd have been no use to him.' My smile felt stiff on my face. 'We're not *policemen*, Sir Anthony, we're not the *taxman*. I'm merely indicating to you certain relationships that stand – as you insist – beyond the law's reach, and were indeed designed – with Percy's active help – to do just that.'

My speech sounded so ill composed to me, so unpointed, that I assumed at first that Bradshaw did not propose to bother with it at all.

And in a way I was right, for he merely shrugged and said, 'Fuck's that got to do with anything?'

'Well, quite a lot actually.' I could feel my blood beginning to rise, and there was nothing I could do to check it. 'We're asking you to lay off. Stop. You've got your knighthood, you're worth a fortune, you have a duty to your country today just as you had twelve years ago. So get out of the Balkans and stop stirring it with the Serbs and stop stirring it in Central Africa, stop offering them guns galore on tick, and stop trying to cash in on wars that may never happen if you and other like-minded spirits keep your fingers out of them. You're British. You've more money in your pocket than most of us will touch in a lifetime. Stop. Just stop. That's all we're asking. Times have changed. We're not playing those games any more.'

For a moment I fancied I had impressed him, for he turned his unlit gaze on me, and looked me over as if I were some-one who might after all be worth buying. Then his interest flickered out again and he relapsed into despondency.

'It's your country talking to you, Bradshaw,' I said, now with real anger. 'For Christ's sake, man, what more do you *need?* Haven't you got even the vestige of a conscience?'

I will give you Bradshaw's reply as I transcribed it, for at Burr's request I had slipped a recorder into my jacket pocket, and Bradshaw's sawing nasal tones ensured a perfect repro-duction. I will give you his voice too, as nearly as I can write it down. He spoke English as if it were his second language, but it was the only one he had. He spoke in what my son Adrian tells me is called 'slur', which is a slack-mouthed Bel-gravia cockney that contrives to make *mice* out of *mouse* and dispenses almost entirely with the formality of pronouns. It has a vocabulary, naturally: nothing rises but it *escalates*, no opportunity is without a *window*, no minor event occurs that is not *sensational*. It also has a pedantic inaccuracy which is supposed to distinguish it from the unwashed, and explains gems like 'as for you and I'. But even without my tape recorder, I like to think I would have remembered every word, for his speech was like an evening war-cry from a world I was leaving to itself.

'I'm sorry,' he began, which was a lie to start with. 'Did I understand you were appealing to my *conscience*? Good. Right. Make a statement for the record. Mind? Statement begins here. Point One. There is only one point actually. *I don't give a fart*. The difference between me and other charlies is, *I* admit it. If a horde of niggers – yes, I said niggers, I meant *niggers* – if these *niggers* shot each other dead with my toys tomorrow and I made a bob out of it, great news by me. Because if *I* don't sell 'em the goods, some *other* charlie will. Government used to understand that. If they've gone soft, tough titty on 'em. Point Two. Question: heard what the tobacco boys are up to these days? Flogging off high-toxic tobacco to the fuzzy-wuzzies and telling 'em it makes 'em horny and cures the common cold. Tobacco boys give a fart? Sit at home having nervous breakdowns about spreading lung cancer among the natives? The fuck they do. Doing a little creative selling, period. Take drugs. Don't use 'em personally. Don't need 'em. Never mind. If willing seller is doing business with willing buyer, my advice is step aside, let them slug it out, and bloody good luck to 'em. If drugs don't kill 'em, the atmosphere will or they'll get barbecued by the global warming. British, you said. Matter of fact, rather proud of it. Also rather proud of one's *school*. Empire man. Happens to be the tradition one's inherited. When people get in one's way, I break 'em. Or they break me. Discipline is rather up one's street too, actually. *Order*. Accepting responsibilities of one's class and education, and beating the foreigner at his own game. Thought you people were rather committed to that one, too. Error, apparently. Failure of communication. What one cares about is quality of life. *This* life. *Standards* actually. Old word. Don't care. *These* standards. Pompous, you're thinking. All right, I'm pompous. Fuck you. I'm Pharaoh, right? If a few thousand slaves have to die so that I can build this pyramid, nature. And if they can make *me* die for *their* fucking pyramid, bloody good on 'em. Know what I've got in my cellar? Iron rings. Rusty iron rings, built into the walls when this house was built. Know what they were for? Slaves. *That's* nature too. Original owner of this house – man who *built* this house – man who *paid* for it, man who sent his architect to Italy, learn his trade – that man owned slaves, and had his slave quarters in the cellar of this house. Think there aren't slaves today? Think capital doesn't *depend* on slaves? Jesus Christ, what kind of shop do you run? One doesn't normally talk philosophy, but I'm afraid one doesn't like being preached to either. Won't have it, you see. Not in my house, thank you. Annoys me. Don't bug easily, rather famous for one's cool. But one does have a certain view of nature; one gives work to people and one takes one's share.'

I said nothing, and that is on the tape too.

In the face of an absolute, what can you say? All my life I had battled against an institutionalised evil. It had had a name, and most often a country as well. It had had a corporate purpose, and had met a corporate end. But the evil that stood before me now was a wrecking infant in our own midst, and I became an infant in return, disarmed, speechless and betrayed. For a moment, it was as if my whole life had been fought against the wrong enemy. Then it was as if Bradshaw had personally stolen the fruits of my victory. I remembered Smiley's aphorism about the right people losing the Cold War, and the wrong people winning it, and I thought of repeating it to him as some sort of insult, but I would have been beating the air. I thought of telling him that now we had defeated Communism, we were going to have to set about defeating capitalism, but that wasn't really my point: the evil was not in the system, but in the man. And besides, by then he was asking me whether I wanted to stay to dinner, at which I politely declined, and left.

In the event, it was Burr who gave me dinner, and I am pleased to say I don't remember much about it. Two days later, I turned in my Head Office pass.

You see your face. It's no one you remember. You wonder where you put your love, what you found, what you were after. You want to say: 'I slew the dragon, I left the world a safer place.' You can't really, not these days. Perhaps you never could.

We have a good life, Mabel and I. We don't talk about things we can't change. We don't cross each other. We're civilised. We've bought a cottage on the coast. There's a long garden there I'd like to get my hands on, plant a few trees, make a vista to the sea. There's a sailing club for poor kids I'm involved in; we bring them down from Hackney, they enjoy it. There's a move to draft me for the local council. Mabel does the church. I go back to Holland now and then. I still have a few relations there.

Burr drops in from time to time. I like that in him. He gets on well with Mabel, as you'd expect. He doesn't try to be wise. He chats to her about her watercolours. He's not judgmental. We open a good bottle, cook a chicken. He brings me up to date, drives back to London. Of Smiley, nothing, but that's the way he wanted it. He hates nostalgia, even if he's part of other people's.

There's no such thing as retirement, really. Sometimes there's knowing too much, and not being able to do much about it, but that's just age, I'm sure. I think a lot. I'm stepping out with my reading. I talk to people, ride on buses. I'm a newcomer to the overt world but I'm learning.

Afterword

In *The Secret Pilgrim* I determined to take a last farewell of the Cold War, of George Smiley and all his people, and of certain elusive themes that had been nagging at me through two and a half decades of writing. I wanted to consider who we had been and who we had become, and take a look at the future shape of the two superpowers, now that – with some reluctance on both sides – they had suspended, if only temporarily, their games of Russian roulette. I had already taken leave of the Cold War twice before, in my own mind: in *Smiley's People*, which ended for good, as far as I was concerned, the stand-off between Smiley and Karla; and in *A Perfect Spy*, in which the despairing protagonist neither knows nor cares any longer whether he belongs to East or West.

But the elusive themes still constituted unfinished business. Some of them remained unexplored until later books. Now that the West had dealt with rogue forms of Communism, I wanted to ask, how was it going to deal with rogue forms of capitalism? In *The Secret Pilgrim*, Smiley pops the question, but I didn't really get round to addressing it until *Single & Single* and *The Constant Gardener*. A more banal theme that had always bugged me was the element of human incompetence in the world of espionage. Part of the baggage that a spywriter has to address is the conviction of the man in the street that spies are somehow smarter and more adept at life than are ordinary folk. Spies don't lose their car keys or forget the combination to their safes or accidentally address the new wife by the name of their last one. Well, of course they don't, they're spies, they're trained and all that – hand-picked; well, aren't they? And we tell ourselves this despite the endless news stories of cock-up that reach us by way of disgruntled defectors like Shayler or Tomlinson, or through the daily press; despite brief-cases stuffed with priceless secrets left on the London Underground; and computer disks containing the names of informants picked up in second-hand radio stores.

Even when a Chinook helicopter crashes on its way from Northern Ireland, killing a galaxy of intelligence officers, we seem as a nation reluctant to ask ourselves just how anyone could be such a purblind idiot as to put all these important people on the same flight – even if we discount the fact that the perils of such flights had long been abundantly clear to the evasive Ministry of Defence. *There must be a reason*, we tell ourselves, falling back on our faith in the occult. *Spies do things differently. They're not as daft as we are*. Whereas, as Arthur Koestler said famously of his fellow Jews, spies are the same as us, but more so.

But when from time to time I had tried – for instance in 1963 when I was writing *The Looking Glass War* – to use cock-up rather than conspiracy as the dramatic engine of my story, I failed to take the reader with me. And in a sense I had only myself to blame, for the book before it had been *The Spy Who Came in from the Cold*, in which conspiracy, and conspiracy only, ruled the plot. *First you tell us one thing, now you tell us the opposite*, was the reader's justifiable grouse, and I paid a high price for my presumption, even if I never gave up my personal conviction that incompetence, not conspiracy, is what makes the secret world go round.

So in *The Secret Pilgrim* you get a hyper-nervous young British intelligence officer who leaves a handwritten break-down of his East German spy network on the roof of his car, and thereby destroys both himself and his luckless agents; and a pathologically solitary cypher clerk who deludes himself into believing he is a star Russian-language student, and thus delivers himself to the KGB. The poor clerk wasn't the victim of cock-up exactly, but rather of the fatal triviality of human motive, of the hairline distinction between the harmlessly eccentric and the dangerously insane. Not nearly enough has been written about the phenomenon of apparent sanity among people who turn out to be barking mad. It will be years before anybody is brave enough to put a name to the motive that drove the recently unmasked senior FBI operative, Hanssen, to betray his Service for so long and with such extraordinary devotion, but the signs are that he was an outwardly sane man whose interior reality was mayhem.

But the character who haunts me most in these pages is neither the poor cypher clerk nor the Berlin trainee. Nor even the old soldier, Sergeant Major Hawthorne, who believed that his criminal thug of a son was a loyal British secret agent acting a part; and was allowed to persist in this belief by George Smiley, who gave him a pair of precious gold cufflinks as spurious proof of the boy's service before the secret mast.

It is Hansen. Not the wretched real-life Hanssen of the FBI to whom I have just referred, but Hansen my Dutchman and Asian scholar, Hansen my British agent and lapsed Jesuit priest, whose story you will find in Chapter 9. Very few characters in my writing are drawn from actual people, and those that are tend to be a mishmash of several. Very few episodes have a basis in fact either, though I confess that the story of Smiley's cufflinks is descended from an incident attributed to Sir Maurice Oldfield, once Chief of MI6.

But my character Hansen does for once have a real-life model and his name is François Bizot, a French scholar of Buddhism whom I met first in Cambodia and then in Thailand while I was researching *The Honourable Schoolboy*, and who generously gave me permission to adapt his true-life story to my spurious fictional purposes. And Bizot, I am delighted to say, last year published his own much praised account of the events in his life that I have traduced. And Bizot's book, rightly hailed in France as a masterpiece, called *Le Portail* – the gateway – and winner of a string of French literary prizes, will be published in English next year.

And it is a measure of the amoral ways of us fiction writers – of our secret thefts and wanton misrepresentations – that in my fictional story of Bizot's heroism I make of him precisely the person he emphatically never was. He was not a Western lackey, he was not an imperialist spy masquerading as a Buddhist scholar, he was not the fascist running-dog that Pol Pot and his henchmen would have him be. He was Bizot, nobody's creature but his own – which was why, against all the probabilities of those dreadful times, his Khmer Rouge inquisitors let him go. By sheer determination and force of character, Bizot convinced his would-be executioners of his innocence.

At the time of its publication I dedicated *The Secret Pilgrim* to Alec Guinness in acknowledgement of his portrayal of George Smiley in the BBC television series, and of a modest friendship that persisted until his recent death. But Guinness was always humbled, as I am, by the gap between the world of the imagination and the world of the real. So he would certainly join me in raising a toast to Bizot, a real man among my cast of imaginary souls.

John le Carré
Cornwall, March 2001